SMALL TOWN, BIG MAGIC

SMALL TOWN, BIG MAGIC

HAZEL BECK

GRAYDON
HOUSE

GRAYDON
HOUSE®

Recycling programs
for this product may
not exist in your area.

ISBN-13: 978-1-525-80471-7

Small Town, Big Magic

Graydon House
22 Adelaide St. West, 41st Floor
Toronto, Ontario M5H 4E3, Canada
www.GraydonHouseBooks.com
www.BookClubbish.com

Printed in U.S.A.

For witches past and present, hidden and boldly unhidden.

SMALL TOWN, BIG MAGIC

IF YOU GOOGLE MY NAME—SOMETHING I only do every other Tuesday because ego surfing is an indulgence and I keep my indulgences on a strict schedule— the first twenty hits are about the hanging of Sarah Emerson Wilde in 1692 in Salem, Massachusetts.

Guess why.

Only after all those witch hits—three pages in—will you get to me, Emerson Wilde. Not a tragically executed woman accused of witchcraft by overwrought zealots, but a bookstore owner and chamber of commerce president. The youngest chamber of commerce president in the history of St. Cyprian, Missouri, not that I like to brag.

Men are applauded for embellishing the truth while women are seen as *very confident* for telling the truth—and *very confident* is never a compliment.

If you slog past all the *Crucible* references and sad YouTube videos from disaffected teens with too much eye makeup, you might read about how my committed rejuvenation efforts have brought ten new businesses to St. Cyprian in the past five years. You might read about our Christmas Around the World Festival which, thanks to my hard work and total commitment, brings people from—you guessed it—all around the world. You could read any number of articles about what I've done to help St. Cyprian, because it's not a good day unless I've done something to support the town I love best.

And I pride myself on making every day a good day.

Even if most people read about Sarah and the witch trials and stop there, I know the truth about her. I learned all about my notorious ancestor while researching a presentation for my fourth-grade class.

My peers might have preferred Skip Simon's bold and unlikely claims that he was a direct descendent of the outlaw Jesse James, but learning about Sarah changed my life. The *reality* of Sarah Emerson Wilde is that she was a fierce feminist who wanted to play by her own rules. A nonconformist who wasn't interested in playing the perfect Puritan, and therefore a direct threat to the Powers That Be. Following her own rules, ignoring theirs, and trumpeting her independence got her killed.

Sarah wasn't only a tragic figure. She was also a fierce martyr who would have hated being called either.

In retrospect, it was maybe too much for Miss Timpkin's fourth-grade class.

But ever since then I've considered Sarah my guiding light. I'm proud to have such an exceptional, indomitable woman in my family tree. My great-grandmother times nine, to be precise. I've always felt that I owe it to myself, the Wilde name, and Sarah to be a strong, independent woman who doesn't let the patriarchy or anything else get her down for long.

"And I don't," I announce brightly to the quiet of the early-morning kitchen of my family's historic house.

It's a Tuesday in March and I have plans. I always have plans. It's what I do, but these are particularly epic, even for me. I might have been born too late to speak feminist truth to Puritan patriarchal power, but I have my own calling.

I am here to make St. Cyprian a better place.

Don't laugh.

You can't fix the world until you sort out your own backyard. I intend to do both.

Since my first St. Cyprian community project with my second-grade class, I have put everything I am into this shining jewel of a river town, the people lucky enough to live here, and the shops that carve out their spots on the cobbled streets—like my own intensely independent bookstore.

For all the women who came before me who weren't allowed. Or those who carved out their way and were shunned for it.

Fist pumps optional.

I pump a few on my own in the kitchen, because there are few things in this life that psyche a girl up more than a fist pump. One of those things is coffee. Another is sugar. Combine all three and I'm ready to face the day.

But first I need to face my roommate.

My roomie and best friend, Georgie Pendell, grew up in the rickety old house next door, but moved in with me when she could no longer bear another moment of agony in her parents' house—her dramatic words, not mine. She's been here five years, sprawled out over the third floor and using the extra bedroom I'd assumed she'd make into an office as a library instead.

Mind you, what Georgie calls a library gives me hives. It's an overflowing catastrophe of books piled into tottery towers that she refuses to let me organize for her. The last time I tried to go inside, the door only opened about two inches before hitting one of her stacks.

She insists it's exactly the way she wants it.

And that's fine, because Wilde House is big enough for the both of us. In fact, bigger than we need. With my parents gone living the high life in Europe and my sister's defection to who knows where after our high school graduation, the house had seemed too big. I had been thrown for a loop when both my sister and parents left St. Cyprian within a year of each other—though I'd rallied the way I always do. My sister, Rebekah, had always been a free spirit. My parents had always been socially ambitious—so why not take that as far as it could go on the Continent? I had the town. I had my friends. I got to live in this piece of history with my grandmother. Yet when my grandmother died a few years later and left me here alone, the old house felt like an ominous, rattling thing that might swallow me whole. Winter had seemed to seep in, cruel and unforgiving. The halls had seemed too long, the lights too dim.

Possibly I was grieving. The loss of Grandma. The loss of my family, who I knew had their reasons for staying away, in Rebekah's case because she always had reasons no matter how little she communicated those reasons. Or returning only for the funeral, in my parents' case, and then rushing back to their European adventure.

It felt a little stormy there for a while.

My silly, happy, eccentric best friend moving in has been like letting in the sunshine.

Organizational challenges aside, having her here makes these early mornings with the whole of Wilde House creaking around me, like it's singing its own song while I wake, feel less...lonely.

Not that I allow loneliness in my life. I swat it down like an obnoxious fly anytime it pops up. Because loneliness is a betrayal of all the women who came before me and I am not going to be the Wilde who lets them down. I'm the current caretaker of this landmark of a house that's been in my family some three hundred years, since the first Wilde wisely made the long trek away from the Massachusetts Colony and settled down in this part of Missouri where two great rivers meet, the Mississippi and the Missouri. I like the idea of roots that deep and rivers that tangle together. I like this house that towers above me with its uneven floors and oddly shaped rooms. I like where it sits in town, on one end of Main Street like a punctuation mark.

And I really like that my best friend is always right here, within reach.

Because before I head off to my beloved Confluence Books today, I need to get Georgie on board for an Official Friend Meeting tonight. Being a young, ambitious, independent woman in charge of the chamber of commerce in the most charming river town in Missouri—and therefore America—comes with its challenges. A strong leader knows when to lean in to her community, and I do. My friends are always the first people I turn to when I need some help.

I tell myself that I would do that even if my family was still here. That my friends *are* my family. My parents and sister are the black sheep—not me. Their leaving, their lack of contact entirely or bright, shallow, early-morning messages from abroad is their choice.

And their loss.

My friends stayed. They love St. Cyprian and loved my grandmother too. They are mine, and I am theirs. Just like this town I love so much.

Still, sometimes I like to make a gathering *official* because that makes it more likely we'll get to the constructive advice more quickly.

I head for the curving narrow stairs that will take me up into the house's turret. It's never been my favorite part of the house—it makes me think of princesses and fairy tales and other embarrassingly romantic things that have no place in a practical, independent life—but it suits Georgie to the bone. Like it was made for her.

I eye the newel post as I start up the stairs because it's shaped like a grinning dragon and I've never understood it. The Wildes are the least fanciful people alive. Pragmatism and quiet determination would be our coat of arms if we had such a thing, but we're Midwesterners, thank you. Coats of arms are far too showy.

The dragon grins at me like it knows things I don't.

"That is unlikely," I tell it, then close my eyes, despairing of myself.

There is no room in my life for the kind of whimsy that results in discussions with inanimate objects. Especially a dragon. A sometimes creepy dragon who hunches at the foot of the banister like he's guarding the house.

"Stop it," I mutter at myself—and possibly at him—as I head upstairs.

Once on the third floor, I eye Georgie's library door as I pass it, itching to get in there and establish some order, but sometimes friendship comes before logic. Or intelligible shelving systems. At the end of the hall, her bedroom door is ajar, and I can see Georgie herself sitting on the wood-planked floor facing the two huge turret windows that take up most of the outside wall. They are flung wide open to the cool spring air and she has her face lifted to the sunrise.

Her curly red hair swirls around her, and she's wearing enough bracelets on her wrist to perform a symphony of tinkling metal sounds. Like the half hippie, half free spirit she claims to be.

Georgie's family also has roots in Puritan Massachusetts witch trials but unlike me, she *loves* getting lost in all that witchcraft nonsense. She pretends she has various supernatural powers to annoy me, but mostly she likes the trappings. What she solemnly calls *crystal lore* and *sage burning*. She likes to talk to her cat as if he can understand her and claims his meows are detailed replies that she, naturally, can comprehend perfectly. And she steadfastly claims to believe that Ellowyn, one of our other closest friends, can brew teas that cure colds, repair broken hearts, and curse weak-willed men.

There's something comforting about how Georgie wholeheartedly embraces the silliness, like this daily ritual of hers. The morning light streams in, making the colorful crystals she's arranged around her in a circle glow.

As I stand in the doorway, she gets to her feet and begins to collect her debris. Her crystals are the only item she owns that I have ever seen her keep in some kind of order. I used to try to help her pick up the various rocks, but she would tell me things like I put the malachite with the quartz and *everyone knows that's wrong*, or that reds and blues shouldn't touch on Wednesdays, *obviously*. I finally gave up.

I'll admit that sometimes I have to shove my hands in my pockets to keep from helping again anyway.

"What brings you to my lair this early in the morning?" she asks without looking at me. I know this is to give the impression that she *divined my presence* when it's more likely she heard the creaky board out in the hallway.

She does something dramatic with her fingers in the air, and at the same time a breeze shifts through the wind chimes she has hanging in her windows. A funny little coincidence.

I ignore it. "You're free tonight, right?"

"Sadly no. In a shocking twist that will surprise everyone who's ever met me or seen me attempt to dance, I'm running away to Spain, where I will dedicate myself to the study of flamenco. And possibly also tapas and wine."

In other words, yes, she's free.

"I need to call a meeting."

Georgie sighs and looks over her shoulder at me. "Not every get-together needs to be a meeting with a cause."

I smile winsomely at her. "But some do."

"Is this about those flyers I helped you put up yesterday?"

I smile even more broadly. If there was an award for best flyer, that one would win it. But then, I'm excellent at flyers. "That flyer was about the new and improved Redbud Festival, Georgie."

"Yes, I know. I also know that anytime you try to *new and improve* something in this town, the plague that is Skip Simon descends on you like the locust he is."

"He hasn't. Yet."

"But he will."

He will. He always does.

I sigh. "Yes, he will. He can't resist. But I don't want to fight him." *This time* is implied. "I want to find a way to get through to him. Preferably without embarrassing him in front of the whole town."

Because the only thing I've ever been able to do when it came to Skip Simon, from another old and well-to-do local family here in St. Cyprian like mine, was embarrass him.

Publicly.

His unearned victory against me in fourth grade notwithstanding.

There was the kickball game. You'd think a grown man wouldn't still be mad that a girl had *accidentally* smashed his face with a kickball in gym class, both breaking his nose and making him the laughingstock of the fifth grade, but Skip had brought it up at least twice in the past six months alone.

There was the olive branch incident. Except it wasn't an olive branch. It was an extra helping of the fish sticks from the cafeteria that everyone knew he loved. I'd thought he'd find those fish sticks within the hour and maybe we could bury the hatchet. Instead, he'd come back from a week's vacation—that he claimed was the flu, but he had a tan from lying on the beach in Mexico—to find everyone calling him Stinky Simon. And hadn't believed I'd been out that same week because I really did come down with the flu before I could take the fish sticks offering back out of his locker.

There was the unfortunate field trip to Mark Twain's Boyhood Home in Hannibal. The riverboat incident a year later. The ninth-grade intercom thing that even my own friends didn't entirely believe was an accident, but how was I supposed to know that it could be so easily turned on? Or that Skip and his freshman year girlfriend would choose to use that room to make out in?

Classmates made unfortunate slurping sounds at him for years.

Then there'd been prom. Our parents had urged us to go together despite the many years of discord. They thought our two old St. Cyprian families should be friendlier, and obviously my rebellious sister wasn't the one to approach for cordiality of any kind. And when they'd had a few drinks, our parents tended to wax rhapsodic about how they'd always had hopes for Skip and me.

Neither Skip nor I shared these hopes.

But we'd agreed all the same, because St. Cyprian is a small town. And because it made sense to make an effort. Okay, that was me, but he was briefly less jerky about things. We even called our awkward plans *peace talks*.

Then I stood him up.

It was an accident, but no one believed that.

My position, then and now, is that when your always-problematic sister "loses" your favorite science teacher's chinchilla, you can hardly be concerned about a *dance*. You initiate search and rescue, in a prom dress, because it's the poor, lost chinchilla that matters. And given that I was the one who found Mr. Churchilla, you'd think Skip would have forgiven me.

But he didn't. Especially when the rumor went around that I'd always plotted to stand him up. As if I would descend to playing teen rom-com movie games with *Skip*. Plus, there was another rumor that Skip himself had actually been planning to embarrass me with something far more cringe-worthy than his choice of white tuxedo.

I wish I could say we'd left such silly adolescent issues behind, but on the day of Skip's coronation—I mean, election, if you could call it that when his grand and formidable mother basically forced everyone she knows into voting for her precious spoiled baby—as mayor of St. Cyprian, I led a town cleanup service project. I had no idea the cleaning substance we'd used in the community center would make the floor abnormally slippery. *I* was wearing shoes with decent treads.

But Skip was not. He tripped, fell flat on his face and, yes, broke his nose again.

Yes, he blamed me.

The harder I tried to be nice to Skip, the worse I seemed to embarrass him. Over time, he moved on from any actual incidents to simply blaming me by rote. If there is any bad word breathed about him on the cobbled streets of St. Cyprian, he assumes it's my fault.

But he's the *mayor*. What mayor is universally adored? Welcome to politics.

An argument he does not find compelling, sadly. I've tried.

Skip might not believe this, but while he can certainly schmooze with the best of them, he isn't liked by all and sundry. He is mayor here because his family is powerful and because he vowed to keep the town *as it is*. The sad truth is, no matter how many progressive folks live here, a great many people in the greater St. Cyprian area are afraid of change.

That doesn't mean they like Skip personally. Yet somehow the blame for any negativity aimed at him or his office or his campaign gets put on my shoulders. When he decides I'm wrong, which is pretty much anytime I get out there and try to change things for the better, he *really* goes after me.

This is why I need my friends to help me brainstorm ways to deal with Skip's eventual, inevitable response to my new ideas for the Redbud Festival. Because I'm certainly not going to stop trying to improve St. Cyprian and its tourist-attracting, revenue-producing festivals to appease Mayor Stinky Simon.

I've said nothing, and Georgie has stood there *studying* me. Which means her response will be one I do not like.

Sure enough, Georgie nods as if she's *seen something*. She goes to her bag of crystals and takes one out. Then she places the shiny black stone in my palm. "Keep this with you."

"You know I don't believe in this stuff," I say, somewhat desperately. We're usually good at letting each other be who we are. She lets me march around being bossy and anal. I let her waft around being fanciful and disorganized.

I feel like surrendering to crystals is blurring these lines.

"I know," she says gently, her other hand coming over mine. There's no lecture, just a gentle squeeze. "Humor me today."

"Fine." I slip the rock into my pocket. "Tonight?"

"I'll make the brownies."

"Perfect." Because there is nothing more perfect than a plan coming together, unless it also comes together with gooey chocolate goodness.

Now I've got to get the rest of our little group on board before I open my bookstore. Because my friends are awesome, by definition, and each one of them brings specific skill sets to this kind of meeting. I need them all.

My cousin, Zander Rivers, is a ferryman like the rest of his part of the family. He always lightens the mood and makes everyone laugh, especially when I'm being *intense*. He always thinks I'm being *intense*, by the way.

But Zander is even more key to these town domination meetings thanks to his evenings at St. Cyprian's townie bar. He always knows what the gossip is. And knowing what people in town think, and what they're saying, makes it easier for me to do things that really are what's best for them.

Not in a paternalistic, condescending Skip Simon way. In a collaborative, *it-takes-a-village* way.

Ellowyn Good, on the other hand, is particularly vicious and vindictive—traits I don't share, but deeply appreciate. Especially because Georgie is very talented at taking Ellowyn's usually extreme ideas and softening them. Then making Ellowyn think it was her idea all along. Georgie also always supplies the sweets, which helps, because sugar helps everything.

And Jacob North...

I suddenly feel hot and try to cover it with my smile as I leave Georgie's room.

I tell myself it's temper as I march down the hall toward the stairs. Jacob is maddening. I've spent years telling myself that every resistance—or community service project, call it what you will—needs a Jacob to point out the flaws in a plan. Every single flaw in every single plan, endlessly. I tell myself, as I often do, that Jacob is not a dour pessimist.

He's *cool-headed* and *rooted in reality*. Both necessary counter-balances to Ellowyn's dark imaginings, Georgie's airiness, Zander's comedy routines, and what Jacob likes to call my *delusions of grandeur*.

"Necessary counterbalances are necessary," I mutter as I hit the stairs.

I text Zander as I walk down to the first floor. He'll catch Jacob on the ferry and tell him the evening's plans, and—bonus—I won't have to hear Jacob's initial complaints. I'd text Ellowyn too, but she never checks her phone, so I'll have to stop by her store on the way to mine.

I grab my jacket in a nod to the still-capricious spring weather and sling my messenger bag over my shoulder, then I step outside and pause the way I always do.

Because I love St. Cyprian and I like to take it in.

From my front door I can see down the length of Main Street, a redbrick straight shot as if some man was trying to prove he had dominance over the curving, wild Missouri River. Like men do. Buildings made of local limestone and brick, and even the odd wood-paneled cottage, are crowded on either side of the street and almost all of them are on the historic register. Storefronts boast big windows and swing-ing signs declaring their names and cute logos. This time of year, the sidewalks are cluttered with chalkboard signs and sturdy pots of early-blooming flowers.

I set off with the same song in my heart that's swelled in me since I was a kid.

St. Cyprian is mine and I am St. Cyprian's.

I've never cared much if people find that odd. And they do, which is why I've learned to keep it to myself. Mostly.

The sun is shining bright today and everything looks a little sparkly from the rain last night. I wave at Holly Bishop through the window of her coffee shop and bakery and share a greeting with Gus Howe, out sweeping the sidewalk in front of his antique store.

I'll never understand why my parents chose Europe or why my sister ran away. This is home. It's *beautiful* and better still, ours. I can practically feel the history rise up from the brick-lined streets.

My history. *Wilde* history. The real family history that has nothing to do with hanging for witchcraft back east, but is instead all about strong, determined women who wanted to make each generation a little better for the next. I have a responsibility to that history. To my grandmother, who created Confluence Books when her grandmother passed a drugstore down to her, who had inherited it in turn from *her* grandmother— a full-on badass who'd run a gun shop and trading post here when St. Cyprian was the frontier.

I stop at Ellowyn's tea shop, *Tea & No Sympathy*. Outside, it's a serviceable two-story brick building with Ellowyn's apartment stacked above the shop. It was built in the 1800s, so it's not one of the older buildings in a town that was settled in the 1700s. Inside, it looks like a charming little European cottage. White walls and paned windows open with luxurious flowerpots on their sills. Teas line the back wall in big antique jars, making you feel like you're walking into a country apothecary. Possibly circa 1802.

Ellowyn's selling point is the idea that her teas can cure things. Any and all things, like they're magic potions. Silly for people to believe, but a smart business move, because the tourists who flock here love the idea that a novelty tea set from a local shop can cure what ails them. I always appreciate a smart business move.

Though I have learned not to liken Ellowyn's "curated tea blends" to things like fortune-telling, palm reading, or Tarot cards. It makes her testy.

Ellowyn appears from the back in a black apron with her blond hair tied into a swirling mass on the top of her head. "Since when do you want tea?"

"Good morning to you too." She only looks at me, expressionless, so I drop my shiny chamber of commerce smile. "Since you ignore your phone, I stopped by to see if you're free tonight."

Ellowyn narrows her eyes at me. "For what?"

"Now, Wynnie," I say in as placating a tone as possible, using the nickname she would kill anyone else for speaking out loud.

"Don't *Wynnie* me. I don't want to be roped into putting up flyers or picking up litter all over town or volunteering for some deadly dull committee."

Her position has never made any sense to me. "Even though all of those things help you as a business owner in this town?"

"Even though."

I sigh. Sometimes it seems like I'm the only one who cares about our town, but there's no point having that fight for the millionth time. I know at the end of the day Ellowyn cares about *me*. That means she'll help on this, the way she always helps, even if she has to be dragged in, kicking and screaming.

Not always figuratively.

"I need to figure out how to head Skip off at the pass," I say. "But in a way that does not end with our illustrious mayor embarrassed in front of a hundred people, again, and hating me even more than he already does."

Ellowyn continues to fuss around with her tea, in and out of bags. She takes different leaves from a selection of jars and pours hot water over them, so a fragrant cloud of steam rises up between us. I breathe it in and feel my shoulders relax. Slightly.

"But embarrassing Skip is one of the things you do best. And also one of my favorite things about you." She shoots me a grin.

"Be that as it may, embarrassing Skip only makes *my* life harder. I need help."

Ellowyn *humphs*, but I know she'll relent. She always does.

"Take this." She hands me the tea she's just made in a to-go cup.

She waits for me to ask what it is. I don't. She'll tell me it's been specially brewed to *cleanse my aura* or *support my moon connection* or something equally woo-woo and ridiculous. I prefer not to know rather than have to pretend it isn't all absurd.

"Thanks," I say with a smile instead. A genuine smile. "Tonight at six?"

"Is Georgie making brownies?"

"You know it."

"I'll be there." But her smile borders on evil. "Though I can't promise my ideas won't be about how to embarrass Skip even *more* than usual. He's a dick."

I try to look disapproving, but I can't. She only speaks the sad truth. Skip *is* a dick.

On the other hand, as one of Ellowyn's oldest friends, I feel like it's my duty not to encourage her *I Am the Night* thing too much.

Either way, I'm smiling as I walk out of her shop and head down Main Street to mine.

Confluence Books sits in one of the oldest buildings in St. Cyprian. A white brick structure with a green roof and shutters around each of the four windows—the big, arched storefront window on the ground floor and the three smaller windows upstairs. The thick wooden door is a bright, cheery red. There's a balcony on the second floor, currently a simple wrought iron black, but I always think about painting it a bright color in the spring before things really start to bloom.

This year my focus has been on a new and improved Redbud Festival, so I haven't had the time. Because I love Confluence Books with my whole heart, but my role in the community sometimes takes precedence over the projects I'd like to do here. As long as I sell books, and I do, the cosmetic details can wait.

I step inside this building that's been in my family for generations. I turn the book-shaped sign on the door from *Closed* to *Open* and gaze around the main floor of the bookstore with satisfaction. My grandmother would be proud.

And despite the inevitable showdown with Skip, I feel good.

Because I love that my friends will help me come up with scenarios to handle our obnoxious mayor, but I have a secret weapon.

I'm Emerson Wilde, last in a line of powerful women, and I can accomplish anything.

MORNINGS IN THE BOOKSHOP ARE SLOW DUR-
ing the week, so I spend my Sunday evenings plotting out
how I'll spend my mornings before the customers show up
in the planner I carry everywhere with me. Georgie likes to
make fun of what she calls *the trendy planner life* but she spends
her days immersed in history at the local history museum
her family has run forever. The only dates she keeps track
of happened centuries ago.

I live in the present. That requires planning. And possibly
also encouraging stickers—don't judge.

As I drink Ellowyn's concoction—sweet and spicy and, it
pains me to admit, actually delicious, for a change—I take a
moment because being here makes me happy. And happiness
is the one thing that can't be planned. It has to be grabbed
and savored.

I've kept the store set up just as Grandma had, except I
got rid of the ridiculous New Age and *metaphysical* section.

If people want *that* kind of fiction, they can order it online, with my blessing.

That is not something I say lightly as an independent bookstore owner.

Grandma made the bookstore look like a home, encouraging customers to treat it like an extension of theirs. The lower level is decorated like a parlor. Couches and tables are piled high with comfort genre reads and antique lamps. In the back, there is a children's area set up like a child's bedroom, complete with a tent that looks like a canopy bed that Georgie has been known to commandeer after hours.

Upstairs a room is outfitted like a kitchen and filled with cookbooks on shelves and spilling out of the antique wood stove. Next to the kitchen area, a shelf was built around the window that looks out over Main Street and appears more like a nook in a garden shed than a bookshelf. Some shelves hold gardening tools, a mix of fake and real plants, and the rest hold the gardening selection, from coffee table books with to-die-for photographs of peonies to how-to guides.

I go ahead and take a few of the books and props downstairs. I already put up flyers and updated the city tourism website, but that doesn't mean I can't also have a display in my own store for the Redbud Festival, which is only a week away now.

Usually, the Redbud Festival is our lowest turnout of the year for festivals. Some blame spring's capricious weather. Others claim the draw of the unique trees isn't exactly universal, because there are always haters. But my new ideas for this year are sure to put the Redbud Festival on par with our other seasonal festivals. Nothing beats our Trick or Treat Halloween Extravaganza or our Christmas Around the World season, but that doesn't mean Redbud can't improve.

Because the Draconian Redbud tree *only* grows here in

the greater St. Cyprian area, right where the Mississippi and Missouri Rivers meet. We get people who come from all over to see it as it's the only redbud species that appears pink during the day and white at night. Hard-core botanists love the uniqueness of our redbud season, though, I will admit, the *floods* of people who show up for Halloween and Christmas have yet to discover the charm of our trees.

I want to open it up beyond the botanists. I've worked hard to get a bunch of business owners on board with adding a nighttime component. Fairy lights and sidewalk sales, all paying homage to our one-and-only tree variety, will lure people in. I'm sure of it.

As I'm finishing up the display, the first customers of the day walk in. Two female friends toting coffee cups even though the sign clearly says no food or drink. They won't buy anything. I've been in the business long enough to sense a sale or the lack thereof by the way someone walks into the store.

My second set of customers comes in not that much later, a young family. They'll buy a book each for the kids. I take some time to point them in the right direction—I inherited my grandmother's knack for that kind of thing. She always knew the exact right book to put in a customer's hand.

Once I've checked them out, I get back to working on my redbud-themed display. I've got a stack of books about redbuds and our local trees, a small pot I've arranged gardening tools in like a bouquet, and I'm thinking about how I can put a flyer for the festival somewhere in the display when I hear a low, familiar voice saying my name.

And *feel* it, but I ignore that part.

I look up to see Jacob North standing in the doorway of my store. This is a surprise. Jacob and I might be friends, but he doesn't make the trek into town very often during the week. He lives across the river on a farm and he doesn't have time for excursions. Except when he comes over on Saturdays to run his stand at the farmer's market with his dark hair faintly rumpled, his broad shoulders far wider than Bernie the cheese guy's, and that about-to-scowl look that is his trademark on his objectively attractive face.

Just like now.

I smile at him, though he doesn't smile back. I don't take this personally, because Jacob has never been much of a *smiler*. He's a solemn guy. Some would call him curmudgeonly and humorless, but they don't know him. He is *also* an upstanding, loyal friend…who takes life way too seriously.

And that's coming from me, the type A queen. A crown I wear proudly.

"Corrinne wanted to meet me here," he says, like he feels the need to excuse his presence. He's still standing in the doorway, hands in his pockets.

But I focus on the Corrinne part. "Oh, is she finally considering local food?"

Corrinne Martin is the chef at the oldest restaurant in St. Cyprian. A small, casual place with American fare and only a handful of tables shoved into a historic building and, weather permitting, its delightfully uneven patio outside.

While Jacob supplied local ingredients from his farm to two of the newer restaurants in town, Corrinne had been stubborn about making the switch over to higher priced ingredients, even if they were local and better.

Because local is always better. Especially *our* local.

"She finally is. I think she wanted to meet here so you can talk her into it."

I've been trying to talk Corrinne into using Jacob for years, but Jacob is the actual farmer. "Isn't that your job?"

"She'll feel better if she has your blessing. You know that."

I can't help but grin. It's been my goal to get all the business owners in St. Cyprian to look at me as someone they can come to for help, advice, a sympathetic ear. I've worked hard to earn the reputation of a smart businesswoman who cares about this town and the businesses in it. To be available to anyone who needs help or advice, and to always have the businesses' and town's best interests at heart.

People don't just trust me—they believe in me. It took some time. A young woman always needs time to prove she knows what she's doing, unlike certain mayors who simply announce they're up to the job and win in a landslide, but I've put the time in. The more I've helped my fellow business owners, the more they look to me for advice. I was right to focus on that.

I love having Jacob affirm it.

"You know I'll support you," I tell him. "It would be a real attraction for tourists if we could boast that all our restaurants are stocked by local suppliers. It'll help the farmer's market too."

I know Jacob doesn't need me to go on about either of those things. He's been an integral part of it all, but he's also a very taciturn human being. He doesn't talk much and loves nothing more than to let a silence stretch out.

I do not.

"Have you given any more thought to goat yoga this summer?" I ask innocently.

Maybe not so innocently.

He looks at me without moving a muscle. "I am not facilitating your internet nonsense."

He will. Once I find the right tactic, Jacob will come through with his goats, because Jacob always comes through.

"Goat yoga isn't internet nonsense, Jacob. Since when did you become a boomer?" His expression shifts closer to a real scowl and I hurry to continue. "Science has proved both yoga and animals can lower your blood pressure, calm anxiety, and center your thinking."

All things Jacob could use, though I know better than to say it. I try to picture him doing yoga, which is hilarious all on its own. He's so...big and *masculine*. Nothing like the lithe suburbanites in fashionable spandex who usually partake around here.

Still, I can't help myself. The image of Jacob in spandex with a goat on his back is too much. "Maybe you should try it."

"Maybe you'd like some llamas too," he says, his voice dripping in sarcasm.

But why should that be sarcastic? "Tempting. Llamas *are* very popular, but they can't really get on your back the way the goats can."

He studies me and I wonder when he moved so much farther into the shop. "How small do you think my goats are?"

And suddenly I am...not thinking about goats.

We're interrupted when Corrinne bustles into the store. *Thank God.* She looks haphazard as always, tendrils of gray curly hair spiraling out from under a ball cap that boasts the name of her restaurant. She must have been baking this morning, because she forgot to take her apron off. Sometimes I wonder how she can keep track of a restaurant kitchen when she always seems to be at her wit's end, but the restaurant has excellent ratings on all the online review and travel sites.

I check. For every business in town. Weekly.

She's an asset to St. Cyprian, and if she lets Jacob supply a good chunk of her ingredient list, I'll only have to convince her to use Holly's bakery for her bread supply to be able to advertise that all our restaurants are part of the 25-Mile Eat Local movement.

Which I will then blast all over the internet to lure in all the hipsters from Cherokee Street in St. Louis. It isn't enough to know your existing customer base—a chamber of commerce president must always be trying to expand it.

"Jacob says you're considering using North Farms food for the restaurant," I say instead of a more conventional greeting. Because I'm already coming up with new campaigns in my head.

Corrinne huffs. "It's a price increase. I'll have to raise my menu prices to offset it, and you know how much my regulars will hate that. I depend on them in the off season."

"Yes, absolutely. And those are all valid concerns." I move to Corrinne to slip my arm around her shoulders and begin to guide her toward where Jacob is standing. "I imagine you'll hear some grumbling, but you'll still be able to boast the most reasonable prices in St. Cyprian *and* the surrounding areas with such an excellent product. Grumbles will quickly turn to satisfied customers once again."

Corrinne nods. "I know you're right, Emerson. I just really hate change. And risk. The Lunch House is...my everything."

I give her a friendly squeeze as we stop in front of Jacob. "Change and risk are *hard*. If they were easy, everyone would effortlessly succeed at whatever businesses they have half a mind to run, and we both know they don't. You have lasted in St. Cyprian this long because even when it's hard, you stick with it. I've learned a lot from you, Corrinne."

Corrinne looks at me, her face crinkled into a smile. "I needed that reassurance." She gives me a quick hug, then turns to Jacob. Her gaze gets sharp and I can see the organized chef who knows what she's doing come alive. "All right, Jacob. Let's talk."

They move into the parlor area. I've often encouraged business owners who don't have a good space of their own to meet here. It's a quiet place, and I'm always on hand to help facilitate. It's good to watch Jacob and Corrinne bend their heads together and do something I *know* will help both their businesses.

And the town.

A few customers trickle in and I greet them and help where I can. When my bell tinkles again as Jacob and Corrinne are finishing up, I look at the door and inwardly wince.

"Skip." I thought I'd have at least another twenty-four hours to prepare as Skip isn't usually up on looking at the town website, or my many flyer stations throughout the town. Someone must have showed him.

The likely culprits, a few of the more excitable members of the chamber of commerce, walk in behind him. They're doing a terrible job of hiding their smirks and eager eyes. They pretend they're looking at books, but what they really want is to see a Skip and Emerson showdown.

"Perhaps you'd like to explain this," he says, brandishing one of my excellent flyers for the Redbud Festival's new nighttime extravaganza.

I try to remember all the best tips for professional encounters I've ever read. A kind smile, a clear message. He's not going to rile me, because I know what I'm doing is good and is going to be even better for our town. *Our* town.

I remind myself that Skip has to care about St. Cyprian to be its mayor. Maybe we care differently, but, fundamentally, we want the same things.

If only I could make it clear to him that my way is better, I'm sure we could get past all this silly tension.

The lurking chamber of commerce peanut gallery doesn't help.

I try to *exude calm*. "The other business owners and I want to expand the Redbud Festival to reach beyond the botanists. By including a nighttime portion, we make it more of a community-wide event. Twinkly lights and sales will bring people in. The restaurants and bars will keep them fed and happy. The ferry will run an extra boat to take them back and forth—"

Skip sneers. "So this is all a ploy to help your uncle and cousin make money."

I don't let that accusation rouse my temper. Somehow. "The Rivers family will benefit, but so will every business owner who participates. Everyone in the Main Street coalition agreed."

"I'm the mayor, and I did not agree."

I fear I am beginning to exude something less than calm, but every conflict resolution article I've studied emphasizes how important calm is. "You're not a business owner, Skip. You're a politician. This isn't your domain—it's mine." That wasn't smart. I know that when his cheeks start to redden, always a telltale sign that he's about to have a tantrum. I summon my professional smile from somewhere and attempt to look placating. "Now, Skip, you know as well as anyone that my only goal is to make St. Cyprian a better place. That means more profitable businesses and *that* means bringing in more tourists, especially during the off season."

"You can't do this without my approval. End of story."

He is mistaken. But then, I doubt he's read the town code the way I have. Annually.

"It's already done," I say firmly, my smile slipping a little.

Skip prefers to play golf and ride in convertibles in parades and pretend to be important rather than actually *work*. It suits me fine. I'm not a politician. But when he decides to interfere—because *I've* decided we need to change things—it's always like this. Fraught with the land mines of all the years of embarrassment.

He can't compromise. He can't concede. In his head, he *has* to win. He has to beat me for the sake of his fragile male ego.

I understand. I do. And I wish I could let him, so we could all move on, but the town is too important. This festival *matters*.

"It's happening." I shove my hands into my pockets so they can't curl into fists, and there's Georgie's stone. I wrap my fingers around it and hold on. "With all the required permits and town approval. There's nothing you can do about it."

A couple of people are whispering, someone else is snickering, and as those sounds move through the air, Skip's face gets redder and redder.

"You don't think there's anything I can do?"

"Skip, that's not a challenge. I only meant—"

"I'd watch your back, Emerson."

Skip points his finger at me like he's about to jab me in the shoulder with it.

The rock in my hand gets...hot, and as I'm trying to figure out why, Jacob is suddenly standing between us.

"I wouldn't," he says to Skip.

That's all he says. But there's something about the way he stands there, arms crossed and gaze direct, that has Skip fuming. You can practically *see* anger arcing between the two of them in a bright flash.

But that's all the tension in the room getting to me and making my imagination run wild. Just like the rock, hot and throbbing in my hand.

"My money's on Jacob," someone says from behind me.

"Mine too," I say, and then wince, because obviously that was the absolute wrong way to go about making peace with Skip.

But *honestly*.

"You want to take this outside, North?" Skip demands, his face now an impressive shade of purply red.

Jacob only raises an eyebrow. "Do *you*?"

The crowd is full-on giggling and whispering now. Skip's mean, but he's no physical specimen. Even with his inflated ego, he has to know Jacob could take him. Probably with a hand tied behind his back.

Soon enough Skip does what men who think they're far more important than they actually are always do.

He retreats.

He slams out through the shop door, leaving the crowd laughing and talking about him as he goes. Another embarrassment he'll put at my feet, I have no doubt.

I let out a long breath. Jacob's interference, however personally thrilling, didn't do anything to change the situation. Like many a privileged man before him, Skip will run home and pout to his mother, who will in turn try to use her money and influence to make my life harder. But this isn't Salem and there aren't whispers of witchcraft in the air over St. Cyprian. So, unlike Sarah, I won't be hanged.

This is why I have my friends coming over tonight. We need a Skip plan. Not because I worry what Skip will do to me, but because I worry what he'll do to the Redbud Festival. He's a petty, petty man.

"He shouldn't be threatening you like that," Jacob says darkly.

I take my hands out of my pockets and wave it away. I try to wave the whole unfortunate interaction away. "I always seem to make a fool out of him when I'm not trying to— not that he believes that."

"He deserves to be made a fool of, and in this case, it wasn't you making a fool out of him."

"But he'll blame me," I say with a sigh. "Somehow, he always blames me and then he takes that out on me and I want to find *some* way to call a truce. It's what's best for the town. The most important thing is what's best for St. Cyprian, and I *know* an extended Redbud Festival is going to help." I look up at Jacob, who's still standing there with his arms crossed, anger still crackling from him like he's a live wire. I don't want to think about Jacob *crackling*. "I'll see you tonight?"

Jacob nods, shortly, but he's still glaring after Skip. "Yeah, I'll be there."

And he is. That night, Jacob and Zander show up together, about ten minutes before Ellowyn waltzes in covered in black, shroud-like layers. No one knocks. Wilde House has been open to my friends since we were kids. My grandmother insisted on it.

I ordered the pizza and Georgie made her brownies, so we settle ourselves in the big living room like we've done since middle school. The only person missing is Rebekah, but I hardly think about my runaway sister anymore.

Almost never, really. She left. Her choice. She refuses contact. Her prerogative. If it feels like betrayal…

Well, I can't control people. Pity, that.

A stone hearth made of local limestone dominates the room. It's original to the house, and the panel wall above is decorated with colorful stones to make a mosaic of a star. Georgie must have started the fire while I was paying the pizza delivery guy. The flickering light makes the walls dance with shadows and the comforting scent of wood fire fills the room.

"Holly was all abuzz about the showdown you and Skip had when I got my afternoon coffee today," Georgie says, taking a big bite of pizza from her spot curled up in a big leather armchair.

I grimace, because nothing in this town ever stays private

or even rational. People love to gossip, and the game of St. Cyprian telephone will tell everyone that I beat Skip to a bloody pulp in the alley behind my bookstore by tomorrow.

He will *really* hate that.

"It wasn't a showdown. It was a discussion." I can't mitigate the rumors in town, but I can mitigate the way my friends exacerbate the problem. Jacob snorts and I glare at him. He's standing in the corner with his plate of pizza. No matter how many times he's been in this house, he never seems comfortable, and he always positions himself next to an exit like he's ready to bolt. "You didn't help stepping in between us and playing bodyguard."

"You were going to fight?" Ellowyn is suddenly interested. "You and Skip?"

"I bet Holly was telling everyone it was an all-out brawl, but no." I make a face. "He was just jabbing his finger at me and then Jacob got between us like Captain America and told him not to."

Everyone goes quiet, and there's a strange tension in the room that I'm familiar with, but have never spent too much time trying to parse. They look at Jacob like protecting me *means* something, when of course it doesn't.

Yes, there was a time in high school I thought Jacob might have been into me, but we grew up and never acted on anything. We're friends. Who would want to risk a friendship when *attraction* is so fleeting?

"I need options on how to keep Skip from interfering with the festival," I say, bringing everyone back to the important task at hand.

Because otherwise I might be tempted to talk about what it was like when Jacob stepped in, the *electricity* of it all and the hot stone, and I don't think that's a great idea. Because maybe I was into him too, back in high school, but we're adults now.

"We could always poison Skip," Ellowyn suggests.

She's stretched out on the large couch, making sure no one can sit next to her. Except Georgie's cat, Octavius, who's curled into the corner cleaning himself as he watches the proceedings. He looks desperately bored. He always looks desperately bored.

"Ellowyn."

"Well, we *could*," Ellowyn insists, widening her eyes at me. "Specifically, I could."

"I'm not interested in anything illegal. I'm interested in finding a way to reason with him."

"You'll never reason with him," Georgie points out. "There is no reasoning with a spoiled child."

I let out a huff of breath because that's true. "Okay, maybe not reason. But a peace offering. If he lets me handle the Redbud Festival, I'll… What?"

Ellowyn snaps her fingers as though she's had a brilliant idea. "Organize a fight between Skip and Jacob. Sell tickets, take bets. The town would be rich. No Redbud Festival necessary."

"Always so bloodthirsty," Zander points out from where he sits on the hearth, pizza already demolished.

Ellowyn lifts a brow in his direction and the usual tension hums between them. "When it's called for, yes."

"Because you get to decide that." Zander isn't laughing any longer. "Judge and jury."

"I'm the boss of me, Zander." Ellowyn's gaze is cool. "You should try it."

"Maybe you could give Skip some job," Georgie says, rolling her eyes at Ellowyn and Zander and their traditional bickering.

I take great pride in the fact that though my cousin and

Ellowyn broke each other's hearts back in high school, they've never asked me to take sides. We're a friend group, no matter how destroyed they were after their breakup and no matter how many bad feelings still exist between them. And no matter how many times I've tried to facilitate some healing between them, I might add, yet have been denied.

"Like grand master of turning on the lights," Georgie continues. "He can give a little mayoral speech and make himself feel important."

I consider it. Feeling important *is* Skip's only goal as mayor, as far as I can tell. "That could work. He does love a speech."

"He wouldn't take the offer from her," Jacob says gruffly.

Which bursts my bubble, because it's true. I'd try to ask Skip to make a grand speech and end up accidentally pantsing him in front of his mother. I suppress a shudder at the thought.

"This is ridiculous," I mutter. "Skip may be a man-baby, but *I* am an adult."

Everyone nods, of course. Because it's true.

Zander takes a brownie off the platter. "Maybe someone else on the chamber of commerce can ask. Holly Bishop handles Skip pretty well."

My cousin's skill at reading people is right on the mark, as usual. "He'd still know it was from me, but he could save some face. It's worth a shot." I look over at Jacob, waiting for him to point out ten more reasons it is not, in fact, worth a shot. But for once, he says nothing.

Okay then. It's not a foolproof plan, maybe, but it's *something*.

We talk some more, stuff ourselves, and then everyone begins to go their separate ways. Zander has to get to the bar. Jacob has to get back to his animals. Georgie claims the crystals are calling her.

When Ellowyn leans in to give me a hug goodbye, she whispers, "Consider poison."

I won't, but for a second I do wish I had Georgie's fanciful mind. It would be handy to imagine I could put some kind of spell on Skip. I wouldn't turn him into a toad, necessarily. I'd just get him to see the wisdom of doing what I want.

Or get him to love St. Cyprian the way I do, which is the same thing.

But there is no easy magic, only hard work, I think as I tidy up the living room and then wash up the dishes. My grandmother used to say that all the time. Like her, I've never been afraid to put in the time and work my butt off if it gets me where I want to go.

"No one thought you could win chamber of commerce president either," I remind myself over the sound of the water pouring into the sink. "And now look."

And I find myself grinning, because I know what Skip doesn't and never has. Come hell or high water, if it takes me to my grave, I'm going to find a way to win him over.

One way or another, a Wilde always wins.

SKIP DOES NOT TAKE THE OLIVE BRANCH. NOT from me, and not from Holly, though she makes a valiant effort.

That's not exactly unusual.

But he doesn't show his hand either. That is *very* unusual.

Usually I don't have to worry about Skip. He has all the stealth of a charging bull. But he's quiet. *Everything* is quiet this whole week, and as the Redbud Festival approaches, I am a bundle of nerves. I don't *show* it, of course, but it's sitting in me like an overactive chinchilla.

And I know more about chinchillas than I'd like.

The morning before the festival, I'm lying in bed waiting for my 5:00 a.m. alarm to go off. I haven't been able to sleep much. Too much going on. Too much stress.

Too many repeats of that same old dream I always have of my sister. Rebekah and me somewhere in this house, having strange conversations we never had before she left. Last night's was odder than usual, us huddled near the confluence as a storm raged around us. Me asking her to stay and fight. Her asking me to save myself and run. But I don't know what she'd be fighting for or what I'd be running from. Or why a fox led me one way, and a raven led her another.

Something is in the air. Not like…*vibes* or any of the things Georgie would call it. It's a logical response to everything that's going on. Because things aren't right. Skip is planning *something*, and I don't know what it is.

All I can do is move forward with *my* plans, I tell myself. For the nine millionth time. Everything is ready for the festival tomorrow and I've made as many overtures to Skip Simon, and his significantly more fearsome mother, as I can.

Once the Redbud Festival is a success, I'll have time to sleep and relax.

Until the summer season starts up—but I have a whole, ruthlessly indexed binder for that, carefully filed in my home office.

My phone chimes—not my normal alarm, but a call— jolting me upright. It's far too early for a *good-news* call. I don't recognize the number, but it's local and it might have something to do with the festival, so I answer.

"Hope I didn't wake you, Emerson," comes the very last voice I ever want to hear in my ear.

Much less while I'm in my bed.

Skip.

Everything inside of me goes a little cold, but I pull myself together and smile at the wall. A trick I learned long ago to sound upbeat and happy on the phone. "Are you calling because you want to be our grand master after all? I could help you write a speech if you need—"

"I'm not going to be your grand master." I don't like how he says that, but he's still talking. "I feel it's my duty as mayor to let you in on a little rumor I heard this morning."

The cold inside edges toward full-blown panic, but I keep my voice even. "Rumor? Before five in the morning?"

"Just a few whispers that something bad happened at the cemetery last night with your precious redbuds. Sad. You should probably go check it out."

"What do you mean?"

"I honestly don't know. It was something I overheard, but I knew you'd want to go check on it right away."

He sounds so *smug*. I don't even bother with saying goodbye—I just hang up. I jump out of bed and throw on some clothes. I don't want to wake Georgie up. She's not a morning person, and I'll see what's what before I start dragging people into it.

My mind races as I head downstairs. I'm going to get there and it's going to be nothing, clearly. Or maybe it's a joke. Maybe Skip is playing a joke on me.

I hesitate at the back door. This could be Skip finally taking the opportunity to embarrass me. To enact his revenge.

Maybe I should wait. Call Zander and have him scout it out on one of his ferry trips rather than go racing across the river myself. I could call Jacob. He lives on that side of the river and that makes him my friend closest to the cemetery, but I...don't want to call Jacob. Not when I'm uncertain about something.

I like to keep my interactions with Jacob based on facts, not feelings.

Besides, all of those options require waiting, and I can't. I'm not sure I'm physically capable. I blow out a breath and decide, what the hell, I'll just go.

If Skip's got an ambush set up, how bad can it be? Maybe it will be embarrassing, but what Skip doesn't understand is I don't embarrass easily. Not when I know I'm in the right and *especially not* when it might benefit the town. I once dressed in a chicken costume at a town council meeting. That's how seriously I take my mission.

And hey, maybe if Skip gets a shot in, he'll feel better about himself and leave me and my ideas alone. Maybe this is the best thing I can do for the Redbud Festival.

I leave Georgie a note that I went to the cemetery to check on the redbuds. I do not tell her why. Then I throw myself out the back door of Wilde House. I march through the backyard, heading for the riverfront below. The yard is a steep hill, and Georgie and I have taken a let-nature-handle-it approach to the landscaping. I make my way through the run-of-the-mill, regular old Missouri redbuds hinting at budding. Then the tall prairie grasses. Past all that—and more of Georgie's crystals hanging from some of the giant, ancient cottonwood tree branches than I remember being there before—is a staircase built into the slope that takes our yard down to the river. My great-great-great-grandfather installed the steps so he could walk right to the riverbank every morning.

I like to think of him coming down and greeting the great Missouri River every day. It reminds me of my own ritual on the front step, taking in the town. I like a lot less the family legend that one night he'd woken up and inexplicably walked down these same stairs, then straight into the river to drown.

I shiver a little as I reach the riverbank. Georgie would call it a *genetically passed memory*. I call it an overactive imagination brought on by Skip-induced stress.

Instead of going all the way down to the water, I cut across a strip of grass and then onto the bike path that ribbons along the length of the river. It eventually takes me to the large parking lot for the ferry. Zander's side of the family—aptly named Rivers—owns and runs the ferry business that connects the Missouri side of the river to the Illinois side. It allows people who want to live on the Missouri side and pay cheaper taxes, but work their jobs on the Illinois side, to cross here instead of driving miles out of their way to find a bridge. It also allows tourists to go back and forth—to Missouri for the small-town charm of St. Cyprian and to Illinois for a scenic farmland drive or U-pick orchards.

My uncle Zack is manning the ferry this early in the morning, and I'm glad I don't have to explain to Zander that Skip did something, then called to goad me into reacting. Or that he's playing a prank on me and I'm letting my worry over the festival override my concerns about what the prank might be. It's not a trap if you know you're walking into it, right?

Zander would take a dim view of all of this.

And I *have* to check on the Draconian Redbuds. They are the crowning glory of the redbud festival. The entire reason there even *is* a redbud festival. I'd rather have Skip dump pig's blood on me or whatever he's got up his sleeve than spend my morning worried about what he *might* have done to them.

Besides, it can't be something truly serious. If Skip was going to hurt me, he would have done it years ago. The bottom line is Skip is a coward.

I am not.

"Early morning for you, Em," Uncle Zack greets me. He only has two cars on the open flat of the ferry this early, and I'm the only pedestrian.

I wish I'd thought to bring coffee with me. "I wanted to check on the redbuds before I have to open the store."

My uncle is about as likely to stand around talking about trees and festivals as he is to announce that the ferry has gone nudist. Secretly, I suspect he thinks I'm a bit off, but I'm fond of him anyway. He's a fixture in this town, and he takes his legacy as a Rivers seriously. I appreciate that in anyone, but especially a relative. Then there's his devotion to my aunt, my mother's sister, who's been suffering from a disease no one wants to name, but I can only assume is cancer of some kind.

He's a good man. Better yet, he doesn't comment on the redbuds. He goes and collects the fare from the two drivers, then heads back to me.

"Pretty cold yet. You want to come sit in the pilot room with me?"

I shake my head. "I'm all right. On the way back I will."

He nods, then disappears into his little room where he'll guide the small ferry boat over the water to the Illinois side. The engine rumbles to life and we begin the slow chug across the wide river.

I stand out against the railing. It *is* cold, but that helps keep me centered. Whatever prank Skip is going to pull is going to be childish at best, and my redbuds will be fine. The festival will go on as planned. I will preside over all of it serenely.

Positive visualization is one of the things I give myself stickers for in my planner, FYI.

See it, then be it, I chant at myself.

The river is high, the brown waters rippling in front of the ferry, the banks swollen and muddy. But trees line the river and in the distance I can see the confluence, a term that I've never thought does justice to the fact of two mighty riverways meeting and mingling. The Mississippi and Missouri in an age-old dance. If I squint, it almost looks like there has to be another river out there too, mixing and melding and making something new.

That's the kind of magic I believe in.

I suck in a deep breath and let the river-scented air settle me the way it always does. I used to have dreams of swimming out into the middle of the confluence and going down beneath the surface. My sister informed me they were just nightmares when I told her about it, but she didn't understand.

My river dreams were never nightmares. They were always joyful, even when it seemed like I was drowning.

I always knew better. I always knew I was going to rise.

No matter what Skip has in store for me, I'll withstand it. I'll handle his little reindeer game and pull off my festival, and when the tourists stampede into town bringing revenue for all, I promise that I will *try* to be gracious.

When Uncle Zack lands the boat, I wait for him to open the gate. The cars lurch forward onto the bank where mud changes to concrete that leads to the highway. I wave at my uncle and take the muddy trail along the river toward the cemetery.

It's the oldest cemetery in the area and is where all the grand old St. Cyprian families, including my own, are buried to this day.

But even more important, it's where the Draconian Redbuds bloom.

The hike isn't easy this morning, thanks to all the spring mud where the trail should be, and I narrowly miss sliding and falling three times before I make it up the hill to the cemetery. If we get any more rain, I'm going to have to install a guardrail and put out warning signs for people to watch their step. Perhaps have a council member guide people up the trail.

I catch myself from slipping one more time, then I hesitate outside the wrought iron gates. *St. Cyprian Cemetery* is written in gold metal in the archway at its entrance. It looks old and imposing, faintly gothic, and is attached to no church or funeral parlor. It's just a cemetery close to the river and far away from most everything else except farms.

An eerie location, sure, but who knows what it was like back in the 1700s when they first started burying their people here?

I usually find it charming. *Atmospheric.*

I blame Skip for ruining what should be a perfectly lovely morning.

I push away my unease and charge ahead, pulling open the gate. I have things to do and silly fears about dead people beneath my feet—some of them my own relatives—cannot be entertained.

The redbud cluster is on the far side of the cemetery and as I head there, I look out over the river below. It's high for this time of year. Too much more rain and the ferries will start having trouble running in floodwater with all the hidden hazards and drowned docks—and *that* will be a problem for tourism, all right.

We're a river town and we know how to deal with flooding, but that doesn't mean I like it.

I keep walking.

My first hint that something is amiss is the gravestones. Around here we have a peculiar local tradition of having animal statuary with our gravestones, like guardians for our dead. But the stone creatures…are in the wrong place.

There's a cat on my grandmother's grave when there should be a fox.

My mouth feels dry, and that makes my pulse pick up. I suddenly start to feel like I'm in one of those upsettingly realistic dreams. Though mine are usually about showing up at important meetings naked and unprepared, not graveyard shenanigans.

How can stone animals hop graves? It doesn't make sense, especially because when I go closer to look, the cat where my grandmother's fox should be hasn't been broken or damaged, the way it would have to be if it was moved. It's just…a stone cat, sitting there as if it's always been there.

My stomach ties itself into intricate knots, and I have to breathe out a few times, hard.

Even Skip couldn't pull *this* off. Could he?

I decide that even if he could, the graves aren't my concern right now. I'll come back to that. I'll come back to it and it'll make sense. I'll find a reasonable explanation.

Or I'll wake the hell up.

I pinch myself on the inside of my wrist and it hurts, so I march myself over to the redbud cluster. The *famous* redbud cluster.

But my footsteps slow and my throat closes up when I make it over the last gentle hill, because I need, suddenly and desperately, for what I'm seeing to be a nightmare.

The trees have been hacked to pieces. Blooms scattered on the ground and stomped into the mud. They're still white, but the sun is out, so they should be pink.

It can't be, but I crouch and touch one splintered limb and it feels as real as anything. Tears threaten, but I blink them back.

Rage is a much better reaction for the situation. It feels almost healing. I jerk my phone out of my jacket pocket and punch the number from this morning.

"Hello," Skip answers cheerfully.

"How could you do this?"

I want to cry. Maybe I am crying. I can't believe he'd be this small and vicious. To me, sure. I can take it. But how could he hurt the town this way when he's supposed to be its mayor? Because of some stupid feud he's been mad about since fourth grade, or because—like so many people around here—he hates change?

Or because he's a spoiled baby, like Georgie said. But I'm the responsible adult in this situation. The businesswoman rooted in reality with a duty to my town and all the business owners involved in the festival.

But damn it, this *hurts*.

"Emerson? Is that you?" He's enjoying himself. I can hear it. "I don't know what you're talking about."

There's such *glee* in his voice.

"You...you did this. The cemetery. And you chopped up all the trees."

"The redbud trees? Did someone cut down your fancy redbuds, Emerson?"

My hands are cold. My throat aches. I concentrate on how angry I am instead. "*You* did it, Skip. How could you... *Why* would you?"

"Sounds like you've got *quite* a mess on your hands." He makes a tsking sound. "I'd be careful about blaming me for petty vandalism. I have a lawyer on retainer, you know."

But I'm having a hard time concentrating on Skip's oily voice in my ear. Something is happening all around me. I stand up, frowning, as dark clouds slink across the sun.

Storms, I tell myself. Though there were none in the forecast.

"Is everything okay, Emerson?" Skip practically purrs. "Or has something...got your tongue?"

"What?"

I'm only half listening, totally confused because the darkness gets thicker and thicker, until I can barely see. I look up at the sky, but it's black as night.

My heart begins to thump loudly in my chest, the beat echoing in my ears. My fingers feel nerveless and it becomes a little too hard to catch my breath. The phone slips out of my grasp and lands with a thud in what seems to be a dark mist on the ground. Thick and boiling.

Don't be silly, Emerson, I snap at myself. *It's just a storm.*

Just a storm, and I should get back to the ferry before it kicks into gear. I look over at the hill to the north of the cemetery. Or I could call Jacob and have him help me.

Am I really going to ask Jacob to help me...with a storm?

I'm a born and bred Midwesterner. I'm not afraid of *storms*.

Then I begin to see tiny dots of light in all this black.

At first, I try to convince myself they're lightning bugs, even though lightning bugs are out of season. And also, it's morning.

But the lights are too...red.

Too much like eyes.

Maybe there's some animal I'm not familiar with that has eyes that glow red, I reason, a little desperately. Some odd species of possum. A certain kind of rat.

And maybe, for some reason, there are suddenly a whole lot of strange possum eyes in a graveyard at six o'clock in the morning. Hell, maybe they moved all the gravestone guardians for their own nefarious possum reasons.

It's possible I'm becoming hysterical.

But then it doesn't matter what I'm doing as the red lights begin to move.

Toward me.

Closer. Then closer. And there are *so many* of them.

No rain. No thunder. Just the dark and the red, red eyes.

"Stay back!" I yell.

I even pick up a hunk of branch from one of the splintered redbud trees and hurl it at them. My palms are sweaty and my aim is off, but it should be enough to scare them away. Or at least slow them down.

Wake up, I order myself.

But there's only a terrible hissing noise, like knives beneath my skin. The air is getting darker and too thick to breathe.

The horrible red eyes draw closer.

It's a storm. They're just possums hidden by the dark. I'm shaking and I try to convince myself there's a chill in the air, but it's terror, through and through.

I'm dreaming. I squeeze my eyes shut, sure that when I count to five and reopen them everything will be back to normal. The graveyard will be pretty and calm. Or I'll still be in my bed, waiting for my alarm to go off.

All this will be gone when I open my eyes. I know it will. But it's not.

When I look again, the black all around me is worse. The red eyes are still there, and my stomach twists as I begin to see the nightmarish bodies the eyes are connected to—

They jump.

I can finally see that their bodies are actually too big to be possums. They're more like dogs, giant, muscular dogs, which would be scary enough, but their faces aren't canine.

They're all too human.

And they're coming right for me.

4

SOMETHING EXPLODES AROUND ME IN TIME
with my scream of horror. Like lightning, followed by a
rumble that *isn't* thunder no matter how much I want it to
be. I cover my head with my arms, sort of like a standing
tornado drill.

Relief floods through me at the thought. It's a tornado.
That *must* be it. Sure, I've lived through a few near misses
and never seen this kind of blackness or fog or *red eyes*, but
it's the most reasonable explanation. So reasonable that I almost laugh at myself for imagining it could be anything else.

When nothing else happens around me—no explosions,
no lights, no teeth rending my flesh, just the heavy cold press
of that swirling black—I slowly lower my arms and survey
the weather. Because certainly those creatures with human
faces were a panic-induced hallucination.

But I don't see a funnel cloud. No green tinge to the sky
that so often precedes severe weather. The dog-bodied and
human-faced nightmares are still there, but a new…animal

stands between their approach and me. This one doesn't have red eyes. It's a giant deer, of all things, with a huge rack of antlers. Fighting off the wave of horror jumping at me, slicing through their bodies with thick horns that glow gold. Every time its antlers stab through the red-eyed nightmare jumping at me, they turn to ash and disappear.

I let out that laugh. My imagination has certainly lost its tether to reality.

And then a man *lands* in front of me. Sort of like a superhero in one of those needlessly long and overly loud action movies. But this is no Superman.

It's Jacob.

It's a relief to see him standing there, even if he's glowing like the deer. *Glowing.* I'm not relieved because I think he'll save me—I'm certainly not that patriarchal—but because I really know it's a dream now. A familiar one at that. How many times have I dreamed of Jacob saving me? Or the reverse? My subconscious is all about equal opportunity saving. When Jacob is involved anyway.

But it confirms that I am, in fact, dreaming.

I take my first full breath since I saw a stone cat where a fox should be.

Jacob looks back at me, and his green eyes are...luminescent. I prefer cold, hard facts with him, but it's feeling that slams through me—too many feelings to parse. Too strong to catalog away and deal with rationally. So vivid they almost feel like memories.

Too real, a voice that sounds suspiciously like my own whispers around me. Inside me. *Remember this, Emerson. Remember.*

I haven't the slightest idea what I'm supposed to remember, but Jacob points at me and draws a circle in the air with his finger. When I look down at my feet, a line drawn in the damp earth appears. A circle carved around me like the one Jacob drew in the air. The black fog that had tendriled around my feet, thick like ropes, now circles me but keeps its distance. Like it can't get past the line on the ground.

I look back up at Jacob. He's chanting words I don't understand but feel familiar all the same. Like a lullaby in a foreign language. Like a memory I can't quite access. A soothing echo, though I couldn't say of what. I want to repeat the words, feel their shape in my mouth as I make the sounds.

I find my mouth *is* moving in the silly song I sing to myself. *St. Cyprian is mine and I am St. Cyprian's.* And there's a warmth deep inside of me that centers itself in my belly, growing outward in a strange tingling. But I can't focus on what's happening inside of me when Jacob is standing there in the midst of swirls of dark fog, the deer beside him fighting off the red-eyed creatures that only seem to multiply. Their human-like mouths full of bigger, sharper teeth as they snarl and snap.

Jacob holds up his hand toward the sun, which is now hidden behind the thick, forbidding clouds. The oversized deer is fighting off wave after wave of the creatures. Jacob's eyes, glowing green, are still on me. He's still chanting words, and my mouth seems to move with his.

St. Cyprian is mine and I am St. Cyprian's, I think. Maybe I say it. And maybe there are other words, too, layered in and around the comfortable ones I know so well.

"Stay in the circle," he orders me, a sharp command that's so unlike him. But then so are the glowing eyes and the magical deer—Dream Jacob is a whole mood. "That's all you have to do, Emerson. Stay in the circle. Do you understand?"

This feels far more vivid than any dream I've ever had. *Maybe it's a hallucination*, I think. Maybe Skip drugged me before he hacked my redbuds all to pieces. I'm not conversant on typical drug trip visuals, because I, naturally, just said no to recreational drugs back in the day. Unlike some.

I don't really know why I'm thinking of my sister again, at a time like this. Maybe I'm following her lead and enjoying a mental break, one of my pet theories for why she ran away—

Another thundering roar echoes around us, shaking the very ground. My knees buckle. And suddenly there's a light in Jacob's hand, shaped like a sword, as if he conjured it from the very sun. A sun sword.

Jacob swipes the sword through the black fog. Light scrapes against dark like nails on a chalkboard, a deep rasp of a scream, but Jacob keeps pushing forward. When he hits one of the creatures with his light-sword, the snarling, red-eyed doglike thing turns to smoke and black ash rains to the ground.

I can smell it. Burnt hair and something *wrong* beneath it, like decay. I can't remember ever dreaming *smells* before.

Still in my circle, I look over at the huge deer. It's still taking out as many of the horrible beings as Jacob does with its glowing antlers. I can see more of the nasty things now, thanks to Jacob's blazing sword. I can see their faces...and I really wish I couldn't. My stomach cramps into queasiness, because they have those horrid doglike bodies and red eyes, and that's bad enough. But it's the human faces, twisted into grotesque fury, that make me feel sick. I can taste my own fear. My eyes even water. Their muscles bunch, saliva drips from their sharp teeth, and the sounds they make...

I shudder and I can't stop shuddering. Nothing earthly about the snarls and growls. Nothing okay.

No matter how Jacob and the deer fight, the creatures keep coming. Multiplying. Until the two of them are surrounded.

I know this isn't real. The circle around me is simply a line in the dirt. It doesn't mean anything. And those creatures aren't real. If they attack me, no matter how scary it is, I'll wake up. It'll all be over.

But I don't move. I'm paralyzed and my usual pep talks aren't working. The thought of a fist pump seems obscene.

One creature hurls itself at Jacob, rears back as it clings to him, then sinks its sharp teeth deep into his arm. I can't bite back a scream even though I know it's an illusion. I can *hear* the snarling and, I swear, the actual tearing of his flesh—

But all Jacob does is grunt and run his sword into its back.

It's like a dance. A fight sequence in the kind of horror movie I would never watch.

"This isn't real," I mutter out loud. "It isn't *real*."

Another monster lunges, scraping its long, pointed claws down Jacob's chest. And the gash it leaves looks entirely too real. I can practically feel the searing pain myself. I rub my own chest, my breath coming in pants. My heart is beating so hard it's thundering in my ears, louder than anything going on around me.

My stomach hurts. My eyes are damp. This isn't real—but worse, this isn't *me*.

Jacob is hurt and here I am standing by like a scared little child. Even in a dream, I can't let these things *devour* him. His sleeve is torn where he's been bitten. His chest has a giant claw mark across it, ragged and bloody. Every time he kills a creature, it disappears in a groan of black smoke, but there are so many.

Too many.

I have to help. I have to *do* something. It's simply not in me to watch Jacob suffer. Not anybody—but especially not Jacob. And since it's only a dream, why not charge into the fray? Why not take charge? It's what I *do*.

I take a step outside the boundary carved around me.

"Get back in the circle!" Jacob shouts, plunging his sword of light into one of the awful *things* charging him. Then another, and another.

But he's bleeding. No matter how fictional it all is, it feels wrong to hide in that circle.

I move through the dark fog that clings like a sticky swamp and smells even worse. It takes all the strength I have to lift up a leg and put one foot in front of the other, but I fight through it. It takes too long, forever, to move in Jacob's direction. I don't even know what my plan is if—when—I make it to him. *I* certainly don't have a sun sword.

But I have to help.

When I finally fight my way almost to his side, a lifetime later, I stop suddenly. I rub my palms over my face but my eyes stay gritty. And what I see doesn't change. The bites and gashes on his body are already healing. Right in front of me. I watch the skin slowly stitch itself back together, leaving a scar for only a moment or two, and then nothing.

My stomach swoops. Shock. Denial. *It's just a dream.* Surely this is proof. But there's something else too. I forget everything going on around me. Odd dream whispers slither through my mind. Flashes of memories. Whatever drugs Skip gave me.

I don't know what I'm doing, only that I *have* to do it. I reach forward and touch the place where the blood trails down from the now fully healed bite mark on Jacob's arm.

"Emerson." His voice feels like a whisper *inside* me rather than an audible uttering from his mouth.

The blood I touch bubbles, turns gold on my fingertips, and then sparkles. I can only stare at it, mesmerized, as something warm and prickling swims through me. I feel a... strength. A light.

Power, something inside of me whispers.

I look up, and though the dark fog and the hideous creatures remain, the light washes me clean. It brings me clarity. The deer and Jacob are fighting off the creatures that lunge for *me*. At *me*. Jacob tries to draw another circle, but a surge of darkness stops him. One of the creatures latches on to his sword arm by the teeth. He tries to fight it off, but he can't. Where there was one, there are five. Then five more.

"Stay behind me!" Jacob grits out.

But I know we're losing. Jacob is protecting *me*. I don't know why these *things* want to harm me, but they do. And Jacob is the only thing standing in their way while I do *nothing*. It's a dream, sure, but we're losing and I'm the reason.

Wildes don't lose. We rise.

A terrible growl has me whirling around, my back to Jacob's as one of the awful beasts lunges for me—no deer or Jacob standing between us this time. With a look on its twisted human face that I'm sure is a kind of sickening triumph.

All I can think to do is hold out my hands, wishing all these nightmare dogs would simply die.

Just...*die*.

I squeeze my eyes shut and fervently tell myself to wake up as I hold out my palms to the beast lunging at me and all its revolting cousins. I even say it out loud. "Die!"

And I brace myself for impact. I don't have a sword like Jacob. Antlers like the deer.

I'm defenseless.

I refuse to accept that. No Wilde woman is *defenseless*. It took the Salem witch trials to kill Sarah Wilde when shame wouldn't do the trick. I do not intend to die without defending myself in my own damn dream.

I hold out my palms, prepared to fight. To brawl. To do whatever it takes.

"Die!" I shout, my eyes screwed shut and all my *will* focused out, focused hard and bright and *now*—

There's a bloodcurdling scream, the sound of a ripe, uneasy splashing, and then quiet.

I wait for the rending. Claws and fangs. The pain.

But there's only silence and that smell of dead things, thick and old.

When nothing happens, I open my eyes. I look down at my feet. An oily black substance covers the ground, staining the earth like a spill. But there are no monsters. No more black fog. Just a spring morning, colder than before.

Did I do that? I look at my hands.

They're glowing, the way Jacob was before.

Jacob.

I whirl around, sure he'll have disappeared in a puff of dream smoke like those monsters. Like the deer. But he's there. He's him.

There's still blood all over him, but those terrible wounds are healed. Most of them are completely gone, only the ripped fabric of his shirt to show they'd ever been there. That glow remains. That aura. A ring around not only him, but the both of us.

Like a kind of shimmering hug, but Jacob and I don't hug.

"What just happened?" I demand. Because thinking about hugging Jacob makes me feel too many things that remind me of high school and why I don't *feel* around him. And because I obviously haven't woken up yet.

And because none of this feels like a dream.

"I don't know." Jacob's breathing is ragged, and despite the fact his injuries have outwardly healed he looks...gray. Like the fight and that impossible healing has cost him.

"Emerson!"

I turn to see Georgie rushing toward me, her scarves and skirts flowing behind her, and the sight of her in all her bright colors is startling here, where the ground is still that dark swamp. Then Ellowyn appears out of thin air, literally. Quickly followed by Zander.

I blink, my knees feeling wobbly again.

They're all talking at the same time. Interrogating me and Jacob.

But I can't get past that out of *nowhere*, they're all here in the cemetery with us. Standing in the oily black residue on the ground. The sun shines above us, like there was never any storm.

For once in my life, I don't have the first clue what to say.

I decide, again, that this is a dream. I dream about my friends all the time. *Dream, dream, dream*, I chant at myself, though deep down, I'm starting to think that maybe—

But no. That's impossible. All of this is impossible and I am Emerson Wilde. I don't do impossible.

"You could have gotten here sooner," Jacob says, sagging against Zander, alarmingly, as if he needs the support to help him remain upright.

"We didn't hear you until just—"

"We came as soon as we—"

"How did you—"

They all trail off and look at me.

"Emerson." Georgie's voice is a breathy whisper. "Your eyes."

I reach up and touch my face as if that will give me any clue as to what she sees—what they all see—that has their mouths dropping open.

Except Jacob. He looks grim. The gray pallor is fading and he's standing straight again. Like Superman once more. Like all that was real.

"She killed them," he tells them, staring at me with an emotion I can't read in his eyes. It's almost like pride. "In one blast. Adlets. Actual adlets, as nasty as the books always said they were. They attacked us and she killed them all with a *blast*."

"Adlets…" Georgie whispers, with a frown, like that word means something to her. It does not mean anything to me. But it makes everything feel that much more real that those things have a name.

My friends are looking at each other now, like they know something, understand something, I don't.

Because they *do* understand, clearly. Because here we stand and I haven't woken up. Because everyone seems to see what I see instead of gently informing me I've had a break with reality—and sanity.

"Adlets," I say with great authority that I don't feel. For once. "That are now sludge on the ground."

No one contradicts me.

That is…not better.

"We have to get out of here," Zander says in a low, urgent tone. "Ellowyn?"

She nods. "I'll clean up. You guys take the conquering heroes to Jacob's. Safest at his place, off the bricks but thoroughly charmed, don't you think?"

They all nod.

I nod too, like any of what she's said makes sense. *Off the bricks. Charmed.*

Zander places his hand on Jacob's shoulder. "Let's go, hero."

Jacob tries to shrug off Zander's hand. "I can handle it," he insists.

I accept, grudgingly, that I really don't like not knowing what's happening.

"Not after all the healing you must have done you can't," Zander is saying to Jacob.

Then he looks up and they're suddenly gone.

Just…gone.

I'm staring at nothing but blue sky. Until I feel dizzy.

I can't seem to get a full breath. I can't seem to *wake up*.

Georgie slides her arm around my shoulders. "Come on, Em." Her voice is gentle in a way I don't recognize. When I know Georgie as well as I know me. When I know every single thing about her. "We'll try to explain everything as best we can at Jacob's."

I frown at her. "How—"

Something washes over me. An odd prickling feeling, then a *whoosh* of air, like a gust of wind. Like I'm catapulting through the air at top speed.

And then I'm not.

I'm standing firmly on the ground again, Georgie's arm still around me.

But we're standing in Jacob's living room instead of the cemetery. There's a fire in the hearth. Jacob is sitting in an old-looking leather armchair, no longer gray but not his usual gruff and scowly self either. Not that I've made a study. Zander is over by the fire looking uncharacteristically pensive.

And I'm *standing in the middle of Jacob's living room.*

As if I *flew* here. In the *air.*

Georgie's skirts and hair flying all around as we *flew.*

"One of you needs to tell me what the hell is going on," I say.

But my voice is weak. Not like me at all.

I'm either going to be sick or I'm going to pass out. I can't decide which one's more embarrassing before the world goes black.

MY EYES FLUTTER OPEN AND AN OVERWHELM-
ing wave of relief sweeps through me. It really was a dream.
Or the drugs have worn off at last. Whatever it is, everything is back to *normal*.

I am me again. Unmagical but unstoppable and—

I scowl directly above me. That is not my ceiling. The
cushions underneath me are not a part of my bed, and the
flannel blanket tucked around me is definitely not mine.
It smells like springtime, woodsmoke, and rich earth. *Like
Jacob*, something in me hums, like a knowing in my bones.

I don't make a move to sit up. Part of me hopes that if I
sit still enough, a rational thought will finally take hold of
me and deliver me from whatever psychological breakdown
this is. I take one breath. Another. Then I can't take it any
longer. My curiosity gets the better of me and I finally turn
my head to better take stock of my situation.

Before I really freak out.

I'm still in Jacob's living room, but now I'm laid out on

his couch. My friends are around me in various states of disarray. Jacob is still lounging in that chair when I'm sure I've never seen him *lounge* a day in his life. He has a ceramic mug in his hands that he only sips from when Ellowyn gives him a death stare.

Georgie is pacing with a pent-up, nonfluttery energy I've never seen in her, like there are more parts of her I don't know. Zander stands by the fire looking stiff and burdened, not easygoing at all. And Ellowyn sits at my feet, something like...*fear* stamped across her features when she's not dispensing her trademark glares all around.

Evidence that everything really is different makes me feel a little lightheaded, even though I'm already lying down.

Jacob is the first to notice that I've woken up. His gaze meets mine and I can tell he's searching for something on my face, in me, but I don't know what.

I open my mouth to say something, but nothing comes out.

Something that's almost as unreal as...everything else. I remember *whooshing* through the air and then finding myself here when I should have been in the cemetery. I remember stone statues on the wrong graves. I remember a carpet of chopped-up redbud trees and red eyes in a sudden black fog and—

"You're awake." Ellowyn climbs to her feet. "I'll get your tea."

I do not want tea, but I don't dare argue with Ellowyn when she has that stern look on her face. She holds out her hand like a mug might magically appear if she wills it, but Jacob shakes his head. Ellowyn frowns at him, but she stalks out of the room without saying anything.

My friends are having entire conversations in front of me

without saying a word. Without me gleaning any understanding whatsoever. It's as disorienting as anything else.

"What happened?" I ask. Carefully.

"You passed out," Zander says curtly. As if this was a grave affront. To him.

But I'm the one affronted. "I do not *pass out* in a neurasthenic swoon like some beleaguered Victorian in a corset, surrounded by yellow wallpaper and dreaming of wading into the sea, Zander."

His brows rise. "Spontaneous nap, then?"

"Don't be snarky," Georgie scolds him. She smiles weakly at me and takes Ellowyn's seat at my feet. "We're all just a little confused, Em."

They're confused. I'm having trouble forming words, but they're *confused*.

Ellowyn returns with a mug of tea that matches Jacob's. I recognize the mugs as ceramic masterpieces made by Ellowyn's mother that Ellowyn sells at Tea & No Sympathy. Local products. I approve.

And, frankly, I'm a little surprised that Jacob North bought such whimsical things. Even though they're excellent, superior quality. They don't exactly match the rest of the old, converted farmhouse, all deep leather and various takes on plaid.

For the first time since I set foot in that graveyard, I feel myself relax. I'm still me. I'm still Emerson Wilde. I'm still committed to St. Cyprian and all its works. That old song winds its way through my head like a charm.

Now if the world could go back to making sense.

Ellowyn hands me the tea she's made and looks me in the eye before she relinquishes it. "Drink every last drop."

"You should have let me make it," Jacob mutters.

She glares at him again. "I used your herbs, Healer."

I'm distracted by yet another interaction I don't understand, by that word. *Healer.* Another one of those odd sensations moves through me. Like a dream that disturbed me but I've forgotten since waking up.

I remind myself that I'm awake now. And that maybe it really was all a dream. Maybe there was poisoned pizza or psychotic breaks—or maybe I just fell, hit my head on my grandmother's gravestone, imagined a cat where a fox should be, and dreamed up a great, big, terrible storm. My friends came to find me thanks to the note I left Georgie, they took me to Jacob's place because it's closest, and any moment now they'll launch into that whole *you-need-to-learn-how-to-manage-your-stress-better* thing they do like clockwork, at least four times a year. A few promises to really take up yoga this time—with or without Jacob's goats—and I should be on my way to open my store and figure out how to save my festival.

All is well. I am fine.

I'm so relieved it almost feels like I might cry, except I never cry, because a woman's tears are too often weaponized against her.

I sit up abruptly then, waving off Georgie and Ellowyn as they fall all over themselves to help me. Maybe I did pass out a little, but I feel strong now. Alert.

Strangely so, in fact.

I frown down at the tea in my hands. It does *not* smell good and I make a face before I remember how much Ellowyn hates it when I do that. Today she only rolls her eyes. She wiggles her fingers, very casually, and the smell of the tea changes.

Just like that.

And all my rationalizations crumble inside me.

Because I didn't imagine that.

I find myself hoping I'm having a stroke, but when I touch my lips I find no drooping.

Damn it.

"Someone make all of this make sense for me," I say then, using my best authoritative chamber-of-commerce-president voice.

Georgie opens her mouth, but Ellowyn holds up one of her *apparently magical* fingers. "Jacob should explain it." Georgie starts to protest but Ellowyn shrugs. "You'll be too emotional. I'll be too blunt. Zander will crack too many jokes, or even more disturbing, none at all. Jacob will explain it succinctly, with all the pertinent facts."

All eyes turn to Jacob, even my own. He doesn't look *pleased* about Ellowyn's explanation, but they all seem to agree in that silently communicative way they have that I make a note to be outraged about later. He sets aside his mug. His usual rigid posture is back, that careful way of holding himself just out of reach even as he leans forward and rests his elbows on his knees.

He seems to consider his words and the room is utterly silent while he does it, like everyone is holding their breath.

I know I am.

"It's hard to know where to start, but Ellowyn is right," he says, sounding gravelly. And grave. "This is bigger than what happened at the cemetery today. And you like facts, so I suppose I have to start at the beginning."

What happened at the cemetery today, he said. Like it was all...a real thing. I look down at my hands. They're not glowing any longer, but that odd buzzing inside of me—like I've been electrocuted—hasn't stopped.

Jacob waits until I look up at him again. "St. Cyprian is a haven for witches, though we are accepting of any magical beings willing to follow our rules."

I laugh. I can't help it. Witches and magical beings. *We*

and *our* and *Jacob* of all people saying that sentence with an utter seriousness that doesn't compute.

But no one else laughs or even cracks a smile.

"Halloween isn't until October," I say, but still. No laughter. No grins to indicate this is a joke. The electricity inside me surges higher.

"We live among humans, but hidden, so to speak," he continues. Using that voice of his I know so well, but the words make no sense. "To avoid witch trials and hangings and the other nasty things humans tend to do when they find us."

"Sarah Wilde," I whisper, a discordant note sounding within me. *Sarah Wilde*. Hanged for witchcraft. A thing that doesn't exist. She was a woman out there fighting the good fight centuries ago. She was—*is*—my hero. My belief in her power—her not-magical, strong-woman power—is the cornerstone of my life.

But Jacob nods. "Like Sarah, and the rest of them in Salem. And other places the world over. Our ancestors finally learned that it doesn't work. Humans and witches mixed together always ends in pitchforks. They retreated here to build something different, and we have. But building a world within a world and keeping it secret comes with a lot of rules. To keep us and our ways safe."

He's giving the pertinent facts, maybe—a lot of facts that sound like fairy tales—but he is skirting around the most critical fact. "You're saying I'm a witch?" I ask flatly.

Witch. A *witch*. I think about those creatures coming after me and Jacob and that deer fighting them off. The white-hot feeling that blasted through me when I yelled at them to die. The buzz inside me I can't shake.

"We're all witches," Georgie says in that gentle way people use when they admit something they've done wrong.

In a sea of WTF, I cling to that. Her guilt.

Because if I'm a witch and they're all witches too, I have to look at my friends and wonder... "You've been keeping *witchcraft* a secret for twenty-eight years?"

"No," Jacob says. Firmly.

I open my mouth to argue with him, but he continues. Like a professor delivering a lecture.

When that is usually my role.

"For their first eighteen years of life, any witch born into St. Cyprian society is taught the ways of magic," Professor Jacob tells me, his green gaze not glowing now, but still intense. "We are trained, educated, and prepared. No matter how powerful or how weak our magic is, we're given eighteen years to develop it. But there are some, whether because of diluted blood lines or other mishaps, who have no magic. No matter how hard they might work to develop it."

I don't miss the odd way Zander looks at Ellowyn, but I can't concentrate on their issues right now. Georgie's hand resting on my knee tenses. No one in the room seems to know where to look. Certainly not at me.

"In your eighteenth year, a test is administered," Jacob continues. "It determines your level of power and, if you aren't genetically predisposed already, what type of witch you'll be. What role you'll serve in the community."

This part is familiar enough. I've read the back cover copy of all those New Age books I refuse to stock. "Like hedge witches and kitchen witches?"

"No," Jacob says darkly, the way he sounds when we talk about llamas. "I do not mean that."

"Hedge witch and kitchen witch and river witch are all like your astrological sign or enneagram stuff, I guess," Georgie tells me. "The witch version of personality quizzes on the internet that humans can take too, and then think they're doing spells when they talk nicely to a tomato plant."

"Real witch designations aren't cute," Zander agrees.

"They don't come with stickers and adorable Pinterest boards," Ellowyn says. "It's more blood magic and binding spells and the odd unbreakable curse."

There's a small silence. Georgie pats my leg in her awkward, yet comforting way. "Though there *should* be stickers," she says. Loyally.

And this all feels so normal, topic aside, that it's the first moment that something shifts enough inside me that I think, *Holy shit, we might actually be witches.*

Jacob sighs. He's still sitting in that formal way of his, but everyone quiets and gazes expectantly at him, so I do too.

"If a genetic witch doesn't meet the required level of power, they're given two options," he tells me. "One is exile. You must leave, never attempt to practice or engage in magic, and never come back home unless special permission is granted."

"Rebekah," I whisper from that same place inside me— that same sudden shift. Witches and magic and all this is crazy, clearly, but in one sense it finally gives me an answer. Why did my sister abandon me? Why has she never come back? We were always different, born on the first and last day of the same year. She wanted a rebellion and I wanted responsibility, but we were close all the same. I've never understood why she left. Maybe I want to believe what Jacob's telling me because it gives me a reason at last.

If she was exiled, she didn't just run away. She *had* to leave. She wasn't *allowed* to come back home. I want this with every molecule of my being, but to believe Rebekah was exiled, I have to accept the rest of what Jacob is telling me.

Maybe I really do want to believe.

Jacob nods, sympathetically. "Yes, Rebekah chose exile when she was labeled spell dim."

I blink. "That sounds pejorative."

Zander belts out a bitter laugh. "That's because it is."

I want to chase down that term some more, but I focus on the bigger picture. And frown. "But I'm still here. Not in exile."

"The other option when labeled spell dim is what amounts to a memory wipe," Jacob tells me. And no one moves, but I can feel the tension rise all around me. "You're stripped of all magical memories. You can stay in St. Cyprian, exist within our world, but you're rendered blind to it. You remember people, places, things, but from a human perspective. It's a safety measure, to avoid humans getting too close to the truth."

"You're saying I took the mind-wipe option?" I'm incredulous. Obviously, I'd never leave St. Cyprian, but when would I ever accept *mind wiping?* A new thought jumps at me. Was I someone else entirely before...*wiping my mind?*

Jacob's mouth curves, ever so slightly, the kind of rare smile he usually hides from me. Reminding me of that odd look in his eyes when he said, *she killed them all with a blast.* "You know yourself, Emerson. Surely you know you tried to create your own, third option."

"*Tried.* That signifies failure." I wave my arms around me, at all of them. At all their secrets. "*This* means I failed."

Jacob's expression sobers, and no one will look at me anymore.

"The Joywood, our ruling coven, did not care for your third option, and you were..." He trails off. And while Ellowyn had said Jacob wouldn't be emotional, this is some kind of emotion. I can see it on his face, and I can feel it like a shaking thing, deep inside. "They broke protocol, and instead of performing your mind wipe at the appropriate ceremony, did it then and there."

"Jacob tried to stop—"

Jacob glares at Georgie, who immediately clamps her mouth shut.

"Are they the evil witches?" I demand, maybe a little outraged. "With the *mind wiping*?"

Jacob makes a noise but Zander shakes his head. "They're not evil. Necessarily. Witch law is harsh, that's all. Because it's that or Salem all over again."

"What was done was done," Jacob says evenly. "You got to stay in St. Cyprian. And we weren't allowed to tell you who you really are. We've all taken great pains to avoid outright lying to you, Emerson, but we are bound by St. Cyprian law."

"Which we're breaking now," Zander points out. "The punishment for breaking the law is exile if we're lucky. A mind wipe if we're not. Or, you know, worse than that if the Joywood are feeling spicy."

"She displayed power," Jacob snaps, with a surprising amount of all that emotion he's not supposed to have. And never has had in as long as I can remember.

I blink as the phrase *mind wipe* kicks around inside of me. What can I actually remember?

"She *killed* those adlets," Jacob continues. "I watched her do it, and even now, look at her eyes."

"What is wrong with my eyes?" I demand. Or maybe yelp.

Georgie hands me a mirror. I don't know where it came from. It's just suddenly in her hand and then in mine.

I look down and nearly drop the mirror. Slowly, I reach up to touch the skin next to each eye that has, until now, always been the same. But they aren't *my* eyes anymore. Not the serviceable brown I've been looking at my whole life. "They're gold," I whisper.

"It happened when…" Jacob trails off, not so much emotion this time as his usual discomfort with things. *Or things that are me*, something in me counters.

"When what?" Ellowyn presses.

But I know what he means. I felt it. "Jacob was bleeding. I reached out and touched his wound, but it had already healed. The blood was still there and..." I drop the mirror in Georgie's lap and surge to my feet. "This is ridiculous. I don't know what's going on, but—"

I cut myself off. Because the facts are the facts. I haven't woken up. My friends, who I have always trusted completely, are telling me that they're witches—that we're *all* witches of some kind. And I've read this story in books, haven't I? A girl wakes up with powers in a world that has hidden them away for some reason. I might be older than your average young adult heroine, but is it so different?

I'm suddenly very happy with my not-so-private YA paranormal addiction over the years. Because I know how this goes. Do I want to be the kind of person who flails around and denies everything and wails that it can't be true? Or do I want to be the kind of woman who sucks up her new reality, figures it out, and makes it work?

The answer is clear, because witches or no witches, I'm still me.

"Do you want us to prove it to you?" Georgie asks gently. Trying to make this easier on me, I can tell.

I almost say no. After all, there's nothing to prove. I don't believe in witches. But I also don't believe my friends would make up this insane story. Or would loom around looking so sincere while I'm clearly having trouble taking it in. If it was a joke, Georgie, the weak link, would have broken a long time ago.

What I know is that these people—*my* people—love me.

I know this without question. It doesn't matter what I can remember. My heart knows.

And then there's what I witnessed with my own eyes.

"Yes," I say. "I want proof. I want to *see* it." I want to know what *we* can do.

They exchange glances, then they all move to stand, shoulder to shoulder, in front of me. They each hold out their right hand. They whisper, in easy unison, simple words: *"Give us light, for this night."*

A *ping* of recollection inside of me warms, as they repeat it. Over and over. Together. As one.

Is this...*power*?

Is it a memory?

One after the next, in each of their palms, a small ball of fire sparks to life. Hovering above their skin. Real light. Real heat.

Each is a slightly different shade of gold, each a slightly different size, but they all hold this...*thing* above their palms. Out to me, like an offering.

Something inside me clicks into place.

This is magic. The kind that isn't supposed to exist. I reach out to touch the nearest ball of light, cupped in Georgie's palm, but it's hot. If I touch it, it will burn.

For a moment I have a foggy kind of vision. My grandmother in the bookstore. Laughing with the reflection of a ball of light in her dark eyes, like maybe I was holding one out to her. But I don't *remember* that. It didn't happen.

Or my memories of magic were wiped. Erased. Looking down the row of glowing orbs before me, how can I keep trying to deny it? Magic exists. Right here in my best friends' hands.

I look up from their quiet light show to find Jacob. I look above the ball of fire in his palm, up to his face, which I thought I knew so well. His eyes are glowing, though not with the same power as when we'd been in the cemetery. This is faint. A vague touch of luminescence to the green of his eyes.

I feel it everywhere, though.

"It's a lot," he says, but his lips don't move. It's like his voice is in my head. He did that in the cemetery too, I suddenly remember. "But you're Emerson Wilde. You can handle it."

I inhale, sharply, but I let out that breath slow. And in control. Because he's right. I'm Emerson Wilde and I can do anything. I already have.

"Of course I can." I have to. I will.

I've been called a word that rhymes with *witch* enough times, because that's the plight of an ambitious woman. I've owned it. I will own this too.

"Now the real question is who sent those adlets, and why." Zander extinguishes his light first and looks at me, frowning. There's a barely restrained rage inside of him I don't recognize inside my easygoing cousin. "But let's start with the basics, now that we've covered the whole secret-identity thing. What the hell were you doing in the cemetery this morning, Emerson?"

6

THAT IS NOT A QUESTION I REALLY WANT TO answer, but as my friends stare at me with various levels of concern etched into their faces, I know I'm not going to be able to hide the fact Skip basically taunted me into going to the cemetery.

Skip.

Skip? Could he be…

Surely not.

"I wanted to check on the redbuds." And then I forget about why I was there. I forget about who sent me because the reality of what happened this morning slaps me. Hard. "*My redbuds.* They're shredded. The festival. What am I going to do?"

"Emerson…" Jacob sounds choked.

But Georgie is laughing. "Only you, Em."

"Find out you're a witch, worry about a festival." Ellowyn sighs, clearly despairing of me. But who else can take care of my festival? The town might be full of witches, but I don't

recall anyone else stepping up to take on town event planning. Nor do I recall any *magicking* of tasks, though now that
I think about it, I have always doubted Zander's claims that
he personally papered the outlying neighborhoods with my
various flyers. Magic makes a lot more sense than him actually trekking about out there on foot.

"She's right," Jacob says, back to his stoic self. This feels
like solid ground again. As I am usually right. "People are
going to expect her. Any minute now she should be opening her store, right on time, and badgering everyone about
tonight."

"I do not *badger*—"

Jacob's eyes hit mine and I stop talking. A rarity, but then,
they're still so *bright*. "Until we have more understanding of
what happened, we don't have time for this."

But Zander is shaking his head, that uncharacteristic anger
still shrouded around him. "We need to know. Why did you
want to check on the redbuds, Em? This morning, before
the sun was up, without telling anyone?"

"I left a note," I offer.

I look from Zander to Georgie. Then to Ellowyn. Then
finally back to Jacob. But none of them look inclined to drop
this. Which feels unfair, especially after I've taken the whole
they-lied-to-me-for-a-decade thing so well. I remind myself
that I am the heroine who embraces her call to adventure,
not the one who runs screaming in the other direction. Or
hides her head in the sand. No matter how attractive both
options seem right now.

I clear my throat. "I just wanted to make sure everything
was in its place." Not a lie. But an evasion. In the moment I
might have felt righteously compelled to check on my redbuds alone, but in retrospect, I feel like a bit of an idiot and I
don't plan on *wallowing* in that feeling. I wouldn't know how.

"Because?" Zander asks, arms crossed over his chest.

It sounds a lot like an accusation.

"I often check on things before the start of a festival," I tell him loftily. "Maybe you've met me? I'm your cousin Emerson, famously anal since birth."

"Really? At 6:00 a.m.? That's overly anal, Em. Even for you."

He eyes me like I'm being shady. Making me fidget like I'm being shady when I certainly am not.

I sigh, because I don't know much about magic, but I have a fairly good idea of how this conversation is going to go. "I had a phone call this morning that…prompted me to worry about the state of my redbuds."

"You didn't tell me you were going anywhere," Georgie says, and her accusation sounds soft and a little hurt. But it's an accusation all the same.

"I left a note," I say again.

"Who called you?" Ellowyn asks. She's not angry like Zander, but that directness of hers has the same effect.

I could lie. I could hedge, but they all know me too well. They know I don't fly off the handle. When I have real concerns I rally the troops. Form a plan.

I don't go racing across rivers into graveyards at the break of dawn without a reason.

"Skip," I mutter.

I can tell immediately no one expected that answer. That they had no idea Skip was involved. I think about the smug way he spoke to me on the phone. Something creepy moves over me. I think about magic. Witches. Did he send those things after me?

Can he…summon nightmares and dispatch them to do his bidding? The same man who can't manage to pass a single local ordinance?

Part of me doesn't want to ask, because most of me doesn't want to know. "Is Skip Simon a witch?" I sound a little shrieky to my own ears.

"Yes," Georgie says with a groan. "And he's the witch you'd expect. Told everyone his familiar was a little-known jaguar for years when, in fact, it's a sad little weasel named Steflemon. Totally the magical equivalent of a convenient Canadian girlfriend."

She glances around the room and clears her throat. "Do we really think Skip is behind the attack?" She's not asking me. She's looking over at Jacob, who looks deep in thought.

I decide to solve things the way I always do.

"Can't we just go to this coven-wood-thingy and tell them I have power and get my memories back? If we go now, we can get it all done before the festival. The bookstore might not open in time, but won't the witches all understand?"

I'm a *witch*. Horrible Skip Simon is a *witch*. Sarah Wilde was actually a *witch*. I could get used to this.

Everyone looks at me and I'm not used to this kind of look. Like they all know more than I do and possibly even feel sorry for me. Like I'm the one flailing around in the dark. It dawns on me that I have been this whole time, but didn't recognize it.

I do not care for this realization.

"We can't tell anyone," Jacob says quietly, but there's a note of steel in his tone. Like this isn't just his preference, as a man who likes to live across the river and avoid conflict by waiting it out, not that I have feelings about him, because I don't.

Except I remember that what happened between us in high school—or didn't—maybe isn't what actually happened. Or didn't. I make a mental note to circle back to that later, possibly while alone, and freak out.

But first there's an argument just waiting for me to win.

"What do you mean? If I have power, if I'm actually a witch, can't they undo their mind-wipe thing, which, talk about dubious consent. Then once I remember, I can—"

"If Skip was the one trying to hurt you, it isn't that simple," Ellowyn says.

"Why?"

They all exchange looks. *In-the-know* looks that make me feel like an outsider. Like a child. I hate it, but I don't know what to do about it.

Yet.

"The Joywood doesn't just rule St. Cyprian. They're the ruling body of all witchdom—across the world. Elected, cycle after cycle, to be our ruling coven. Only full covens can rule and a full coven is seven witches, led by a Warrior—a type of witch," Georgie explains patiently. "Carol Simon is the Joywood's Warrior, and as such, she is basically in charge of all of witchdom—and has been for a very long time."

I try to take that unexpected blow on board. Because Carol Simon is a formidable woman, the first person mentioned so far that I have no trouble believing is a witch. She's also Skip's mother. So. Yes. That could be a problem.

"She will protect Skip," Zander says, so serious and certain that I'm reminded of the ways Ellowyn used to torture me by telling me she found my cousin *hot*. "Believe me. It's not safe for you if they know. Not until we understand what happened."

"Skip comes by his tantrums over being proved wrong honestly. Just like last time, Carol won't let you talk yourself out of this," Jacob says.

I try to remember being mind wiped, but I can't. It's a complete blank.

"But I don't remember last time," I say to Jacob.

He holds my gaze, all that green so direct, so intense. So

different than the Jacob I thought I knew. Something in me hums. "I do," he says.

Then he turns to Georgie. "Get Emerson to the bookstore. But first, clean her up and teach her a quick glamour. Ellowyn and I will handle the redbuds. We should be able to minimize the damage, maybe even fix it. Zander—"

But my cousin is shaking his head. "I've got to get to my shift at the ferry or Dad will ask questions. We have to keep this between us for now."

"The fewer people involved, the better," Jacob agrees. "Be on the lookout. Watch for someone who might be looking for signs that Emerson was attacked. We can't be too careful."

I stare at Jacob, over there issuing orders like some kind of general. Like me. "You're certainly Mr. Take Charge when you want to be."

Jacob looks slightly taken aback, and I'm not sure why that surprises him. Everyone clearly jumps to do Jacob's bidding. In this world, he's in charge, when in the human world, I've always considered myself the organizer, the doer, the go-getter. Apparently, in the witch world, that responsibility falls to Jacob.

Apparently, I've decided to embrace the witch world as a reality, but I ignore that shift because I'm not sure what to do about not being in charge. Surely, once I get my feet under me with all this magical stuff, that'll be *my* role. It's the role I was born for.

The truth of this settles around me like an old friend.

"If we can't go to the Joywood, there are other options," Ellowyn is saying, and though I don't know what the options are, I can tell by the pointed way she says it that no one else is going to like them.

And they don't.

"No," Zander says firmly at the same time Jacob does. A chorus of *nos* and a spike of tension.

Ellowyn seems unbothered. "He's an option. He'd know."

"Nicholas Frost is a traitor," Zander replies harshly. "And I for one don't want a traitor's help with anything."

"This is delicate," Jacob agrees. "Frost can't be trusted."

They say this like *Nicholas Frost* is a name we all know. "Who?"

Georgie slides her arm around my shoulders, like she did back at the cemetery. "Come on, Em. We need to go home before we head to the bookstore. Let them argue about practicalities."

I frown at the idea of Jacob and Zander—or anyone—arguing and making decisions without me, but Georgie tightens her grip as I start for the door.

This is when it occurs to me that we're not going to walk down to the ferry like we usually do.

"This way is better," she says.

Inside my head.

Then we're in the air again. Just like before. It's not the kind of flying I would have imagined, Peter Pan arms and soaring to and fro. No chanting, like they did to create the light balls. It's simply that *whoosh* of air, a moment of feeling weightless, and then standing in the place we're going.

This time it's Georgie's turret.

She immediately lets me go and begins to race around her room, crystals clanking, scarves floating, and wind chimes moving in violent shakes. "There's so much to do and so little time," she mutters. "We have to hide those eyes of yours. One look and everyone will know."

"Maybe I want them to know."

Because women should claim their power. We all know who benefits when they don't, and it isn't us.

Georgie shakes her head solemnly. "It's too dangerous. Because it's not supposed to be possible. You're not supposed to have the faintest hint of power, much less be able to smite down a few myths without any training."

I nod as if this makes sense, but I privately think that this witch world might need a little revolution, because I've always been powerful, thank you. No matter what color my eyes are.

But I keep this to myself as Georgie forms a circle of crystals around us, arranging candles and whispering words that feel like a spell… I suppose because they are.

Huh.

I've made fun of her for this. Rolled my eyes at it all, but it's real. It's *real*. I feel it humming around us and deep inside me.

Haven't you always? asks a voice from somewhere in all that humming that reminds me of my grandmother.

Georgie directs me to stand in the center of the crystals. She steps in with me, taking long, deep breaths, then takes my hands in hers. She breathes out, then looks right at me. "We'll do a quick glamour to hide the gold eyes from everyone." Her own eyes are shiny. "You'll repeat after me, focusing on that center feeling of heat. Of energy. I'm guiding you, but you're the one doing the spell."

"Why do you chant for this, but not to fly? Why do I need spells when I killed those adlets with nothing but the word *die*?"

Georgie considers. "There are different ways we use our power," she says, and I can tell she's choosing her words carefully. To impart me with the most understanding as she can. "Flying is…basic. Elemental. It is within us. The best way I can think to explain it is that words or thoughts or crystals are aids—and you use the ones that best help you harness the power you're trying to use. Internal things, solitary things can often be done without words, just focus. External things— glamours and fire and protections often need words or aids. But they don't have to be special or grand. Focusing your fear and your power on those adlets and saying the word *die* aloud was enough to accomplish what you wanted to do."

I wish that made more sense than it does. "Isn't there some sort of manual I can read?" I ask, trying not to sound petulant.

Georgie smiles warmly. "It's not quite so straightforward as a manual, but don't fret. We'll teach you. You'll practice. It'll make sense to you again." As she talks me through it all, tears begin to fall onto her cheeks.

I'm baffled. "Why are you crying?"

She fights for a smile. "We always knew there was something inside you, Em, but we didn't know what to do about it. So I never thought I'd be here. Wholly me, with you. Wholly us and who we are." She shakes her head, overcome by an emotion I can't access because I haven't been waiting for this. "It's been such a long ten years."

"I don't know how to...be magical," I confess, feeling perilously close to tears myself. And I am not one to admit I might not be awesome at something.

"Emerson," my best friend says, squeezing my hands, "you may not have known you were a witch. But you have always been magic."

JUST THIS MORNING I WOULD HAVE TOLD YOU I knew *everything* about St. Cyprian and its residents. And while I might have accepted that my friends possess inner lives they don't necessarily share with me, I would have been *certain* that none of their revelations could surprise me. That's how well I know them, I would have said.

Obviously, mythical creature attacks and witchcraft has made that certainty feel a little rocky.

But this town is still *mine*, the redbud festival is my baby, and assassination attempts aside, I have things to do. I am still Emerson Wilde, and if I have to keep repeating that to myself to keep my balance and sanity, so be it.

Georgie has led me through a spell. Words said together, her holding my hands, guiding some feeling inside of me that feels familiar and foreign all at once.

She encourages me to say the words with her, over and over.

"Hide that which none shall see. Help me mask what's inside of me."

But it's the *feeling* that seems to matter over the words. The words are something like a framework, a mindfulness exercise to focus the magic inside of me on our end goal.

Magic. Just there. Inside of me.

"Good," Georgie says, smiling her encouragement. She hands me a mirror.

I stare at myself in the gem-encrusted mirror longer than I should. I have looked at the same face for twenty-eight years, so sure I knew myself inside and out too.

But even as I think that, I also think, *I do*. Whatever with witches, I have always been *me*. I hold on to that simple truth.

And *me* needs answers. So very many answers. Answers I don't have time for. Not yet. It doesn't seem fair, but I have a festival to run. I have a life to lead. Maybe I was attacked, but Jacob saved me.

And then I saved us.

Jacob. I have faith in myself and in my town and, therefore, in this whole witchcraft business if that's a part of those things. But I can't seem to find my footing when it comes to Jacob. I had my dealings with him down to a science, but now...

I have a flash of that Superman landing and feel myself... blush.

But I never blush.

Maybe there's something lurking in the memories I can't access that's causing this...slight lack of confidence I have when it comes to the man. "So are the memories I have...fake?"

Georgie frowns as she grabs a colorful tote bag from the doorknob of her overstuffed library. We head downstairs as she considers. Her hands glide over the banister. Walking when we could fly.

Fly.

We can *fly*.

"*Fake* isn't the word I'd use. Sometimes you'd talk about

a thing that happened and in your memories it was like…
dissecting a frog in biology class when really it was practicing
woodland spells or something. Or you'd remember a simple
ferry ride when we'd been practicing spells at the confluence. The mind wipe doesn't change things exactly—it just
strips the magic from them."

We reach the bottom of the stairs. I release the banister,
making sure not to touch the newel post—a habit so in-
grained I don't even think about it.

Welcome home, Emerson.

It's a voice I don't recognize. I whirl around. No one's
here. "Georgie, did you hear that?"

"Oh, that's just Azrael."

She waves at the newel post. Its dark black onyx eyeballs
seem to gleam, but they aren't *eyes.* They're just crystals. The
dragon's mouth is peeled back in the same grin that's always
been carved in the wood. And I am somehow simultane-
ously creeped out and…almost comforted.

"It's some enchantment or another one of your ancestors made, I think. I've done a little research on it, but keep
coming up empty. More important research to do now," she
mutters to herself, propelling me forward, across the front
hall. I'm not usually so biddable, but I let her lead me along
this time.

I tell myself it's a reasonable reaction to my newel post
having a name. And it knowing mine.

And the whole part where it was *talking to me.*

"We'll need to come up with an excuse for why you're
late opening the bookstore. Someone will ask. People pay
way too much attention to you." She barrels for the door,
reminding me more of me than Georgie. So much of this is
unsettling, but I decide to feel complimented that my town
of *witches* pays as much attention to me as I do to it.

"Whatever magic Skip used was blocked, somehow. None of us on this side of the river heard you calling for us."

"I wasn't calling for you." How could I have been *calling* for anyone when I was too busy trying to wake up? And terrified?

Images of dark fog and red eyes wash through me, but I shove them aside.

Georgie looks back at me. She pauses before she opens the front door. "You were. You do." Her frown deepens. "All witches can. It's not so much power as…connection. We're connected to you. Even with you mind wiped, that didn't go away. You're not conscious of it, so you don't control it like we do, so we should have felt it. But we had no sense anything was going on for most of the attack. We're in tune with you, so we'd feel it first. We feel it every time Susan Martingale chases you down to talk about the flower boxes on Main Street. An actual attack should have lit us all up. It's really not good that it didn't."

She flings open the door and I have no choice but to grab my bag—already packed for the day and waiting on the hall bench, since I do that every night before bed—who doesn't?—and follow her outside. Into the sunshiny day with a hint of a bite in the air, but spring nonetheless.

"Too many questions," she mutters, and I know she's talking to herself because this is exactly how she acts when she has a big research project. Muttering about *focusing* and *centering*— and I do know her. Of course I do.

"Right now we need to figure what on earth would keep Emerson Wilde from opening her store on time," Georgie is muttering under her breath as we take to the sidewalk. "Because *someone* is going to ask."

But I can't focus on the disruption to my routine—that, obviously, could only have been caused by a supernatural occurrence like the one earlier, complete with monsters, since a plan is power and I stick to mine—because something about the bricks beneath my feet feels all wrong. I'm overcorrecting for dips and unevenness that I *see*, but don't *feel* beneath my feet.

Georgie takes my arm. "It's a mask. They're all over the place. When it comes to masks and glamours, you'll need the words. Just say, *'Reveal to me what I should see,'* and you'll see the real bricks, not just feel them."

Real bricks. *Masks.* Spells that I can work because... because I'm a witch.

I'm a freaking *witch.*

I shake my head, but it doesn't get any clearer. Or less witchy. I repeat Georgie's words and...

The bricks are suddenly different. The same, but not. The old bricks I thought I knew so well, cracked and worn, are even and practically gleaming. Like they haven't aged in the century since they were put down.

"The excuse would have to be some bigger responsibil- ity," Georgie continues to muse as we walk swiftly down the street toward the bookstore, still talking about excusing my unprecedented tardiness. I can't lift my gaze from the bricks. "Helping someone probably. Maybe we could claim Jacob had a farm emergency."

I snort inelegantly, forgetting about the bricks. "I think ev- eryone knows I'd be the last person Jacob called for *farm* help."

"Something with the ferry. You're practically a Rivers. Rivers adjacent."

I shake my head. "Not unless we want to ask Uncle Zack to lie for me."

Georgie looks thoughtful. "Your uncle didn't come either. And he was *on* the river."

"Uncle Zack doesn't ever stop the ferry unless the weather makes him. You know what he's like."

I've always taken pride in my relatives' commitment to their duties and responsibilities—and their timetables.

But Georgie's shaking her head. "This isn't about ferry schedules. Whoever did this—whoever sent those monsters after you—hid it from all of witchkind, or more people would have come to see what was happening. More people would have *felt* that power surge. *Your* power surge."

Power surge. I look down at my hands. *Power.* And I don't have a clue how to really work it yet. For the first time in my life, I'm at a disadvantage.

I don't know what to do with that.

Except plow ahead. Isn't that always the answer?

Well. It's always *my* answer.

We arrive at the bookstore and I look up at all that is familiar and real—power aside. No matter how wrapped up in town projects or council business I might get, at the end of the day, Confluence Books has always been my heart. Because of my grandmother, because of the *history* of it all, because it's *ours*.

I have to wonder if some of the answers are right here where they always are—just with more magic than usual. Because if there's magic in St. Cyprian, there's magic in this bookshop. The magic is here. It has to be.

And I thought Grandma was magic my whole life, so…

"My grandmother was a witch," I whisper.

Georgie smiles fondly, though she glances around quickly, presumably to make sure no one is around to hear us. "Of course she was."

For a moment I feel almost vindicated, but then a raw sense of loss hits me. Hard. That my grandmother isn't here to teach me. That Rebekah isn't here to help me. That my parents left their lost daughters on this continent, all on their own. I frown. "Rebekah was exiled. Grandma died." That still hurts to say. I push on. "But my parents…?"

Georgie sighs as I unlock the door and she follows me inside. "They *are* doing critical witch work in Germany. There's an important witch colony there, and as Praeceptors—that's our word for teachers, basically—they're imparting wisdom."

"Imparting wisdom doesn't seem like a great excuse for abandoning their child and town and *life*." Because Georgie's excuses are why they're somewhere else—not why they never visit and barely tolerate phone calls.

I've never stopped trying to reach them, but after Grandma died, I realized it was time to set boundaries. I stopped waiting for them to see *me*. Want me.

"They're very powerful, prominent witches, Em. To have two children who weren't even magical must have been crushing. It's actually considered an indictment of the bloodline, which neither of them took well."

That sounds…suitably dramatic and witchy. *An indictment of the bloodline.* It also fits. I knew I was a disappointment to my parents. I could never understand why *I'd* be an embarrassment. Now I know. Better still, I know they were wrong.

I wish it made me feel better about them leaving me here.

"You don't think anyone but us knows what happened?" I ask as I flick on the lights and fire up the computer. But as it hums to life, I look at my hands. I can't help it. I've changed my eye color and killed mythical creatures. What other amazing things can I do? Something tugs at me, and I remember what she said as we were leaving the house. "You said that I was calling for you. That I do that." I sound dubious because I do not call for help. I convene committees. She knows this as well as I do. "And you all heard me, eventually, even though I was all the way across the river in the old cemetery."

"*Heard* isn't the right word," she says, regarding me from the other side of the counter. "It's more that we *felt* you, but not until it was over. It shouldn't work like that. People should have sensed something as big as an *adlet* attack."

She says that the way someone might say *a Godzilla attack*. Or *a Bigfoot attack*.

I swallow a bit harder than necessary.

"And the rest of us should have felt your distress, and Jacob's pain. But it's like someone blocked it all out, and that shouldn't be possible."

I don't fully understand all this *blocked* business, but Georgie looks seriously concerned, so I try to arrange my face to the same approximate level of worry. Normally I would comfort her or assure her in some way, but nothing is normal.

And worse, I'm suddenly aware of something...*whispering* at me.

I look around wildly, trying to find the source. My heart is beating in overdrive like there are more hideous monsters out to kill me, and I realize I'm looking for evil red eyes on the new-release table.

I hadn't really thought about a repeat performance until this moment. My mouth goes dry.

You beat the first ones without even trying.

Right. *Right.* I certainly did. And when I take a moment to consider it, these new whispers don't feel threatening. Scary and weird, sure, like a trickle of cold water down my back, but not like anything is out to get me.

I take a breath, and it's like they're calling to me. Drawing me out from behind the counter and deeper into the shop. I vaguely hear Georgie call my name, but it's like a window suddenly separates us.

Emerson, Rebekah. First of the year. Last of the year.

I see my grandmother standing where the Missouri History section usually is. Grandma is standing before Rebekah and me. Rebekah is seven and I'm eight. I know I'm eight because that was the summer I insisted on wearing glasses I didn't need.

This isn't my memory. Or it isn't *quite* my memory. I seem to remember sitting like this in front of Grandma while she read a *Mrs. Piggle-Wiggle* book to us. But she isn't reading in this…memory or vision or whatever it is. She's speaking to us. Touching our foreheads.

Chanting, like my friends did back at Jacob's house.

Blood of my blood. Heart of my heart.

I'm not just seeing this play out before me, like watching a movie of something that never happened to me. I feel it like it actually happened. Like it's a memory. *The real memory*, something in me asserts. Threaded through with magic.

I can hear Georgie calling me, from far away, but I want to stay right here. With Grandma. With Rebekah, who is widening her eyes at the child version of me in this memory, speaking to me in our own, private language. With this new magic that isn't new at all.

A tear trips over and onto my cheek, and Grandma looks over at me. At adult Emerson. She reaches out, but she's too far away, and yet I still feel her sigh brush across my cheek and her finger wipe away my tear as if she's here.

Right here.

"Grandma," I whisper, all the loss and bewilderment, magic and *I miss you*, right there in my voice.

Be strong, sweet pea. You're a Wilde.

And then she's gone, and so are younger Rebekah and me, and I can feel Georgie's hand on my shoulder.

"Em. *Em.*" She gives me a shake, looking a little wild-eyed. "Breathe."

I finally do, and realize my lungs are burning. Like I'd been drowning. I gasp for air. "I saw—"

"Nothing," Georgie retorts fiercely. And in my head, I

realize belatedly. "Remember, Emerson. You see nothing. You know nothing."

"But—" I say. Out loud.

"Nothing," Georgie shoots right back.

The bell over my door tinkles then, announcing a customer. And for the first time in my entire career as a businesswoman, I want to chase a potential sale away.

Especially when I see who it is.

"Emerson. I was *so* worried. You didn't open up on time." Maeve Mather stands there, her absurd panda head purse clutched in her hands and a strangely triumphant gleam in her eye.

Maeve Mather and her questionable accessories have been a trial forever. She and my grandmother did *not* get along. Maeve once tried to start a rival bookstore and, when it didn't work out, claimed my grandmother sabotaged her store, when the truth was that Maeve had used her father's deep pockets to fund a store that catered only to her specific taste, thus running her own business into the ground. Not that she could be told that unpalatable truth.

She's had it out for Confluence Books ever since.

"Em was out saving a chinchilla again," Georgie confides, then smiles at Maeve in her typically dizzy way. Forcing me to wonder if she does that on purpose. On demand. Is everything a mask? "Not her responsibility, but you know our Emerson. Responsible to the core."

"You look rather disheveled, Emerson." She sounds pleased. Or certainly not sympathetic anyway. "That is for certain."

I try to focus. To think. To be present in this moment instead of the past, and I definitely do not look back over to the Missouri History section.

"Were you looking for a book, Maeve?" I know she isn't. I also know she'll bristle.

Her nose goes into the air, right on cue. "This festival of yours is very important," she chides me, as if I might have missed that. Despite coming up with it myself. "If you're late for any of the preceremony meetings today, that would be a disaster."

"Luckily, I'm never late."

"You are this morning." She jabs a finger toward the old clock on the wall. It's shaped like a fox, its bushy tail twitching back and forth to the seconds. It's always been there, but for the first time I connect the dots. Grandma also has a fox on her grave. Or she usually does.

"I wasn't late, Maeve. I was actually right on time."

"That's late for you."

"On a normal day, but today is not a normal day." I remind myself to smile. Then I remind myself to make it serene, not edgy. "It's the Redbud Festival and I had to check on everything this morning before I came in, despite the renegade chinchillas. It's what I do."

As comebacks go it's not scathing, but it is true. And would be almost entirely true whether or not I'd discovered that I was a witch today, which feels like a win. I begin to feel solid again. Me-ish.

Maeve sniffs. "I'll see you at noon, then. We'll need to go over Skip's speech."

I tear my gaze away from the fox. "Skip's...what?"

"Honestly, Emerson, get your head out of the chinchilla nest." Maeve tuts at me like I'm a child, which I can't blame on the witch thing. She's always talked to me this way. It's just more irritating now that I know I could smite her down. With my hands. Maybe. "He said you begged him to give a ceremonial opening speech. As the leading members of the Redbud committee, we'll need to go over it to make sure it's fitting for the occasion. You know how he likes to go off on tangents."

I nod, because I do know this. Just like I know she only likes to join town committees so she can swan about the festivals, claiming privileges. After all the actual work is done.

"Of course," I murmur.

Except… Skip refused the speech. More critically, Skip was behind the adlet attack that was maybe supposed to kill me. Maybe. Probably. But I'm still here. I'm still alive.

Maeve leaves, no doubt to inform the entire town that the unstoppable Emerson Wilde is chasing chinchillas once again, but I'm still trying to wrap my head around Skip. And the speech that I distinctly remember that he scoffed at giving.

"What was that?" Georgie asks, brow knitted again in another frown. Another one of today's weirdnesses has been all this time in the presence of a Georgie who doesn't smile constantly. It's like she's inside out.

"I don't like to speak ill of another woman," I say, "because the sisterhood is for support, but Maeve has never met a moment that she couldn't make into an opera."

"Not Maeve. Before. It was like you put a bubble around yourself." She points to where I saw Grandma and Rebekah. "I couldn't get to you."

That startles me. I felt the wall, or window, or whatever it was, but I didn't think *I* made it. It just seemed to happen. "I didn't… If I did that, I didn't mean to."

Unease ripples through me, but I can't let it take hold. Things are strange. Finding out I'm a witch with *magic powers* will take some getting used to. No point in panicking.

I repeat that a few times. To make sure it takes.

"I wish we had time to figure out what was going on before Ostara," Georgie mutters.

"Ostara?"

"It's the real festival."

"My festival is pretty real." I feel stung. Or maybe I'm frustrated that there's this whole world I don't understand, right here where my safe, tidy, *awesome* world is supposed to be."

Georgie reaches out and smooths her palm over my arm. "Of course it is, but the Redbud Festival is for humans. Ostara is for us."

Us.

"The Redbuds are part of it. When we have a festival, there's an influx of witchkind, so we need a mortal festival to happen at the same time to cover it. All the town's festivals are distractions to keep the humans from looking too closely at our rites and holy days and things."

So much subterfuge. Perfectly formed bricks hiding beneath a glamour. Witches among humans. Witches stripped of magic memories.

I focus on the important part. "Historically," I say.

"Historically?"

"Maybe *historically* the town festivals were to cover up... witch things." She stares at me. I stare back. "Because, obviously, Georgie, since I've been chamber of commerce president, *my* festivals are fantastic in their own right. Aren't they?"

My best friend laughs. "Obviously."

We can both pretend I'm joking, but it still feels like a touchstone. Like I'm still me, no matter what I can smite. I smile back at her. "What is Ost...Oysteria?"

"Ostara—" she pronounces the word distinctly "—is the celebration of the spring equinox. Groups come together to celebrate the changing of the seasons instead of, say, Thanksgiving. Depending on what you need, you might offer something or ask for something, and often with Ostara we simply... reset. Cleanse ourselves for a new season, leaving the old behind. It helps keep the world in balance. Or it's supposed to."

I want to chase up that last part, but her hand is still on my arm. And like back in her turret, she looks like she's going to cry again. "And this year you'll be with us again."

She says that like I should know why that's so important to her.

Georgie has been my best friend for as long as I can remember. I've never wanted to pull away from her. Never wanted to withdraw or find some distance. Until this moment. I want time and space to work this out, but I can't have it.

There's a festival to plan. Skip's speech to approve, apparently. Spring equinoxes and adlets and in my spare time, my family's historic bookshop to run. When all that's handled, maybe I can spend some time digging around in how today has changed all my relationships.

Or changed my impression of my relationships, that is.

"Thanks for walking me over, but I can take it from here," I tell her. Briskly. "If anyone else asks why I was late, I'll just use the chinchilla excuse. No worries."

Georgie's frown is back. "I can't leave you alone."

"Don't be ridiculous."

She shakes her head slightly, like she can't believe what I'm saying. "This is so dangerous. *So* dangerous. You have no idea how much trouble you're in."

"Were the snarling, fanged, nightmare dogs trying to chew me up not enough of a clue?"

"Em."

"You aren't giving me enough credit, Georgie. I survived."

Georgie firms her lips and she doesn't say a word, but I know exactly what she's thinking. *Sometimes you give yourself too much credit.*

But I have always believed that a woman's best and biggest champion should be herself. The world sure isn't going to step up and cheer on its own. I won against those adlets today.

Me. Maybe Jacob held them off for a time, but I'm the one who smited them. Smote them?

Either way, I did it, and I'm not supposed to have any magic.

"You can't be alone until we have a better idea of what's going on," Georgie is telling me.

"For God's sake, Georgie," I snap. "I don't think crystals and rainbows could have fought off those things. Do you?"

She jerks back, taking her hand with her.

And I wish I could say that today's extraordinary events are what made me decide to be an asshole to my best friend, but I know better. I'm a lot of *A*-words. *Anal. Accomplished. Ambitious. Amazing.* And, sadly, occasionally an asshole too.

Normally Georgie looks like a kicked puppy and nothing makes me feel worse. I open my mouth to start my usual apologies, but her face changes.

Less kicked puppy. More…hardass.

I don't recognize her.

"I realize you're not used to being so out of your depth," she says coolly. "It will be frustrating for you to lean on us, I'm sure. But this is how it has to be, Emerson. You don't have the slightest idea how much damage you can do. For once in your life you need to do what you're told."

I would normally balk at the suggestion, from anyone, that I should fall in line, but this is Georgie. And Georgie has never talked to me this way. Ever.

I don't know what to do about it. I don't know what to *do*, and that is simply unacceptable.

So when a customer comes in—witch or human, I couldn't tell you and I don't know that I care—I do the only thing I can. I smile broadly and welcome them to Confluence Books.

8

I HAVE A STEADY STREAM OF CUSTOMERS, most in town for the Redbud Festival. Maybe I shouldn't assume that. Maybe they're all witches, here for Ostara.

The festival for *us*.

When I have a few minutes to myself, I google "witches" and "latent power" and any other combination of words I can come up with. I look up "adlets," then quickly close the browser window when I see drawings of creatures that look *exactly* like what tried to take me down.

Up close, they are even more hideous and nausea inducing than I remember.

I don't speak directly to Georgie after her *orders*, and she doesn't leave. She sits in a chair and reads. Not from any of the books I carry in the shop, but from books she pulls out of the tote bag she brought.

We don't usually fight. Neither of us are any good at it. Usually.

I try to summon any other memories of my grandmother

using that same magic—but nothing happens. Anytime I think I'm close, another customer comes in.

I smile and nod and sell books. I watch the clock because I'm still me and there's no way I'm missing whatever Maeve and Skip have in store for me at noon.

Is Maeve Mather in all her pinched-faced, thin-lipped nastiness a witch too? I glance over at Georgie, who looks entirely too *at her ease*, reading happily as if wholly *unbothered* that we're at odds. I should be able to ask her what I want to know, but as long as she's *babysitting* I…can't.

I *really* dislike being told what to do.

You know yourself, Emerson, Jacob had said today, that green gaze of his so steady on mine. *Surely you know you tried to create your own, third option.*

It's true that I'm out of my depth here. I'm not so full of myself that I don't get that. But I'm not an infant. I never was. The me-I-can't-remember was trying to talk magical authorities into my way of thinking when I was still an actual kid.

I don't like being treated like the child *they* can remember I clearly wasn't.

I'm the one with all this *stuff* in me. Now that I know, it's all that I can feel. It's all I want to talk about, all I want to do, so that even tending to my shop seems like an imposition—and that never happens.

Something is going to have to change. Because I've changed.

I can give them a day, I tell myself. Magnanimously. But then they're going to have to catch up.

At eleven thirty, I begin to gather my things, because I would rather get eaten by monsters than let Maeve Mather call me tardy twice. Georgie looks up from her book and begins to pack up, but no. *No.*

"You can't come with me," I tell her, maybe a little too shortly.

Maybe a little too much like an order, in fact.

"Give me a break, Emerson," she says, the tone so exasperated that she reminds me of my mother. I have an odd flash—not like the full-on memory of Grandma with me and Rebekah—but more like a glimpse. Of my mother glaring at me, and *I know*, somewhere deep down, that it's because I didn't do some magical thing right. I don't know what thing, I don't know why, I only know she's mad that I'm not as amazing as she thought I'd be.

It doesn't leave me much room to be nice to my best friend. "I need someone to watch the store."

"You usually close for lunch."

"Not during the Redbud Festival." I meet her glare with a steely gaze of my own. "Stay here. Watch the store. Please."

I tack on that last word in a manner that I am aware is less than gracious. Yet I can't seem to help myself.

She looks hurt, which is marginally better than that un-Georgie hardness. But I *feel* hurt. And I don't know how to bridge this gap.

Georgie makes a resigned sort of sound and comes over to the cash register. "Do you have the crystal I gave you the other day?"

I pull the black rock out of my bag. She smiles, if a little sadly. "Hold on to it while you're around Skip, okay? Just… be careful."

"You don't need to worry about me."

"I thought I didn't, and then creatures that aren't supposed to exist tried to kill you in a sacred place, and someone made sure you couldn't call for help."

Something like guilt wells up inside of me. As frustrated as I am with Georgie and how she's treating me, I know she's doing it because she's afraid for my safety. For me. Because she loves me.

But I don't know how to be coddled. I'm not sure I could accept it even if I did know how. "I killed those things, when I didn't even know what I was."

"Who," Georgie corrects me.

"Who?" I echo impatiently.

She doesn't blink. "Being a witch isn't *what* you are, Emerson. It is *who* you are. An elemental part of what makes you… *you*. You didn't need to know you were one—you didn't need magic to become one. It is *who* you are."

I don't fully understand that, but I don't want to be upset with Georgie anymore. My heart can't take it. So I nod. And though I don't give in, I give her arm a squeeze. "I'll be careful," I promise.

By which I mean, I'll be careful alone. Without some kind of magical babysitter.

Georgie smiles, but it's small. And unhappy. But she doesn't argue.

I exit the store and breathe in the early afternoon air. It is *spring*. I am a *witch*. I am even more amazing than I thought. Things are good.

Well. Except for strange memories of my perpetually disappointed mother. And other memories of better things that still hurt. And that whole someone—*Skip Simon*—trying to kill me part. I ruminate on that as I march my way to the town green. It's a little more brown than green this early in spring, a rolling area of grass just a ways up from the riverbank.

I glance at the river, then stare. It's where it always is, the muddy brown it's supposed to be. But something shimmers in the air above it. And in the distance, where the two rivers are supposed to be merging, the way they always do, something else is happening. It's foggy or blurry or something I can't see clearly and when I try it physically hurts and I have to look away.

But then I remember what Georgie told me.

I inhale, focus, and whisper the words she gave me. *"Reveal to me what I should see."*

Like magic—because it is magic—the fog slowly lifts, my vision gradually clears, and there's an entire third river, rippling in the sunlight and joining with the other two.

My heart slams against my chest, its beat thundering in my ears. I gasp for air. I may even stumble, but I'm holding Georgie's stone in my hand and it grows hot. Steadying me. Reminding me.

No one can know.

I have to act like I always act and gawking at the river is *not* me. I suck in a breath, rip my gaze away from the new river, and then focus on the green again.

Maeve is already there with Corrinne. Maeve is always the emcee for our introduction to the festivities, crowning of our May queens and Halloween pumpkins, et cetera, et cetera. I'd do it, but I've always got too much to handle behind the scenes and Maeve *loves* the attention. Corrinne is head of the decorating committee and while I wouldn't say anyone actually *gets along* with Maeve, Corrinne knows best how to handle her, no doubt because of all her experience with obnoxious customers at the Lunch House. I always pair them together on festival work.

I walk toward them now, a new question like a mantra in my head. *Who's a witch and who isn't?* If I chant those words Georgie gave me, will gold eyes appear? Will I be able to see who can create magic and who can't?

But I don't know what witches know. Will they be able to tell what I'm doing? I don't dare do anything.

When I get to the gazebo, Skip is standing on the stage,

almost like he's practicing the speech he said he wouldn't do. In typical Skip fashion. Looking out smugly to the non-existent crowd. Surveying his kingdom like some kind of holy conqueror.

A lick of anger ignites inside of me, and almost as if he *feels* it, his gaze cuts to mine.

Pure, unadulterated shock slackens his face.

I will admit I find this satisfying. I march toward him, thinking of his voice on the phone. Smug and gross. And then what came after. What *should have* happened to me.

But I refuse to be cowed by any man and especially not by the likes of Skip Simon. Just like I refuse to entertain any lingering, yucky feelings of violation for what he failed to do to me. Still, the only thing keeping me from flying into accusations is the hot crystal in my hand.

"Emerson," he says when I take the stairs to stand on stage with him. With *shock*, then what looks like a slow, growing fury. In red. On his round face. Which is no match for mine. "What are you doing here?"

He's surprised to see me, so Maeve didn't mention me. He's surprised to see me, so I *know* he's behind what happened, but I can't fully accept that a man as ineffectual and childish as Skip almost won. Would have, if my power hadn't shown up the way it did.

I choose to feel stronger because of what actually happened, not weak about what could have happened. Because it didn't.

I'm tempted to try one of those balls of light that my friends showed me. I'm tempted to wiggle my fingers at him and see what magic pops up. Because not only did he *fail* to hurt me or get rid of me or whatever, but he awakened all *this*.

Maybe I should see what I can do. All over him.

The stone burns my hand.

With tremendous restraint that he does not deserve, I do not throw light balls at Skip's head. I tell myself that whatever is inside me is mine. No matter what reawakened it. Because it was *me* who fought through that fog to get to Jacob.

It was me who handled it.

"I'm here for our meeting, of course," I say brightly, smiling so widely my cheeks hurt. "Maeve mentioned you'd changed your mind about giving a speech. I'm thrilled."

He stares at me, gaping like a fish out of water, and maybe I'm more spiteful and petty than I ever gave myself credit for, because I enjoy that too. I can't wait to tell Ellowyn. I feel as smug as he sounded this morning. I lean forward conspiratorially. He's still gaping, but he leans in too, like he can't help himself.

"Some joke getting me to run over to the cemetery first thing this morning," I whisper. "But you shouldn't have bothered." I smile at him. Perhaps a bit pointedly.

Skip narrows his eyes. He's now that mottled shade of red I'm so familiar with.

"I'll admit, you had me worried," I continue, needing to needle him. Not *wanting* to, but it's a compulsion. As hot and demanding as the power that shot out of me and killed those adlets. "You clearly went to some trouble to make it look like someone attacked those trees. You really had me going, I'll admit." My laugh sounds canned. And maybe this is all too pointed, but I can't bring myself to care, no matter how that stone *burns* at me. "Luckily, when I took a moment, I realized it was one of your jokes."

"You know me," he grits out. "Such a jokester."

I feel like we have what's almost a moment there. In which all his not-really-jokes-at-all seem to loom large in the spring sunshine, every one more disturbing than the last, and now all I want to know is what *really* happened. Did I accidentally magic off his junk or something in the second grade? Because why else would he hate me *this much*?

I'm annoyed I can't just ask.

"Maeve tells me you have a speech," I say instead. Brightly. I clap my hands together. "Can't wait to hear it. The festivities really kick off at five, so if we could speed this along. I've got a lot to do and not much time to do it."

I wave at Maeve and Corrinne, who are watching us, looking vaguely amused. They've seen the Skip and Emerson show before after all.

I think it's deeply unfair that everyone knows the words to the songs in this show and I don't. I didn't even know it was a musical. All I know is a questionably dubbed version of my own life—and my own red-faced nemesis.

"You'll hear my speech when everyone else does," Skip says in his usual supercilious way. It feels almost shocking to me, because it's so normal. Just Skip, no spells.

"I don't need to approve it or anything. I only need to know the general gist of what you plan to say about the festival. You weren't very supportive just a few days ago. No need to be childish, right?"

"Childish?" He puffs out his chest. "I could show you childish, Emerson."

That would be redundant, I want to say, but the hot rock in my hand stops me. And now that I understand there's *magic*, in me, in Georgie, in her crystals, I realize it's a warning system of some kind. I'll have to grill Georgie on how it works before I agree to carry it around again.

And then maybe carry more.

I may not like being told what to do, but I also hope I never ignore a useful tool when it's offered.

"Oh good, here's your bodyguard," Skip says, glaring behind me. "Always there to stand between you and the trouble you cause, isn't he?"

I look over my shoulder and see Jacob approaching, looking thunderous. But I don't focus on Jacob's uninvited arrival and trademark bad mood. I look back at Skip. "Bodyguard? What does that mean?"

Skip smirks. "I don't know. Why don't you ask your boyfriend?"

Boyfriend. I look back at Jacob, almost against my will. I wouldn't have thought anything of Skip's snide comment, but I know there are things I don't understand. Don't remember. Was something actually going on between Jacob and me before I got mind wiped?

I feel much too hot, suddenly. Not from the stone, for a change.

"Emerson." Jacob bites out my name, and I can tell by the way he glares at me that he's mad at me for something. I want to tell him to join the club.

I also want to pretend that I don't care, but can't quite get there. I'm not my sister, who had always elevated not caring to an art form.

Jacob is frowning at Skip, looking even less amused, and it's refreshing to see that same flash of violence and thirst for revenge in Jacob that I feel inside. Even if he controls it.

He does not greet Skip.

"What are you doing on this side of the river, North? Not enough dirt on your side?" Skip demands, probably peevish because Jacob didn't acknowledge him. Skip really likes to be acknowledged. As he will be the first to remind you, he is the mayor.

"I've got a lunch meeting with Felix and a couple other members of the town council to discuss the continuing flooding issues," Jacob returns, his voice even and perfectly controlled. "A meeting you should be attending yourself, shouldn't you? Mr. Mayor?"

Skip's lip curls. "What do you care about that over there on your precious, protected hill?"

Jacob's stare is so cold it's a wonder icicles don't form in the air. "Emerson strong-armed me onto the flood committee two years ago to see if I could explain some of the imbalances we've been seeing in the rivers, the crops. Since I am still a simple farmer."

I have the distinct impression that he wants to say something more about *imbalances*. Does he mean climate change? Or does he mean people? But Skip is openly scoffing at Jacob.

"Some simple farmer."

Jacob studies him. "Don't you pay attention to your town's committees? Or your town's very pressing environmental concerns? It's *your* town, isn't it? Pretty sure I remember that on a campaign poster."

"I prefer not to be led around by my dick, North, but that's me," Skip sneers. Possibly confirming that I didn't eunuch him as a baby witch.

Jacob does nothing, but Skip lets out a little yelp of pain and nearly jumps off the stage. I make a note to learn that spell too.

"I'll handle my speech, Emerson," Skip tells me, through his teeth. "It's none of your business. *I'm* the mayor, not you."

"I didn't run for mayor," I say with a little smile, the way I always do.

Because obviously if I had, he wouldn't be the mayor.

Skip confirms this by literally baring his teeth at me, then storms out of the gazebo.

I turn to Jacob. "What did you do to him?"

Jacob watches, still glaring, as Skip sidles up next to Maeve. Like a little boy seeking someone's protection from a bully. When Skip *is* the bully.

I've never understood how that isn't obvious. I mutter those revealing words, but nothing changes. There's only Skip and Maeve's *concerned* face.

Jacob still isn't saying anything. To me.

"I *know* he sent those adlets after me, but how could such a sniveling coward accomplish such a thing?" I ask.

"I don't know." It's clear the question bothers Jacob as much as it does me. "But I'm going to find out."

"*We* are going to find out."

He looks down at me. "Speaking of *we*, Emerson, you can't be alone." He takes my arm like I'm a toddler who's run away and he's going to return me to my mother, like it or not. "Certainly not with him. Have some common sense."

"*Common sense?*" I'm so shocked by his offensive, patronizing bullshit that I barely notice he's marching me back across the green in the direction of the bookstore.

Like said naughty toddler.

I want to kill him, but on the off chance that my thoughts alone can lead to smiting, I ratchet that urge back. Piously, because he doesn't deserve my consideration while acting like he thinks he's my father.

Jacob North is not my father.

Even though he's lecturing me. "Georgie said you insisted on coming over here alone, when anyone with the faintest shred of common sense would know that after this morning there could be a threat around any corner. I thought she must have misunderstood, but here you are."

"So you came running. In your role as my bodyguard?"

He shoots me a look I can't read. Green and stormy. "Call it what you want. I already fought for you once today. You're welcome. You can thank me by not going out and *taunting* the guy who tried to kill us both."

"You may recall, Jacob, that I'm the one who actually neutralized said threat. Feel free to thank *me* at any time."

He looks down at me. He releases my arm. There's something bleak in his expression, but I don't understand it.

And I am sick to death of not understanding.

"What happened between us in high school?" I blurt out.

And regret it instantly, but I can't take it back.

There's an almost unnoticeable hitch in Jacob's stride, but he walks on, if a little more stiffly than before. "What?"

"High school. I don't remember it right, obviously. Skip said—"

Jacob stops and skewers with me with such an incredulous look I don't finish. "Please tell me you didn't just say *'Skip said'* to me as if that's a viable addition to *any* conversation."

"Obviously I can't trust him. That's why I'm trying to clarify with you. Someone I do trust. But you're being weird about it." I go to poke him in the chest, but something stops me. Possibly the fact I want to punch him. Possibly because I...don't actually want to *punch* him. "I always thought..."

But I can't finish that sentence.

"Thought what?" He's just standing there in the middle of the sidewalk, arms crossed. All closed off and imposing.

Imposing enough I can't quite seem to form the words. The real words. "That we were *friends* in high school."

"We were."

He offers nothing more. And I feel certain he knows what I'm getting at, but won't give me an inch. See also: treating me like a toddler who he knows better than. That lick of anger is back, this time aimed right at Jacob.

"But not more than that?" I demand, though I hate the way my voice sounds higher pitched than it should. When it's a perfectly fair question I have every right to ask.

He raises an eyebrow and says *nothing*. I want to throttle

him, and I wonder for a moment if I really could. If I could best Jacob the same way I bested those adlets.

But I don't really want that. I only want to prove…something. I hate that everything has changed, but I still don't know anything. I more than hate it.

It feels *bleak* suddenly, even with magic. Even with Georgie so happy I have it when I'm not being awful to her because she knows things I don't. Suddenly I feel stripped completely clean of every last shred of strength I've been holding on to. "You don't know what it's like to be the one who can't remember things. Things everybody else, including *Skip Simon*, clearly all know. It's bullshit."

I'm far too close to tears. I'm alone, in a way I've never fully understood before. That I must always have been this alone, but never realized it, is worse. It feels more violating than Skip sending his little hellhounds after me.

Because it's not just that the people I love most know things I don't. It's that they know—they remember—a *me* that I don't.

Jacob is looking at me like he knows exactly what it's like to feel torn in half. And exposed.

"Maybe not," he says. His voice is rough enough that it makes my eyes go bright—but I do not cry. I do *not*. "But you don't know what it's like to be the one who remembers."

"I didn't ask for this." And suddenly I'm as close to breaking as I've been all day, in all this insanity. And it's in front of *Jacob*.

"Neither did I. But I dealt with it. We all dealt with it." He sounds angry, but what echoes inside me feels like pain. Like it's ours. Like we share it. "Nothing happened between us in high school. Except that we were very dumb and you paid the price while I did not."

He acts as if that's a good enough explanation.

"You have to tell me what that means."

What we felt. I want to know what we *felt*.

His mouth curves, but it's not a smile. "Not today I don't."

And then he just *disappears*. Poof. Gone.

I gasp out loud at the air where he was standing, then gape around in all directions, because surely someone saw. Surely he just gave away everything.

Suddenly I'm desperate to keep my own secret.

But I'm not standing out on Main Street. Somehow I'm in an alley between the bookstore and the neighboring building, hidden away from all of St. Cyprian's prying eyes.

Did we walk here? Did he *poof* me here? I want to scream in frustration, but I still have a bookstore to run and a festival to facilitate. *I* can't go disappearing when the conversation doesn't suit me.

Bastard.

"And I guess you left me alone after all," I mutter in accusation to the spot where he was, but when I turn Ellowyn is standing there in the alley's entrance, Main Street behind her.

She smiles sheepishly. "Not quite."

9

I TRY TO TELL MYSELF I SHOULD BE GRATE-
ful my friends are here to take care of me. They know so
much that I don't after all. I should be so glad.

But I can't get there. I feel betrayed. I feel beat down. "So,
you heard all of that?" I ask Ellowyn, partly out of embarrassment. And partly out of wondering what I can get her
to tell me that Jacob won't.

I walk toward Ellowyn. She shrugs. "Not all of it."

I join her at the mouth of the alley and we step back into
the sunlight. "What parts?"

Ellowyn smiles. "Did you know that men lie twice as
much as women?"

I've always found Ellowyn's habit of spouting random,
disturbing facts, always about why men are terrible, kind
of comical. Everyone should have a walking encyclopedia
of the evils of the patriarchy on hand. Plus, she delivers
these fun facts so happily. It's both creepy and hilarious—an
Ellowyn specialty.

But it lands differently now, in this new world. Because everything is different. "What is that?" I ask.

"What is what?"

"I used to think it was a joke. A small comedy routine about the patriarchy, so I'm obviously the target audience. But it's not, is it?"

We stare at each other in the bright glare of the spring sunshine. Cars bump by on the bricks. I hear shop doors open and close, bells jangling. And the longer we stand there, the more I think that she's not going to answer me.

In some ways, Ellowyn is the biggest mystery to me in our little group. She was always tighter with Rebekah. She had her whole thing with Zander—though who knows what actually happened versus what I remember. She is a font of arcane knowledge and talks openly—often over tea—about things like poisoning our enemies or how a person might effectively dispose of a body as if *body disposal* is a situation that might spontaneously arise on any random Tuesday.

That little personality quirk sits a bit differently, now that I think about it. Because who knows what might magically arise? For any reason?

Maybe nothing is what it seems.

I'm not sure if I want Ellowyn to answer me or do her usual thing and redirect.

We walk toward the bookshop's front door and I get the feeling she's sizing me up too. Maybe doing the same sort of math.

"It's not a comedy routine," she tells me when we reach the step outside Confluence. "It's a curse."

She sails into the shop as if that's a complete answer. I follow. Georgie is talking to a customer in the corner and I know I should take over, but I want Ellowyn to keep talking to me. Since she's the first person to actually talk to me like I'm still *me*.

I herd her into the back room and lock the door behind us.

Ellowyn leans back against the nearest stack of boxes and crosses her arms.

"A curse," I repeat, very carefully. Giving her ample time to correct me if I've misheard. She does not. "A *curse*?"

"A curse," she confirms. And shrugs when I gape at her. "I can't lie. That's the curse. Like that Jim Carrey movie, but less fun. So, instead, I deflect. Regaling the world with mankind's many, *many* flaws seems like the best choice to express myself."

"Someone actually *cursed* you. Like an actual, magical curse."

"To be distinguished from a hex. Because a hex can wear off, but curses never do."

"But…how? Who? *Why?*"

"How? Accidentally," Ellowyn says, ticking the questions off with her fingers. "Who? My mother. Why? Because she cursed my father when she found out he was a cheating liar who lies and cheats." She wiggles her three fingers. "And it turns out when you curse someone's blood it affects, you know, the daughter who shares that blood."

"That sounds horrible, Wynnie."

I know it is, because she doesn't make a face at that nickname. "I mean, it's not awesome."

"When?"

Her head droops a little, like a physical rendition of a sigh. "High school. You try being a teenage girl who can't tell even the tiniest white lie. I can't recommend the experience."

I try to take this in. All the ramifications. "But you still have a relationship with your mother. Don't you?"

"That's the thing about magic," Ellowyn says softly. "It's all fun and games. Until it isn't. And some things you can't take back."

I swallow over the sudden lump in my throat. And when another wave of emotion hits me out of nowhere, I go with it.

"Thank you," I say, all choked up. I step across the small stockroom and hug her. When I step back, she looks horrified—which, at least, is normal.

Ellowyn is not tactile.

She frowns at me. "What was that assault about?"

"You're the only one who's answered any questions directly today."

"Can't lie. It's a curse." She grins, but I see the emotion beneath her usual cool bravado.

And I realize...we all are who we've always been. Georgie wants everyone to be okay. Ellowyn wants to plaster over her more complicated feelings with an edgy comment and a face of stone. Zander wants to pretend everything is okay and even easy to hide the serious parts of him inside. Jacob wants to protect everyone—whether that's from actual monsters or the pain of failure—he's there to try to stop it.

I, naturally, want to be in charge, to mold the world to my will, because I always know the best way forward. I just do.

This might be the first time in my life that the next step isn't clear to me. That I don't know what to do. "I don't know how to do this. *I* don't know how to do...any of this."

In a day filled with disconcerting and disorienting things, one after the next, this somehow feels like the breaking point. I sink into the nearest chair.

"Maybe give yourself a break, Em," Ellowyn suggests after a moment, her voice softer than usual. "It's only been a few hours since your whole world got turned around. It would be weird if you *did* know what to do. Even you." She straightens, then reaches over and pats my shoulder. Awkwardly.

Coming from Ellowyn, it's more comforting than a hug might have been from anyone else.

I close my eyes for a moment, hoping my old certainty returns in force. But mostly there's a growing pit of...something in my stomach. Something I've felt before, but it's been so long I thought I'd eradicated it.

Self-doubt.

When I'd been *sure* I'd wiped it all out after my first few years of climbing that chamber of commerce ladder.

"Since we'll all be together tonight for Ostara anyway, and there's extra magic in the air for the holiday, everyone is going to want to do a summoning tonight," Ellowyn tells me. This, too, feels like a gift, because she's definitely not talking to me like I'm a child. We could be having any normal, everyday conversation. If we weren't talking about a *summoning*.

"What's a summoning?"

Ellowyn blinks as if surprised I have to ask. For a moment, her expression softens and reminds me of what Georgie said. *It's been such a long ten years.*

But it's gone before I can react, hardened away into typical Ellowyn. "All witches have a designation—what we're especially good at. What…things our power lends itself to. Jacob is a Healer from a family of Healers. They take care of any witchkind needing healing in the area. Maybe it won't surprise you to learn that Georgie's a Historian. Zander and all the Rivers are Guardians. They take care of the rivers and the confluence—who comes, who goes. And I'm a Summoner. I can summon spirits, spells, sacred or profane objects, whatever."

"Right," I say, very knowledgeably. "That stuff. All of it."

She smiles a little. "A summoning is when a Summoner attempts to reach the past spirits who are open to communication to offer us some guidance. I'm a connection to the past. What we really need is a Diviner—someone who can see the future."

"Naturally," I say, because doesn't everyone wish they could see the future? At least sometimes?

"Though I suppose, to really figure out what's going on with this attack on you, we need a little bit of both." She continues on, clearly talking more to herself than me. "We don't have a Diviner we can trust, but a Summoner is useful. Theoretically. But if you're relying on *me* to be your Summoner…"

She trails off, looking at me as if she expects me to get it. But I don't.

"Why shouldn't I rely on you?"

"I'm not like you guys, Em." I still don't get it. She sighs. "You're all full-blood witches. I'm only a half witch."

She's a half witch, but she somehow ended up with her memories and her magic and even a curse. When my parents are both powerful witches, according to Georgie, yet Rebekah and I were a disappointment. How does that work? "But…you weren't mind wiped or exiled."

"Well, no, I have enough power. Some half witches don't have any power. Some have a lot. Power isn't math. The Joywood try to make it into that, try to simplify with their tests and their mind wipes, but no one has ever been able to explain *why* some witches are born with more power or less. It just is. But the Joywood survive because people like simple. People like math. It's much harder to fight, to admit things are complicated. To need to sacrifice something."

I nod along with all of this. I might not understand power, but I understand simple and difficult solutions—and the way public opinion affects both.

"But if you're powerful enough, why does it matter that you're a half witch? Why shouldn't we depend on you?"

She waves a hand, and there's a strange brittleness to the Ellowyn I know. Like her typical bravado is cracked. "Half witches have a tendency to be more…volatile, regardless of power level. Control is the issue with me. I'm not going to blow something up or summon a demon or anything, don't worry. But you might want to manage your expectations, because I might make a mess of things. It happens. I can handle everyone else's disappointment. Years of practice and the expectations of a half witch. I'm not sure I'm up to yours."

I want to comfort her, even if I don't understand this confession she's making. But this is Ellowyn. Tough. Sardonic. Unamused. *Cursed*, apparently. She looks like even a hint of kindness or comfort might break her in two.

"Luckily for you, I have no expectations about *summonings*," I tell her. "And if everyone has roles...what am I?"

"The roles are determined in different ways. Healers and Guardians are genetic positions known from early on. The rest, once you've passed the power test and aren't labeled spell dim, you take the positions test."

"I *excel* at tests."

Ellowyn grins at me, and I know I did the right thing in ignoring the open wound. "That you do, and if I was a betting woman? The witch who struck down some adlets before she even knew she had power is almost certainly a Warrior."

I like the sound of that. "I don't know what that means either," I say. "But it feels right, I won't lie."

Because haven't I always been a warrior?

Ellowyn leaves me and I spend the rest of the day in my normal blur on a festival day. Questions that need answering, fires that need putting out. But this time it feels like there are two of me running around. The normal me is the one *doing* the things the way I always do. Yet there's an outside observer watching. Me. St. Cyprian. The people I've always known.

Watching, studying. Always looking for some sign. Some glimpse into this new-to-me magical world that I can only see bits and pieces of.

Georgie and I are careful with one another and if I spend any time thinking about that, it hurts, but luckily I don't have much time to *think*. Or even to be frustrated that one of my friends is constantly within arm's reach. Guarding me. *Babysitting* me.

Once, when I'm in the middle of talking to another committee member, Gil Redd, about the lighting element not working, I feel a cold chill skitter down my spine. Yet there's no breeze. I look around, and across the street, Skip is standing there.

Just standing there at the head of an alley between two shops, the river behind him.

He's staring at me. He does nothing else. Just stares, and I can't seem to look away. People walk through our eyeline, but his gaze is on mine and I'm stuck. Frozen.

Is he...doing something to me?

When he disappears, I blink. Once. I stay frozen, though this feels more of my own accord. I stare at the place where he was standing. Someone walks through the space and I turn my head to watch them continue walking down the street.

And my heart is beating too hard, telling me it was a narrow escape.

Gil gets the lights fixed as the sun is going down. All around us, the shops have stayed open, the restaurants are full, and the town is hopping. If I had to guess, I've doubled the turnout from last year. I should be giddy with the glow of success.

But I can't get there. It's like I'm seeing everything through a window again, and this time the glass is thicker. And as I think that, I know what I have to do.

It's the *wrong* thing to do. It goes against everything I am, everything I believe, because it's certainly not the *dutiful* thing to do, but I'm walking out before I even fully realize it. Away from the store, leaving Georgie hanging with my customers, without telling her what I'm doing. I still have that last meeting with the business owners before the evening's festivities really take off. I walk toward the ferry loading dock, knowing I have things to do in town. And as irritated as I am with my friends for treating me like fragile glass, I should let someone know what I'm doing. Anything else is careless and I'm never careless.

But I don't do any of the things I should. I walk. All the way onto the ferry. The sun slips below the horizon and the sky is a pearly pink that will fade quickly.

So quickly, by the time the engine roars to life and the ferry begins to chug across the river, it's dark.

The ferry itself is packed with people headed over to see the cemetery redbuds that Ellowyn assured me were taken care of, and I can see that there is a line of cars on the other side waiting to return. *Success. Look at my success.*

But I don't smile. No fist pumping here. It's like I'm someone else. I stare out into the dark of night at the water. The moon stretches out across the rippling river like a beacon of light. I inhale the cold night air, I look at the twinkling stars above, and for a moment I am still.

St. Cyprian is mine and I am St. Cyprian's.

It's like something lifts off of me then. A weight. A fog. I pull my phone out of my pocket and text Georgie an apology, promising I'll be back before closing. I breathe again, letting the star shine wash over me like a bath.

Today has been a *lot*. But I'm a Warrior and I live for *a lot*. I need to get better at handling the witchy version of it.

"Why isn't anyone with you?" Zander demands, appearing next to me without me realizing he's left the pilot booth. I was in such a fog that I didn't realize he was on the ferry at all, and I should have, since I have all the ferry schedules memorized.

I decide then and there that I will not allow my witch self to be a flake. I'd rather let a conjured monster eat me alive—and having narrowly avoided that fate this morning, I know I mean that.

I glance over at my cousin and, big surprise, he's scowling. So far witch Zander leaves a lot to be desired. "You're with me."

"You know what I mean, Emerson. You're heading right into…" He trails off, then looks around the boat as if there's a reason for alarm when all I see are botanists. He lowers his voice. "I can't walk with you to the cemetery. We're too busy."

I tell myself this is concern. Love. I reach out and squeeze his arm. "I don't need you to walk me anywhere. Really."

I've never seen him like this. So tightly wound and protective. So…worried, I realize, with surprise.

Then again, I've never been attacked before. He's never had to play the overprotective cousin, because the biggest threat that's ever been laid at my door before now is Skip. And Skip has been constantly sad and annoying since the fourth-grade showdown, but he's never been *dangerous*.

Until now.

How did Skip *manage to send those adlets after me?*

"You have to take this more seriously," Zander lectures me, and I want to point out that I've said that to *him* approximately seven hundred thousand times in our lives. But he's so *grave*, and I made such a hash of it with Georgie that I try to be better this time. I try really hard.

"I'm taking it seriously."

"Yeah, but you're not. Because here you are. All alone on the river."

"I'm taking it seriously, Zander." I lift a shoulder. "But it's possible I'm taking it a little less slowly than you are."

It's funny, really. Because they all knew the truth all along. The only thing that's changed is me knowing. More evidence that I'm a badass Warrior, I think smugly. I can adapt *this quickly* to new information, new powers, and a whole new identity.

But then, none of them ever truly appreciated my years of training in the cutthroat trenches of student body politics at St. Cyprian High.

Instead of lecturing me further, Zander pulls a chain from around his neck. I'm trying to remember him ever wearing a necklace before, but I draw a blank. Yet the way he takes it off makes it clear the thing is a part of him. A part he hid from me.

I frown down at it as he holds it between us, nursing another round of hurt feelings, but I stop them before they can really take hold. Because there are three pendants hanging from the leather chain that feel *right* when I touch them. Three wide, curved pieces of hammered metal. Copper. Silver. Gold.

And I know what they are. Three rivers. Our three rivers.

I don't say this out loud. I can sense that Zander would freak if I did—because there are too many botanists milling around. And because there are only supposed to be two rivers touching here.

He puts the leather chain over my head. "Do not take this off."

"What is it?"

"Protection."

"Georgie has me weighted down with crystals."

"The more the better," he mutters. "If I don't see you on *my* boat in fifteen minutes, I'm sending everyone after you."

I salute. "Yes, sir."

He mutters something else I prefer not to hear and stalks off, but I know he's keeping his eye on me even as he pilots the boat into land. Even while he chats with drivers, or flirts with the women who are forever sidling up to him.

Most of the visitors have driven their cars onto the ferry,

but they have to park at the dockside lot and walk up to the cemetery on the same path I take. I do not think about taking this same, muddy path this morning. I do not think about what was waiting for me in the cemetery. I do not—and this is easier than it might have been, because everything looks different now. It's dark. And the lights set up along the trail give off a faint blue glow. I suppose it could feel eerie but there's a warmth to these guiding lights in the March night. It feels like tradition, like ritual.

Like magic.

I smile a little, because *magic exists.* And I can do it. I know my friends are focused on the danger, on the questions, but surely there's time for some joy too. Walking in a group of happy strangers toward redbuds that change color in the dark seems like the perfect time for it.

I reach the cemetery with the group, but peel off after we walk through the iron gate. And I brace myself as I approach my grandmother's grave, prepared for anything. A stone walrus. No stone creatures at all—

But when I get there, I find the usual fox on top of her headstone, the way it's been since the day we buried her. No cat to be seen. Just my grandmother's extraordinary life, reduced to two dates and a dash. *At least she lived a long time,* I tell myself the way I always do. *A very long time.*

I gaze at the familiar fox. For a moment, I'm deeply relieved.

Then I wonder why they were switched at all. Why was Skip rearranging statuary when he had trees to butcher and hellhounds to raise?

I make a note to ask…someone. I turn around to head for the redbuds I last saw in hacked-up pieces, but stop when I see the stone lamb that's always been right where it is now, snuggled up on the grave of one Agatha Merriwether North, one of Jacob's formidable female ancestors.

Any thought of Jacob makes me warmer, but that's not what gets me. What gets me are the stone creatures themselves.

Because if we're witches, maybe these animals aren't just a cute, small-town dose of eccentricity.

Witches have familiars, don't they?

Something in me rings deep, like a bell. A bone-level knowing. It's not that I remember—I *know*.

These are familiars, not statues. Beings being celebrated and remembered here, not mere curiosities.

I reach back and put my hand on my grandmother's fox... and I swear I feel it give off the fox version of a happy purr.

But Georgie's crystal is hot in my pocket, Zander's three rivers are warm against my chest, and I don't react. Just in case someone is watching me.

I have to assume someone always is, don't I?

I make my way to the redbuds, the carnage from this morning flashing in my head.

People are already crowded around the trees when I reach them. Strangers. A few townspeople I recognize.

Witch or not? Witch or not? The words echo like a chant in my head I have to work to push away, because the point isn't who's a witch here. The point is so many people showed up. Despite the events of this morning, my festival expansion succeeded, exactly as planned. Attendance is exceeding my highest expectations and I'm confident all these botanists and festivalgoers will head back across the river to eat, drink, and make merry in town.

I should be turning cartwheels. Instead, I'm looking for witch tells in the faces of everyone I see.

I move closer and really look at my poor trees. Whatever Jacob and Ellowyn did this morning not only got rid of the signs of any fight or struggle, but repaired the damage. The redbuds are here where they belong, lush and blooming white now that the sun has gone down.

Are they magic too?

"Emerson."

I nearly jump out of my skin, so focused on the gleaming white blooms that I haven't been paying attention to the world around me, which isn't wise when a person is simply an awesome human woman. It's even more unwise when a person also happens to be a secretly powerful witch. I glance toward the voice's owner, already smiling like the chamber of commerce president I am.

Carol Simon is standing next to me with her own warm smile. Carol Simon, who has always been an illustrious presence in this town, but who I'm now meant to believe is the most powerful witch in the world. And I do believe it, though she doesn't look terrifying, or even particularly powerful. She doesn't *look* like a witch. She's wearing her signature pearls and a twin set. Most women of formidable midlife go in for ruthless bobs, but not Carol. I used to think her long, wavy, always slightly unkempt hair was a charming gesture toward the bohemian. A little devil-may-care touch of drama in our Carol.

Now I wonder if her hair is *bewitched* somehow. Or the source of her power—is that a thing? Or—

"You've created quite a successful festival out of our trusty redbuds," she's saying.

For a minute I can't stop thinking about her power, her *hair*, and my nearly overwhelming, nearly uncontrollable impulse to shout out that word my friends kept using. *Joywood*. Just to see what happens. Forget she's supposedly the most powerful witch in the world.

I don't do this. Somehow. Instead, for a minute, I bask in the compliment. "It's pretty great, isn't it?"

"Your grandmother would be proud."

A lump forms in my throat, but I speak past it. "I think she would."

Carol lets out a little chuckle. "It's certainly more than she could manage."

I open my mouth to agree, but then the words hit me. I blink up at Carol. "What?"

Another chuckle. She pushes back her hair, frizzing slightly in the night air.

"Darling, your grandmother was... Well, a decent enough businesswoman when given the right push." Carol isn't even looking at me as she speaks these falsehoods. She keeps her eyes on the group of people gathered around the redbuds. "But she didn't have what you have. You must know that she could never have pulled off what you've done here."

I've never been more insulted by a compliment in my whole life. So insulted—so shocked by the offhandedness of the insult—I can't even find the words. I simply gape at her.

She turns her gaze to me. And maybe I'm imagining it, because surely she ought to be hiding the truth about herself from supposedly powerless me, but her eyes seem to glow a little in the dark. "Now, don't be sulky. I'm giving you a compliment. Nothing wrong with being a cut above your grandmother, is there?"

But I'm not. There's no comparison. We are different people in different times, but even if we weren't, Grandma was a wonder. I've never felt the need to compare myself to her.

I do feel the sudden need to punch Carol in the face. It washes over me so intensely that for a moment I see red. Literally.

"Maybe she could have been something if she hadn't given so much of herself over to your grandfather and her little family," Carol continues merrily. "Always giving and giving and giving. Never standing for herself. But women of her era were like that, weren't they?"

I want to scream at her. I want to tell her what I know about my family, so much that my tongue feels weird in my mouth. My fingers cramp from not taking a swing at her. Inside, that seed of power unfurls—

Suddenly, I'm aware of three bands of pain against my chest. Zander's necklace. And the scalding heat of Georgie's stone in my pocket.

I breathe. The crisis passes. Or the tide ebbs a little anyway.

"You've always made smart decisions, Emerson." Carol squeezes my shoulder and smiles. "You chose dedication to this town rather than dedication to your fractured family, and that's so unusual. Especially in girls your age. I admire it."

I do not for one moment believe Carol Simon admires a thing about me, but her hand is on my shoulder. That tide inside me roars in—

I am St. Cyprian's and St. Cyprian is mine, I chant to myself.

Carol chuckles again. I feel frozen, almost, the way I did when I saw Skip glowering at me from across the street earlier.

But I make myself smile like my life depends on it.

"Thank you, Carol," I say. I sound like someone who means that. Like the me who would have meant it yesterday. "I really appreciate you saying that."

She squeezes my shoulder again and I feel a kind of bright light spear through me, a kind of high-beam flashlight.

And I know that no matter what, whatever she's looking for, I can't let her find it.

Every warning and admonition my friends gave me today swirls around inside me. Every single plea to tread carefully that I ignored. And everything inside me wants to fight, the way I did this morning—but almost too much.

It almost feels like I'm being *pushed* to fight.

But one thing that has always been true of me, no spells necessary, is that I do not like to be pushed.

Wildes do not follow the crowd. They lead.

And after dealing with the town council, the chamber of commerce, and assorted citizenry here, I can state with confidence that I *can't* be pushed. I don't *need* to push back.

Women bend, because they can.

Because they'll be accused of *pushiness* anyway.

Might as well smile, agree, then do as I like.

The way I always do, even if it's not the town bureaucracy I'm dealing with tonight, but the head of a secret witch government. Who doesn't need to know how little I like what she said about my grandmother, much less that I know who I am now.

I know. That's what matters.

I beam at Carol like we're having a sappy moment. That tide in me recedes. She gives me a kind sort of look that still manages to feel searching. But then she excuses herself.

Leaving me to stand in the same cemetery where I almost died this morning, wondering if I imagined...all that.

And if I didn't, what, exactly, I'm planning to do with this creepy, witchy, clearly very dangerous new magical life. When what I should be doing is taking a victory lap for pulling off the most successful redbud festival of all time.

Tomorrow, I promise myself, and then I get out of there.

I'M BACK ON ZANDER'S FERRY WITHIN MY AL-
lotted fifteen minutes. He doesn't come and talk to me this
time, just gives me a satisfied nod from inside the pilot room.
Once on land again, I head back to the bookstore to find
a crowd of chattering tourists and Georgie looking a little
frazzled.

"I am really not cut out for customer service," she says to
me when I approach. "I go off on tangents and that is not
what people want from a bookseller, it turns out."

"I'm sure you were terrific," I say, trying to sound reassuring.

Her eyes widen. "Em. I was not."

I know I need to thank her. Profusely. And then I need to
apologize even more profusely. And *then* try to tell her how
much I've relied on the stone she gave me—the very one I
mocked, the way I've always mocked her crystal lore nonsense.

But I don't know how to do any of that.

So instead I step around the counter and wrap my arms
around her. She hugs me back, hard, and I know all is forgiven.

"How did the redbuds look?" she asks.

I pull back, a wave of gratitude moving through me. Because she's her. My Georgie, no matter what. "Good," I manage to say.

I might have lost a lot—Grandma to death, my parents to their pride, Rebekah to exile—but look what I have. Real friends. A family I've made myself.

"You're frowning," Georgie points out. "Usually a good festival has you dancing on the ceiling." Her eyes gleam as she leans in closer so no one can overhear. "A thing you'll be able to make literal these days."

I do like the idea of *literally* dancing on ceilings, it has to be said. But not tonight. Not after my trip to the cemetery. "Carol Simon was there," I say.

Georgie looks alarmed. Deeply alarmed. "You didn't give yourself away, did you?"

"I don't think so. She didn't turn me into a horned toad, so."

Georgie makes a face. "That's the thing about Carol," she mutters.

"That her hair is magical?" I ask in a low voice. Maybe a little too intensely.

"What? Her *hair*?"

"Never mind." I tuck my new theory away. "What were you going to say?"

"Just that she *seems* nice and kindly and approachable. Until she turns your entire extended family into plague-stricken rats for a winter, just to make a point."

"She...does that?" I had been kidding about the horned toads. I think.

"She can do all kinds of things," Georgie says very quietly, her gaze disconcertingly dark. "She's the head witch in charge."

I try to process that as I ring up the customers who form a line at the counter. And I'm still working on it later, when the crowd is gone. I take a pass through the store to neaten, rearrange, and find, then remove, the inevitable sticky food items that always end up on the shelves.

"We need to make sure to tell the others about Carol tonight," Georgie says when the last customer leaves and I lock the door on the longest day in recent memory. I woke up the same old me. Now I'm…still me, but secretly superpowered. *And* I sold a ton of books.

"Until we know what's going on, you're going to have to make sure we know all the weird stuff. Maybe we can figure out the pattern."

Weird stuff. Skip. The cemetery—this morning and tonight. Adlets and stone foxes and *glowing eyes*. The compulsion I've felt twice now to get on the ferry. Spells and glamours and *Carol Simon* with her possibly magic frizz. Familiars. Monsters. Bricks and mind wipes and Sarah Wilde, feminist hero *and* martyred, murdered witch after all. "What *isn't* weird?"

Georgie smiles a little sheepishly. "Fair enough." She points to the fox clock. "It's ten. Are we all closed up? We need to head on over to Jacob's while the moon is still high."

As usual, his name is like heat.

"Jacob's? Why?" I ask with studied casualness. I ignore the part about the height of the moon, because witches.

"We often do our rituals out on the farm because he has all that room and the land has been charmed forever," she tells me while I shut down the computer and then switch off the lights. "Especially Ostara."

"Of course," I say, not actually rolling my eyes. "*Obviously* for Ostara."

Georgie laughs, standing by the door with her red hair everywhere. "Ostara is a celebration of spring. Of balance."

I wave her out of the door and close it behind us.

She shoves her hands in her pockets and her head tilts back

as she studies the streetlamp nearest us. "It's about the earth coming alive again. The beginning of more light than dark, rebirth, renewal. No better place than a farm to really experience all of that."

"And we just...get together with our loved ones and celebrate?"

"More or less," Georgie agrees. "We could join the crowd. A lot of witches don't need or want only loved ones, but ever since high school we've just...done it together. Our own little mini coven—just the six of us. Well, five now."

It takes me a moment, but I realize the sixth would have been Rebekah.

"She should know," I say, surprised at how quickly emotion clogs my throat.

Georgie doesn't need an explanation, but she doesn't agree with me or jump to witch-summon Rebekah. "Exile is as serious as a mindwipe, Em. She *can't* contact you, or you're both punished. Vice versa too."

I think about my dream—Rebekah wanting me to run, me wanting her to fight. Was that really a dream, or was it a memory? Only Rebekah knows.

But my sister's safety outweighs everything I want to know, everything I want to do. Maybe I'll figure out a way to let her know I *am* magic, but I'm not going to risk her life for my own gain.

Never.

"I know it's sad," Georgie says, because she likely misses Rebekah too. "But you're here, and there's so much more to show you. Magic, real magic, isn't about tricks and hexes and little glamours. It's about connecting. To the earth, the moon. The divine within, the rivers without."

Three rivers, I think then, Zander's pendants like three

points of light against my chest. I don't know why I don't say something.

"You'll see," she promises me again. She loops her arm through mine as we walk back to Wilde House in the dark. The lights in all the shops are out all along Main Street. The ravages of the festival have been cleaned up thanks to my crew. Tomorrow will be an average day here in St. Cyprian. Meaning, it will be fantastic.

I smile to myself. *Except I'm a witch*.

"Did you hear Skip's speech?" Georgie asks.

"Can you believe I forgot about his dumb speech?" I can't believe it. I never forget...anything. Especially when it involves the idiot who thinks I'm his nemesis.

"According to all accounts, he was shockingly mayoral."

I wrinkle up my nose. "That's the creepiest thing yet today."

We both laugh at that. My laughter fades as we approach Wilde House. It's a shadowy figure, rising high above its section of Main Street, big and imposing. And apparently it has housed witches for *centuries*. It's funny how so much of what I feel for the town, for my own Wilde history, doesn't really change with this new knowledge about who and what we are. It only shifts.

Maybe the house itself is magic. That dragon newel post *did* talk to me after all. What else is in there I haven't noticed? Is there magic in the walls?

But I don't have time to search. Once we're inside, Georgie heads for her turret, talking nonstop about what we'll need for our ceremony, which I'm secretly hoping will involve cloaks and altars and dramatic techno music. Sadly, she only gathers crystals and what looks like bundles of herbs. Still talking about *energy* and *balance* and whatever else when I want to know about Warrior things. Like smiting. And bubonic rats.

"Ellowyn said she's going to...summon something," I offer when she stops to breathe.

Georgie pauses in the act of putting crystals in her bag, but only for a moment. "She'll try. And maybe we'll get something to explain the adlets and Skip, you never know. What would *really* help is a Diviner. But Ellowyn might be able to pull this off herself."

"You don't know any Diviners you trust?" Maybe they're like accountants. Thick on the ground, yet a really good one is a treasure.

Maybe I shouldn't assume a Diviner is a *person*.

Georgie shakes her head. "Not here. Not yet. They're rare." She pats her bag, then reaches out for my hand. "All right, we're ready to fly."

I pull gently away. "Is this something I should know how to do myself?"

Meaning, this is something I really, really want to know how to do myself. Who wouldn't want to *fly*?

Georgie blinks. "I guess now's as good a time as any." She glances at the bright crystal bound in leather she wears wrapped around one wrist. Like it's a watch. "Zander will be busy with the ferry until eleven. We've got some time for a misstep or two."

Suddenly it seems less fun. "Missteps?"

Before my eyes, Georgie changes from her usual dizzy self. She suddenly looks...wise. Like all the books she reads and the research she does has made her a kind of professor.

"Your magic is a muscle," she tells me. "You're going to have to learn how to build it. And part of the process is accepting that you'll make mistakes sometimes. You can't expect that the first time you flex a new muscle, it will be perfect."

Georgie watches me carefully as if she doesn't trust my reaction to that. As well she shouldn't. I am well-known for preferring perfection. What I've never understood are people who claim they don't—

But that's a very old argument we don't need to rehash here and now.

"You know I'm an if-at-first-you-don't-succeed-try-try-again type." Learn, grow, dominate. If I was a tattoo sort of person, I might imprint those words on my skin.

"I know, but you're usually so good at, well…everything."

"That isn't necessarily true," I say modestly.

Possibly it's false modesty.

Georgie raises an eyebrow at me, but doesn't argue. "A transportation spell doesn't require a lot of words or magic. Like I said earlier, it's internal. Just you. What it requires is focus. You picture where you want to go in your mind. You focus on that. And when you begin to feel the heat of power deep inside, you close your eyes and will yourself to go."

"That's it?"

"That's it." Georgie steps back and I know she's keeping herself from holding on to me. She's giving me space to do it myself, even if it means failure.

I don't intend to fail. But I don't tell her that.

"On the off-chance you land somewhere unfamiliar, you only have to hold on to your crystal and say my name. I'll figure out where you are and come get you."

"Does that happen a lot?"

"Only in the beginning. Once you're used to it, it's like breathing. You only wind up somewhere else if your focus is fractured." She laughs in a way that suggests she could tell me a lot of stories, but she doesn't. "Once it's a daily practice, you'll know better than to try to fly with a fractured focus."

Fly. I want to laugh. We're talking about *flying.*

I close my eyes and bring to mind Jacob's house. I focus on that, picture it.

"Just hold on to the image the whole wa—"

Georgie's last word cuts off as I find myself *whooshing* through the air. It's cold and bright and for a moment my stomach swoops and I feel like I'm going to fall. I almost scream, but Georgie's voice is there. Maybe my grandmother's and Rebekah's and Jacob's too.

Focus.

I squeeze my eyes even tighter and picture Jacob's porch. Wraparound. Wood planked.

My feet hit the ground but I'm so surprised to touch down that they don't hold me up. I tumble with a rush and a thud, facedown in the grass.

Grass, not a wood-planked porch. At least it's not concrete.

But I landed, all in one piece. I take stock. Even though I fell I don't seem to have hurt myself. I push myself up and look around. The moon is shining above me, the stars like a pulsing mass of white. I'm alone in the dark, but I don't feel afraid. I don't quite recognize where I am, but it smells like a farm. Earth and animals and the river in the distance. This has to be Jacob's land. I'm about to sit up and twist around to see if I can make out Jacob's house somewhere around me, but I hear something rustling out there in the dark.

I sit up fast. And then I see glowing eyes.

I jump to my feet.

I suck in a breath to scream, but the glowing isn't evil and red. It's a deep gold. Like my eyes were earlier. A creature moves toward me cautiously, stepping out of the shadows and into the moonlight, where I can make out its shape.

A giant…dog, I suppose. A real dog. Not one of those hideous, man-faced creatures from this morning. And I would tell you that I'm not a dog person, but there I am, climbing to my feet and stretching out my hands. I feel like I want to cry.

"She's your familiar."

I turn to the sound of Jacob's voice, and I realize I'm closer to his house than I thought. That's his back porch, right there where he's standing. Just a few yards away. I flew better than I thought I did.

And I let that feeling of triumph chase away the remnants of my—totally rational, I tell myself—adlet fear. "My what?" I ask.

I know what the word means. I've seen *Sabrina*—both versions. I was thinking about familiars at the cemetery earlier. But I wasn't thinking about *mine*.

Jacob is answering me. Patiently. "Your familiar. An animal with magic who bonds with a witch and assists a witch in various things. Typically, they appear to you in early childhood. Not as a constant companion always, but there when you call to them or need them."

"Like a personal assistant."

Not likely.

I don't recognize that voice in my head, but something about the way the dog's eyes glow makes me think it was her.

"More spiritual than that," Jacob says, with some amusement, as if he heard the dog speak in my mind as well. But it fades quickly, because this is Jacob. Doomsday always. "Typically speaking, spell dim witches are stripped of theirs."

Spell dim. I *really* don't like that word, but the dog is... "But this is mine?"

"Cassie was nowhere to be found when the Joywood went looking for her."

I hear the pride in the way he says that.

"Because you hid her?" I ask. My hands are still extended toward the dog. My dog. She pads toward me and lets me put my hand on her wolfish head. Then she leans into my touch. And I like it. It fills me with a different kind of warmth. A settling kind.

Home at last. Took you long enough.

"No. She did the running." Jacob looks at the dog. Not at me.

"What did you do?" Because I know he did something. I just know.

He winces a little bit, as if all these things he's done for me—and I know it's *for* me—he never meant for me to know about. "I sent her off to my sister in Montana. She would have been here earlier, but both my sister and I cautioned patience. Until we knew more."

Georgie walks out of the back door onto the porch and stands next to Jacob. "There you are. You made it on your first try! Of course you did. And Cassie's here."

She makes a cooing sort of noise at the dog, who whines in approval and settles her head a little more firmly against my palm.

"Do we…all have animals?" I ask, thinking of the gravestone guardians.

"Pretty much." Georgie grins. "It may shock you to learn that Octavius is mine."

The cat in question jumps onto the porch railing and twitches his tail. At me, I feel.

"Zander has an eagle, Ellowyn an owl," Jacob continues. "You'll meet them."

Ellowyn appears and mutters something darkly about Harry Potter ruining everything.

"What about you?" I ask Jacob.

He gestures toward the corn field behind me, and there's the deer I remember from our fight. "That's Murphy," he offers.

I stare at the deer I last saw using his antlers to kill adlets on my behalf. "He helped us."

Jacob nods. "That's what familiars do. Help. Advise. And when necessary, protect."

But he sounds unduly gruff. I can't stop staring at the deer. Even without his antlers glowing, he's an impressive size. A regal, majestic figure standing there before me.

I feel compelled to say something. *Do something.* This animal fought and bled for me. But all I have is a simple, whispered "Thank you."

Murphy inclines his head, regally. Like he understands.

I turn back to my friends, my hand still on this dog. On *my* dog. Cassie. And I see Zander has taken his place on the porch. I feel like they're all waiting for me to do or say something, the way I would if this was a pizza night. And because I normally would, I do.

"All right," I say brightly. "Who's ready for the best Ostara *ever?*"

Everyone laughs—and not because it's funny. Because it's one hundred percent Emerson Wilde doing her thing.

Maybe I'm not the only one invested in me being me.

They all come off the porch, down into the yard. Moonlight shines on us from above. The animals keep close.

"First, we want to block our magic," Jacob tells me as we walk side by side through the night. "We don't usually have to, but someone might feel the extra burst of power you bring to our circle."

"Am I going to have to hide forever?" I ask.

A reasonable question, I think, but everyone gets quiet. And there are clearly *glances*, which I didn't like all that much *before* I knew that they were *telepathing* at each other.

No one is in *my* head. And that's fine. I know they're wrong. I also know that if I say so, there will be a fight, so I keep it to myself.

"Let's see what we figure out tonight," Georgie says in her let's-keep-the-peace tone. "The familiars will keep watch over the circle. They'll make sure our block stays intact."

The deer, the dog, the two birds, and a sleepy-looking Octavius arrange themselves around us. Facing outward. They really are watching, I see. Guarding us.

And I must have crossed some kind of internal line, because I don't question any of this. A circle beneath the moon. Our own, personal zoo.

That time I *flew*.

"We light the candle first," Georgie says, taking a tall, fat green candle out of her bag. She hands it to Jacob.

"Emerson should do it," Ellowyn argues.

All eyes turn to me. Jacob's expression is carefully neutral. Georgie looks weepy, and at least I can read her again—every time I do something magical, she's overcome with emotion. Zander looks concerned.

"If she's our Warrior, she should light the candle," Ellowyn says firmly.

"Emerson isn't a Warrior." Zander frowns at Jacob. "She wanted to be a Healer."

"Not exactly, and she wasn't one." There's something very weighty about the way Jacob says that. But he hands me the candle. "Ellowyn is right. Emerson killed the adlets. She's the town's champion. Why wouldn't she be our Warrior?"

He asks these questions of our friends, but his eyes are holding mine while he says it. Glowing from within.

Our Warrior. The town's champion. Feels right, frankly.

But I can't get over Zander's lack of faith in me. I turn to scowl at him. "Why do you hate a woman in power? Does it make you feel small?"

Ellowyn makes a choking sound. Zander rolls his eyes. "This is a lot of responsibility for someone who had no magic when she woke up this morning. That's all."

"Responsibility is what I *do*."

"This is too much, too fast," he retorts. "It's dangerous. And your memory is *flawed*."

I want to demand to know what is flawed about my memory, but someone else speaks first.

"We should be more careful—is that what you mean?" Ellowyn asks sweetly from somewhere in the dark. Too sweetly. "Wouldn't want to move too fast?"

"Someone has to be the voice of reason," Zander growls back at her.

"Since when is that you?" Ellowyn returns, and it feels a bit like they're having their own argument that has nothing to do with me.

"Since you all lost your grip on reality, apparently." But his demeanor changes. He smiles. Lifts his palms in a gesture of defeat. "But y'all go ahead and do what you want."

I know when he brings out that *y'all* all is *not* well.

"Guys," Georgie says softly. "Let's focus."

She puts a gold plate in the grass. Everyone arranges themselves around it in a kind of circle. Even more obviously a circle. Except Ellowyn, who sits down cross-legged next to the plate.

"First, we light the candle," Georgie says, nodding at me as I hold the candle. She's arranging things on the plate next to Ellowyn. Crystals, bundles of herbs, eggs, seedlings wrapped up in colorful ribbons.

I frown down at the candle. "I don't have a match."

My friends all look at each other.

"We tend to handle that ourselves," Jacob says.

"But I—"

Jacob puts his hand over mine. Something arcs through me—maybe through *us*, though he doesn't flinch like I do.

"It's a simple spell," Jacob says, his voice low and deep in my ear. Almost like we're alone out here. I have to remind myself that we...are not. "You think about the heat inside, and you think to yourself, *'Heat within, flame without,'* then you blow that power out. Onto the wick."

"It's all about focus," Georgie adds, still piling things up on the plate. "Think. Do. Easy as breathing."

Easy as breathing, I tell myself.

Jacob is still right here. "Focus on the wick. Let those words sink into that power inside of you. *Heat within, flame without.* Then breathe out. Not too hard. Not too much. I don't need my house set on fire."

I scowl at him, but there's a half smile on his face. He's teasing me.

I decide that's acceptable and ignore it when I blush a little.

I turn my gaze to the candle. Jacob keeps his hand over mine and I want to freak out a little bit about the *touching*, but instead I focus on the wick. On the power inside. On heat. On flame. *Heat within, flame without.* I breathe out.

The wick ignites and I meet Jacob's gaze through the flame. His hand is still on mine, but I know he didn't do it. Guided it maybe, but that flame is mine.

Mine.

I await applause, but when none is forthcoming, fall back on congratulating myself. No one has to tell me I'm a quick study. I know I am.

"Now, we'll make the circle," Georgie says. "Since Ellowyn is going to do some summoning, she'll be in the center to protect her."

"To protect you all," Ellowyn mutters.

Jacob's hand slowly slides away from mine. I want to reach out and grab it, but I don't, and I congratulate myself for that act of tremendous restraint too.

Those of us in the circle take distinct positions around Ellowyn and her plate. Georgie reaches out, palm up, and Zander puts a hand to her palm. She does the same to Jacob on the other side, then they reach their palms out to me.

I put my palm to Zander's first. It seems safer somehow to start with my cousin. There's a zip of something when we touch. Like an electrical shock, but more invigorating. *That's not so bad*, I think. Jacob is waiting on my other side, patiently holding his hand out.

I can't say why I hesitate. There's something inside of me that just...doesn't want to place my palm to Jacob's. Not like this, with everybody watching. It was bad enough before, to light the candle. I'm still too hot but this time, everyone can see.

But fear is unacceptable.

I'm a witch. I'm a *Warrior*.

I fit my palm to Jacob's.

It's a shock—not like the small zip of something when I touched my hand to Zander's. It's a *blast*. Like this morning, a bolt of heat. Of *power*, but it controls me rather than the other way around. It arcs right through me like I'm little more than a conductor. I can't control it. I can barely manage to stay on my feet. It's too big and too much. Too hot.

I want to let go, collapse, get away from this all-encompassing firestorm.

"Open your eyes," Jacob grits out.

I try. I really do. But I can barely *do* anything. I can barely move and some part of me doesn't want to.

I fight and I manage to get one eye open, then I look at where Jacob's and my hands are joined.

His hand is burning. *Flames* are enveloping it. I try to pull my hand away, sure I'm doing this to him, but he holds firm.

"Focus. Breathe. Do not let go."

But I'm hurting him. I *know* I'm hurting him. Letting go would stop that.

So will controlling it, Emerson. Open your eyes. Focus. Breathe. Do not let go.

Jacob repeats those words in my head, over and over again, until I have to. I have to open my eyes to the circle we've made.

To the candle in the center, its flame high and too bright. Ellowyn in the center, waiting on me.

They're all waiting on me to control it. To make this magic my own.

To join them, at last.

Focus.

To create this circle that will help her do her thing.

Breathe.

The flames around Jacob's hand start to fade. As they retreat, I see the nasty burns all over his flesh and I don't know if I want to sob or throw up because *I've hurt him*—

But even as I watch, the burned, blackened skin is rippling, changing, knitting itself back together.

Healing.

Do not let go.

I stare at the candle standing in the middle of the plate. I focus on the surge and scream inside me that wants to control me. But *I* am in control. Always.

Magic, mayhem, or St. Cyprian town politics—*I* am in charge.

I don't know how or when it settles, but it does. I feel it like a breath we all take, then let out, together.

As if we're one.

Ellowyn nods, then closes her eyes. She rests the backs of her hands on her knees. She tilts her head back and her hair falls behind her, glistening near silver in the moonlight. She chants something I can't make out.

I'm not sure she's speaking English.

Light begins to spill from her—her hair, her fingertips, her eyes. A bright, golden, pulsing light that reaches up to the moon as moonlight seems to reach down to her. Until they dance and meld, and become one intense glow.

I can hear Ellowyn saying words, murmuring to someone

or something only she can see. I sneak a quick look around the circle, but everyone is focused on the center. Not necessarily Ellowyn. The candle. The plate of crystals and what have you. But all three of them are focused.

I need to find that focus too. To breathe. To harness this power coursing through me. Not only to keep it from hurting Jacob, but to *use* it. To strengthen our circle. To lend it to whatever Ellowyn is trying to do.

Summon things. Find answers.

Isn't this what I've wanted all day?

And then she screams.

It's a scrape of pure agony against the dark.

I try to rush forward, but Jacob grips my hand, making me involuntarily clench down on Zander's. Georgie belts out a rush of words and the candle goes out.

We all let go and basically throw ourselves at Ellowyn's crumpled form. Zander gets there first. There's a moment where the fear and pain is so stark on Zander's face that I can't reach for Ellowyn myself.

He cradles her head up off the ground, whispering something to her none of us hear.

Then she rolls away from him. "Don't touch me," she manages to say, though her voice is weak and shaky.

I kneel next to her and manage to get a hold of her hand. Georgie starts rubbing her back, whispering calming words. Zander stands, backs away, looking so stricken I wish I could comfort him too.

But Ellowyn is moaning quietly, in visible pain.

I look up at Jacob. He's the Healer. He has to fix her. "Surely there's something you can do."

Jacob squats down in front of her, but even lying there on the ground in clear pain, Ellowyn glares at him. "Don't you dare heal me, North. Just give me a minute or I'll lose it."

"Lose what?" I demand.

"Whatever she saw. Whatever she summoned." Jacob makes a dark sort of sound. "She won't be able to tell us what it is if I go in and heal her."

"But she's hurting." It claws at me like it's my own wound.

Ellowyn struggles to sit up. I want to push her back down, or magic her into a bed, but Georgie helps her and Ellowyn keeps her steady grip on my hand.

"Hurting is part of the price," she says. She flicks a glance at Zander, who even now looks too grim in the light of the moon.

"What did you see?" Jacob asks Ellowyn now that she's sitting up.

I might have snapped at him to give her a second, but I can see what he's trying to do. The quicker Ellowyn tells us what she saw, the quicker he can take the pain away.

"More than I usually do." She's sitting on her own now, without support from Georgie, but she still clutches my hand. She gives me a wobbly smile. "That's down to your magic, Em. You expanded our reach."

"Meaning it's my fault you're hurt."

She shakes her head. "No. It isn't."

I want to argue but then I remember: she can't lie.

Ellowyn inhales deeply, lifting her face to the moon like she did during the ritual. She sits there like that for a minute or two, and I get the feeling that she's soaking in the moon's rays. And that it's helping her.

This is the kind of woo-woo stuff I would usually laugh at, but it's been a long day. And I'm currently standing in a magic circle, surrounded by guardian familiars.

Ellowyn's owl hoots. At me.

I don't laugh.

"It's still just pieces that don't make sense," Ellowyn is saying. "We need a Diviner."

"We'll make sense of everything," Georgie says firmly. "Let's get you inside."

Georgie and I help Ellowyn to her feet. She isn't steady, so we each take an arm and walk her back to Jacob's house. I wonder why we're not *whooshing* her inside, but maybe there's something in the moonlight and the fresh air.

Because we walk slowly, but with every step, she seems a lot stronger. By the time she hits the porch, she's walking on her own.

Jacob has everything from the ceremony cleaned up with the snap of a finger and then appears ahead of us, opening his back door and gesturing Georgie and Ellowyn inside.

I glance back at Zander, who's still standing in the same spot, looking after Ellowyn with an expression on his face I tell myself I can't decipher. But I know longing and regret when I see it. "Are you coming?"

"Yeah," he says, then has to clear his throat. "I'm coming."

He doesn't explain himself. I don't ask.

But when he reaches my side, he bumps his arm against mine, and the smile he aims at me is the one I know. Engaging. Fun. Off-handedly handsome. *Zander.*

So I return it with one of my own, happy and carefree.

We don't fool each other, maybe, but things feel lighter all the same.

And then, together, we walk into Jacob's old farmhouse, leaving the heaviness behind with the moon.

11

JACOB MAKES ELLOWYN TEA, AND WE GET HER
situated on the couch, much like I was this morning.

Was that only this morning? It seems impossible. Like I've
lived a month in one day, but here we are. No time to wish
I was the kind of person who indulges in naps. I'm a *witch*.
I've just taken part in my first ritual. Now it's time to dis-
sect the results with my people—are they my coven now?
Are we a *coven* now?—and I'm here for it.

Dissecting data is my love language.

"I saw Skip," Ellowyn says, hands wrapped around her
mug. I'm sitting on one side of her with Georgie on the other.
Jacob and Zander both pace the room. Two caged animals
with nowhere to put their excess energy.

But they both go still when Ellowyn says Skip's name.

"That part was clear. I asked the spirits to show me what
they could, what they knew, what would help. And I saw
Skip first. I couldn't see *where* he was. He was shrouded, but

it was him." She inhales deeply. "He offered blood to something or someone, and got something dark in return."

"Adlets?"

Ellowyn shrugs. "I don't know. I couldn't see it clearly. Only that it was a transaction. A dark, blooded transaction. I didn't see any of it clearly enough to be certain that it was the adlets he was bargaining for. Or *only* the adlets. But we all know adlets aren't supposed to exist, so it makes sense, doesn't it? Only him bartering in blood and souls could make the adlets."

"Actually, I've been reading up on adlets since this morning," Georgie says. "The lore behind them."

"Mom used to tell us many a boogeyman adlet story," Zander says dismissively. "Like they were real, but we always just laughed her off."

I laugh. "I'm sorry, you're—*we're*—witches, and you think some...dog-man creature can't exist?"

"Not every story or mythical creature is real just because we are," Georgie cautions me. "But adlets *might* have been. In old texts, adlets were a sign of magical imbalance. A symptom of darker forces gaining power."

Zander and Jacob exchange a look.

"Yes, Skip could have sold his blood or soul or something to the dark powers. I feel like Ellowyn's vision makes that probable. But it's also possible that any adlets he unleashed exist because..." She trails off and looks at Jacob, so I do too. "Because of the imbalance."

Before I can ask what that means, Jacob leans in to focus on Ellowyn. "Is that all you saw?"

Ellowyn sips her tea. "No." Her forehead puckers and she looks into her mug. "The rest didn't make sense, but that somehow made it feel...more important? Even though the vision showed Skip being an evil dickweasel bartering in black magic, that was almost a footnote. Who's surprised he'd trade something you're not supposed to trade for evil?"

She shivers a little and Georgie and I move in closer as if we can warm her up, protect her from what she saw.

"I saw the rivers rising." She glances at Jacob in particular, though his back is to us. "And rising. Into the streets. Into the shops. It wouldn't stop. Nothing anyone could do could stop it."

"A flood is coming?" I'm already thinking about sandbag chains and boarding up windows and whatever else we can do to protect St. Cyprian, the way we've had to many times before. That's life in a river town. And surely with magic we could stop a catastrophic weather event before it started— especially with advance notice like this.

I had no idea Ellowyn could predict the weather. I wonder if I have such useful skills.

"No, not exactly." Ellowyn sounds tired, but much like earlier at the bookstore, she's direct. There's no hemming and hawing. She tells me what I need to know, and I've always loved her, but I'm not sure I've ever appreciated her this much before. "Like I explained earlier. Summoners can access the past, not the future. And even then, I can only see what the spirits want me to see. What they could give me to see. But not what's coming. So, it wasn't a vision of what could be. At most it was a vision of what was."

"St. Cyprian has never flooded like that," Georgie says softly.

"No. Not that we know of." Jacob turns back to us, looking so very grave. "I've seen that vision too. In a dream."

Something about the way he says that makes me think it wasn't one dream. But a routine occurrence.

"So…a flood is coming," I repeat.

"It doesn't feel…current, in my dream," Jacob says. He looks at Ellowyn for agreement.

Ellowyn seems to consider this. "There were no cars. I couldn't make out any of the shops or houses. They're more a blurred mass. But I saw a ferry."

She flicks a glance at Zander, but quickly looks back to her tea.

"Are you sure it was St. Cyprian?" I ask gently.

Ellowyn frowns at me. "Of course. It was familiar. The river. The path alongside it. The ferry."

Jacob nods. "Yes, my dream was the same. Blurry, but it has to be St. Cyprian. Where else could it be?"

"The ferry," Ellowyn murmurs. "That part wasn't blurry. It was clear. The boat was clear." She squints as if she's looking at it right now. "Something was off."

"The shape of it. It's too small," Jacob says, sounding like he's just realized it himself.

"Yes," Ellowyn agrees. "And there's no place for an engine. And… The writing on the ferryboat wasn't English."

"What was it?"

Ellowyn shakes her head. "I don't know, but not English."

"German," Georgie says quietly. "There was a flood, in the witchlore. There's no human record of it, but there are stories handed down—witch to witch—of the terrible flood at Passau. At the destruction back in the 1400s or so. It couldn't be stopped and it was seen as a bad omen because it was something to do with magic, not with the earth. All our records start in the aftermath of that."

"The spirits showed me an old flood?" Ellowyn sounds disgruntled.

"Because a new flood is coming," Jacob says grimly. "It's a warning."

"But what does that have to do with Skip trying to kill me and me suddenly accessing my power?"

My friends exchange glances. Careful, cautious glances I wouldn't have noticed a day ago. But I'm different now. Everything is different now.

"Do you think me finding my power is going to cause a flood?" I ask my friends.

There's a beat of silence—just a shade too long—before Georgie says, "Of course not."

She's the only one.

"What we're talking about, what Jacob and I have been trying to convince the Joywood of for years now, is that there's an imbalance in the confluence," Zander says. "Adlets. You awakening powers you weren't supposed to have. That's all imbalance."

I know he doesn't mean it like it's my fault. I'm a symptom, not a cause.

But I don't want to be either.

"Maybe that explains what Skip's trying to do," Zander offers. "Handle the imbalance."

Ellowyn makes a point of turning to glare at him. "You can't honestly think Skip is doing something *noble*."

"Of course not. The noble thing wouldn't be to *kill* Emerson, especially not with dark magic. But if he's convinced himself he'll be a hero…" Zander shrugs. "The spirits showed Skip getting dark magic and a flood. Something connects it."

Everyone is quiet, a silence so oppressive I find it hard to even take a breath.

When Zander speaks again, his voice is cold and firm. "What this tells us is that we can't tell anyone. You have to keep your power hidden, Em. If anyone thinks you might be the reason for the imbalance, that's even more dangerous."

"Always a fucking Guardian," Ellowyn mutters.

"Yes, that is who I am," Zander replies, in the hardest voice I've ever heard him use. "Who I will *always* be and have always been and—"

"She isn't the reason." Jacob sounds firm. He's staring at the fire, and I can't read the expression drawing harsh lines on his profile as the flames flicker over him.

"It makes sense," Zander continues. "She's a Rivers relation. A connection to the confluence. Latent power. Someone trying to stop—"

"She isn't the damn reason," Jacob growls. He turns back to us. "I would know. That imbalance in the earth, in the confluence, in everything isn't coming from *her*, or any one person. We can't discount symptoms and she's part of that, but she isn't the *cause*." He looks at me. "I would know."

My heart shudders there in my chest. I don't know what I feel, everything is too *jangly* inside of me. All I know is I want to believe Jacob because I like to think of myself as a solution, never a problem.

"It's been a long day," Georgie murmurs, placatingly. "We all need some rest. No one is quite acting like themselves."

"I am," I mutter, but no one hears me. They're shuffling about, preparing for a flight back to their individual homes. Having muttered conversations, or, in some cases, just glaring.

"Let me help," Georgie is saying to Ellowyn. "You aren't up to it yet. Why don't you stay with us? Just for tonight."

I know Ellowyn must be feeling really off because she readily agrees instead of pretending she's bulletproof. Georgie holds out a hand to me. "Come on, Em."

I shake my head. "I'll be there soon."

"Em. You shouldn't be alone. Really. It's not safe."

I look over at my cousin, who's standing stiffly by the big picture window in Jacob's living room. "I need to talk to Zander," I whisper. "I'm sure Jacob can babysit my flight home if it makes you feel better. Just get Ellowyn tucked into bed. I'll be there soon."

Georgie looks uncertain, and Ellowyn rolls her eyes, but one glance at Jacob seems to assure them that I won't be going anywhere without a bodyguard. By this point, Zander is heading out the door, leaving me to hurry to follow him outside.

I make it to the porch in time to see Zander hold out an arm. A giant bald eagle swoops down from above, swift and magnificent, and lands with light precision. On my cousin. It's spectacular. And clearly commonplace, which makes it even more breathtaking to me. But something tells me he's about to magic them both away, so I speak up before he disappears. "Zander. Wait."

Zander turns to face me. He looks at me like he's considering vanishing anyway.

"I'll only follow you." Because I can do that now. No big deal.

"I've got things to do, Em," he says, then murmurs something to the eagle, who shoots back up into the night sky in a smooth rush of size and strength.

I focus on my cousin. "Good for you. I've got things to say." I finally stopped trying to solve the rift between Zander and Ellowyn years ago, and part of me thinks I should stick to that.

But they've hurt each other today. And I somehow understand them both and not at all. And I simply need to help.

It's who I am.

"I don't mind you being my guardian."

He sighs and shakes his head. "Hell, Em."

"But—"

"Please, no buts."

"You don't get to make proclamations. And sniping at Ellowyn—"

"Do not go there." I have never heard Zander speak quite so forcefully to me—or maybe anyone, even drunk idiots at his bar—as he does when I say Ellowyn's name.

"We just need to work together on this. I love you both. I hate to see you both hurting."

He says nothing. I'm not sure why I thought this would go differently than it always has. Faulty memory or not, I know the past ten years has been fraught for them.

"The rivers *are* rising, Emerson. Mom is mysteriously ill. This imbalance isn't new—Jacob and I have taken it to the Joywood more times than we can count. But they wave it off. Blame the humans for polluting our power sources, but that isn't it. I've always known that isn't it and now I know. Something *changed* when those adlets came after you." He pauses, staring off at something I can't see. It takes him a moment to focus on me again. "I don't know what it was. I don't know how to guard against it, and worst of all, I know you'd do anything—sacrifice anything—to fix it. Maybe we all would. That's what scares me."

That word bites at me. That's what *scares* him. When Zander has always been the most fearless of us. Reckless, I would have said a day ago. Never afraid to dive off a bluff into the river, or climb a tree far too high when we were young. All things I suppose weren't as dangerous when you had magic at your disposal, but still.

But this isn't…silly tricks and stupid boy nonsense. This is real. Floods and Aunt Zelda being sick. Life and death.

"All of this connects, and that means it's bigger than me. Than us. It's too big and there's nothing I can do and…" He struggles with something then. Some emotion bigger than I've ever seen in him. "We're going to lose her to this."

I don't have to ask to know he means his mother. In my

magic-stripped mind I figured Aunt Zelda was fighting cancer, but this sounds…different. "Zan—"

"No one can cure it. Jacob has taken her case to every Healer he knows, but they all say the same thing. That he can stave it off, make her comfortable, but he can't rid her of it—whatever it is." He rubs a hand over his face. "Witches don't die this young. Hell, it was a shock when your grandmother died when she was only one hundred and thirty."

"One hundred and *what*?" Her gravestone had her at ninety-five.

But he's not really listening to me. "I'm glad you have power, Emerson. Truly. It's who you are. It's how it always should have been. But it's another indication of this same dark spiral. Another sign things are bad. The more things pop up like this, the closer it gets, whatever it is."

"So, we'll fight it."

He only shakes his head, but he almost smiles while he does it. "I suppose you really are our Warrior, but even Warriors have to know that *fight* doesn't always mean *win*."

"I know I don't…know things like you do," I say. A hard thing to admit, even if true. "And maybe I'm flying blind here, but there is always, *always* something that can be done. If Jacob keeps helping Aunt Zelda, it means he thinks he can find an answer. If the spirits are showing Ellowyn this flood, it means they think we can do something about it, right?"

"If any of us knew the spirits' intentions," Zander says bitterly, "we wouldn't spend all this time staggering around, casting spells in the dark, would we?"

"But I have power, and maybe that's an answer in and of itself." I reach out, kind of wanting to shake him, but all I do is give his forearm a little friendly squeeze. "You have to have faith."

"I don't know how much faith I've got left."

This time I do shake him. Or his arm anyway. He's big.

"Look at me. *I have power.* I faced dark magic that should have killed me, but I won. That's not imbalance. If anything, it's counterbalance. Anything can happen, Zander. Anything." He doesn't roll his eyes or pull away, and I take this as a sign of encouragement. "But we have to believe. We have to try. We can't fight among ourselves when there are actual monsters in our midst. We have to trust one another. Believe in one another. There's real magic in that. There always has been."

His mouth curves ever so slightly. "Some things never change, I guess. *You* never change, do you?"

"Think of all I've done *without* magic, Zander." I grin. "Just imagine what I'm going to do *with* it."

He steps back, scrubs his hands over his face again, and I realize how tired he looks. It makes me think about how much he's been holding inside. How since Aunt Zelda started to feel poorly, I've seen all that lightheartedness inside of him get dimmer and dimmer.

It doesn't require magic to see.

But now that I have magic, it's clear to me that he's hidden the bulk of it.

Presumably with some kind of spell. All that pain and worry and fear about his mother, and now everything else, kept carefully locked away. But fear can't be kept locked away. It only grows, cracking through the façade and making itself known.

The bald eagle swoops down again, this time perching on Zander's shoulder. They both look at me with eyes that glimmer gold. "Thanks for the pep talk, Em," Zander says.

I'm not sure he really is all that grateful, but I smile anyway. "See you tomorrow."

And then he's gone in a flash of light and a little whoosh of air.

I breathe in the dark night and admit that the talk with Zander has left me feeling…tender. Aunt Zelda has something wrong with her that Jacob is trying to cure. My grandmother was one hundred and thirty times more awesome than I thought. St. Cyprian needs me *even more* than I thought it did.

And my cousin is deeper than he likes to pretend.

I hear the sound of something approaching on four legs and my heart leaps to my throat, but it's not a new set of red-eyed monsters.

It's Cassie. My dog. *My familiar.*

I kneel down and she wags her tail and most of her body, wiggling as she comes to me. I rub my palm down the impossible length of her. "You're awfully big for a dog, aren't you?"

She doesn't make a sound, but I get the distinct impression of laughter. I don't quite understand the purpose of a familiar. A guard dog? A friend?

Either way, I like patting her.

I half expect her to speak up and answer, but she merely sits with me and lets me pet her until I hear the back door creak open behind me.

"She'll have to stay here," Jacob says apologetically. When I look back, he's standing on the porch, his hands in his pockets. "Easier for her to stay out of sight. Someone in town could recognize her and that would be dangerous for you both."

Maybe I already suspected that. But it makes me a little more sad than it should, because I only just remembered her. Or feel as if I ought to remember her. I give her one last scratch behind the ears. She barks in a reply I understand perfectly.

Then I turn to face Jacob. "You'll watch after her?"

"I will." He holds my gaze and it's *weighty*. Which isn't new, precisely, but it seems to be happening a lot more than usual. He comes down into the yard and holds out a hand. There's a reluctance in the gesture, and I feel an equal reluctance inside of me.

Fear, maybe. But laced straight through with fire.

"Why can't I transport myself?" I ask. Not at all petulantly.

"Because Skip has dark magic, Emerson. We'll be lucky if those adlets are all he throws at you. I know you bristle at having people take care of you, but you're going to have to let us protect you for the time being. In whatever ways we can."

I want to argue. Or tell him I don't need a lecture. But I have the sinking sensation he's right.

In all the ways that matter, I've only been a witch for one day. I still don't remember everything. And a smart woman knows that the best way to lead is to listen.

Jacob doesn't move any closer. He just holds his hand out. And waits.

And for a dizzying, disorienting moment, I don't know exactly what I want. Because I want too much.

His eyes are so green. My mouth is so dry.

I put my hand into his and his grip is so firm. So warm. There's that *whoosh* of air, and I don't know where *he* intended to land us, but I'm thinking about how exhausted I am and how I just want to go to bed.

And that's right where we land. Standing hand in hand. Staring at my large, hastily made bed *in my bedroom*.

Jacob looks shocked to his core, and I realize that by picturing where I wanted to be…*I* took over. *I'm* the one who transported us.

Perhaps not to the smartest, safest spot.

He pulls his hand from mine and takes a step back before

he seems to realize what he's doing. He stops, straightens his shoulders, and studies me with his patented, disapproving Jacob frown.

I smile.

His frown gets full-on scowly.

"I need you to be more careful, Emerson. What Ellowyn saw proves Skip isn't afraid to shed his own blood to wield dark magic. We have to take this seriously. This is why he lured you off the bricks."

"The bricks?"

"St. Cyprian is built on bricks imbued with protective magic," he explains. "Dark magic is forbidden in the historic district. It's also impossible. It's a safe place for all magical creatures. No feuds, no blood barters. Nothing bad on the bricks. So, he lured you to the cemetery. Off the bricks. Unprotected."

"The cemetery isn't sacred? Isn't protected?" That just seems wrong.

"There's only so much protecting you can do. At some point, witches have their own free will. Even if it's dark magic." Jacob is always so pragmatic. I think it still seems wrong.

"What is this dark magic?"

"Evil," Jacob says simply. "You can't have power without those who are consumed by it. Demons and witches who've sold their souls. They need blood to survive. If you offer it, you will be consumed by the dark—by everything wrong within you. Blood is memory. It isn't just you. It's all who came before. Blood is sacred. If you sacrifice it to evil, you may find immeasurable power, but you will never have a soul again."

That is suitably...awful.

"I realize you're used to being in charge," he continues.

Lecturing me. "Doing things on your own, but it's different now."

He's right about that. Everything is different now. "I know Skip hates me. I never understood why we were adversaries without magic, but why would he be so against me if he had magic and I didn't? Isn't that like…stamping on ants?"

Mind you, if I was an ant, I'd be the queen. And unlikely to get stamped on, but I digress.

Jacob stands by the door, looking like he wants to toss it open and escape. But he doesn't. "He's a bully. It's not that mysterious."

"I guess. I feel like we're missing something."

"I feel like we're missing everything."

I study him. Always so thoughtful and careful with his words. Always so certain to point out the flaws in a plan… not because the plan has flaws, I understand, but because he's always trying to avoid mistakes.

I realize for the first time in my adult life—because maybe this is something I knew during my magical childhood— that, clearly, Jacob failed at something. Terribly. What else would lead him to this place? I have the sinking suspicion it has to do with me.

I've never failed in any major way. The one time I supposedly failed—that magic test, according to reports—I don't even remember it. You could say that failure formed me, in the sense of altering my memories. But it didn't form *me*, because, thanks to mind wipe, it didn't leave marks.

But I get it, finally. Jacob is all marks.

"Is there really no way for me to get my memories back?" I ask softly.

"The Joywood's magic is the most powerful magic in the world," Jacob says, and I don't think I'm imagining that he sounds regretful. "To undo that kind of magic would take... Well, it would take the Joywood."

"And they're off limits?"

"We can't risk drawing their attention," he says. "At least not yet. This imbalance, this impending flood, is something I've been trying to warn them about for years. They don't listen. Some might say they're sticking their heads in the sand because they don't believe it can happen here, but..."

"You think it's purposeful."

"I don't know what to think. I only know we have to be careful and cautious. Keeping you safe is the number one priority."

I frown. "St. Cyprian is the number one priority."

He sighs. Exasperated with *me* as much as he is with the situation. But that's pretty much par for our course. And he's here.

He's always been right here.

I move toward him, drawn by too many things to name. "I'd be nothing without St. Cyprian. *St Cyprian is mine and I am St. Cyprian's.*"

Jacob looks at me a little strangely. Contained, still, because he's always so contained. I want to know why. What holds him back? Is it rooted in the past—our past—like so many other things I can't remember?

"Tell me something from back then. Something real, not mind wiped."

"Like what?"

"Anything." Anything at all. Everything.

He stares at me for the longest time. So long the breath seems to back up in my lungs.

"You once tried to turn me into a toad."

That is...not what I expected.

"I always wondered what that memory was for you, stripped of magic," he says.

"How old were we?" I frown. I *failed* at turning him into a toad? It makes me want to try again. Now.

I don't.

But only because I don't know how. Looking at him and picturing a toad doesn't make it happen.

"We were thirteen or so," Jacob says. "You were trying to put together a healing spell with some of my herbs. I told you that you had it wrong. You said I couldn't prove you were wrong until you tried it out. I pointed out that you'd likely kill someone if you tried it out the way it was."

"My memories of you always being a party pooper are disturbingly accurate, then." I think back to age thirteen. I try to access the feeling of wanting to turn someone into a toad, but I come up empty. "And there are too many memories of me wanting to cause you physical harm."

He laughs. A deep, rare, intoxicating sound. I drift a little closer. I don't think he notices.

"It was summer. A sunny day at my parents' farm." Something in his expression changes, from fond nostalgia to...a deeper thing. Hurt, maybe? "At the time, you thought you might be a Healer. *We* thought that, so you'd come over to the farm almost every day and try to work on healing spells."

The summer when I was thirteen, I do remember spending a lot of time with Jacob. "In my memories, you were tutoring me about the local flora and fauna."

"Flora and fauna?"

"*I'm* not the one who replaced my real memories with fake ones. It was for a Girl Scout patch."

"I guess that makes sense. We did a lot of herb work. I'm just not sure why a thirteen-year-old would want lectures on flora and fauna from another thirteen-year-old all summer long."

I know why, but I don't say it. "I don't recall wanting to turn you into a toad. I do recall that one day you were being your condescending self and I tossed you into the pond."

He grins. "Yeah, that was you trying to turn me into a toad. I warded it off though."

"But still wound up in the pond?" I sniff. "*Did* you ward me off?"

"An unexpected dip is better than being amphibious. What else do you remember?"

I frown, trying to pull up the images. But it's kind of foggy. I can't seem to tease out the details. I only remember Jacob standing in that pond. "You didn't turn *me* into a toad."

"Of course not. You were weaker than me." I narrow my eyes at him, but he only shrugs. "My magic was stronger. It wouldn't have been fair."

But there's something about the way he says that. It isn't the whole story. "Somehow I ended up in the pond too." I remember sensations more than any actual memories, and I lean into them.

His mouth twitches. "Yes, *somehow* you did."

"Fair, my ass."

He laughs and it's hard to hold on to any kind of irritation when he does that, when he looks at me with that smile and his eyes so warm.

For a moment, I think he has to be lying to me about nothing happening between us. Surely this feeling inside of me means what I think it means. But I can't imagine Jacob lying either.

He looks down at me, as if cataloging all the ways I look different than that day almost fifteen years ago.

"I almost kissed you," he says quietly, so quietly I almost wonder if he didn't plan on saying it out loud.

"No way," I whisper. Not because I don't believe it. But because I want, desperately, not only to believe it—but to remember it.

"Don't remember that part, do you?" He sounds amused.

I feel too…edgy to be amused.

"Of course I don't remember. Mind wipe for the win, again. What stopped you?"

Jacob crosses his arms. "There was something in the air. Like the spirits, pushing us apart."

I wait for him to laugh, but he doesn't. "That's ridiculous."

He shrugs, but like he expected this reaction from me. "That's what it felt like."

"Did I feel it too?"

"I'm not sure. I didn't ask. And you never said anything either way. I figured you didn't read the moment the way I did. Do you remember any of it?"

I try to think back. To put myself into the girl who was in that pond. Who tried to turn Jacob into a toad. A summer day. Thirteen. Spirits pushing us apart, an almost-kiss.

I can imagine it, but I can't *remember* it. All I have is what I remember, without magic. Meanwhile I'm staring at Jacob and I can't help but think there *could* be magic here. Right here.

"You could test that theory," I manage to say though my throat is dry. "Reading the moment. The spirits pushing us apart."

His gaze drops to my mouth, so I know he considers it. He has to consider it. My heart beats like an echoing drum.

I am burning hot. Everywhere.

But his expression grows serious, and even before he straightens—making it seem like he's moved far, far away from me without moving at all—I can tell he's made his decision.

"Jacob..." I begin, maybe *this close* to *pleading* with him.

"Good night, Emerson," he says quietly, and then he's gone.

Like an old dream I've had many times before. One that usually comes with relief. I did not blur the line and everything gets to go on as it always has. That's always been a good thing.

But there's no relief tonight. Only an odd pang of *wanting* I'm going to have to do something about.

Just as soon as I figure out how to save us from a potential flood.

12

WHEN MY ALARM GOES OFF THE NEXT MORN-
ing, I think I'd rather give up all my newfound magic than
actually wake up. But I have a bookstore to run and magic
to learn and dark forces to thwart.

And I don't believe in the snooze button.

No matter how much I'd like another few hours of rest.

Dutifully, I crawl out of bed. I don't have the energy to
make it, but I do anyway, because making your bed every
morning sets you up to conquer your day. I don't feel much
like a conqueror this morning. I didn't pack my bag last night,
or shower. The list of things I'll need to do this morning
that I usually handle the night before seems insurmountable.

Coffee, I tell myself, like a prayer. *Coffee will make everything doable.*

I trudge out of my room and start for the kitchen. Surely
all this witch stuff means I can whip up some coffee and food
in a manner of seconds. And shouldn't I be able to snap my
fingers and pack my usual bag?

I walk down the stairs, considering that. So far everything I've been taught has been all about focus and visualization and a centering in my power—things I'm very familiar with *without* magic. So, I think of my bag. What I usually take with me for a day on the mean streets of St. Cyprian: all three daily planners for self, store, and chamber of commerce. Keys. Extra cardigan in case any customers are cold. First aid kit in the event of any accidents or scraped knees in my vicinity. The pile of crystals Georgie has bestowed upon me over the years. My clipboard with all my freshly printed, weekly updated to-do lists—one for the town, one for business and books, and personalized ones for other business owners, family, and friends that I like to sneak into their hands and bags when they're not looking. I center myself in that heat deep inside.

I give the spell words I think make sense. *Make it so*, I think, and it feels like…magic.

I don't remember closing my eyes, but when I open them, my bag that wasn't sitting on the bench near the door…now is.

To say this pleases me is putting it mildly. Though if it's filled with, say, rocks, I'll deal with that later.

"I'm a witch," I tell Azrael, the newel post dragon.

And I don't know if I'm pleased or disappointed when it doesn't respond.

I march into the kitchen. Ellowyn is already there. She's sitting at the kitchen table, slumped over it with her eyes closed.

"Aren't we fresh as daisies," Ellowyn says as I enter, barely lifting her head off the table.

"I could hardly crawl out of bed," I say through a yawn. "I don't know what's wrong with me."

"Being a witch is a lot of work." Ellowyn lifts a hand,

makes a dramatic twirl of a finger, and two mugs appear on the table. She points to the one not in front of her. "That should help."

I take a seat and peer into the mug. Not coffee. I'm not even sure it's tea.

"Trust me." Ellowyn shoves her blond hair back, then sits up enough that she can take a sip from her own mug.

I am dubious.

Georgie shuffles in, looking even more of a morning mess than usual. "Magic me too," she says to Ellowyn. And another mug appears where Georgie collapses into a chair. "I was up half the night reading up on the stories of the Passau flood, trying to draw any kind of correlation with what you saw, Ellowyn."

She blows on her drink. "Anything?"

"Not yet."

"Can't you just do a spell to find out what you want to know?" I ask, wondering if I could snap a plate of bacon and eggs out of thin air. And some actual coffee.

Georgie points at the fridge and then the stove and says a few muttered words. Things begin to move. A carton of eggs floats out of the fridge. A skillet appears on the stovetop. "Magic is fine and dandy, but food is still better when it's made. Doesn't mean you can't use a little help. And no, I can't cast a spell to find what I need because I don't know what I need. Much like cooking, I can get help, but doing it is part of the process."

As someone who admires hard work and getting my hands dirty, I think there's something kind of amazing and cool about that. As an exhausted woman who wants answers, it just sounds like magic might be kind of pointless.

I don't say this. I don't know what witches find offensive.

"So," Georgie says, sipping from her mug. She pins me

with a glance and a smile far too innocent to be genuine. "I heard two sets of footsteps last night when you got home."

I feel the strangest sensation. Like a heat creeping up my cheeks. Like *embarrassment* when I have absolutely nothing to be embarrassed about. Especially considering my room is *below* Georgie's.

"Finally going for it?" Ellowyn asks, as if it has always been inevitable that I would one day *go for it.*

I open my mouth to deny it, like I always would have denied it before. No feelings about Jacob. No thinking too much about Jacob. But I'm a witch now. A Warrior.

I may not remember, but I know.

And I also really don't care for the word *finally.* Like everybody's been waiting for me to hurry up and get a clue.

But what I do is smile. Maybe a little smugly.

They both gaze back at me like it's Christmas and I've just unveiled my Friend Advent Calendar, an annual tradition.

"Emerson," Georgie whispers. "Did something happen?"

"We talked," I say demurely. I lower my gaze to whatever's in my mug, then take a big swig. Then another. Only then do I say, "Jacob says there wasn't anything between us in high school, and I believe him, but..."

"We always got the feeling there was something going on between you two back then," Georgie says at once, a little breathlessly, as if she's *that* excited that things are changing with Jacob and me. "But if it had been as simple as getting together, you would have told us."

"Especially during my idiot phase," Ellowyn chimes in. She's always called her high school relationship with Zander her *idiot phase,* but it lands wrong today.

"He was worried about you last night," I tell her, trying to sound neutral. "Genuinely."

Ellowyn's expression darkens. "Look, I'll put up with him

because he's your cousin and your friend and all, but when it feels like I've been torn in half, the last thing I need is my ex looming around."

"If it was that bad, we shouldn't do it again," I say earnestly, because while no one will admit it, surely adding my power to things is what made it so hard on her.

"Some pain is the price." Ellowyn shrugs. "Maybe what you need is a full witch."

"*A full witch,*" Georgie mutters, rolling her eyes. "Hecate wept."

I'm about to get deeper into it, but the ancient doorbell gongs loudly, making all of us at the kitchen table sit up a little straighter.

No one rings that doorbell. Certainly not this early. "I'll get it," I tell them.

I get to my feet, surprised at how much better I feel when I move. I don't feel totally restored, but Ellowyn's drink did help clear some of the cobwebs and that heavy body feeling. I would say I'm at eighty-five percent capacity. Which is obviously one hundred eighty-five percent better than most. I am me after all.

I pull open the thick, heavy front door expecting to find a lost delivery person or a St. Cyprian business owner needing some help before stores open. One time Joanne Walters appeared on this very doorstep at 5:00 a.m. on a Monday morning in October to discuss the inclusive holiday decorations we put up on the lampposts along Main Street each year. She was opposed.

A chamber of commerce president must always be prepared.

But I am not prepared for Skip.

"Skip?" I can only stare at the smiling man on my porch

who *looks* like Skip, but can't be, because he's smiling. At me. And holding flowers.

Pretty flowers at that. Clearly from our local River Girls Florist, not that questionable place out on the highway.

"Morning, Emerson," he greets me cheerfully. *Warmly.* "These are for you."

He pushes the bouquet of flowers into my hands. Obviously my only thought is: poison. Surely if I smell them, I'm going to die.

"What is happening?" I demand, which is not easy while holding my breath.

I do not throw the bouquet away from me. Or at him. Somehow.

Skip Simon continues to *smile* at me. Like he's a completely different person. Or I am. And I don't mean in a magical way. I mean like maybe I woke up as one of those unfortunate girls in high school who professed to find him hot.

"The festival was a success. A boon for the town. You were right, as you so often are." I'm pretty sure I can see a hardness in that alarming smile now, behind the alarming flowers. "It's time to stop playing petty games and accept that we could work together to do some real good."

"I've been saying that for years, Skip," I point out, because I can't help myself.

"Have you, Em?"

I don't like the way my name is shortened when said in that voice and I couldn't say why. It's the nickname people use. Even if he never has. But I can't say anything because... *What?*

Another toothy smile. "Are you free for dinner?"

"Free for... What?"

"Dinner. I think we should sit down and talk about all the ways we can make ourselves a team. For the town."

My mouth is ajar. Yet no words are coming out. Because for once in my life I've been rendered fully and utterly speechless.

By Skip Simon. Standing on my doorstep, smiling. Pleasantly enough, I guess. Wanting to *have dinner* and discuss how we can *work together*. Maybe I should revisit the notion that this is really all a dream.

Because two mornings in succession dealing with Skip Simon's whiplash nonsense seems like it could only be a dream. A bad one.

I'm not sure that Skip bearing flowers is better than a legion of adlets. I prefer monsters I can fight.

"You want to…meet for dinner," I say carefully. Because maybe I'm not understanding him, having never become fluent in douche. "To talk. About working together."

"I want to *take* you to dinner," Skip corrects, political smile firmly in place. Less edgy, just as gross. "To bury the hatchet, Em. Maybe forge a new path ahead. You and me."

Which sounds less like a business meeting and more… personal. I feel a little nauseated, but also confounded by the sudden turnabout. And suspicious. Very, very suspicious.

I therefore have no choice but to agree.

"I…suppose."

"Tonight, then?"

"Tonight? Don't be silly." I reach for my bag and find my planner. I flip through the pages to find the current week. "I have a meeting or volunteer work every night this week." I move to next week. "I could do next Friday."

There is a cold, hard pause. He stands so still I almost wonder if he's a robot who's malfunctioned. Maybe he's been cursed? Surely, something isn't right.

But eventually his mouth curves into a tight smile. "I can certainly make that work if you need to be difficult."

I don't even know how to take offense to that comment, because this is all too weird. "Um." It's hard to get my face to work the way it should. I can't even imagine what expression must be on it. "Okay?"

He nods firmly and turns to leave. Whistling. I slowly close the door, peering at the flowers and inspecting them for deadly bugs that might jump out and sting me. Maybe a poisonous fog that will turn into those adlet things.

"Emerson," Georgie says, and I look up to find my friends standing out of view by the stairs, clearly having watched the whole thing. "Did Skip Simon just ask you out on a date?"

I wrinkle my nose. "Ew. No. Maybe?"

Ellowyn looks revolted. And betrayed. "You said *yes*."

"I said yes. I had to say yes. I have to figure out what game he's playing." I study the flowers. "Do you think these are going to kill me?"

Georgie takes them from me and holds her hand over them. Her frown deepens and I assume she's going to tell me I'm already dead.

"They're clean."

She hands them off to Ellowyn, who closes her eyes as she touches each stem. When she opens her eyes, she's frowning as well. "It's a bouquet of flowers. No magic at all."

We all study the colorful blooms. A riot of gerbera daisies. I actually like them—and I'm deeply uneasy at the notion that it's possible for Skip Simon to give me lovely flowers.

"I think we should burn them. In a ritual sacrifice." Ellowyn frowns at the pink-and-purple flowers. "Can't be too careful."

"I'll leave that to you two. I still have to get ready for the day."

Georgie's hand closes over my wrist as I attempt to sweep past her. "You can't go to dinner with him."

"Why not?"

"Because it's Skip Simon. *Skip Simon* bearing *flowers*, which should be the end of the conversation." She shakes her head at me. "Remember when he tried to kill you yesterday? Then showed up in Ellowyn's vision, all decked out in dark magic?"

"The way I see it, he's sucking up to me for a reason." I think I sound perfectly rational and levelheaded. Meaning I feel Georgie's *you-have-lost-it* expression is unfair, but I choose to rise above it. "I want to know what the reason is. I'm never going to find out if I blow him off."

"He wants you to die, Emerson. Remember the last time he was nice to you? He wanted to *Carrie* you at the prom."

"Was there a chinchilla in the magical version?" I ask.

Georgie ignores me. "He wasn't kidding then and he's not playing now."

"Maybe," I agree. "But he's had years to make that happen. And didn't, until yesterday."

"That we know of. He was using black magic. That means all bets are off. He could do anything. You should avoid him like the plague."

"You said he can't use it on the bricks. I'm safe on the bricks." I look over at Ellowyn. Who can't lie. I wish I'd known that all along. A useful tool, that. "I'm safe on the bricks, aren't I?"

She gets that look on her face. "Did you know that the word *boy* means something like servant or farm worker in Anglo-Saxon?"

"See?" I say to Georgie. "Besides, you'll know where I am. Safer to talk to him this way than to meet him in a dark, brickless alley with his dark magic and more monsters."

"This is a terrible idea," Georgie grumbles. "The men in your life are going to hate it more than we do."

"You mean the servants and farmworkers?" I shrug. "We won't tell them."

"Oh, that is not going to go over well," Georgie predicts. But I ignore her and head upstairs. I don't need permission from the *men in my life* to do anything.

I get ready for the day, unaccountably frustrated with myself for letting yesterday get so far away from me. This witch business is really going to have to be plotted out further in advance from here on out. Are the rituals usually scheduled? I need to make all the relevant notes.

When I finally get to the store, Georgie is my shadow. And I understand that my friends want to protect me. I do. As more seasoned witches, they have a better shot at warding off threats. Presumably. But that doesn't mean it doesn't rankle to feel like a small child who needs to be looked after. *All. The. Time.*

I'm used to doing my own thing.

"Don't you have your own work to do?" I ask Georgie as I put cash in the register. I attempt to sound friendly instead of childishly peeved.

"My uncle is handling the museum as I'm deeply involved in a very important research project. Which I can do from here." She's spread out in the workspace of the shop, looking as if she's working from her own home office. There's an inviting air to it, actually. People looking in the window will think this is a place they can settle in and relax.

I graciously allow it.

And I'm right, Georgie's presence draws people in. As the morning passes I do a brisk business, thanks to that and to the sunny spring day outside. Sunny days mean foot traffic out on the street. And no doubt some of the people who stayed over in town after last night's festival.

In a lull, I crack open my planners and think about the

next chamber of commerce meeting, two weeks from now. We'll need to pool together numbers and see how we all fared. I'll need to make notes about next year's festival—what worked, what didn't work, what needs to improve. I'll need to provide my usual, detailed spreadsheets to show exactly how amazing it all was—even with Carol's weirdness about my grandmother. And I guess I'll need to make sure I have a plan for facing Carol and her cronies too, in case there's further social weirdness.

To be distinguished from Carol's *coven* and their *witchiness*.

And somewhere along the line I need to learn more about witches, magic, and the potential of town-ending floods. I also make a note to find out who else is in the Joywood with Carol.

When I finish organizing my life back into recognizable shape, I look around the store. But no one is here except Georgie and me. "Is there a spell to put more hours in a day?"

Georgie looks up from her old leather books. So obviously full of information about floods and witches and magic that I don't know how I never caught on before now. "Sorry, even witches can't mess with the passage of time. At least, we shouldn't, because it always comes back to haunt you. If you steal time, you lose time." She smiles fondly. "That's a witch nursery rhyme."

"I've got a lunch meeting with the May Day Festival committee—" It occurs to me if human St. Cyprian has a May Day Festival, witches have their own. "What's May Day for us?"

"Beltane." Georgie's smile goes strangely devious. "Oh, I can hardly wait." Her expression sobers. "I'm not on the committee, but—"

"I know you guys want to protect me. I appreciate it." I'm trying anyway. "But I have to be able to walk down Main

Street on my own sometimes. Surely having one of you *constantly* around is suspicious enough."

Georgie sighs, and I can tell she wants to argue. But she looks at Octavius curled up next to her. They seem to have a conversation. I wish I could have Cassie with me. I wish I could be *me* out loud. I do not like all this hiding.

But first things first and all that.

"All right. Be careful. If you feel threatened at all, simply call out. Think of us, and we'll come."

I nod and grab my bag while Georgie whispers things—spells? Charms? Curses?—as I flip the sign over to Closed and leave her and her magic behind.

I walk down the road and notice that perched on the sign to Ellowyn's shop is the snowy white owl from the night before. Watching me.

Hello. You don't really need to spy on me. I wonder if the owl understands what I'm trying to think at her.

The white head inclines. Grandly. *You're welcome*, I hear in my head.

That *would* be Ellowyn's familiar.

Before I'm past *Tea & No Sympathy* I hear my name being called. Skip. Again. He falls into step next to me. Smiling.

Maybe *he's* under some kind of magic spell.

If so, someone should have cursed him years ago.

Skip reaches out and does the unthinkable. He slings his arm over my shoulders like we're old buddies, used to walking side-by-side.

I think about calling out for Georgie, but his words stop me.

"Can we expect a visit from your bodyguard?" he asks, and though his voice is light, there's a flash of something darker in his eyes.

I'm confused at first, but then I remember his angry display at the gazebo yesterday. I carefully slide away from his arm. "Do you mean Jacob?"

"He always seems to show up when we're together, doesn't he? Like he doesn't trust us on our own."

I have to work very hard not to pull a face and/or heave. *As if* something might *happen* between Skip and me if Jacob wasn't there—he must be delusional.

"I'm not in charge of what Jacob chooses to do or where he chooses to go," I tell him. With admirable calm, if I say so myself. "And we're not together. I'm walking to my meeting."

Skip snorts, but before I can tell him this is a waste of time if he's only going to be insulting, he smiles at me.

"I thought I'd stop by the meeting myself."

"But…why?"

"Mother was so pleased with the festival last night, I thought I could help out with this one and maybe she would show me even half as much attention as she gives our great Emerson Wilde."

I remember Carol's hand on my shoulder and *how badly* I'd wanted to explode right then and there. I remember her weird intensity and the things she said about Grandma. I try *not* to think about how childish Skip sounds whining about his mommy not giving him enough attention.

"I'm glad she was pleased," I make myself say. "It was a great success. I think most everyone was happy with the results."

I do not say *I told you so*, though I want to. The event speaks for itself. It was crowded. I sold books. Businesses prospered. Why? Because even in the face of magical adversity and discovering my true nature, I'm damn good at my job.

Skip nods as if I've said something profound. He waves merrily at a couple of St. Cyprian residents who pass on the sidewalk—after they stop dead and stare at the two of us.

"Mother is often pleased and impressed by you," Skip continues. "For a very long time I let that bother me."

"But all of a sudden you're fine with it?" It certainly doesn't sound like it.

He looks off into the distance, and thoughtful Skip is…not better. "There are some things you can fight, Emerson, and some things you can't. I don't want to end up like Nicholas Frost up in that mansion on the hill, decaying into dust. I want a say in what happens. If we find a way to have a say together, then I want that."

There's that name again. Nicholas Frost. The traitor. I try to act calm. Casually confused, that's all. I stop in front of the Lunch House, where I'm meeting Holly, Gil and the ironically named Happy Ambrose Ford. "Nicholas Frost?" I ask, working on a casually vague smile. "I don't think I know him, which seems odd. I know everyone."

Skip frowns. It seems to take a long time, then he frowns even deeper. For some reason I start thinking about the way Muppet faces fold in on themselves, and have to fight off a shudder.

"He's…dead. Old. An old dead guy. Ghost story." Skip shifts on his feet. He clears his throat. Then he gives me that wide smile again and it's even creepier this time. "Not even that interesting. Just a story."

"Is that why I can't get the house razed?" Because I know the eyesore on the hill. I've been petitioning to have it condemned and torn down for years.

Skip holds up a manly, patriarchal hand that, in the spirit of our new friendship, I do not try to burn with fire. "You don't have to worry about all that, Emerson. Really. In fact, allow me."

"Allow you?"

"I'll look into it for you. The building *is* an eyesore. I'll see what I can do about it. As mayor, I'm sure I can move something along."

I don't have the slightest idea how to respond to that. He's spent years fighting me about doing something with the old mansion on the hill, overlooking the town and the river. I don't want it *razed*, exactly. The cost of restoring it would be astronomical, but it's a beautiful old house that could also be a historical monument with a little TLC. Though I haven't been able to get it on the historical register either. I've tried.

Now that I think about it, that old Victorian mansion is the one place in town where I'm always stopped. Even the people who are usually behind me when it comes to town rejuvenation efforts try to persuade me away from dealing with the house on the hill.

Nicholas Frost. Who is he? My friends call him a traitor, but clearly he lives here in St. Cyprian anyway. A witch of some kind, I'm guessing. In that old, crumbling house. And people don't want to boot him out of it.

Why not?

Skip is staring at me expectantly. I don't actually imagine he'll do anything about the house. But why not pretend I believe he might? "I'd be *so* appreciative," I say. "Finally!"

"I knew it," he says, clapping his palms together. Like a seal. "You just need a firm hand, don't you, Em?"

I want to throw a punch at his weaselly face. But I don't, because I'm a lady. And more importantly, a Warrior.

He's still talking manfully at me. "You just want someone to take the reins for you. *That's* what you've been looking for. *I* will take care of the house for you." He pats my shoulder. "Don't you worry about a thing," he says.

He is enraging. And gross. But at least I recognize this Skip.

And still everything is so desperately *wrong* I don't even

lecture him about the very notion of *a firm hand*, the paternalistic horror that underpins that phrase, or the misogyny
that practically drips from him.

Not to mention, if I *did* find myself in need of a firm hand,
it would not be his.

It would never be his.

"I'm so pleased you've had this change of heart," I offer
instead.

My teeth hurt when I speak. I unclench them.

Skip reaches across the space between us and takes my hand
in his. It's cold and clammy. I want to pull my hand away, but
part of me is too shocked to move. *Why* is he *touching* me?
All I can do is stare at his bony hand. At his flesh *touching me*,
which feels like *things* crawling all over me.

"Everything changed yesterday, Emerson," he tells me in
a low voice.

My instinct is to flinch, but I manage to hold myself still at
the last second. I can't let on that things might have changed
for *me* yesterday. Even if he knows, or guesses, I need to pretend I don't. On that I can agree with my friends.

"How?" I ask.

"I saw the light." He smiles, and there *is* a warmth to it,
but it creeps me out. "We can't survive this alone. We need
each other."

This isn't Skip. I can't shake that feeling. Whoever is speaking, whoever is *touching* me...it isn't the Skip I know. And he's
speaking of survival, like he knows something bad is coming.
Like destruction. Maybe that flood. *We can't survive* this *alone.*

I clear my throat and try to sound like myself. "That's a
lovely sentiment, Skip. Truly. But what can't we survive?"

He keeps staring at me a little blankly.

"You know what I mean," he says after a while, still with
his small hand on mine. And the sensation of *bad touch* crawl-

ing all over me. "Just general survival. Small towns like ours are always in danger of falling apart and fading away. I didn't fully realize that until I saw all your hard work come to fruition last night."

Which continues to not make sense. Skip has seen dozens and dozens of my plans come to fruition and pay off. Helping St. Cyprian is what I do. Hello.

What he does is…golf? I think?

And apparently dabble in the dark arts?

But as hard as it is for me not to scream, run, or vomit, I know I need to agree with him to keep this odd peace. Because he's said two interesting things. Nicholas Frost. And that something's coming we'll need to survive. Best to agree with him and see what else I might be able to find out.

"Oh look, there's Holly," I say, pointing through the window of the Lunch House, where Holly Bishop is staring at us. She's obviously here for the meeting. She's also a little openmouthed, with her phone out like she was taking a picture of Skip holding my hand.

I want to throw myself through the window and slap that phone from her hand, but I restrain myself.

Skip lets go and pats his pockets. "I'm getting a call. Might have to skip this meeting after all, but I'll see you next Friday. For dinner. I'll pick you up at six."

I nod. Too hard. And a little too long, but Skip pulls out his phone and holds it to his ear. He begins to talk, yammering on and walking away.

I stand where I am, right outside the restaurant, trying to rid myself of the gross, creepy-crawly feeling that's settled over me. Because I have a meeting to attend and I take my meetings seriously.

I'll figure out how to deal with Skip and our gross, fateful dinner later.

I tell myself a little sticker session with my planners and a liberal application of washi tape will set me to rights. But as I move for the Lunch House's front door, I look past the shops, past Wilde House, up the length of Main Street and beyond. Up to the top of the hill, where an old, dilapidated Victorian mansion sits. A complete eyesore, lording its dilapidated state over my beautiful town the way it has my whole life.

It's a tragedy.

And, possibly, the source of some answers.

THE REST OF THE DAY IS MOSTLY NORMAL. I
close up the bookstore, Georgie and I head home, and
Ellowyn comes over for dinner. They talk to me about magic.
They show me how to do what they call *everyday spells* and
teach me all the words. They show me simple charms and
glamours. How to wave a hand to do household chores and
so on.

"You don't really think I *mop*, do you?" Georgie makes
a face.

"Mopping is meditative," I retort.

Ellowyn shakes her head at me while she works a piece of
wood with a too-sharp knife. "You're adorable."

I practice the spells they teach me, messing up both more
and less than I like, and they answer all my questions.

Well. Almost. I have questions they can't answer. Or won't.
But I'm not the kind of woman who gives up after one no.
Or even a careful redirect.

"Who is Nicholas Frost and why is he a traitor?"

They exchange a glance. Georgie looks pensive. "You know as well as I do that she'll only go out and try to find her own answers," she says. To Ellowyn. "And the guys are so touchy about him when really, we don't *know* he's a traitor."

Ellowyn's mouth firms. "You don't get to be immortal by doing anything *good*."

I clear my throat. "So...he's immortal, then? An immortal traitor who lives in a falling-down house on the top of a hill overlooking town, kind of like a big *fuck you*?"

Ellowyn makes a face that basically says, *Yes. That.*

Georgie sighs. "Nicholas Frost is a witch. A very, very ancient witch. A Praeceptor. Like your parents."

"A teacher," I say, remembering.

"Kind of, but with broader implications." Georgie sits back in her chair. "In a traditional coven, the Praeceptor takes the coven's shared knowledge and figures out how to utilize it—meaning, like, how to cast the right spells and build new magic. The Praeceptor would also be responsible for teaching the coven's followers too. If the coven had followers."

The minute she says this, I know who the Joywood's Praeceptor is.

"Gil Redd," I say. "That pompous windbag."

Ellowyn nods. "The very one."

"Though he's actually pretty great with lights. In fairness." He did all the lights for the Redbud Festival. And with minimal lecturing.

"Nicholas Frost isn't just *a* Praeceptor," Georgie continues. "He's *the* Praeceptor. When people aren't making themselves hysterical over his immortality, he's widely held to be responsible for the creation and implementation of not only the coven system as we know it—"

"Responsible?" Ellowyn queries. "Or complicit?"

Georgie ignores her. "—but a number of witchkind's most beloved rituals. Like the pubertatum."

"The test I failed," I say. "Except check it out. I'm powerful after all."

I try not to sound smug and fail at that too.

Georgie's book turns its own pages and she closes it absently with a little wave of two fingers. "He's become his very own ghost story. No one sees him anymore."

"Just that ridiculous raven of his. And the house, of course." Ellowyn looks aggrieved. "Uglier by the year and no one else's magic can cover up that kind of glamour."

"Why is he immortal?" Or maybe the question is *how*.

Georgie shrugs. "No one knows. They just know that he is and there are all kinds of conspiracy theories about it. Something people overlook when you're actively helping witchkind. Not so much when you're a mysterious hermit. Who clearly takes pleasure in that monument to himself up there."

"How long has he been around?"

"Too long," Ellowyn mutters.

"Forever," Georgie says at the same time.

"So…he could have been around since the last big flood? He could have survived that German deal? He could have all the answers from personal experience?"

"He could." Georgie says that like it's never occurred to her before. "I guess."

"He could also turn us into insects with a snap of his fingers," Ellowyn protests. "And would. He's probably sitting up there waiting for the flood to happen so we'll all go away and he can do whatever immortals do when the world ends. Party?"

"Make a new one," I retort. "What else is there to do?"

"Emerson Wilde," Ellowyn says. "The only witch around who would use immortality to *work*."

Georgie is nodding. "There have always been whispers of black magic around Nicholas Frost. He might even be where Skip got the adlets." She reaches out and pats one of my planners, because it's closer than my hand. "I know you want answers. We do too. But this is all delicate until we have more information." She pulls her hand back and waves open her book again. "I'll find it."

But I'm not convinced. I know Georgie believes in her books above all else. Usually I'd agree with her, but she hasn't found anything yet. She said herself no witch books exist prior to this flood from however many years ago.

And I get what they're saying about this guy.

Yet if we know someone was actually *there*, or could have been, why tread so carefully? Doesn't saving the town rank above being cautious?

I already know my answer.

"I know that look." Georgie gives me a stern glare. "Leave Nicholas Frost alone, Emerson. I mean it."

I have no intention of leaving such a resource alone. That would be abandoning everything I am and all I stand for. But clearly I can't get through to them either. I'll have to handle this my way.

Still, I make what I hope sounds like an assenting sort of noise.

"I've got to get going," Ellowyn says a while later, pushing away from the table. "It's only going to get colder on the walk home."

"Why are you walking?" I ask, baffled. "You can *fly*."

"I like to walk," Ellowyn says as if that was a strange question to ask. She nudges Georgie. "Thanks for dinner."

Georgie waves a hand and a stuffed Ziploc bag floats over to Ellowyn, who plucks it out of the air. "Brownies?"

"You know it."

"You're the best." Ellowyn glances at me and jerks her chin, a silent signal to follow her.

I do. Intrigued.

"Are you sure you should walk home alone?" I ask, following her out of the kitchen toward the front hall.

"Bricks, Em. Besides, Ruth always has an eye out." Ruth, her owl. Her familiar. We get to the door. "Here." Ellowyn hands her piece of wood over to me. It now looks exactly like a wolf, or a dog. Cassie, in fact. A cute little wood knickknack of Cassie.

"Wynnie." I'm grinning ear to ear. "It's beautiful."

"You can't have Cassie here in case someone sees her, but if you're in trouble and you can't reach us because you're blocked, you might be able to reach her with this."

I gaze at her. Innocently. "How could I be in trouble when you're constantly spying on me?"

"I'm sure you'll find a way." She puts her hands on my shoulders, a rare physical gesture. "But I wish you could trust us."

"I trust you."

"With your life maybe, but not with anything else."

I frown, but Ellowyn steps outside and closes the door in my face before I can come up with a retort. I look down at the pretty little figurine she made me, and though it's got magic in it, clearly, it wasn't made *with* magic. There's something special about that, I think.

I say good night to Georgie, though she barely lifts her head from her book. I know she's putting in overtime trying to figure this out. Trying to find answers in the past to help us face the future.

But why are we putting it all on Georgie and her library collection? Someone who might have been *alive* for the last big flood might know what this all means. What's he going to do if I go ask him for some answers? Send some adlets after me?

Been there, done that.

Still, Ellowyn's words frustrate me as I lie in bed. I trust my friends with my life *and* in all things. It's just that sometimes they're a little too willing to go along with the status quo when a spark is what's needed.

I've always been more than ready to light that spark. Why should this be different?

I toss and turn, because I can't help who I am. I'm a doer. Not a wait-and-see-er. Not the sort of person to let everyone else handle it just because they might know more, remember more. I need to *act*. I always have.

But I also hope I'm not the too-stupid-to-live heroine in too many of the books I've read, who is flatly told to stay away from the haunted house and traipses right into her peril.

I decide then and there if I wake up before my alarm, before sunrise, it'll be a sign. An *omen*. To go talk to Nicholas Frost and see if an immortal witch might answer more questions than regular witches do.

If I sleep until my alarm, I'll do as directed by my friends, have a normal morning, and wait for Georgie to find some answers in history.

I'm up at four.

It's a sign. An *omen*. Who am I to argue?

I get up and get ready quietly. I write Georgie a note that I've gone to the store early, which I certainly plan to do— loaded down with protection crystals, spells and a promise to stay on the bricks. Surely the house on the hill is considered on the bricks.

I slip out of the house while the world is still dark. The moon shines down on Main, making it look like a silvery river. Parallel to the river it follows, a fourth river of moon.

In the distance, the three rivers join together, a black, churning mass.

I frown a little. Surely that isn't right. The black and the churning. I feel something inside of me pull tight, as if I'm... drawn to the mess and tangle and weight out there. I even begin to walk to the ferry, instead of up the hill—

But something stops me. Reminds me. Centers me.

The hot crystals, the dog figurine in my pocket, Zander's necklace, my grandmother's words:

St. Cyprian is mine and I am St. Cyprian's.

The bricks are safe. The rivers, maybe not. I stop heading for the water and look up at my destination. The house on the hill. I keep my eye on it, the ghostly skeleton of what was once a lovely home—I've seen the pictures after all. The pictures from a century ago that make what's become of the house even more of an outrage.

But historical homes are expensive to keep up, much less renovate. Usually bought up by land developers who will shove a twenty-five-house subdivision on the lot, this one has remained untouched. Untouched and uncared for, I think as I start up the hill. Which makes even less sense now that I know who owns it. Surely an immortal witch should have a few ancient coins invested somewhere. Or, at the very least, should be capable of magicking up a few home renovations.

Oh, I think. *Magic.*

Like the kind that hides the three rivers meeting so humans see only two. Like the kind that showed me a perfectly level street and sidewalk instead of the slightly run-down, uneven bricks I knew in my decade of nonmagical life.

I'm suddenly convinced the house has to be the same kind of magical sleight of hand. Didn't Ellowyn say as much? As I climb the hill, I think about what must exist behind the mask of magic. I keep my hand on the dog figurine in my pocket and pretend it really is Cassie by my side.

Something shivers across my skin as I reach the top of the hill. The uncomfortable feeling of being watched, judged, threatened. Though when I look around, I see an old Victorian behind a suitably weathered iron fence, and nothing else save a few bare trees. The hint of dawn to the east. Wind kicking up ripples on the surface of the rivers. The lights of St. Cyprian down below.

As if I've never been more alone or more exposed.

I lift my chin and say the words, *"Reveal to me what I should see."*

Nothing happens. The sun is beginning to rise behind the old, creaking house, and the light makes its state of disrepair even more apparent.

I frown at the house. He can't possibly live in this…pile of sadness. It's impossible. There aren't doors or windows. It's basically a skeleton. Debris on the floors inside, visible from the street. Giant holes in the walls. Is an immortal witch camping out in all this wreckage? I don't believe it.

I focus on the house, on that warmth inside of me that seems to grow stronger every hour. *"Reveal to me what I should see,"* I say again, more intently.

Something flickers, maybe the house itself, and there's the glimmer of something so bright I have to close my eyes. But when I open them again, the house is as it was. Determinedly old and decaying.

But there was a flash of something. I saw it. And I won't give up. I beat back those adlets and I can see behind this facade too. I take a quick look around to make sure there's still nothing and no one around. Then I close my eyes, focus on that energy inside me, and hold out my hands the way I did in the cemetery.

I imagine harnessing that warmth and light and *power.* I picture it coming out of my palms. *"Reveal to me what I should see,"* I say. Out loud and in my head.

I can feel the flow of it. The bright, glorious light of it. And when I open my eyes, I see I did it again, because there it is. The real house—I'm sure of it. A mansion sparkling in a glorious spring sunrise. Natural beauty and magic so brilliant I gasp. As much at the spectacle as the sudden appearance of a man on the porch as if he's a part of that light.

Though he's tall and imposing in a black cloak. Beautiful like the rest, but cold. He looks at me with a vaguely raised eyebrow, reminding me of what Ellowyn said. That he could crush us like insects. "Do you *mind*?"

I blink once. Not quite the greeting I expected. "Mr. Frost?"

He doesn't confirm or deny, but it has to be him. *This* is what an immortal witch would look like, I'm sure. A black-cloaked blade, cutting through the morning light.

Also, he's not the crypt keeper I expected someone ancient to be. He would be hot if he wasn't so...terrifying.

"Who might you be?" he asks.

I can't characterize the look on his face as a sneer, but it could teach condescension to a parade of sneers. I'm too impressed to be offended.

"I'm Emerson Wilde." I don't expect him to know me, necessarily, if he's been absent from local politics and events of late. But if it's true that my parents are such powerful witches, he might know them. Or my grandmother, who I refuse to believe was a disappointment, no matter what Carol Simon says. If he's so old and has been here so long, he must understand what it means to be a Wilde in St. Cyprian.

He narrows his eyes at me, studying me like I'm indeed some sort of insect pinned to a board. "The last Wilde girl

who intruded upon my privacy was…different," he murmurs. I assume he means some Wilde ancestress. "Difficult.
Why are you here, Emerson Wilde?"

"I think you can help me."

His laugh is deep and dark. "I can help you, certainly.
Why would I want to?"

I scramble for an answer that isn't a stuttering mess. Because I feel certain this man won't tolerate indecision or uncertainty, and I have too much pride to show it. "Out of
nowhere, I've found a whole hell of a lot of power. It may
have…started something." I swallow, then go for it. "A flood
might be coming."

His eyes gleam.

"What's coming has nothing to do with you," he says,
but he's studying me with a certain amount of consideration
I find promising.

"The timing of all this is coincidental, then?"

Now he looks bored. A kind of warning shiver creeps
down my neck. "The timing of what?"

"I think you must know enough to know I'm a witch
who's not supposed to have powers. Yet I do."

He gives the impression of shrugging, though he doesn't
move. I hear the rustling of wings and see a remarkably large
crow on the roof, watching this. Watching *me*.

Then I remember what else Ellowyn said and correct myself. That's a raven. And a familiar.

"You'd be surprised at how little I care," Nicholas Frost
tells me.

But caring and knowing are two different things. I don't
point that out to him, as he doesn't strike me as the kind of
man who likes to have a mortal, witch or not, point things
out to him.

"I know something bad is coming. Suddenly I have powers. I'm supposed to believe it's a coincidence?"

"That's not the word I'd use." He shrugs negligently, and this time I see him do it. He must want me to. "But again, I can hardly be bothered to use any words. Now, stop annoying the grown-ups and—"

He opens the front door with a wave of his hand, like he's going to make a more dramatic exit by walking away. Like disappearing would seem tedious after he appeared that way.

I center myself and wave my own hand, closing the door with a resounding slam.

He has the audacity to yawn.

I can do better than that, I think. It's about focus. And energy. And keeping him here until he answers my questions. I need to block the house somehow. I hold out my hands and imagine—imagine—

A forest of thorn bushes. I may have all the appropriate skepticism of *Sleeping Beauty*'s consent issues, to name but one part of the feminist critique that fairy tale begs for, but the sad little yard begins to look exactly like the scene before Prince Phillip cuts his way through. The thorny bushes envelop the entire house.

Pretty impressive if I do say so myself. Let him get through *that*.

Nicholas Frost, immortal witch, flicks his wrist and it all disappears. Without closing his eyes or having to work at it. He simply *flicks* away all that magic I just made.

But he doesn't go inside or disappear. I know he could.

I take that as encouragement.

"You aren't the first."

"The first what?" I ask, desperate for any kind of answer. For some kind of win. I came here to get *answers*. To do something, anything. To move forward. He has to give me *something.*

He nods. "You're likely the last, but worlds come and go, Emerson Wilde. With tedious frequency. Why fight for this one?"

"Because it's ours."

The entire world around us is still—so still I'm afraid to take my next breath. It's like he's frozen something. Time. Space. Everything.

And then there's a book in my hands. A big, heavy book that looks older than the ones Georgie has had her head in for days. I struggle to hold the weight of it.

"Fight for it, then. I dare you." Then he does something with his hands or maybe just his eyebrow and I'm falling. Through the sky, through the air. I land with a kind of cushioned crash in a field of…something, flat on my ass.

The book is still in my hands, now heavy against my chest. But I haven't the slightest idea where I am as I gape up at the bright morning sky above me.

I'm filled with sheer delight that I'm alive.

I think.

Until I hear Jacob's voice saying my name with a mix of concern and confusion. He kneels next to me. "Are you all right?"

And I get it then.

That bastard dropped me at Jacob's farm with an ancient book I can't explain having in my possession. Except with the truth about my secret dawn trip to the house on the hill that *no one* is going to like.

Particularly not Jacob.

14

I DON'T KNOW WHAT TO SAY TO JACOB, AND since I'm not one hundred percent sure where I landed, I look around. It has to be one of his fields. The earth is turned over and there are even some small green shoots coming up through the dark earth. Spring literally springing before me.

"I'm sorry," I say. Because the best offense is often an apology. I don't make the rules—though I should. "I didn't mean to land there."

"Clearly." He helps me to my feet, by tugging me up by the elbows, then frowns at the massive book that's now between us. "What's that?"

Is there a way I can explain this without explaining it? "It's a book."

Cassie pads over and settles herself at my feet. Jacob eyes us both suspiciously.

"A very old-looking book. I've never seen it before, but I recognize that symbol."

He points to the cover. I look down at the emblem there.

Stamped into the leather is a gold embossed symbol. Bold lines that whisper of that power I felt up on the hill. Ancient. Full. *Sure.*

"Oh, hey. Look at that."

"It's the Frost family crest. Not that I've ever heard of any family members but him." He stands there, clearly waiting for me to explain, but I know he knows already. His eyes are cold and his jaw is tight, but he waits for me to explain.

I'm not sure why that breaks my heart a little bit. "Jacob…"

"Don't beat around the bush. Don't try to make it more palatable. Just tell me what you did."

I do not care for the way he says *"what you did,"* like I'm a toddler who got into the pantry and spilled all the cereal. Like he's the *parent* in this situation.

"I did what I had to do," I return firmly. Because I *did.* And maybe Nicholas Frost didn't give me any answers, but he didn't try to hurt me. And he gave me a book that might just help.

If he hadn't dropped me off at *Jacob's,* I'd be at Confluence looking through it as we speak. No doubt finding answers and solving all our problems, like the boss I am.

You could use a dose of humility, child.

I blink at Cassie. Before I can retort to her snide comment, Jacob is demanding more answers.

"And what did you have to do?" Jacob asks, and it's worse than the scolding parental tone. It's tired. Devoid of any emotion. Like I've beaten him down somehow.

Which isn't fair. Probably.

"I had a few questions for Nicholas Frost, the only immortal witch around here, as far as I know. None of my *friends* would answer those questions for me. Instead you all talked in circles around me and put a line in the sand without discussion. I didn't like that, so I took matters into my own hands."

He stands so *still*, I can barely manage a breath.

"Did you tell anyone what you were doing?"

"Weird," I drawl. "Last time I checked, I was an adult."

"Last time *I* checked, you were a hardheaded woman who's been aware she's a witch for all of a *day* and can't get it through your thick skull that you might not know everything." His voice isn't lacking emotion any longer. He's angry and trying to beat it back.

My heart does a little double take in my chest. Perhaps I shouldn't be *quite* so flippant.

Wow, you think?

Snarky familiars leave a *lot* to be desired. So I ignore her and focus on Jacob.

I go for placating when I reply. "He might have answers. He's been around how long? I don't know why—"

"What he might do is get us all killed, Emerson."

"Don't be silly."

"You can't go charging in alone. Have you learned nothing? He could have killed you where you stood with a snap of his fingers."

"You guys said the bricks were safe. I was on the safe bricks."

"We said *wait*," he explodes, and it *is* an explosion. I've seen him angry. Or I thought I had. This is pure fury. His eyes glow. His *hands* glow. Cassie growls in warning at my feet, her hackles rising.

But Jacob is beyond hearing that. He's beyond warning. He is quite literally incandescent with rage. "We said be patient. We said be *careful*, Emerson. Because this is *life-or-death*. Not just for you. For *all of us*. Don't you understand you're putting us *all* in danger?"

I can feel the blood drain out of me. I might not understand that statement, but I know Jacob doesn't exaggerate, even when he's being ridiculously overprotective. "What?"

"If we make the wrong step here, there are any number of punishments we could face. All of us who know about you and haven't told the Joywood would be considered equally guilty. Exile and mind wiping are only a start. Those are *nice* punishments. All Frost has to do is tell them you came to him. That's *it*."

He slashes his hand through the air.

It's a bomb. I feel it detonate deep inside of me. I thought my friends were just trying to protect me, but... Oh God. What have I done? "No one told me I might..."

But they *have* told me. Maybe not directly, but I think about what Georgie said about Rebekah. That telling her would endanger us *both*. It's not just exile that's life-and-death. I should have realized that.

I want to be angry they didn't say it in so many words. Blame them. If I'd had all the information, I never would have put them in danger.

Wouldn't you? a voice inside me asks. Or maybe it's Cassie. I don't know anymore. I'm untethered in the horror of my realizations.

They didn't want to tell me straight out. Not because they think I can't handle it, but because they don't want to put that responsibility on me—to worry about *their* well-being. They don't want me to think they're in danger because of me when they're all so happy—Georgie's face flashes in my mind—*so* happy that I've found my real power.

That doesn't change the fact that my power puts them at risk. Going to Nicholas Frost was a mistake. A desperately awful mistake if that cold, mocking man sells me out. I know with every cell in my body that if he decides to do it, he will. Without a care in the world. I repress a shiver as I think about how easily he waved away my attempts to contain him.

"I'm sorry," I manage to croak. I'm desperately holding on to the tears, but Jacob is so angry, and I, for once, am so very in the wrong. And reminded of what Ellowyn said to me about her mother cursing her.

That's the thing about magic. It's all fun and games. Until it isn't. And some things you can't take back.

"I didn't mean…" But my voice breaks. I can't seem to get ahold of the tide inside of me that just overflows.

I don't want my friends to be in danger because of me and what I am and what I know. That isn't right or fair for anyone. Tears start to fall and I'm quite certain I've never cried in front of Jacob before. Crying is *not* my MO, but endangering my friends…

"Emerson. Don't do that. Please. Just…" He swears under his breath as he pulls me to him. He clearly doesn't *like* tears, but he knows how to deal with them. He rubs my back and starts murmuring reassuring words that don't quite make sense in the moment.

But I know it'll be okay. We'll make it okay, even if I did mess up. Because he's holding me. Making promises. And no matter how angry he is, he doesn't turn away.

And at least this is honest. He let me see his anger. I'm letting him see my tears. It's not awkward pizza parties any longer. It's real, no matter what happens.

It's not exactly a comforting realization, but it makes me feel better.

He pulls back when it seems I've gotten it together and uses the rough pads of his thumbs to brush away the tears on my cheeks. My hair is tangled around his fingers. And my heart feels bloody and bruised and I hate myself a little bit for that…

But Jacob is touching my face. All gentleness and care. Angry with me, sure, but he doesn't want to see me cry.

"I really am sorry," I manage as I stem the tide of stupid tears. I feel embarrassed enough to *want* to pull away, but I don't.

"I know," he says. "We all need to be better about honesty. You deserve that. We're all so used to trying to protect *you*, but you know everything now. Trying to protect you seems to be having the opposite effect. So, I'm sorry too. It's still so new, to have you…"

He trails off and never finishes the sentence. His hands are still on my face, and for all his outbursts about how I don't listen or think, he doesn't seem frustrated any longer. He's looking at me like he did last night. Our breath mingling. The flecks of gold and blue hidden in the green of his eyes. So sturdy, so *good*.

His hands are on my *face* and he hasn't let me go. I can't stand the idea he'll disappear again. Let this stretch out and then just *poof* at the onset of *almost*. Didn't I decide last night that I would go for it? I would fight for something?

But the flood. The timing. The sensible thing to do is leave this for another day when things are more settled. And I have always prided myself on being sensible.

But I don't step back.

And he doesn't disappear.

"What is this?" I ask, my voice little more than a whisper.

"What?"

"This, Jacob." I indicate *us*. "You told me there was nothing romantic between us. I believe that you're not lying to me. But I have to believe what I feel too."

He takes the book I'm still clutching out of my hands. He looks at it with a frown, then sets it on the ground next to

Cassie, who places a careful paw on the cover like she thinks it might make a break for the river.

"Jacob—" I begin again.

"I'm not saying we didn't have feelings for each other."

I don't like the past tense, but I tell myself that's not the most important factor right now. "Then what are you saying?"

He returns his gaze to me, like he's weighing what he'll say. What's *acceptable* for me to know.

And I'm so freaking tired of this.

I reach out and grab his arm. I need that connection. "Tell me the truth. All of it. You just said we need to be better about honesty."

"I've been honest," he replies with a little frown.

"You've been careful."

His mouth curves. And it's rueful more than joyful, but I'll take it. "I have been. It's who I am." He looks up at the sky for a moment, then lets out a long breath. But he doesn't dislodge my grip on him. "High school. Feelings. Attraction. Sure, it was all there. But you had a plan. A timeline for... Well, I don't know what you'd call it. Everything, I suppose. I did not fit in to that plan. And I didn't try to. I'm not putting that on you, to be clear. You didn't fit into my plans either. Healers are supposed to be with Healers, and I wasn't about to upend the order of things."

But the order of things is upended, I want to argue. And yet wasn't I just talking myself out of this moment? Putting the danger and the flood and my own plans first? How can I blame him for doing the same? That isn't fair.

Still, I'm not a saint. I might blame him a *little*.

"And we had bigger plans," he continues. "You can't remember and I didn't want to tell you now because I was afraid you'd...well, be you."

I scowl, my old umbrage coming back like it's the cavalry, here to save me. "What does that mean?"

He sighs and does something. Flicks his hand and there's...a kind of bubble around us. I can't see through it, and I get instantly that no one can see—or *hear*—inside it. It's just the two of us, not even Cassie. Like the world doesn't exist. He moves closer to me, his voice low, his eyes so *serious*. "Back in high school, you wanted to start a rival coven to the Joywood. You thought we could do better, be better. I agreed. I was all in."

He delivers this like he expects me to reel away in shock or horror. But maybe that's the benefit of my memory situation. What I think is, *Hell yeah, we could do better.* I don't even need the details. "Did we get everyone else on board?"

"We didn't tell them. It was too dangerous. Borderline treason. It was just us. We had to have everything in place before we risked involving everyone. We didn't count on..."

He sighs.

"On what?" I prompt him.

"The pubertatum. You being pronounced spell dim and mind wiped. It never occurred to any of us that it was even a possibility. You've always been a force, Emerson."

I sift through what he's telling me and I suppose it makes some sense. I thought it was silly teenage unrequited-love stuff. I thought it was all about near kisses in ponds. When it was rival covens and treason.

That does sound a bit more like me.

But what I feel in the here and now doesn't have anything to do with *that*. If it did, I wouldn't be standing here wanting to drown in the heat radiating off of Jacob's body. I'd already be home, neck-deep in the book Nicholas Frost gave me.

Instead I'm here, in a bubble, wanting things I can hardly name.

Because there are so many of them.

"I don't have a plan anymore," I tell him. "Or a timeline. It's kind of out the window, what with the whole witch thing, murderous monsters, a flood, my whole life is a lie, and stuff."

"You will soon enough. You always do." But he still doesn't disappear. He traces a strand of hair down my temple and then delicately tucks it behind my ear. "Emerson."

That's all he says. Part of me wants to tell him to stop being a coward, and then that same part of me wonders why *I'm* being a coward. I could easily initiate a kiss.

But there's a heavy weight in my chest, wrapped all around me like a fraught hug. Like this is the most important moment of my life. In this moment, everything changes. After this, nothing will be the same.

Yet everything has already changed. I don't have the control I once did. I can't charge ahead, like Jacob accused me of doing, because there are real, life-or-death consequences for people I love.

My plans are out the window, and while Jacob is right—I'll find new ones, because it's who I am—I don't want timelines anymore. I want this.

I want him.

Everything will change if I choose it.

I want it to change.

"Me too," he says, answering out loud what I thought was only in my head, but then it doesn't matter because he puts his lips to mine.

And it's everything. More than.

He tastes like rain and heat. His mouth is hard and soft and fits mine so well it's like a slick dance. And I've never liked dancing this much.

I've never liked *anything* this much.

I may never like anything else, ever again.

He holds me like I'm his, so I hold him in return. Because we're in this together. Mouths learning the shape of each other, new tastes and textures. *At last*, echoing with every bolt of pleasure, our hearts beating as one.

One.

Kissing Jacob is worth almost getting torn to shreds in a graveyard.

Kissing Jacob is worth anything. Everything.

At first I think the distant rumbling is simply our hearts. Or maybe a physiological response to *finally* having Jacob's mouth on mine. I have spent as long as I can remember concentrating on facts, not feelings, when it comes to him—and now I know why.

But no. I realize the earth is literally shaking beneath us. Violently, not romantically. I pull my mouth from Jacob's and look down at the ground. It's not moving, but everything seems to shake so hard I can barely keep my footing. Jacob holds me steady until it stops.

"What was that?" I ask, my breath still not getting back to normal. The kiss? The earthquake? Surely the kiss didn't cause it.

Though I can't pretend I'll be all that surprised if it did.

"I think that's what we were afraid of," he says, rueful again, but his hands are still curled around my arms. Holding me tight and close.

"I'm not afraid of anything," I hear myself say, because what could touch us here? In this perfect moment. In a literal bubble.

He rests his forehead on mine. "I am."

I want to assure him everything is fine. What could be finer than this? Than *us*, at last? Maybe back then I *was* afraid, of this or of having my plans upended. But I'm not now. He shouldn't be either.

I open my mouth to tell him exactly that, but a sharp bolt of pain explodes inside my head. I cry out, my legs crumpling under me, but Jacob holds me up.

"Emerson."

The pain is all-encompassing. I can feel a kind of fog floating around in my head, while another internal force tries to beat it back. Push it away. There's a battle going on inside my brain, but no matter who lands a blow, it hurts. It's excruciating, and I can't seem to find a way to make it stop. I hang limply in Jacob's arms and let the fight roll over me, through me.

I can hear Jacob calling my name, but it's from far away and I can't reach it. Dimly, I can feel Cassie's cold nose on my neck. But I can't reach them.

Then there's relief, a small, bright shaft of it. I manage a breath. Another. I'm laid out on the ground and Jacob's palm is on my forehead.

Jacob is healing me. But I can hear how hard he's breathing. I can hear the groan deep inside of him. He's trying to fight back the fog, but he can't.

"Stop," I try to say. Even though I'm in desperate pain, I can't stand the thought of something hurting him on my account.

But whatever he's doing, it's helping the light win. The fog is being beaten back. It's a painful process, but something is…happening.

Something so huge that I want to escape it, afraid it might destroy me as it swells high, coming at me anyway—

I remember.

It washes over me, waves and waves of sparkly light. The coven, *our* coven. Whispering with Jacob in corners, because we were going to change the world. Tossing him into that pond, the almost-kiss interrupted—not by spirits but my own fear that if I let him kiss me, everything would change.

Nothing could change until I was ready, because I had a whole world to change first.

I feel Jacob bear down. He's fighting the fog harder, as if he understands that it's what's keeping the rest of my magical memories at bay. But it's hurting him. It's costing too much.

"Stop. *Stop*." I manage to say it louder, firmer each time. "Jacob, please."

I push at his hand. I'm too weak to push it off, but he finally lets go.

And I can breathe again. I can feel his hand in mine. Slowly, slowly, the pain recedes and I manage to open my eyes. I have to blink the blurry vision away to see that the spring morning looks totally normal around us. Pretty, even. His bubble is gone. The pain is gone.

But I still remember.

I look over at him. My hand is still in his. He's sitting on the grass, looking as gray as he did after the battle with the adlets. Only he's not healing deep cuts or bites. He simply tried to fight something within me.

For me.

I still have a headache, but it's a dull throb rather than the slicing, debilitating pain from before. I manage to sit up with his help. I feel weak and fragile and yet...not.

"What was that?" I ask.

"I went in to heal you. I didn't see anything external, so it had to be internal. There was a thick fog around your brain. The mind wipe, maybe?" He frowns a little, deep in thought. "It had to be the spell—your obliviscor. I've never dealt with anyone with a mind wipe before. I've never seen anything like it, and it was strong. Thick and strong, but we were beating it back together." He shakes his head. "I shouldn't be able to undo Carol's spell, even with my healing skills. She's more powerful than I am. She's the *most* powerful."

"Unless she isn't." I grab on to him. I need him to see what I see, feel what I feel. "Unless she isn't more powerful than *we* are. Jacob, we had plans once."

"We did."

I don't understand why it sounds so *past tense* when he says it. "Nothing has changed. In fact—"

He moves so that he can take me by the shoulders even though we're both still sitting on the ground. His little bubble is gone, but Cassie is next to us guarding the book, and I see Murphy the deer in the distance, watching us with careful eyes.

We're protected. There's something truly comforting—and amazing—about that.

"Everything has changed, Em," Jacob says, bringing my gaze back to him. His green eyes are grave. "I know the consequences now. They're untenable."

But he doesn't understand.

"I remember things," I tell him.

"This is bigger than high school *what-ifs*," he says repressively.

But I don't do repression.

"Jacob." I wait for him to look at me. "I can *remember*. I can remember magic."

15

JACOB DOESN'T SAY ANYTHING AT FIRST. HIS
complexion is slowly regaining a healthy hue. I want to ask
him what it's like to heal someone. To lose something in
the process. I want to somehow make sense of the gravity
of what he does.

But there are so many other things to deal with here.

"What magic, specifically?" Jacob asks. His hands don't
leave my shoulders.

I close my eyes as if that will give me the answer to his
question. It's not like the memories washed over me in some
kind of catalog. It's more that when I think about things
he's mentioned, I can now bring up the memories that include magic.

"I remember the things you've told me, mostly. The toad
and pond incident. Talking about covens. You helping me…
bring a plant back to life?"

He nods, his gaze intense. "What about the pubertatum?
The obliviscor?"

I search back, but graduation is still very much unmagical. Rebekah disappearing is just her running away. My grandmother… I squeeze my eyes shut and try to think of something my grandmother would have showed me, taught me, said to me about witches. I remember what I saw in the bookstore, but most of the other things that come to mind are normal things. Breakfasts together, walks along the river. Sometimes I think I can almost see the spark of something underneath the memory, but it fades away when I try to focus on it.

I shake my head. "No, not yet. Maybe it will come back over time."

"I can bring more back. If you let me. I was fighting it off."

And hurting in the process. I want my memories back like I want my next breath, but all I can see is Jacob pale and weak when he tries to save me. Using everything he has, everything he is.

I can't stand the thought that he would take on physical pain because of me. *For* me. It's an awful thing to watch the people you care about *physically hurt* because of you, and as much as I want my magical memories back, I can live without them if this is what they cost. I've already lived without them.

"Maybe," I say, because I know he wants to help me. "Not now. It was too much. You went all gray again."

"I'm fine."

"Now you are," I point out. I get to my feet because I'm afraid if I stay seated with his hands on my shoulders, looking at me like he'd fight the whole world to give me this one thing—knowing he *would*—I might give in.

He gets to his feet too, back to his normal self. Tall and strong and in control. Whatever he lost, he's regained. Maybe I could let him get in there and fight back that fog—

But what if he lost?

I can't have that.

"The pain is temporary, Emerson." It's like he's reading me again. "Pain can be withstood. It can be worth the cost."

"Ellowyn said that too," I say, though my voice comes out like a whisper. *Pain is the price*, she'd said. I think Jacob might be worth any price.

But I'm not so sure about old memories that don't really change anything anyway.

He takes a step toward me, all earnest and imploring. "Then let me help you get your memories back."

I can't say no. He won't take no for an answer, because he knows me too well. I have to find a more careful way around this. "I will. But we're out here. We need to be more careful. Isn't that what you've been telling me for the past...day?" I look up at the sky, where the sun is now shining in full, re-alization dawning on me. "The store. Georgie!"

"Georgie knows you're here."

I blink at him. He shrugs. "I knew she'd worry, so I told her the minute you crash landed."

"Told her like...with your magic? Does your deer deliver messages, like a carrier...deer?"

He pats his pocket. "I do use a phone from time to time, Em."

Though there's a gravity to the way he's holding himself, it doesn't come out in his voice.

I stand here for a second taking in the moment, because it's not just that I got some magical memories back. It's not just that Jacob was somehow *inside me*, fighting the fog around my brain.

Jacob kissed me and the ground shook. What does that mean? It's lowering to realize I'm too afraid to ask.

He raises an eyebrow at me as we stand here, feet apart,

not saying anything. There's something almost amused in his expression. "Speechless?"

I shake my hair back, trying to regain some equilibrium. "You wish."

He crosses that distance, puts his hand on my face. "No. That wouldn't be you." But he drops his hand. "I don't want to hurt you again."

"It wasn't the kiss that hurt." I'm not totally certain that's the truth, and the timing isn't in my favor. But it's what I *want* to be the truth, and I'm very good at making the things I want happen.

Still, he doesn't kiss me. Just stands here *within reach*, and I could close the distance. In fact, why shouldn't I? But he steps back.

"I'm not going to do anything different than I did last time. So, until you're good with that, it will have to wait." He holds out his hand and the book leaps into it. He gives it to me. "Frost shouldn't have this book and he definitely shouldn't have given it to you. I don't know what game he's playing, and I don't trust him. But…he'll be in just as much trouble if he takes this to the Joywood. Then again, he is immortal, so I'm not sure trouble really matters to him."

Right. Nicholas Frost. Endangering my friends. Potential floods.

So why am I mostly just irritated that Jacob won't kiss me?

"Get to Confluence before opening. I'll do some investigating." His fingers trail down my cheek. "Call one of your dinner meetings for tonight."

"That's not really what I want to do tonight, *Jacob*."

Jacob grins. *Grins.* "First things first, *Emerson*. Get everyone at your house. We'll see where we stand." He frowns at the book in my hand. "Be careful with that. We don't know what Frost's angle is."

I think about the interaction I had with the mysterious man. Thorns and ravens and his whole black-cloaked thing. "I'm not sure he really has an angle. He seemed wholly uninterested."

Jacob's frown doesn't lift. It deepens. He's clearly not reassured by that information. And I wish I could find a way to make him not worry about me. But then I'd need to stop worrying about him.

He mutters something under his breath, then closes a fist. Something sparkles around it, catching the sun as he holds it out to me. "Put this on that chain Zander gave you."

"What is it?"

"Protection."

It looks like a little charm, the kind fluffier women than I've ever been put on bracelets while wearing lots of pastels. "I'm not going to be able to walk with all the stuff you guys have given me."

"But *I* haven't given you anything yet. Protection is about layers. The more layers, the more you're protected."

I take the little charm and reach back to unclasp the chain, but the tiny lever evades me. Jacob rolls his eyes, snaps his fingers, and then the charm is on the chain. "We need to do some basic witchcraft lessons, Emerson."

"If any of those lessons include stopping time so I have the hours upon hours I need to do all of this—run my normal life, stop a flood, et cetera—I'm all in."

"We'll find the time. But not now. You'll be late to open the store and people will talk. You go on now. I'll see you tonight." He stands away from me, hands clasped behind his back. Purposefully keeping himself from touching me.

I suppose I could be offended, but the whole *clasping* part gives me the impression he *wants* to touch me. But he's afraid the pain will come back. And *I'm* afraid that if it does, he'd do anything to fight back that fog for me. Too much.

It's the nature of *us*, I suppose, all these unspoken fears ruling how we dance around each other. But look what happened when we stopped: Jacob kissed me. The earth shook. I *remembered*.

I look down at the chain. The charm he put there looks like a flower crystallized in something clear. A tiny bluebell, maybe? Pretty, and like a normal piece of jewelry. Not protection crystals and amulets and mysterious teas.

"What kind of protection is this?"

"Complicated to explain, and you've got to get to the bookstore."

"Right." The store, and explaining to Georgie what I did, and how I got this book. I'm not looking forward to it, but it can't be put off.

I look at Jacob—still holding himself resolutely apart from me. We're going to have to find a new dance, him and me. Without fear. Without this *caution* so engrained in who we are. But I need some time to slot that into place in my brain.

"I'll see you tonight, Emerson," he says quietly.

I don't know what to say to that. *You're damn right you will* seems silly. So I simply nod. I think about the store. I picture it, holding on to that core of energy inside me. I feel the wind, the *whoosh*. And when I open my eyes, I'm standing in the middle of Confluence Books with the big, old book in my hands.

Damn, that's *cool*.

Georgie is already situated in the lounge chair with books in her lap, and Ellowyn is standing behind my counter, flipping through a book on serial killers. They both look up at me when I land.

Then they both close their books and say nothing. Just look at me, clearly waiting for an explanation.

I should lead with the book and Nicholas Frost and apologies.

"Jacob kissed me," I blurt out instead. I don't get quite the shocked response I'm hoping for. "And I remembered some things."

"What kind of things?" Ellowyn asks.

At the same time Georgie asks, "What was it like?"

The earth shook. I can't bring myself to say it, even to my friends. It seems so...silly, even if it's true. And we're dealing with real issues. Floods and immortals and danger. Real danger, some of it caused by me.

They've come to stand next to me, questions and interest in their eyes, but not surprise.

"That doesn't come as a shock?" I ask. I may have expected at least *one* squeal. So I could pretend to be too mature for it.

Ellowyn and Georgie look at each other. Then back to me. "Which part?" Georgie asks carefully.

I frown at her. "Any of the parts."

She smiles. Indulgently. "Not really. The memories coming back, well, it's you. That you'd find a way to get them back felt inevitable."

"And the kissing?"

"That's about fifteen years overdue," Ellowyn says dismissively. "But what do memories returning and finally kissing Jacob have to do with each other?"

I recount the morning. The Jacob part of it. I'll get to Nicholas Frost, eventually. The kiss, the memories I managed to find. I explain Jacob trying to heal me, and then I let my friends in on what I wouldn't admit to Jacob. "It's like the pain started because of the kiss."

Georgie nods along. "That makes sense."

"It does?"

"We can put aside the simple answer that would horrify you and focus on the fact that a kiss is a connection. Jacob being a Healer means he has a more…open connection, I guess you'd say, to other people than most. So that opened connection combined both your powers and allowed him to do something we would have thought was impossible." She waves a hand. "It seems obvious now."

That sounds all fine and dandy, but… "What's the answer that would horrify me?"

Georgie hesitates. Ellowyn doesn't.

"Fate," she says firmly. "The kind that shakes the earth."

I frown at her. "You don't believe in fate."

She shrugs. "I don't…*not*."

"I know you're going to take this like someone is controlling your life and then rail against the emotional labor of expectations or whatever, but that isn't fate," Georgie says.

"Then what is?" I can save my lecture about the tyranny of expectations for another day.

"The opportunity," she replies.

"That doesn't make any sense—*life* is the opportunity. No fate necessary."

"No," Georgie replies, her gaze something like stern. "Life is life. Being alive. Fate is the existence of opportunities that make other things happen. Like, let's say fate made you a lock and Jacob a key. It's not *determined* that his key will ever find your lock, even if it's meant. You have to do the work and make the choices to…"

"Stick the key in her?" Ellowyn asks, grinning.

"Choose each other," Georgie says firmly. But she smiles a little as she glances back to me. "Where you want things stuck is up to you."

I can't think about sticking anything anywhere at the moment.

But then, of course, I do.

"What's the book?" Ellowyn asks. She squints at it. "Isn't that the Frost crest?"

I tell them the story, more carefully, but they don't have the explosive reaction Jacob did. Maybe because I sound contrite. Maybe because women aren't as emotional as men. Or maybe because they're too enthralled by the book. Georgie is already paging through it, caressing the binding like a lover.

Once I explain what fully happened when I went to see Nicholas Frost, Georgie considers what I tell her. Then she looks up at me, a serious expression on her face. "This book shouldn't exist."

"Is there a banned-books list for witches?" I perk up. "I should do a low-key display. I could—"

"Witches aren't excitable humans," Ellowyn says. "We don't ban books. We do put curses on them and smite our enemies out of existence, along with their books, but banning? That's for the magicless. And dull."

Georgie carefully slides her finger across the faded black script on the page before her. "It says it's from the 1400s. I'll have to do a more involved translation spell to get to the bottom of all of it, but books like this aren't supposed to have survived the flood in Passau. Incalculable amounts of knowledge were lost."

"What does it mean that he still has it?"

Georgie shakes her head. "I don't know. But this is what I'll focus on today."

"He gave it to Em. Shouldn't she be the one to read it?"

Georgie blinks. "You're right. She should."

"I don't know how," I remind her.

"I'll show you." She looks excited at the prospect.

"Maybe we could all do it together," I suggest. "Jacob wanted me to call a dinner meeting."

"Jacob's calling your meetings now?" Georgie looks even more excited. She peers at me. "Are you sure all you did was kiss?"

Very sure, sadly. "Can we focus on the task at hand?" I reply primly.

"We could try a summoning spell." Ellowyn doesn't seem happy about the idea. "This would be a good place. The store is very protected."

I look around the little shop I know so well. "Protected?"

"A building that's been owned by witches since they built it in the eighteenth century? There are all sorts of protection spells weaved into the walls. The very foundations. By every witch who's ever owned it." Ellowyn glances around like she can see all that weaving. "Knowing your grandmother, she weaved in particular spells to protect you, too. Specifically."

I want to ask so many follow-up questions that I don't know where to start.

"Get everyone to come here," Ellowyn tells me. "Tell Zander to handle food." She turns to Georgie. "We'll need the guys to do some kind of blocking spell. Don't you think?"

Georgie nods. "Definitely."

"I don't want to be a part of another ritual where you all do all the work and I do nothing," I say.

But Ellowyn is shaking her head. "This won't be like last time. You're the one who the information needs to be revealed to. It's more like I'll be lending you what summoning power I can channel to get to that information."

"And I'm more the…administrator," Georgie says. "Just watching to make sure everything goes as it should. We'll have Jacob and Zander block the magic from being felt outside the walls, which is important until we figure out Skip's end game in trying to kill you."

"I've got to get to my shop," Ellowyn says.

We agree to meet later and I move toward the register, telling myself it's time to focus on work now. I need to figure out how I'm going to balance all this witch stuff with reality, since book deliveries wait for no woman. But Georgie follows me over to the counter. Then stares at me with a dreamy smile on her face.

"What?"

She grabs my hands. "How *was* it?"

I could pretend I don't know what she means, but it's Georgie. I open my mouth to say something, though I'm not sure what. No word or description seems to be right. How could I possibly capture it? And Georgie's talk about *fate* has left me...uncomfortable.

But whether fate was involved or it wasn't, Jacob's kiss was... "I guess now that I know it's all real, I'd call it magical."

Georgie makes a little squealing noise, and then she's doing a little jig while still holding my hands. I will admit this is satisfying. "I knew it had to happen *someday*, and it helped you get your memories back? That might be the most romantic thing I've ever heard."

"I could have done without the debilitating pain." But I'm smiling. And Jacob's and Ellowyn's shared sentiment echoes in my mind. Pain is the price, but it's worth it.

Jacob is worth it.

"Feelings can help make magic stronger," Georgie says, postjig. She squeezes my hands, then drops them. "And we're going to need all the strength we can get."

Before I can absorb that, the door opens, the bell tinkles, and in walks Carol.

"You forgot to flip your sign to Open, dear," says the head

of the Joywood who might yet kill us all for crimes-against-witch-law infractions. She speaks in a lilting sort of way, and her hair is extrafrizzy today.

I also forgot to unlock my door, but apparently *she* can break any rules of civility, society, and the state of Missouri she likes. I manage a smile. "Morning, Carol. Are you here to browse or can I help you with something?"

"I was hoping you could help me find a gift to give to my new grand-niece," Carol says, looking the way she always has to me. Kind and vaguely dotty, which, I realize slowly, is the way she wants me to see her. The mind-wiped, might-as-well-be-human me, that is. "It's her first birthday. Something age appropriate but educational."

"Of course." I don't look at Georgie, who's gone alarmingly still, all deer-in-headlights because that's how little game she has. Thank goodness her job has never required her to sell anything, because she'd be terrible at it. I bypass her and lead Carol to the kids' section.

"Skip mentioned you two have a date," she says as I shepherd her to the best board book selection in St. Charles County.

A date is not what I'd call it, but I smile as brightly as I can manage. "We're having dinner next week. He wanted to forge a new path forward. Peace and working together and all that fun stuff." I pull out one of my favorite books to suggest to customers, particularly grandmother types. "What about this?"

Carol looks at me. She is studying me, not the book. It feels as if she's trying to look *through* me, and I get the sense she'd be able to, and easily—but there's some force working against her. The necklace I'm wearing, the crystals I'm carrying, the carved dog in my pocket. Maybe even the floorboard and the walls.

I am protected, so I hold Carol's gaze with a pleasant smile on my face as if I don't feel any of it.

"No, I don't think that's quite right," she says mildly, look-ing at the book. I put it back on the shelf. "My son can be im-pulsive, Emerson, but you know this. You grew up together."

"I don't think there's anything impulsive about us work-ing together to better the town, Carol." I hold up another children's book. "It's what I've always wanted."

"She already has that one," she tells me with a wave of her hand, and the overly mesmerizing rings she wears. Plus the jangling bracelets, bristling with charms. She's even wear-ing pastels.

It feels like a portent.

"Now, it's none of my business, of course," Carol says with a tinkling laugh. "But I want you to be careful. You and Skip aren't likely to get along together for very long, are you? You're very different people."

Does she *know* her son wants to hurt me? Is she trying to warn me? *Protect* me? My friends are afraid of Carol and what she can do, but what if she can *help*?

Isn't she supposed to be the most powerful witch in the world?

I almost say something. Not the full truth, but a small hint that something has happened—

But then I remember this morning, and Jacob. Maybe it's time to remember that I'm not alone in this. My friends de-serve a say too, especially if my choices might kill us all. I am all about choices.

"I appreciate your candor, Carol," I say. "My knee-jerk reaction is to tell you that *of course* the mayor and the cham-ber of commerce president can find a way to work together. For the town. But I'll take your concerns on board. We all remember the prom."

Carol smiles. She holds out her hand and one of the early-reader books jumps into it. Just an inch or two, so that if I didn't know magic existed, I'd still be able to convince myself it was some sort of optical illusion.

But I do know magic exists. Did she just…perform magic in front of me? On purpose? Or was I not supposed to see her do it? I remind myself that she's the witchiest of all the witches. Then I shake my head, not needing to fake confusion, because I am beyond confused. Still, I ring her up the way I would any other customer, human or magical, and say goodbye. Georgie comes out of her frozen state as she leaves. We both watch her walk past the window. Carol looks back in at us and waves. I wave back.

Georgie bursts into action by waving too. Psychotically. "She suspects something."

"Maybe that's not a bad thing." I didn't get a particularly threatened feeling with Carol. Though it wasn't necessarily a *good* feeling either. It was just weird. At least there were no more disparaging remarks about Grandma. I decide that must be progress.

"Maybe," Georgie agrees, but I can tell she's on the fence. "I don't have anything against Carol personally, except the way she tends to shove Skip into places he doesn't belong. But that's a powerful mother's prerogative, I guess."

"Then why are we so scared of her? Isn't she just…the president?"

She makes a face. "Ever since your impromptu obliviscor, Jacob hasn't trusted her. And the way he described how things went down, I don't blame him. But you have to wonder…"

"What?"

Georgie studies me, like she's not sure I can handle the truth. "Jacob isn't the kind to overreact. Or let his feelings get in the way of common sense. For the most part."

"For the most part?"

"That line has always been a little blurry when it comes to you, Em."

I don't know what to say to that. I've never felt Jacob blurring any lines with me until this morning. But then, my view of the past ten years is somewhat lacking. There's no getting around the memory gap.

I kind of love the idea that he's *blurred lines* all along.

"Jacob tried to fight back the spell." I told her this already, so I get to the key part. "He thinks he could push more and get rid of it altogether."

My best friend's gaze sparkles. "And then you could remember *everything*."

"But I could tell it cost him. Maybe I really could remember everything if he kept going, but is it safe?"

"A Healer heals quickly, but that has its costs too. If he pushes too hard, he could do damage his body doesn't have the means to fix. Normally, I'd trust Jacob to know that line. He's noble, but not stupid."

"You say that like this isn't normal."

"It's not." Georgie's smile is big and wide. "It's you. I think when it comes to *you*, Jacob could be very stupid."

I huff out a breath. "I don't want that."

Georgie only shrugs like it's funny. It's not funny. "I'm not sure he does either. I'm also not sure it's a choice."

Not what I want to hear either.

Georgie considers the window again. "Maybe Carol felt it? Jacob somehow undoing her spell? The timing is weird. I know she bought a book and all, but the fact she *just happened* to come to the store the same morning Jacob manages to undo some of *her* spell? I don't buy the timing."

"Jacob would be in trouble, wouldn't he? If she knew?"

Georgie doesn't answer me right away, and when she turns to smile at me, I know she's lying to me. No, that's too harsh.

She's not going to lie so much as dance around the truth. I can't blame her. She's been doing it for ten years. She's had to do it.

"We all have to be careful." She lets her shoulder touch mine. "But we can't stop looking for answers. It might be dangerous, but isn't everyone in danger if we don't figure out how your power, Skip's dark magic, and an impending world-ending flood all connect?"

"Maybe they don't." But that's wishful thinking. I feel it.

"Maybe," Georgie agrees, in that way she agrees with things she doesn't actually agree with because she always believes there's the possibility of something she doesn't expect. "Maybe the book will give us answers tonight."

The book. I forgot about the book. "Did Carol see it?"

Georgie shakes her head. "No. It disappeared when she walked in."

"It disappeared? By itself?" She nods. "Is that…normal?"

"There's not really any *normal* when it comes to magic books." She points to the book, now sitting on the chair she vacated earlier. "But it's back. That's all that matters."

I'm really not sure it's *all* that matters. Because the deeper we get into this, the more I realize my friends are putting themselves in real danger for me—and I'm not strong enough or educated enough in the matter to do the same.

I need my memories. I need a plan. I need a *list*.

"Everything will come with time," Georgie assures me, as if she can read my thoughts. I remind myself she probably can. "You're a Wilde."

And Wildes rise, I tell myself then.

No matter what—floods or magic or witch trials in gloomy Massachusetts towns filled with vengeful Puritans— sooner or later, even if it takes generations and descendants, we always, always rise.

I PUT IN A FULL, BUSY MORNING AT CONFLU-
ence, then I break to go to the Lunch House for my Lunch
with Leaders meeting—the chamber of commerce's monthly
social gathering with members and business owners considering membership.

Somewhere between appetizers and dessert I realize…
everyone here is a witch. I'm almost positive and I'm not
even sure why. I only know there is power humming through
the room.

It's disorienting. My normal, real life is flipped upside
down, and having to pretend I'm the same is taxing. But I
do it. With my customary smile, naturally. I head back to
the store, and I can feel Ruth the owl's eyes on me the entire
short walk back to Confluence.

Someone is always watching me. Protecting me. This has
been my life for a decade—and the only difference is that
now I know. I see.

Hopefully, I can do a little protecting of myself. No. Not hopefully. I *will*.

When I reopen Confluence after lunch, Georgie is already situated on the couch. I open my mouth to say something to her, but she holds up a hand. She's too deep in her books and doesn't want to be interrupted.

Normal Georgie.

And as cool as it is to fly, normal also feels really good.

I go through the rest of my afternoon and close up the store the way I usually do. I mark things off on my planner and reorder my to-do lists. I make sure to input the notes I had from lunch into their correct file on my phone. I don't let *magic* or *floods* distract me.

I like normal. I like predictable. I like order and control.

And then Jacob walks into my store and I wonder how much I really, truly like those things or how much they provide a certain kind of buffer from the emotions tearing around inside me.

It is six on the dot, as agreed. A punctual man. Be still my wildly beating heart. Yet I don't know what to *say* no matter how much I tell myself he's still just Jacob. Even if I now know what it feels like to be held against the tall, muscular length of him. Even if I now know what a kiss from Jacob *tastes* like. That doesn't change how we talk to each other.

Does it?

Ellowyn whirlwinds in, surveying the room with a scowl. "You've got to be kidding me. Zander's late with the food? I'm starving."

"Can't you just magic yourself a feast?" I ask.

"That's hardly the point," she says with a sniff. She drops her ratty backpack next to Georgie, who immediately begins to pull things out. Ellowyn and Georgie move furniture, discuss the correct placement of everything, set out candles and say things like *but we must honor the center,* which would have made me laugh last week. Tonight, I don't laugh.

Jacob and I stand where we are—him by the door, me behind the counter—and we don't say a word. It feels like my entire chest is in a vise and I don't know how to winch it open.

The door opens one last time to reveal Zander balancing pizza boxes from Redbrick. "Don't start bitching at me," Zander says by way of greeting, looking right at Ellowyn as he dumps the food onto the table.

Ellowyn rolls her eyes, even opens her mouth, presumably to bitch at him because he told her not to—but whatever she sees in Zander's expression stops her. I don't see anything myself, but I might be slightly distracted by the fact Jacob hasn't spoken.

And neither have I.

Which is certainly not *normal.*

"Come on and eat, Em," Georgie encourages me. "You've got to be starving."

I don't *feel* starving. I feel awkward AF. And when has that ever, *ever* been me? I move stiffly over to the open red pizza box. Jacob follows suit.

We eat our pizza, neither one of us adding anything to the conversation, while Georgie recounts Carol's visit this morning, Zander tells us a storm is coming—bad news for the ever-rising rivers—and Ellowyn mentions that Skip came in and bought a tea from her today.

"Why would he buy tea from you if he can make his own?" I ask. "With special Skip spells, or whatever?"

"I have the magic touch." Ellowyn waves a finger like she's inscribing symbols in the air. "And much to his everlasting chagrin, this half witch is far more powerful than him when it comes to spells."

"Don't leave us in suspense. What kind did he buy?" I demand. "Regretful Rooibos?"

"Let me guess, a meditation tea," Georgie offers. "For inner peace. Assuming he has an *inner*."

Ellowyn only smiles mysteriously.

"I'm thinking it had more to do with *enlargement*," Zander says with his usual grin and an overzealous bite of his pizza.

Ellowyn rolls her eyes as Georgie and I pull a face. I definitely do not want to think about Skip enlarging anything.

"Jacob? Your guess?"

But he shakes his head and refuses to play.

"Charm," Ellowyn pronounces with a certain relish.

Everyone blinks.

"Skip has become self-aware and realizes he's about as charming as a rock?" I ask.

"Or he's got someone in mind he wants to impress." Ellowyn waggles her eyebrows at me. "He wants to *charm* you, Em. You lucky duck."

"What does that mean?" Jacob asks. Of *course* that's the first thing he says since arriving.

"You didn't hear about the date?" Ellowyn says, clearly not hearing my *shut-up-now* messages in her head.

Zander crosses his arms over his chest so that he and Jacob match. A wall of masculine disapproval. "Is that a joke?"

"Skip invited me to dinner." I employ my best chamber of commerce smile. "Just a friendly, bury-the-hatchet meal between two St. Cyprian leaders. Like you do."

"You don't though," Zander returns.

"He tried to kill you," Jacob points out, with a calm that surprises me. Or might have if his eyes weren't doing that glowy thing that I can now reasonably assume means he's *pissed*.

"I don't think he knows that I know that, Jacob," I reply

loftily. "I subscribe to the keep-your-enemies-closer method of assassination attempts."

"I'm glad this is funny to you," Jacob growls, in a tone that has me gearing up for a *real* fight.

But Georgie steps between us, metaphorically, by waving her pepperoni slice in the air like a white flag. "You guys can argue about Skip later. Right now, let's try to figure out what Nicholas Frost gave us."

"I trust Frost as much as I trust Skip," Zander says, glaring at me. "Why are we even talking about that traitor?"

"Because of course if *you* think he's a traitor—even if we don't know anything about him except he's immortal—it *must* be true," Ellowyn challenges. I don't get the feeling she's challenging Zander because she truly believes in Nicholas. It's more because she's trying to protect *me*.

"Guys," Georgie says, more forcefully than usual. "We can fight each other, or we can fight what's happening. But we can't do both."

Zander sighs. Jacob says nothing—loudly. But Georgie takes my hand and leads me to the center of the room. Ellowyn looks disgruntled, but follows.

"We'll start with a circle around the two of you," Georgie tells us. "I'll make it. Once it's buttressed and protected, Zander and Jacob will create a bubble. It will block the magic from being seen or felt by any passersby." Her gaze grows stern as she looks from me to Ellowyn and back. "But they can only hold it for so long. So when you hear me tell you to end it, you have to pull back. Both of you."

"Pull back?" I ask.

"Georgie is going to keep us tethered," Ellowyn tells me. "My focus is on the spirits. Yours is on the book. You just relax, let the power flow through you, and trust your instincts. The spirits will do the rest. When you hear Georgie tell you to pull back, you cut the focus off. You let it go."

I assume this will make sense when it's happening, like flying, so I nod.

Ellowyn sinks down to sit cross-legged on the floor and motions for me to do the same. We sit facing each other, knees touching. Between us is the book Frost gave me. Georgie begins to make a circle around us, chanting quiet words of protection and insight. Ellowyn puts her hands on her knees, palms up, and then instructs me to put my hands on top of hers, palms down.

I comply and feel that zinging sensation, reminding me that we're really witches here. Real witches doing real witchcraft— not silly fools pretending someone else is pushing plastic around an Ouija board.

Once Georgie has finished with the circle, she nods to the guys. Zander stands behind Ellowyn, Jacob behind me. I can't see what Jacob does, but Zander holds out his hands— much like I did when I held off the adlets. Slowly, a glowing bubble like the one Jacob created this morning expands to surround us.

"Focus on the book," Ellowyn instructs me. "In your head, ask it for answers. Don't look at me or anyone else. Just the book."

I nod to show I understand, then look down at the book in between us. The dark black leather. The symbol of gold in the center. It's old. It has its own power, clearly. And it has answers.

It must.

Ellowyn begins to speak. She's talking to the spirits, asking them for wisdom and for the power to find what we seek. Our hands grow warm, and I want to look up and see if they're glowing, but she told me not to look. So I don't.

Look at the book. Focus on the book. Ask for answers.

Answers. Please, show us answers. Give me an answer.

I begin to fall into a rhythm in my head. Those words over and over. Power arcing between Ellowyn and me—though I barely feel her, barely think of her. It doesn't even feel like I'm in the store anymore. I'm in the air, but not flying. Alone.

Just me and the book.

There's darkness all around. An increasing blackness that reminds me of those dead adlets. A shiver runs down my spine, but I remember what Ellowyn said. Focus on the book. On the answers we need. The book opens, pages flipping in the wind I don't feel, but then vines begin to slither out of the dark, wrapping around the book.

Stop.

But it doesn't stop. The vines grow thicker, stronger, and yet nothing happens to the book. It grows harder and harder to see.

The necklace around my neck heats against my skin. Dimly, somewhere, I start to make out sounds.

"Let *go*, Emerson!"

Not just Ellowyn, not just Georgie. Everyone. Yelling at me to let go.

I try to look away from the book, from the vines like dread and that creeping blackness. I try to close my eyes, but something is holding me still. Something too dark. Too heavy.

The vines are around me. Holding me in place. Holding me immobile.

They slither up my body, then around my neck. I try to focus on my power, kill the vines like I killed the adlets, but I can't seem to access anything. I fight, but nothing happens. The vines pull tight—but when they touch the necklace Jacob gave me this morning, they change. Weaken, shrivel, then fall away.

It's then I can finally let go. Breathe. I'm in some kind of dank fog, but I think I'm back in the store. The book is gone. I feel more inside my own body.

I might even be me again.

Damn it, Emerson. When are you going to learn to listen? It's Jacob's voice in my head and he's bringing me out of that fog.

I couldn't, I tell him. *I couldn't.*

I fight to open my eyes. The candles are still burning, but the circle is gone. My friends are all looking down at me, laid out on the floor of the bookshop.

"I'm okay," I manage to say, even though my voice is croaky. "I couldn't get to you. I didn't hear you. I was lost."

Ellowyn takes a sharp intake of breath. I can feel Jacob's hands tighten on my shoulders.

"What do you mean?" he asks calmly, though his grip on me suggests he's anything but calm.

"I don't know." But they all look expectant and weirded out in equal measure, so I fumble for the words. "I was in the black. Just me and the book. Black everywhere. Then these vines crept over the book and over me, too. I felt…" I reach up to touch my neck, still throbbing from the noose of vines. Then I slide my hand down and close my hand over the necklace Jacob gave me this morning. "I felt this. Then I heard you. When I tried to let go, it wouldn't let me."

"What wouldn't let you?" Zander asks.

"The vines were trying to choke me. Stop me." We weren't protected, I realize, despite the steps we took. The bubble. Does that mean we couldn't have gotten any answers anyway? "It was a failure, wasn't it?"

Ellowyn shakes her head and points down at the book, now lying next to me. The book that was closed is now open. We all stare at it. Then Ellowyn nudges me and I push myself up to sitting position to take a look, suddenly aware of a kind of…new electric current underlying everything.

"Read it," Ellowyn directs me. "Out loud for the class."

I peer at the script on the open pages. It's flowy and faded and *old*. I feel like I shouldn't know how to read it. It's not English, but somehow…somehow the words arrange themselves in my language. In my understanding.

Jacob is still holding me upright, and I wrap my hand around his arm because I think I'm drawing some of that understanding from him.

"'A Confluence Warrior,'" I read out loud.

"'Their magic cannot be fully wielded unless or until they're faced with dark magic and fight it with the help of a conduit. This fight awakens their power—before caged and hidden. Once awakened, their power is one of the strongest raw forces in the universe. The first step in beating back the dark. The first step in balancing the imbalance. If the light can be wielded. If the right choices are made. The flood of dark can be stopped.'"

There's a silence. I look up. "That sounds a whole lot like me," I say.

"It does," Jacob agrees, and I'm too busy turning that over and over in my head to pay too much attention to his guilty tone.

I'm a…*Confluence Warrior*. I don't feel like any kind of warrior at the moment. My legs are weak and my head is pounding. I'm tired, but I keep staring at those words in a language I shouldn't be able to understand.

Confluence Warrior.

I shake my head, glad Jacob is still making sure I'm upright. "I didn't do any warrioring back there. The only thing that saved me was this necklace." I glance over my shoulder at Jacob, who looks vaguely stricken. "What's a conduit?"

Everyone exchanges glances in that way that's really beginning to grate on my nerves.

"It can mean a few different things," Georgie responds brightly. "In this case, I think it means someone whose magic complements yours. Someone who's...safe. On your side. Jacob was your conduit because you have a connection. Warriors and Healers often have complementary skills. So by fighting together, bleeding together, Jacob..."

"Unlocked the cage around your magic," Jacob says. "I was there. You touched my blood. Blood is memory, power. It unlocked what had been locked inside of you. But it didn't create it, to be clear."

Georgie stares at me, then Jacob. There's more she wants to say, but she doesn't say it. And I'm reminded of her talking about *fate* earlier.

This all seems to wrap around me, tight. Like a new sort of vine.

"Did Skip touch you?" Jacob demands. Out of *nowhere*.

I blink, uncomfortable. I feel oddly guilty, even though I've done absolutely nothing wrong. I've talked to Skip like he was a friend, rather than a nemesis. And Jacob is demanding to know if he *touched me* like he's allowed romantic possessiveness because of one kiss. It's a patriarchal weaponization of scarcity fearmongering—

And what does this have to do with anything? "Yes. We made mad, passionate love on the *sidewalk* while everyone watched."

Jacob looks as pained at that set of images as I'm sure we all feel. "No, not like that. Did he touch you *at all*? Shake hands? Bump shoulders? Anything?"

I think back to Skip walking with me. He had been oddly...*physical*. I wish I could lie about it, but I know now is not the time for my pride. "He put his arm around my shoulders. Took my hand and patted it."

Jacob nods then. "That's how he did it. He put some kind of dark magic in you."

Zander studies me. "You'd feel dark magic *in* her, wouldn't you?"

Everyone is now looking at me like I'm beneath glass. I can't say I like it, but I submit to it, the lingering sensation of those dark vines around my neck keeping me quiet.

"He wouldn't have to put it *in* her, just something *on* her." Ellowyn looks at Georgie, who nods. She grabs Zander's hand, and then Jacob's. They form an interlocking circle around me.

"More circles?" I ask, trying not to sound alarmed.

"Just give us a sec," Ellowyn says, her eyes already glowing. Light is already flowing, arcing around me.

The back of my hand burns, hot and sudden, so I lift it up to inspect it and my jaw drops.

There's a mark. On my hand. Red and ugly—so I know it's nothing normal or good. Besides, it's right where Skip touched me.

My friends drop their connection and Jacob takes my hand in his. He puts his fingers on it, but hisses out a breath. "I'll need to take her to the farm to really fix this."

Georgie makes a noise of agreement. "Go, then. We don't want to risk anything else until the mark is removed. Do you need us?"

"I have to get to the bar," Zander mutters irritably, rubbing his hands over his face.

"Best if I do it alone anyway," Jacob replies. "Clearly, too many suspicions have already been aroused. I'll take her back to the farm. Georgie, Ellowyn—you need to make sure the book is hidden. And we have to be more careful. Something is giving us away and we all know what that could mean."

They all launch into various actions, but I can't move. Not for magical reasons, but because I'm left with a paralyzing realization.

I was wrong.

I made a mistake. I'm the something that gave us away. There's no other explanation. I messed everything up by thinking I could handle Skip Simon and Nicholas Frost and the whole being-a-witch thing, just because I'm me and—

"Emerson?"

I look up at Jacob. His expression is blank. Because he's mad at me. He has to be. If I'd listened to him, to all of them.

"Ready?" he asks.

I swallow hard, but I nod and he takes my hand. Wind. Night sky. And then the farm. Not inside his house as I expected, but in the backyard. The moon shines above, but the rest of the sky is covered in clouds. Thunder even rumbles in the distance, bringing in that storm Zander mentioned. I can almost taste it.

"We'll have to be quick," he mutters to himself.

I look at the moon, at the little wisps of cloud try to tendril over the light, but it's almost like the moonlight is fighting them back. Cassie appears, whining softly. She has no snarky comments. She's simply there.

For me.

I lift up my hand. The mark is still red and ugly. I don't feel it anymore, but I see it. Like a brand. My stomach roils at the thought. "I thought I was safe on the bricks," I say quietly.

Jacob is making things appear. A table. Jars. Candles. "Everything I've been told, taught, believed my whole life says you should be. But he bartered his blood, his soul. The rivers are rising. You're a Confluence Warrior. Maybe the old rules don't matter anymore. Maybe we're *that* out of balance. Regardless, this mark can't hurt you on its own. There was some protection from the bricks. You had to be vulnerable for Skip to be able to reach you through it."

I like the idea of being vulnerable even less than being wrong. "We were protected. You made a bubble. Georgie made a circle. Ellowyn said the bookstore was safe. Centuries of witches made it safe."

"But you weren't protected from within, Em. Only from without."

"From within?"

"We'll get to it. First we have to get the mark off. Come here." When I do, he points to the ground. "Sit."

I do and he sits next to me. He takes my hand and places it on his knee. He traces the mark with some kind of wax or oil, then he places some mixture of dried herbs over it, like a poultice. He chants words and light sparkles from his fingertips. When I look up at his face, it's tight with concentration. He's controlling all that power, making it precise.

So serious. So focused. So gentle.

He uses the light of the moon, his own power, this combination of things. And the mark begins to fade. I feel the power surge all around me. The mark recedes before it, in it. And then it's gone.

Jacob doesn't look as spent as he has after the other healing episodes I've seen. That's good. But the bottom line is he did heal me. He removed the mark. *He's* cleaning up all my messes, over and over again.

And *I'm* the one who apparently has to make all the right choices to beat back the damn dark. I'm the one who's supposed to be a Warrior. Not just any warrior. A Confluence Warrior. An *extraspecial* warrior.

I feel...like someone else. Like a failure. Like I suck. Objectively.

Jacob frowns at me. "What's wrong, Em?"

"Everything I've done since I found out is wrong. Wrong choice after mistake after bad move. You all come in and sweep up my messes, but I just go make new ones. How can I beat back the dark when I'm not making *any* right choices here?"

"You only know about beating back the dark and Confluence Warriors because you went to Nicholas Frost," Jacob says, and he sounds patient. Reasonable. It's enraging. I want him to be as mad at me as I am. "Not every choice you've made is wrong, Emerson, even if we—if *I*—didn't agree with it. And even right choices can include mistakes along the way."

I don't want this either—being treated like I *didn't* make mistakes, when I know I did. "How are you going to absolve me for Skip?"

He sighs, his attention on my hand, still in his. "Ignorance. You're used to thinking of Skip as pointless and ineffectual and in a lot of ways he is. Dark magic is what changes his threat level. None of us thought he'd go so far as to get at you from the inside."

"You were mad at me this morning, and now you're not. Why?"

He gives my hand a squeeze and then does the most surprising thing. He brushes a kiss over where the mark used to be, and my heart stutters. "That he marked you is as much on me as you."

He reaches out and touches the charm he put on my necklace this morning. I remember the vines shrinking back.

"Your grandmother gave that to me after I brought you home and told her about the obliviscor," he tells me now.

"She talked me out of trying to take on the Joywood and gave me that charm to keep for you. She said I'd know when you were ready for it. I never understood why she didn't give it to Georgie or even Ellowyn. And so many times I thought, I should just hand it off to Georgie. She lives with you after all. But I never could. Your grandmother entrusted me with it, so it never felt right."

I peer down at the necklace. The miniature bluebell. My grandmother did love bluebells.

"I should have given it to you the minute you showed power," Jacob says. "Maybe you should have had it all along, but I never thought the time was right. I was waiting for a big sign. But if you'd had it, it would have stopped Skip from marking you."

"I had crystals from Georgie, charms from Ellowyn, and this pendant from Zander. I wasn't unprotected, Jacob."

There's a softness in his green gaze. "Now who's trying to absolve who?"

We're sitting in the grass, the clouds making the moonlight disappear. The two of us in the dark. I don't see them, but I suspect our familiars are somewhere close. It's peaceful here, connected to the land. Watched over by the night sky. It feels safe and protected. It's *restful*.

Self-blame isn't going to get us anywhere, I know that. I have to shake it off and make the right choices from here on out. But I've never felt more lost.

It's a wholly unfamiliar feeling, in fact. No extra time with my planners and lists is going to help.

I think back to the book. My hand is still on Jacob's knee. Jacob, who was there when I fought the dark magic that forged me. Who is the *conduit*.

"What does a conduit really mean?"

Jacob rubs his hand over his beard. "Georgie wasn't lying

to you. It's a complement. A key to help unlock what you already have."

"She wasn't telling me the full truth either."

"There *are* multiple meanings for *conduit*," he says, loyally. "Especially when used in older books, different languages. But the one Georgie is leaving out amounts to what we might call...a soul mate. She probably thought you wouldn't take that information kindly."

"Fate. Soul mates," I mutter, taking my hand off his knee. "Why should I take the idea of some outside force controlling me *kindly*? You wouldn't take *kindly* to fate telling you what to do either."

He frowns up at the last slivers of moonlight. "Except I don't care. Fate. Soul mates. Destiny. Spirits. Magic. I don't care about any of it. I know who I am. What I feel. What I want. If it aligns with all those other powers out there? Great. If not, it doesn't change what action I plan on taking."

I blink, because those words—what amount to a speech coming from Jacob—are some of the truest I've ever felt, deep and right. That's got to be better than fighting fate for the sake of it. Than worrying that every choice and feeling is outside forces pulling the puppet strings. I don't *feel* like a puppet. I feel like the woman I've always been, only more so. And I am all about making my own choices. Even with my decade-long mind wipe and memory transplant, courtesy of the Joywood, I charged along my own path, full speed ahead.

I pull my knees up to my chest. Lightning flashes in the distance. The storm is coming. I can smell the rain, feel the electricity in the air. I've always loved storms—I *am* a Midwesterner after all—but I've never had one feel like peace was on its way.

I rest my chin on my knees and look over at Jacob. He's

still studying the sky. His fingers dance over the grass, like he's communicating with the earth underneath us. I'm not sure I've ever seen *him* look so peaceful either. Even in those memories I can access with magic, there's an edge to him. It's the way he always holds himself so carefully *apart*.

But this is Jacob relaxed. Just him and me and the impending storm. He looks over at me, and for a moment my breath catches there in my lungs. His gaze holds mine.

Serious. True.

"If our fighting the adlets unlocked what you are, fantastic. I'll always be glad I was that key for you. No matter what happens."

I frown a little. What could happen? What would I *want* to happen?

"If I am your conduit, that's only another name for what I've always felt," he tells me, like the night all around us. That deep. That beautiful, like a vow. "It doesn't change anything. For me."

17

I'M RENDERED SPEECHLESS. MAYBE ALSO PARA-lyzed.

Except for the thunder in my heart.

Because Jacob and I don't *do* this. We don't admit things without prompting. Sometimes I push, but he always backs off.

Always.

The first fat raindrop lands on my nose. Another splashes on my arm. Jacob doesn't make a move.

"It's raining," I say dumbly. "We should go inside."

He looks at me as if I'm crazy for suggesting it. "A spring rain? It's great for healing. Growth. It'll be good for you."

"To lie out here in a rainstorm?"

"Nothing better," he says, and then lies back on the grass. Eyes closed, palms up, he just *lies* there as the rain slowly intensifies from droplets, to heavy droplets, on and on until it's pouring.

I don't know what else to do except follow his lead. It

must be some witch thing as I've never seen him *lying around in the grass* during a rainstorm. So I lay myself back too. The earth is cold, the rain is cool, but somehow *I'm* not cold. It's almost like there's a little heater around us.

The rain increases, pelting my face, my body, and soaking me to the bone. I screw my eyes shut and try to breathe through my nose. I'm tense and uncomfortable, about to give up and run for the house. Or think myself into a hot shower.

Then Jacob's hand clasps mine. And everything shifts. We're both lying in the grass, rain pelting down on us. I can hear thunder and occasionally see a flash of light behind my eyelids, but the storm itself is still a ways off.

Jacob's hand is holding mine and a kind of ease flows through me. My shoulders relax. I stop squeezing my eyes shut so tightly. I can breathe easy even as the rain pounds down on us.

Somehow I can feel every drop. Not so much in myself, but in him. Like he's a plant, soaking up the rain, the air, the feel of the wet earth beneath us. *This* is what recharges him, I think. Just like executing the perfect festival recharges me.

I remember what Georgie said when she was trying to avoid the words *soul mates*. Complementary skills, she said. Jacob and I have always fit together like puzzle pieces. My prodding, his patience. My wild ideas, his insistence on coming back to reality. Both too stubborn for our own good so we can't bulldoze over each other.

Is it fate? Or does it just feel like fate?

I turn my head to look at him to find he's already done the same. His eyes glow in the dark, and I wonder if mine do too. I think back to the masking spell Georgie walked me through to hide the gold. To hide who I am.

I don't want that. Not here. Not now. I want to be who I am, fully. In the rain. Next to Jacob. I think about the words

Georgie used, then try to say the opposite. I can feel something slip away—that mask.

Jacob rolls onto his side, propping himself up on one elbow as he studies me. Though it's dark, though it's wet, there's a faint light and a sweet heat encircling us. Maybe he cast a spell. Then again, maybe it's just him.

"Still not used to that," he says, indicating my eyes.

He's soaked through. His hair drips and his clothes cling to him. The thunder rumbling around us is closer now. Lightning crackles through the sky, though it hasn't fully broken. It's building and building, just out of reach.

"This might be a good time to try to get your memories back," Jacob says. "The storm is its own kind of power and protection. It would add to what I can do, or help you do."

I *want* that. With a pain and desire that's hard to breathe through. But there is a cascade of images in my head—Jacob hurting himself to protect me or help me, over and over again. I remember what Georgie said, so carefully. That he could push too hard. That he *would*.

"What if Carol felt it this morning? What if she's suspicious? We can't risk it."

He reaches out and smooths a wet tendril of hair off my cheek. "Carol's going to know eventually."

I want to accept that, because I agree, but something in me—something important and deep inside—knows better. "It isn't the right time. Not yet. Can't you feel that?"

His fingers rest on my temple, warm and gentle. After a few moments he nods. "I can." His fingers trail down my cheek, spreading so much heat I'm surprised the rain doesn't sizzle. "But I waited years for this to feel right, and then the years were taken away."

My breath comes out shuddery. I never expected Jacob to be able to make me weak-kneed with words, but here we are.

There's a wealth of difference in our past ten years. I was wholly unaware anything had changed. I thought we were doing that age-old dance and he was his typically intractable, obstinate self. If the situations were reversed, would I have been able to do what my friends did? Hide the truth for our own good? I don't think I could have. I don't think I would have understood the weight of it. I would have wanted to change it. I would have *insisted* on changing it.

I was sixteen and planning treason. Of course I wouldn't have accepted it if Jacob was mind wiped and I wasn't. No doubt I would have finally paid the price for all my arrogance.

Luckily for me, Jacob was the one who knew the truth. And he was the one who put up that wall between us to keep us both safe. I even understand why he did it. But... "I know you couldn't tell me about the witch stuff, but that didn't mean you couldn't..."

I'm at a loss for words. Nothing seems big enough for this. For us. *Date me? Kiss me?* It all sounds so childish, and maybe we were basically children back then, but we aren't now.

Nothing I'm feeling is remotely childish.

I will take this as my cue to leave. Cassie gets to her feet and lopes away, into the night. I barely notice, because I need Jacob's answer to this. His explanation.

"I don't understand the point of being with someone if you can't be who you really are." He shakes his head. "It was hard enough to be your hands-off friend and still only be half of myself. I can't imagine trying to have a deeper relationship like that."

"You surprise me." I need to remember. Everything. For many reasons, like the fate of the world. And informed consent. But I have to do it without arousing Carol's suspicions. And without getting my friends into serious trouble. Because something inside of me knows that would be bad. Disastrous—and not just personally.

I need to figure out a way to handle all this, to fix all this.

But right now there's Jacob. Right here.

"I'm a man of hidden depths," he tells me, his mouth curving, and I focus on him. Because he doesn't need fixing. He's Jacob, perfect as is.

I laugh while his fingers glide up and down my jawline. "*That* doesn't surprise me. It's when you let it show that I'm surprised."

He makes a noncommittal noise and his gaze is on my mouth. But he doesn't kiss me, and I don't make a move. It's my choice, isn't it? Ball's in my court. He's laid it all on the line. Doesn't that make it my turn?

With a surprising amount of hesitance, I reach up and fit my palm to his cheek. My hand glows—from when he took Skip's dark-magic brand away with his own earthy, stormy magic. I can still feel it—him—inside me, brighter and cleaner and wilder than the spring showers all around us.

"You're my conduit," I say.

"It looks that way."

"And maybe my fate."

His green eyes gleam. "Could be."

"I know I don't remember everything, but I don't remember a time I didn't want to be more than what we were. Even when I told myself I shouldn't, or I had things to accomplish first. It was still there."

"It's still here now." He is no more than a whisper away from my mouth. "I know you don't want me fighting that spell around your brain, but if what happened last time happens now—"

"If it hurts again, don't fix me. I'll be okay."

He frowns. "It isn't that simple. I'm a Healer, Em. It's what I do."

I drink him in. A *Healer*. Like Georgie said the day of the Redbud Festival. Witches aren't *what* we are. Witches are *who* we are, and this mantle of Healer is even more who he is. Jacob *has* to heal. But accepting that I have always known this to be true about him, even without understanding the *whys* or the *witches*, leaves an uncomfortable doubt in my head. "I wouldn't want you to kiss me just because you thought you could give me my memories back."

He gives me that slow smile that might have melted me into a puddle if I'd been standing. And wasn't already sopping wet in the rain. His fingers don't leave my face. My lips heat, tingle, and still he doesn't kiss me.

"I'll never kiss you if I don't mean it, Emerson."

And then, finally, he lowers his mouth to mine.

There's no pain. No wave of memories. There's only him. The rain. He pulls me to him, and I find myself...clinging to a man. *Me*. But isn't it funny? I don't feel powerless. I don't feel less. I don't feel swept away because I'm losing some part of myself.

This is Jacob.

This is a culmination of every good moment, every step back, every careful plan. It's light and it's power. *Power.*

The two of us together are power and light and *right*. I don't want to be anywhere else, feel anything else. I just want this moment, as it stretches out, as it gets hotter. I reach out for him, let every single loud thought be swept away by him.

I lose myself in him by finding us *with* him.

My heart is beating so hard I think it might do damage, but I don't stop kissing him or molding my body to his. I want more. I want so much more.

"Emerson." He's breathless against my mouth.

"Don't stop." I hold on to his shoulders, press my body to his. "We've waited so long. Don't stop it now."

The kiss is wild now. And there's an edge to it. Something unleashed in both of us, different but complementary. He tugs my shirt up, but there are buttons that make it difficult.

Or should. The next second my shirt is off. Gone.

Magic.

I laugh against his mouth. Because yes, this is magic. Finally. *Finally* the kind of magic we should have made a long time ago.

"Shouldn't we go inside?" I ask breathlessly. Because my shirt is off and while it's dark, we are *outside.*

"I'm a farmer," he says with that rare, incandescent wolfish grin. "I do my best work outside."

He presses a kiss to my collarbone. My stomach. He smooths his hands up my side, feeling, learning.

I sigh into the rain. Okay, outside it is. Outside is great.

He removes my pants and I realize he has me at a disadvantage. I'm in my underwear and he's fully clothed. It's hard to think past him kissing me, touching me, but I'll need to focus if I want his clothes off.

I think about that hot ball of power deep inside, and *poof.*

He stops kissing me and looks down. I managed the shirt, but the pants are still resolutely on. Though I think maybe I managed to undo the button.

Jacob looks at me and laughs. "You've come a long way in a short time."

"I meant to get rid of both."

He laughs again, and I want to live in that laugh forever. I don't hear it enough. Or see him smile enough. Part of it is his serious nature, but part of it is how these past ten years have weighed on him. I can see that now.

If I can take some of that weight off here and now, I have to. I need to. I want to.

God, how I want to.

"Allow me," he says, and his pants are gone, just like that.

Then he's kissing me again, our bodies intertwined, rain falling on us and if I'm not imagining things, actually sizzling at the heat of us.

Us.

"Em," he says, breathless. "Have you done this before?"

"Are we making *lists*?" I'm a little lost, but who cares if my brain can't catch up when I feel like this. When Jacob is *finally* touching me this way. "Do people really *make lists* and then *share* them?"

"Gods, no." He looks very earnest. *Concerned*, even. "But unless you've had a secret life, which is very…not you, I'm guessing you don't have a list to make."

"What are you, the purity police?" The rough palms of his hands slide up my legs and I want to…*do things*. All the things. "Why does it matter if I haven't actually gotten around to having sex? It's on my to-do list. One of them."

Jacob pauses. It seems to take him a long, long time to process those words. He pulls back. Stares at me with a weight I don't entirely get. It seems to hum in me. "Of course it is. As long as there's a list."

I lift a shoulder—a naked shoulder, outside, *in the rain*, and I don't even care. "Sex hardly seemed important when I had a whole town to run. Who has time to cater to male egos in the bedroom? I get enough of that in committee meetings, thank you."

He smiles, taking his time with it, and then lowers his forehead to mine. "Em."

And my name in his mouth like that is an incantation.

He gathers me against him, and the rain feels hot. Everything is hot. That power deep inside of me I'm understanding more every day, my skin, our breath tangling together. Because there is us here—the physical being of who we are, the science of desire and the culmination of that, but there is also magic. Power.

A rightness, bigger than anything I would have dreamed. Fate, maybe, but in this moment, I am all for fate.

Then Jacob is *inside* me.

In the startling joy of that, I come to the immediate conclusion that it's all true—the books, the songs, the poetry. People being *very* stupid over this sparkling, all-encompassing journey into what amounts to another world entirely.

I had no idea. I had no idea at all.

Him and me. Together. Tumbling into the unknown. All sparkling light. Like power but better, sweeter. Pulsing through me.

And I could tell you more. I could share every detail. I almost want to—but you know who I am by now. I'm not here for the objectification of women or men or the glorification of sensuality for consumer commodification.

Though let me tell you, any glorification would be underselling this.

Because that storm pales in comparison to the two of us. We put it to shame.

Twice.

Wow, I think, when I'm me again. Just me.

"That about covers it."

I'm really going to have to learn how to manage those inner thoughts.

Jacob stands, naked perfection in the moonlight, and now I know exactly how perfect he really is. He laughs down at me. "Stop objectifying me, Emerson."

I try for regal, though I'm lying on the ground, *naked* and *made new*, no big. "It's simple appreciation, Jacob."

He helps me to my feet, then just runs his hands down my arms. I open my mouth to ask him where we go from here, what this means. Because this has to change everything, doesn't it? I feel as different now as I did after I discovered I was a witch—but we didn't talk about what this might feel like. What we would do in the face of it.

We did not prepare a checklist.

But then, for once, I want to live in this very moment and not worry about anything else.

So that's what I do.

He gathers me up, and in seconds I'm neck-deep in a giant tub full of hot water. Flower petals float in it. Crystals are piled up in one corner, candles lit just about everywhere.

I blink, then look over the edge of the tub. He's pulling a towel from a closet and placing it on the counter.

Sadly, he's also fully dressed.

"You relax and enjoy," he says, reaching for the knob of the door.

"Where are you going?"

"I have to do some quick cleanup. I'll be back. You sit tight."

I frown as he *disappears*. The bath is nice and all, but who wants to sit around? Even with candles and crystals glowing prettily, it seems like a waste of time. I wash my hair and rinse off quickly. But I'm not about to *sit tight*.

I get out of the bath and grab the towel and dry off. *Sitting tight* is not what I do. I can't find anything in the bathroom to wear except the towel, so I wrap it around me and head out into the hall.

There are two other doors in this upstairs hallway. One is

closed and the other is open. I decide I'll be polite and only stick my nose into the open one. For now.

I glance in the open door. It's a bedroom. Fairly large. Very...masculine and therefore spartan. Except for a few spare candles and crystals, but even those are much more pared down than Georgie's usual fare.

"I could get you some of my clothes, but you could also just magic yourself what you'd prefer," Jacob says. He's entered the room behind me, perfectly dry and wearing new clothes.

But the window distracts me from worrying over my own clothes. It's huge, almost the size of the entire wall. Outside, the storm has cleared and the moon and stars cast their silvery light over rolling fields, down to the cemetery and the river, then across the water. The lights of St. Cyprian shine in a cluster that looks especially small and charming, cozied up to the river.

I can make out Wilde House and Confluence and all the other buildings and I get the odd sense that Jacob has spent years standing right here, watching out for me. Always watching out for me.

Not just me. St. Cyprian too.

A well of emotion waves up inside of me. I always thought Jacob didn't care about St. Cyprian. Not really. Not like I do. But he does. "Why do you live up here?" I ask, trying to make my voice sound less choked up and obvious.

And I know things have changed with us because he answers immediately.

"Town living isn't for me," he says. "Or Healers in general. We're introverts on the whole. We need a place to escape to that's quiet, that allows us to connect to the land. Where we can grow what we need to grow and commune with the air, the sky." He comes to stand behind me, wrapping his arms around me, and we both look at the view.

All I can think about is how well we fit. And always have. We always will, I think. Just like this.

Key. Lock. Us.

"You probably want to get back to Wilde House," he says quietly, but it's more of a question than the words make it out to be.

"Not tonight." I lean into him, melting my spine to his front. Letting him hold me. Holding him right back. "Tonight, I want to stay right here."

18

IN THE DEAD OF NIGHT, I'M NO LONGER IN Jacob's bed. And instead of Jacob's steady breathing next to me, I'm alone.

"Emerson, you have to stop doing this."

No, not alone. The voice is so familiar. Like mine, but scratchier.

I open my eyes and I'm in my store. My sister is pacing the length of the bookshop. Her dark hair is wild around her, her arms crossed over her chest. She looks different than the last time I saw her, but the same, and it takes me a few moments to realize the difference is simply…age. The ten years that have passed since I last saw her in person. Not to mention the tattoos and piercings our parents forbade her when we were kids.

"Rebekah."

Sometimes I see her in my dreams, but this is different. Because she looks like she should in this time and place, not just the girl I remember at eighteen.

I don't know what this is. Maybe a dream, though it

doesn't feel like one. A memory? But we're us, in the here and now. Some kind of vision? Maybe...

"You're going to get us both in so much trouble," she's muttering. To me. To the store. To herself. "I don't know why you keep doing this."

But I don't know what I'm doing. I don't know why she's mad. Then again, I've never known why she's mad. She's always mad. I concentrate on delight instead—also, historically, my choice. "Rebekah, you're *here*."

She whirls to face me. "You keep *pulling* me here, Emerson. I've tried to ward you off. Not easy when you can't use magic, in case you wondered. You want me mind wiped too?"

I'm taken back. But a familiar feeling sweeps through me. Sisterly irritation.

"Not everything that happens in the world is an attack on you, Rebekah," I retort.

"Says the person who thinks said world revolves around her," my sister shoots right back.

"Now, now," a new voice says. So familiar my eyes prickle with tears. I turn slowly toward the voice, and there she is. Grandma, standing behind her counter like always. Like she's still here. Alive and well.

"No bickering today, girls," she admonishes us.

Maybe it's a memory. But I look down at myself and I am me in the here and now, not young, not someone else. Rebekah looks as shocked as I feel. And maybe also as moved.

"Grandma," she whispers, and I wonder if it's worse for her, because she's not here every day, surrounded by all these memories and monuments to Grandma and our history. Or because she didn't come home for the funeral—couldn't, I remind myself—and it feels like a weight is lifted off me now that I know why.

"We only have so much time." Grandma holds out her arms. "Come now."

I'm almost too afraid to move. She can't be real. This is a dream. But when I move forward, it's just like it always was. She is real. She is here, wrapping one arm around me and the other around Rebekah.

We're both crying into her shoulders. And as she holds us—really holds us—I can feel the strength in her arms. I can smell her.

"It's time, my dears," she says softly, still holding on to us. "My two sides of a coin. You are the sign. The moment. I've done all I could, and now it is your turn. Be brave. Be strong. Lean on each other. Believe."

"St. Cyprian is mine and I am St. Cyprian's," I say, as if my grandmother drew the words out of me. Because she did. Because those words were the talisman she gave me, long ago. A magical chant—one that survived my mind wipe. I may not have known it was magic, but it was mine. Given to me by her.

"Time is mine until time takes me home," Rebekah whispers. Her own words. Her own chant.

I *remember.* That memory I saw in the bookstore, it was Grandma giving us those words. Those reminders of who we were.

"You are our hope. Never forget you have everything you need. Right here." Grandma pulls back and looks at each of us. She puts a hand on my cheek, then Rebekah's. "I'm always with you."

Then she's gone.

I reach out to where she was with a cry, but there's only air. Rebekah turns to me, eyes full of tears. She opens her mouth to say something, but then she's gone too. Just like Grandma.

I wake up—really wake up—and I'm not at home in Wilde

House. I'm not in Jacob's bed like I should be either. I'm at the cemetery. Kneeling in front of my grandmother's grave, tears streaming down my face. Cassie is curled up next to me. The sun is just beginning to rise over St. Cyprian across the river. The fox seems to regard me too solemnly.

I don't know how I got here, and all I want to do is lie there with Cassie and cry some more. That dream was no memory, no figment of my imagination. I saw and talked to Rebekah. My grandmother was *there*. She touched me.

I try to tell myself I'm being silly. That it was just a very vivid dream, but I can't get over the feeling she was here. Talking to me. And Rebekah.

You are our hope.

I get to my feet. The charm of my grandmother's that Jacob gave me glows against my neck. I lift it up. Something seems different about it, but I don't know what. I suck in a deep breath and wipe my eyes.

When I turn to head back to Jacob's, I realize that he's here. Standing a few yards away, that giant buck by his side. He gives me the time and space and waits for me to walk over to him.

"What happened?" I ask him, and I'm reminded, again, that things are different because I don't try to pretend I'm okay.

His green gaze moves over me like he's checking for more dark marks. "You got up out of bed and started walking out here. Cassie was waiting at the door to walk with you. It seemed peaceful, so I didn't try to wake you up. Just followed at a distance to make sure you were okay." He slides his arm around my shoulder. "Come on. I'll get us back to the house."

"I think I need to walk." I need to breathe fresh air and process what happened. Who I saw. Who I *touched*.

Jacob nods. He takes my hand and we just…walk back toward his house. We walk past the redbuds, still looking healthy and pretty, about to turn from their evening white to their morning pink. We take the path out of the cemetery and into his fields. The morning air is cool, the sky turning pretty shades of pink. The wet after last night's storm doesn't seem to touch us. Everything is quiet, beautiful, and the barbed grief inside of me begins to soften and smooth out.

"What does it mean when people say Rebekah and I are two sides of the same coin? We aren't alike at all."

"I think you know that isn't true. You have your differences, but at your core you're both very similar. That being said, it isn't about your personalities. It's the prophecy."

"There's a *prophecy* about me?" How has no one mentioned this?

"Not necessarily about you. You were born on the first day of the year, Rebekah on the last. It's supposed to mean great power. For any siblings. In any witch family. Sometimes even cousins. But..." He shrugs.

"I do have great power," I remind him.

"Yes. You do," he agrees. "Perhaps Rebekah does too. Perhaps you'll fulfill the prophecy." He says all of this like it's very run-of-the-mill, everyday stuff. Not prophecies and magic. "But the Joywood made sure to make everyone believe you didn't."

Grandma's words come back to me. The feel of her *right there*, and I want to cry again, but not here. Not in front of Jacob.

Cassie trots ahead while Murphy moves quietly off into a field of corn. Jacob holds my hand and says nothing, just walks beside me. It's exactly what I need. By the time we reach the porch, I almost feel normal.

"I hope you're hungry," Jacob says as we walk into the house.

I smell bacon immediately, and my stomach rumbles. "Starving." I follow him to his kitchen, where a veritable banquet is laid out on the big table.

"Farmer's breakfast," he says with a wink. "Courtesy of my mother."

"Your mother?"

"I don't ask questions. Sometimes I wake up and there's a breakfast waiting for me. Today, I'm not going to ask why and just tell myself it's a happy coincidence that there's enough for more than me."

"Do you think your mother knows...?"

He grabs a plate and hands it to me. "I'm not going to ask myself that question, Emerson."

I fill my plate and he fills his and we sit at the table like this is normal. Habit. It feels like we've always done this. I feel like we could.

We eat with Cassie stretched out at my feet. Jacob mentions the storm, the rising river levels. It's a very mundane morning-after conversation, but once I finish my food, he looks at me in that rock-steady way of his and asks, "Do you want to tell me what happened? What got you up?"

"I..." I look down at my plate. Everything is delicious. I'm beyond stuffed. And Jacob has given me the time and space to refuel and settle myself before asking.

My instinct is to declare that I'm fine and change the subject, but I don't.

I look up at him and something inside of me...expands. I'm not sure what this is, what I feel, and I don't particularly care for uncertainty. It makes me uneasy, but his green eyes are like anchors. Keeping me right here in this sweet, happy, safe moment.

I don't mean to start talking, but I do. I tell him about the dream. I have to swallow at the emotion that slams into me. My grandmother was *there*. She hugged me. "Grandma appeared."

Jacob nods as if that makes any kind of sense. "I figured,"

he says when he notices my quizzical look. "Why else the cemetery? Her grave. It had to be your grandmother."

"So it was...it was really her?" I blink back tears again. "She hugged me, Jacob, and I swear it was real."

"It was her spirit, definitely," he tells me. "As for the corporeal form? It's more a kind of projection. Witches can make certain...allowances with their spirit after they've left this world. Not all the time, and conditions have to be right. She can't reach into your dreams whenever she wants or appear, like, at this table. And the magic required from beyond would be a lot harder to wield to get to you all the way across the river in Wilde House. A lot more dangerous too. She probably couldn't reach you until you were sleeping on this side of the river."

Fate. Conduit. It's an uncomfortable feeling to think I'm only here because the universe, or my grandmother, wants me here. Shouldn't I have more of a say than that?

But I look at Jacob, and he's perfect. In every way. Maybe I should trust that fate knows what it's doing. My grandmother, my she-ro, was always sure she knew exactly what she was doing.

"What about Rebekah?" I ask. "She didn't seem like a dream either, and she's not dead." I press my hand into the hollow of my chest. "I would know if she was dead."

"I think it's what she said. Whether you mean to or not, you're drawing her—or her spirit—into your dreams."

I blink. "It really was her."

Jacob nods as if that was a question. "It would make sense. You have a lot of power and you're new to it. We spend years learning how *not* to drag people into our dreams—but you can't remember any of those lessons."

I can't get agitated about my altered memories, because I saw my grandmother and my sister today. I'm not sure how to wrap my head around that. Or the fact I'm sitting at Jacob's kitchen table. Eating a breakfast his mother made. After *having sex* with him last night.

It's enough to have me feeling vaguely light-headed. But that won't work. There's too much to do.

You are our hope.

I get to my feet and take my dishes to the sink. "Thank you for breakfast. Or thank your mom for breakfast, I guess. I can clean—"

He waves a hand and everything disappears. "No need."

I blink at my empty hands and the sparkling, empty table. "That's a handy trick I wish I'd known I could do for the past ten years."

He grins at me and that *expanding* feeling is back, but something else rushes in with it. Pain slithers down from my temples, into my neck. I hiss out a breath.

Jacob is by my side in a second. He puts his hand to my head and I know he's going to try to heal it immediately. Like it's a reflex.

I push him away. "No, don't." Maybe it's silly, but I don't want him rushing in to heal every little pain. I need to feel it. To understand. I hold up my hand to ward him off. "I think things are happening inside of me. Fighting inside of me. That sounds crazy."

Jacob takes another step toward me even as I still hold my hand out. "Let me see."

I open my mouth to argue, but he takes my hand gently. And he isn't prying in or healing or whatever it is he does, I can tell. He's holding my hand, waiting for...permission, I guess. It makes me want to cry. Then kiss him some more.

"I promise, I won't do anything you don't want me to," Jacob promises me. "It's more of a...diagnostic scan."

Better to know, right? And depending on what he sees, we'll know what steps to take. I like *steps*. "All right."

His hand is warm around mine. "Let's go into the living room. It'll be more comfortable."

Jacob settles me on the couch and takes a seat next to me. Cassie pads in from the kitchen, yawns, then sits at my feet.

He takes my hand and situates it with the back resting against his palm. Then he covers my hand with his other one. He slows his breathing, closes his eyes, and I should probably chant witchily or something, but instead I...watch him.

The power simply radiates off him. It takes my breath away. What he can do. Who he is. I feel him, a bright heat around me, inside of me. It's all very calming. I almost feel like drifting off into sleep, but my eyes remain open.

"I think what I'm seeing," he says after a while, his brow furrowing, "is your magic fighting off Carol's from back when she wiped you." He releases my hand. "It's still in you. It doesn't go anywhere. It's like that fog, but there's something of you beating it back."

"But I still can't remember everything. And Skip just... *branded* me. If I'm fighting off Carol's magic, why couldn't I fight off his?"

"It wasn't Skip's magic. It was dark magic he bartered for." The look on his face tells me what he thinks about bartered power. "Maybe with more time you *would* have fought it. The bottom line is that your internal, inherent magic is just as strong as Carol's, Em. If not stronger. And that's not supposed to be possible."

Because of you.

"No," he says, and I realize with a start that what I *thought* and meant as a *private thought* winged its way into his head. Again. I'm really going to need to get a lot better at controlling that.

"Because of us," Jacob says firmly. "The power is within

you. Fighting Skip's dark magic together helped unlock it—that's all."

It wasn't just the fight. Maybe that unlocked my power, but it's the two of us finally getting closer that spurred on the fight within me. He doesn't want to say it, and I don't want to either. It sits there so strangely inside of me. Much like fighting back Carol's spell, this is a fight too—between my belief in free will and controlling my own destiny and the absolute certainty that being with Jacob is *right*.

It's always been right.

I just want to make sure it's my choice.

"So, this fight is going on inside of me? All the time?"

"I think so. Carol's obliviscor ritual is a spell. Because it has to change how you perceive the world—not just destroy or create something—it's ongoing. It sits in you like a fog—a tangible thing, at least to someone like me. If you have little to no power, it sits forever."

"Even if Carol dies?"

Jacob nods. "The spell is the spell. Once created, it's going to exist until someone ends it. In this case, your power is trying to. And certain things give your power a boost. The rituals, the healing, and so on."

"*And so on* meaning sex."

He clears his throat. "Possibly."

I roll my eyes. "Don't be missish about it."

"That's not what I'm being. Since I'm not a twelve-year-old girl."

"Twelve-year-old girls are fierce and *fantastic*, Jacob, so we can agree. You are not one, poised on the cusp of woman-hood and hovering on the verge of entering a society that will do its level best to make her hate herself, yet still capable of joy and childlike wonder."

He knows me, so he ignores that small rant as he gets to

his feet. "The problem is the obliviscor remains shrouded in some mystery—only fully understood by those who have the power to perform it. I can only theorize that Carol might *feel* her spell being fought against. It's unlikely it would just… disappear without her feeling something." He begins to pace a little, like it helps him think to move. "She might not be able to understand the exact source, but she'll begin to suspect."

"I think she already does after yesterday morning's impromptu visit."

Jacob rubs his hand over his beard. "But she left unsure. If she was sure, she would have accused you right there. Maybe your power is hiding it. She feels an imbalance herself— inside of her or her spellwork—but she doesn't know why."

I like the idea my power is protecting me without me being fully cognizant of it all, though I wouldn't mind some stronger understanding and purpose in the here and now. The things I could *do* if I understood more.

Heaven forbid you trust someone beside yourself.

I frown at Cassie, but Jacob is continuing to think aloud.

"But that won't last forever. She'll look into it. She'll figure it out, and when she does…" He trails off. He's still now, looking away from me. Out the living room window, almost as big as the one in his bedroom. But through this one I can only see rolling fields, not the river or the city on the other side. It's a different kind of perfect, here in another part of this beautiful place we get to live.

But we're talking about Carol Simon, who has the right to mind wipe me if she likes. Again.

"When she does?" I prompt him.

Jacob slowly turns back to face me. His expression is grim. "She'll have to accuse all of us. We helped you use power without approval. We hid it from the Joywood. The punishment likely would be to wipe all of us."

"People wouldn't accept that. We're not a bunch of teen-agers any longer."

"It would be seen as merciful, Emerson. We have ruling covens for a reason. Power grabs lead to situations like Salem, when individual covens tried to go it alone. We all take blood oaths to support St. Cyprian."

There's a finality in the way he says that. But then, my oaths have always been to St. Cyprian. Not to Carol Simon.

"I have power though."

"You do."

I stand. I know he doesn't want to hear what I'm about to say, but it's as true now as it was back in what memories I do have of magic. And treason. "It isn't right that we're afraid. It isn't right that we didn't feel comfortable going to them about the mistake they made with me and how *amazing* it is that they were wrong, because I saved both of us."

"Emerson—"

"We had a plan once."

"It came at too great a price."

I know he means that, but... "We're stronger now, Jacob. We could win this time. If we don't try, they *will* win. If we don't fight, we guarantee that we lose."

He rakes his hands through his hair, but he doesn't immediately argue with me. I hope that means he's thinking about what I said. And likely beginning to acknowledge I'm right.

Because I am.

"We have to be ready. We have to prepare. Maybe we lose," I say, though I know we won't. We can't. We can find the answers and fight and win. We were *meant* to, I'm sure of it. Isn't that what my grandmother said? *You are the sign. The moment.* "But we lose if we don't fight. Automatically. So we need to mount an offense, like we always planned. We have to, Jacob."

Because we all know I can't hide my power forever, don't we? It's only a matter of time.

I really hope that he hears *that* thought, but I can't tell. What I can tell is that he doesn't *like* the idea, but he's also not arguing. Not refuting me. Deep down he knows I'm right no matter how much it might worry him. Or so I tell myself as I wait for him to respond.

"Even with a full coven, they'll need help," he says. And I know he's on my side. "They'll want to wipe all of us at once, and to do that they'll need a full moon. A real ritual, not that sudden attack they pulled on you. Something big."

"Couldn't she pick us off one by one?" I ask. "Or the whole Joywood could just...take turns?"

"Yes and no. If she wipes us out altogether, there's less chance that one of us might manage to escape. Run away. Hide. Fight back. She'll want to blight out what she'll see as a rebellion—or at least a repudiation—in one blow. With no warning. And theoretically the other coven members are powerful in their own right, but they don't do things without Carol. They like to move as one. And she likes to have their full power behind her."

I consider all of that. I make a few mental pro and con lists. "When's the next full moon?"

"The sixteenth."

I nod. Decisively. "Then we have two weeks to prepare." To prove we're necessary. Not just to Carol.

But to everyone.

I MARCH INTO THE KITCHEN AT WILDE HOUSE, ready for *all the fights*, to find Georgie is sitting at the table.

"Can I charm a planner?" I demand, as if this is of critical importance to the upcoming battles. In my defense, I feel like it is. "Can I make it self-sticker, for example?"

Georgie looks up from her coffee, eyebrows raised. "That cannot possibly be the first thing you say to me this morning."

I frown at her. "What am I supposed to say?"

"After spending the night at Jacob's? I don't know, *anything* about that."

"Oh, well…" I trail off.

"Wait, wait, wait. Don't start without me." Ellowyn appears right next to the coffeepot. She immediately grabs a mug and begins to fill it. I'm still standing in the entry of the kitchen, holding my uncharmed and unstickered Joan of Arc planner.

Ellowyn takes a seat next to Georgie and they both look at me expectantly.

"You don't want to sit around talking about *boys* when we have more important things to discuss," I say in withering tones. "Have you ever heard of the Bechdel test?"

"Many times," Georgie says sadly. "It's your favorite lecture. I still like boys."

"Em, don't take this the wrong way, but bullshit." Ellowyn crosses her ankles and props her legs on the chair next to her.

"Excuse me?"

"This isn't talking about boys. It's talking about you and Jacob, after years of *painfully* dancing around each other, finally doing something about it. The emotional ramifications are pretty big and important to your actual *life*, so drop the crap and tell us what happened. Because it's your life and we're your friends."

I have to take a moment. Because, well, Ellowyn is right, and mostly I was trying to change the subject because...

It *is* big and important. It was life-altering. And I'm still not sure what to do about that with words like *conduit* and *soul mate* rattling around in my head, making me...itchy.

Jacob might be the man for me, but I'm still working on reconciling this fate stuff. And I don't really feel comfortable putting that into words. Not until I have a better handle on it. A better understanding of what I feel and what it *means*.

I clear my throat. "I spent the night with Jacob, yes."

"Don't be euphemistic, Em. Did he take care of business or not?"

"Ellowyn," Georgie scolds.

Ellowyn shrugs, unfazed. "Well?"

"I... Yes, we had...sex."

"And?" Ellowyn prods. "Good? Bad? Oh no, was it indifferent? That's somehow the worst."

"It was not indifferent," I return, starting to feel edgy and irritable instead of full of purpose. Like I should be. "I don't want to talk about this," I mutter, whirling away. Dissecting it feels too close to... I don't know, but we have work to do.

"It's okay, Em," Georgie says gently, though I hear the distinct sound of her kicking Ellowyn and Ellowyn's feet hitting the ground. "You don't have to tell us anything if you don't want to. If it's private."

Still, when I turn back Ellowyn is smirking at me, like she thinks I'm a coward. A *coward*. And even though I know she's only doing it to get under my skin, it works.

"It was amazing," I declare. "Better than anything I've imagined, and I've imagined plenty. Jacob is *built*, and it was...magic. All that power and whatever else magic is, but physical and us and better."

And oddly enough, I feel better once I say this.

Georgie sighs dreamily and Ellowyn's smirk melts into a smile, and I have the strangest urge to laugh and cry at the same time. I sit down on a chair and lay my head on the table, using poor, martyred Joan as a pillow. "Why is that *terrifying*?"

"Because you can't control him," Ellowyn says, and it isn't just in her usual blunt, tell-the-truth way. There's something like a well of experience behind those words. "Or it."

I raise my head. "I don't need to control him. Or it."

Both my friends give me dubious looks.

"I *don't*."

Ellowyn snorts. "Em. Let me introduce you to yourself. You like control."

"Who doesn't like control? That isn't what's scary. You guys keep talking about fate and all that. That's what's scary."

"Because you think fate might be controlling you?" Georgie asks.

Ellowyn sighs. "You should try a curse."

"It's not that," I mutter.

They don't argue with me, likely because they are right. And I can't control this conversation or the situation or my wildly flailing feelings, and I don't like any of that.

I'd rather point my energies toward a situation I can actually *do something* about. "Can we focus on what's important?" I ask, sounding and feeling delightfully officious.

Georgie looks bewildered. "More important than spending the night with Jacob?"

I ignore her. "Jacob did some kind of diagnostic scan on me——"

"I just bet he did."

I scowl at Ellowyn. "He says I'm fighting back Carol's obliviscor spell on my own. It's sort of happening inside of me. But I'm winning. Which means..."

Ellowyn's self-satisfied smirk fades. "We're all in deep shit."

"But..." I look around the house. This is Wilde House. Surely we're protected here.

Georgie nods, and I don't know if she can read my expressions or if I projected that. "We don't need a bubble here. Say what you need to say."

I sit straighter. "The Joywood can be taken down. Completely. I don't think it's right that we're afraid of them when we should be looking to them to handle this flood, at the very least. Our governing body should be honest. Above fear. They shouldn't go around deciding people are *spell dim*, and then wiping people who don't align with their exact principles, especially when those people are trying to stave off a catastrophe."

I expect the small silence. I'm not expecting it to go on as long as it does.

"You're suggesting *we* fight the Joywood?" Ellowyn asks dubiously. Eventually. "To like...take them down?"

"That's...treason," Georgie whispers. "Not human treason, where there's a court of law and arguments. Witch justice is old-school. Obliteration, a lifetime of torture, you know. The good stuff."

"It's not treason if you pull off the revolution," I reply.

Georgie closes her eyes as if in pain, but Ellowyn studies me with shrewd eyes. "We don't have a full coven. Putting aside the fact we're inexperienced and the Joywood are the ruling coven of the whole, entire world, we'd need a Praeceptor and a Diviner to be at full power."

"Do we need a full coven? Maybe we could fill in those slots after the fact. People will line up."

Assuming people line up for coven slots and maybe audition, and I realize I'm thinking it's like some reality show. What do I know?

"That's...optimistic, Em," Georgie says softly. "And you're assuming all of us *want* to be the ruling coven in the first place."

I stare at her. "Your favorite song is 'Everybody Wants to Rule the World,' Georgie."

She inhales, then lets out a gusty breath. "I don't know. I do know that if Carol has any inkling what's going on we won't have the time to figure it out."

I tell them what Jacob said about full moons. Then I tell them about my "dream" and what my grandmother said to me. "This is why it's up to us to stop the flood. If the flood is dark magic, we won't *have* a Joywood or a town if it wins."

"I don't think the Joywood are going to thank us," Ellowyn says darkly.

"Let's put the Joywood aside for a moment. We need to stop a flood. That's our primary objective."

Ellowyn taps her fingers on the table. "But your grand-mother wasn't talking to just you in your vision. She was talk-ing to you *and* Rebekah. Which means we need Rebekah."

"I thought you guys said she couldn't come back."

"She isn't *supposed* to," Ellowyn says with a shrug. "We also aren't *supposed* to lie to the Joywood. But I'm not going gently into that mind wipe—that's for sure. I'd rather die, thanks."

"I believe that was Emerson's take about ten years ago," Georgie retorts. "And look what happened."

"Be that as it may…" Ellowyn gives me that shrewd look again. "Rebekah always fancied herself a Diviner. Maybe we need her, to make a coven to fight the flood? We'd still be one short, but—"

"Frost," Georgie whispers.

Both Ellowyn and I turn to her. She looks a little pale. Georgie was not built for speaking truth to power in the same way I was, and still I know—I *know*—she belongs right here in the thick of it. For her knowledge alone.

"Nicholas Frost is a Praeceptor. That would, in fact, make us a coven. If we can get Rebekah back. If we could get Frost to join us. We could have a full coven to fight against the flood."

And then stand against the Joywood. But I don't say that out loud, of course, because we are taking one threat at a time.

"I know this isn't fair," I say. "Because of me, because of what I am, you guys have been forced into risk and danger. Maybe there's a lesson in what happened though. I can't talk my way out of a mind wipe. But surely we can *prove* our way out of one."

There's a beat of silence, then Ellowyn nods firmly. We look at Georgie. She grimaces, but nods too.

"Tonight's agenda." I start ticking things off on my fingers. "How do we stop a flood? How do we get Rebekah here without the Joywood knowing? And how on earth do we convince Nicholas Frost to join our coven?"

"All before the potential mind-wipe full moon," Georgie adds. "But no pressure."

My grin widens. "Good news. As you know, I *excel* at deadlines."

ANOTHER FULL DAY ZOOMS BY. BOOKSTORE
business. Chamber of commerce business. I'm checking
things off my to-do lists right and left, and reading through
the book Frost gave me in little increments between all I
have to do.

I have too much on my plate to think about Jacob. About
our night together. About what changes between us from
here on out. Or maybe I think about it too much, but I try
not to, because I'm a grown woman with her own busy life.

Georgie gets a call from her uncle and has to head to the
museum in the afternoon. I convince her that I'm comfortable enough now in my power to protect myself, and promise
to call out if Carol or Skip approach me. But the remainder
of my day passes in an almost normal fashion.

Except that I'm still a witch.

When it's time to close up, I go through my normal ritual,
but I magic the book Frost gave me back to my room in
Wilde House because I don't want to be caught carrying it

around. When I'm finished closing up, I step outside into a pretty spring evening, the sun just beginning to set over the confluence.

Three rivers. Not two. Which makes me look up at the sign hanging above my door. I always thought the logo of Confluence was two rivers, and it doesn't change, no matter how many times I whisper the revealing words.

But I realize I never questioned that third line. I thought it was a crack in the paint. But it's the third river. Narrow, but blue. Purposeful.

I exhale. So many things have always existed right in front of me, without spells or glamours or masks, and I just didn't pay enough attention. I didn't *see*. I didn't understand enough to see.

I shake my head and then turn away from the door. I see Carol come out of a shop across the street at the same time. *Should have magicked home.* But I smile and lift my hand in a wave, then begin to walk home to Wilde House without looking back to see if she wants to talk.

My heart is beating hard and I have to work hard to keep my breathing even and calm. I don't want to face Carol with all of these *thoughts* of floods and treason and magic swirling around inside of me. My acting skills leave something to be desired, and the more I understand this world I'm a part of, the more I'm going to have trouble convincing everyone I'm a clueless, spell-dim, mind-wiped witch.

But Carol doesn't call out, and if she follows me, she does it at a distance.

I look out over at the river as I walk up Main Street. I see Jacob and Zander on the river path, clearly walking toward Wilde House from the ferry. I can't hear them—we're too far away—but they appear to be casually chatting as they walk.

No sense of urgency or *treason* waving off of them like it feels it's waving off of me.

It's one thing to discuss these things in private. It's a lot scarier out here, when Carol or the other Joywood members could be lurking anywhere, ready to wipe us all.

We meet at the porch of Wilde House at about the same time. I know I should greet them both with an easy friendliness for any potential witnesses—and because I'm a grown-ass woman—but I can't seem to look at my cousin. I only look at Jacob. Something inside me is twisting in a million knots, and I do not feel my confident, certain self.

I feel like a stranger. And Jacob says nothing. We just stand on my porch and…stare at each other. As if Zander isn't there at all. I don't know what to say when what I really want to do is disappear with him. For a bit. Maybe a few bits. But we have work to do. Before either of us says anything, Zander makes a sound of disgust and disappears into the house before us.

I open my mouth to say something, *anything* to get rid of this annoying anxiety inside of me, but Jacob speaks first.

"Don't look back, but Carol's watching us from down the street."

It is a physical fight not to look.

"Why don't you pretend to get mad and huff inside?" he says casually.

"Firstly, I don't huff." Jacob's disbelieving expression makes it easy to pretend to get mad. I scowl. Gratefully. "Secondly, why do we want her to think I'm mad at you?"

"I think it's best if Carol doesn't think to wonder why we're all together every night."

Touché. "Fine," I mutter. "I will *pretend* to huff, something I've never once done, and you would never ask a man to pretend to do."

I can tell he's fighting a smile. "I'll walk back to the ferry, then disappear. She'll think I transported home, but I'll transport into Wilde House."

"Fine," I say with enough volume and frustration that anyone walking by—or spying, in Carol's case—would think I'm pissed at Jacob. I step inside and slam the door closed behind me. The slam feels good. I do not *huff*.

I can hear my friends in the living room, so I hang up my coat and sling my bag on the bench, then go to join them.

"Where's Jacob?" Ellowyn asks.

"Practicing subterfuge," I announce, as if it was my idea. "He'll be here in a minute."

There's a spread of sandwiches and salads, so I know Ellowyn handled the food. Not because she loves lighter fare, but because Zander hates it. I begin to wonder if they're going to be able to get along well enough for us to really become a coven, but I suppose that's getting ahead of myself.

Priority one is protecting ourselves and the town. I put food on my plate and settle myself on the couch next to Georgie. Octavius meows and ostentatiously begins to groom himself between us.

Jacob appears after a few more minutes. He fills his plate and sits on the fireplace hearth so that he and Zander look like fireplace sentries.

It strikes me, perhaps more forcefully than it should, that he's not hanging at an exit. He's settled himself in the thick of things. It seems…symbolic somehow. Important. And I am far more moved than I should be by a choice of seat.

We eat. We talk like normal people who do normal things. And once I'm satisfied everyone's had enough dinner and relaxation, I begin the meeting in earnest. Because the amazing thing about being a witch is I can do things like make the

PowerPoint I'm constantly working on in my head appear on the wall—no computer or time hunched over slides needed.

Ellowyn groans. "You did not magic up a witch Powerpoint, Emerson. That is a *disease*."

"It's a time-saver, is what it is." I stand because I always stand when giving presentations. And rolled eyes only spur me on. "Now, our first and foremost goal is to stop this flood." It appears on the wall with a picture of the confluence. "With secondary goals of how to get Rebekah and Nicholas on board." Pictures of Rebekah and Nicholas appear. "Lastly, and least important, how I should handle Skip." I couldn't bear to add Skip's visage to my witch PowerPoint, so I included a picture of his familiar. The weasel.

Jacob makes a subtle motion with his hand. A line appears across my Skip bullet point. "Stay the hell away from him. Problem solved. As for number one—"

"I'm not hiding from Skip Simon." I point at the wall and erase his stupid line.

"How about you accept that the man with dark magic who wants you dead is someone you probably shouldn't seek out," Jacob retorts.

"How about you—"

"Do we need to leave you guys alone to have your lovers' quarrel?" Ellowyn asks, smiling sweetly at us.

We look at her, then each other. I feel the faint hint of embarrassment, but pretend I don't. "This is about all of us," I say. Firmly.

"Can we opt out?" Zander mutters.

"We're starting with number one," I say, smile welded in place. "The flood threatens not just all of our businesses, our livelihoods, but St. Cyprian as a whole. Our entire lives. *And* if St. Cyprian is the center of the witch world like you all say, that means it threatens more than that. Especially if there is historical precedent for a flood like this destroying everything so the careless immortals can start over."

"I studied the book Frost gave you before I gave it back to you," Georgie pipes up, picking up veggies from her salad and eating them with her fingers, like candy. Sometimes I have no idea why we're friends. "Clearly the most important part was that you're a Confluence Warrior, Emerson, but it also mentioned beating the dark back. So I thought there might be something flood related."

"No luck?"

Georgie shakes her head. "We could do another ritual, but the last one was so dangerous that I'm not sure that's smart."

I think about the book and it appears on the table in the center of the living room. I smile winsomely at my friends. Maybe they think this is everyday, domestic magic, but I'm still pretty pleased with my ability to make it happen. Because, hello, *magic.*

"Maybe there's nothing more to be found in it," Zander offers. "I'd think after the ritual we did, we'd know. Or I'd know anyway. Flood stuff is Rivers territory."

"Emerson is connected to the Rivers," Ellowyn says. Coldly.

"Connected, sure, but she's a Wilde through and through."

I want to join the conversation, but the room gets...fuzzy. My friends' voices start to sound like one faraway drone. All the light here begins to sparkle around the book—like there's glitter in the air. Something compels me to stand. To move for the book.

The flower charm on my necklace gets hot against my skin. I touch the book, and it gets hotter. I don't think it's burning me, the way the crystals do when they're warning me—it's simply hot. Power. Magic.

I can vaguely hear my friends calling my name, but I can't

break free from the light. It's light, though—not scary blackness, nasty fogs, or creepy vines. Good light. It feels like…it feels like my grandmother is with me even if I don't see her or hear her like I did this morning.

I take the necklace off my neck and the charm is fairly pulsing with heat. And there's a gold circle the exact same size on the book page. Right next to a drawing of the confluence. Like Zander's pendants.

It doesn't make sense, but does it need to? Does magic make sense or is it just magic?

I press the charms to the drawings on the page. Something rumbles—the ground or something deep within me, I'm not sure—and the book begins to…float.

Georgie rushes forward, but I stop her by holding out my hand. At first I think she stops simply because I wanted her to, but I belatedly realize I'm holding everyone back with *power*.

While the book levitates before us, bathed in gold light. I can hear whispers, not from my friends. Not from me.

Spirits. *Wilde House* spirits.

The pages flutter, shift, and then the book slams to the ground with a loud crash that has me jumping in surprise. Whatever power held back my friends is gone and they're immediately touching me, making sounds of relief. Or just swearing.

Except Georgie, who kneels next to the book.

"Guys," she says, and her voice is only a whisper, but everyone stops talking to look at her. "It's a new page. A brand-new…no, an old page, revealed to us."

Georgie runs her fingers over the script. Her mouth moves as she reads the words to herself. "I think… I think it's a ritual."

Then she looks up at me. "Em. It's an explanation of a ritual that will stop a dark-magic flood."

21

I GLANCE DOWN AT THE CHARMS HANGING around my neck, once again looking like nothing more than some funky necklaces. Then I look around, not sure if I want to gape at Georgie, kneeling there with the book, or rewind to the *how* of it.

I decide that I need to process the appearance of the exact perfect ritual in Frost's enchanted book a little more first.

"Everyone saw how that happened, right?" I manage to ask.

Everyone still clustered around me nods. And mine aren't the only widened eyes.

"Your grandmother. She must have…" But Jacob can't seem to name what Grandma must have done. Even though we all saw it.

"She left clues. That would be shown to us once Emerson got her power." Georgie's voice is filled with wonder. With awe. "She knew what was coming."

"Why didn't she fight it then?" Ellowyn asks.

All eyes turn to me. *Confluence Warrior.*

"This is her fighting," I say. Because I knew—*I knew*—that she was no disappointment. Any more than I was. "She just needed the right weapon."

Haven't I always known? It's up to *me*. I'm *actually* special, and not just because I decided I was, then worked my ass off to do what needed to be done. And beyond. But because of something innate within me. I was made for this. It was always in me. My grandmother knew it years ago despite being told I was spell dim and useless, a stain on the family name. She believed in me—and the charm proves it.

I'm a firm believer that validation comes from within. But I'll admit, I like this acknowledgment from beyond. I like it *a lot*.

Bottom line, this is up to me. Which means I need to take charge. Just like I usually do.

Luckily, I'm good at this too.

"We'll need to translate the ritual, word for word," I say briskly. "Make sure we aren't making any mistakes there. Then we'll each need a copy to study. We can't just leave it up to Georgie or me—it has to be a joint effort." I draw flow charts and assignments in the air as I talk. "Then, no matter what, we'll need to organize whatever is necessary to do the ritual before the potential full-moon group mind wipe. I'm thinking that if we break some dark-magic flood curse, Carol and the Joywood won't be able to punish us *that* much. I'd hope that mind wipes would have to be off the table once we save St. Cyprian."

And won't that be a poetic kind of justice? *No, Carol, you can't deprive me of my magic* again, *because I just saved your world.* I make a note to draft a humble, yet kick-ass, little speech.

Georgie shakes her head, frowning down at the book. "Slight problem. This ritual also needs a full moon."

Though that is definitely a complication, I wave it away.

I *live* for figuring out complications. The more complications, the better. "We'll handle both on the same day, then."

There's an awkward silence, but it's the kind of silence I'm used to. My friends clearly haven't moved on into a sense of purpose like I have. But then, they often need a bit of a pep talk to catch up.

I'm here for them.

"We have to do it, or the ritual wouldn't have been shown to us." I look down at the charms on my necklace and hold them up in the light. "Everything came together at just the right time. You guys gave me the charms to unlock the key to the flood ritual. And my grandma made it happen. Here and now, when we're all together. If that's not fate, Georgie, I don't know what is."

"I agree," Zander says, surprising me. He hasn't exactly been a beacon of support.

"I always wear that pendant. *Always*. I've only..." He shifts uncomfortably, and though he doesn't look at Ellowyn, she suddenly finds a spot on the wall *very* interesting. "I've only ever felt compelled to lend it out once before. And that was more about me. This time, on the ferry, it was like *the pendant* was telling me it needed to go to Em. I thought it was to protect her, but it had to be for this. It *fit*."

Jacob is nodding. "I've had that necklace all these years, ever since Grandma Wilde gave it to me. It never felt like the right time to give it to Emerson. Until now."

Zander crosses his arms, his gaze moving between the book and the charms around my neck. "My pendant is three rivers from the Rivers family. Water. The Wilde charm—a flower—came through Jacob and represents earth. The book hung in the air and was lit up, like fire."

I open my mouth to make a sarcastic remark about this woo-woo summation of what just happened, and possibly direct Zander to my nonexistent New Age section at the bookstore, but everyone else is nodding. *Thoughtfully.*

"The universe is out of balance," Jacob says after a moment. "How long have I been saying this? It wants balance. It craves it. We have to beat back the flood and restore that balance. That's the message."

Neither one of my usual naysayers seems the least bit reluctant or begrudging tonight, and I'm almost rendered speechless by the wave of emotion I feel. It's all truly coming together. *We* are coming together. Without me having to drag certain people kicking and screaming. Or even having to convince them.

Georgie settles in with the book right there on the floor, reading what she can spot-translate to us. Some of it goes over my head—and it's clear I'm going to have to study more witch terminology.

"I want to look at some books I have in my library," Georgie mutters, more to herself than us. "I want to be sure these translations make sense, historically. Translation spells are notoriously tricky. I'll need to do some research before we take this word for word."

"Thanks for telling us how the sausage is made," Ellowyn says dryly. "Translation-wise."

Georgie ignores her. Zander does not, possibly because he's still hungry after six salads and seventeen finger sandwiches. "Because of your vast experience with translation spells?"

"I'm an expert in some spells," she replies. It's clearly a threat. Or a challenge anyway. "Want to see?"

"Why are translation spells tricky?" I ask...no one in particular.

"Context," Jacob offers. Quietly, from beside me. "How you ask—and when you ask—matters as much as what you ask."

I file that away, because it feels important.

Or maybe it's just the way he looks at me when he says it, his gaze so very, very green.

Georgie sits up, nodding as she runs her finger along a few sentences. "It looks like there are different allowances for numbers of participants. That's great news." She grins at us. Mostly at me. "We can do it without a full coven."

"But a full coven would give us more power," Ellowyn points out.

"True," Georgie agrees. "But Emerson brings a considerable amount of once-in-a-generation power that might offset that."

"Rebekah could come home, couldn't she? We could hide her. How do I reach Rebekah?" I study the PowerPoint, currently hovering on the sideboard, cluttered with family photographs.

"You already did reach Rebekah," Jacob points out. "In your dream visit. From what you told me, she didn't seem all that into coming back."

"She was reacting. Now that she's had time to think about it, we can offer protection since we're prepared. I'm sure—"

"She knows the consequences of coming back, Em," Ellowyn says with rare gentleness. "She doesn't want to risk them. You can't strong-arm her into wanting to take on those consequences."

I do not care for that answer. It wouldn't be *strong-arming*. It would be explaining the situation to her. Reassuring her that we can win this time. Reminding her that Grandma called us her two sides of the same coin. First of the year, last of the year—it's a prophecy, and we need to fulfill it.

But I connected with Rebekah all on my own. Without even trying. I can do it again. Maybe this is just some sister stuff that needs my personal, private attention.

"Frost didn't turn us in. He gave us the book, which has

the answer," Ellowyn says, mildly. Too mildly. She gives an elaborate shrug. "Maybe we should approach him."

I glance at Jacob, somehow knowing there will be a scowl on his face. And there is.

"How many times do I need to tell you that he's trouble?" Zander demands. But there's no heat in it.

Everyone's starting to fade, even Zander. And a good leader knows when to break. Even if said leader could go all night and into next week, because who needs sleep when there's a world to save?

But if we get into Nicholas Frost, there will be an argument, and those are bad enough when we're all well rested.

"We'll save items two and three on the agenda for tomorrow," I say, magnanimously. "I think figuring out this ritual takes precedence for the time being."

I am pretty sure I hear Ellowyn mutter, "Thank the fire goddess," as she jumps to her feet. "Send me my copy of the ritual," she says around a yawn. "I'll look it over in the morning when I can think straight."

Georgie agrees and Ellowyn disappears without so much as a goodbye.

"I have to get to my shift at the bar," Zander says, rising. "Do *not* send me a copy in the morning. Send it after noon, when normal people's brains start to work."

Georgie laughs at him and his aversion to early mornings. "You got it."

"Don't forget. Nightly meetings—"

But he's gone before I can finish my admonition.

Leaving me, Georgie, and Jacob sitting in the living room.

Which is instantly…fraught. Because my mind drifts away from the important business of world-saving and mind-retaining to what Jacob and I did last night. And how I invited him to stay here tonight.

My face heats. *You're an adult woman, Emerson*, I tell my-self sternly. *And shame is a tool of oppression. Adult women have lovers spend the night at their house, without getting all red-faced in front of their best friend about it. Get it together.*

"Anyone care for a game of Scrabble?" Georgie asks sweetly.

But I know she's taunting me. It helps undercut the awkwardness, allowing me to focus more on the fact that...I would very much like to have Jacob. Alone. In my room. I would like last night to not be a one-night thing. "Don't you have a ritual to translate?" I return, pointedly.

She laughs. She gets to her feet, frowning down at the book. Then she does a little flourish with her hand and the book begins to float. "Up to the turret," she whispers.

The book begins to move, slowly floating out of the room like it's a sentient being flying up to Georgie's room. And what's amazing is that all I think is that I need to work on the spells she taught me so I can make things soar about the house like my very own Disney movie. Because I'm a witch. She's a witch. We're *witches*.

Georgie follows the floating book, then stops at the door to look at me over her shoulder. The very picture of innocence. "If you're a screamer, make sure to put a soundproof bubble around your room. I wouldn't want to hear anything that would embarrass us all in the morning."

"Hell," Jacob mutters.

I should probably be embarrassed too, but it only makes me laugh. Georgie waves and saunters off, finally leaving Jacob and me alone.

"There are reasons I live by myself," Jacob mutters darkly. But he's studying me, something borderline *mischievous* in his eyes.

He makes a motion with his hand and I skid across the floor, straight into him. He reaches out to keep me from tumbling backward on the recoil from his wall of a chest. Then grins down at me.

I open my mouth to lecture him about power dynamics and consent, but he kisses me instead.

And kissing Jacob has to be the only thing on earth better than a good lecture.

But I don't want to stay here in the living room, where it feels like the eyes of all my ancestors *ever* are on us. I picture my room. I picture Jacob and me in it. Kissing just like this.

We land, a little gracelessly, right in the center of my bedroom. I let out a breathless laugh against his mouth. Then I pull away and look around. I know I did that all on my own. Simple spell or not, no one *taught* me how to bring people along.

"Proud of yourself?"

I let my smile take over. "As a matter of fact, I am."

And why stop there? I lift my hand, but he covers it with his before I can try getting rid of all his clothes in one snap. "No magic yet."

"Easy for you to say. You've always had magic."

But he presses a light kiss to my lips, my jaw, my neck. His hands slide down my arms. Everything inside of me feels a bit like what I saw downstairs. Sparkling gold. Light. Power. All I am, or could be, lit up in a million shining colors.

And. Well. I'm not going to say magic is *overrated*, but maybe it's a good reminder that there's a very simple magic two people can make—whether they're witches or not.

It's surprisingly *easy*, after every fraught moment with Jacob for so many years. To simply touch each other, make love in my bed, curl up together and drift off into an almost dreamless sleep.

Would it have been this easy if we'd acted on what we felt back then? Maybe it isn't fate. Or that we're soul mates or conduits or whatever we are. Maybe we're the simple perfection of a good fit, and fate handled the timing. I can recognize when I'm being slightly strident better than I did at seventeen. Jacob is better at expressing himself than he was back then.

Maybe fate is waiting long enough for the right time to come along.

Maybe we had to get through all that *fraught* to land here.

The truth is, I never really thought something like this could happen. Meeting the perfect partner was on my list of *somedays*, because a strong woman deserves a partner who fits her needs and supports her in everything she does. I could have been happy with my strong and capable self and my friends, naturally, but why shouldn't a leader have it all? If she wants it?

But I always had a very fuzzy picture of what that *someday* might look like. Given that most men of my acquaintance treat ambitious women like a swarm of locusts sent to plague them. Personally.

Jacob's not like that. I like Jacob in my bed. I liked being in his. Maybe that's all that matters right now. And if at some point I want more…well, then I'll ask for it.

Demand it, even.

That's me.

When my alarm goes off the next morning, Jacob is gone. It surprises me how disappointed I feel. Normally I would not have slept through someone getting out of my bed, or so I assume, having little experience in communal sleeping—so I feel certain he did it with witchy sneakiness.

I scowl at the pillow where he *should* have been resting his head, but there's a little note there.

Even witch farmers need to be at the farm bright and early. See you tonight. Check your planner.

   -J

As if I don't check all my planners as a matter of course.

I sit up in my bed. I reach out for my planner, opening my palm to the morning light, and it flies into my hand from its spot on my desk across the room. I flip through to this week and then I can't fight back my grin. On today's box in the evening slot, after tonight's meeting, he's written, *"North Farm."* On tomorrow's entry he's written, *"Wilde House."* Back and forth like that for the rest of the week. Switching off places to spend the night.

Together.

I don't think about what that means for next week. Or the week after that, on into the great, wide future of it all... Okay, I do kind of think about it, possibly in an obsessive fashion, but mainly through a slightly giddy haze.

Because his handwriting is decidedly abrupt and unpretty and kind of ruins the aesthetic of the week's layout, but I can't bring myself to magic it into something more pleasing. I run my fingers over the letters instead, like I'm Georgie trying to glean meaning from ancient texts.

But I know the only meaning that matters.

Whatever we are, or will be, Jacob and I are *finally* on the same page.

Literally.

A FEW DAYS OF LATE-NIGHT MEETINGS AND
of switching back and forth between Jacob's house and mine
each night, and I feel *great*. Others might be drooping here
and there, but I've never felt better. Magic *and* sex? Apart
from the whole impending doom, life really couldn't be much
better. Not that all I've done is explore lust and draw charts
in the air. We've studied the ritual. We've practiced different elements of it. Everyone has taught me different witchy
things I should know, from spells to witch history to current
magical customs, and more.

There are a few hiccups. No one is too psyched about me
going to dinner with Skip tonight. It's a variety of disapproval in four different shades of *Hell no*, but I've stated my
case. I'm not doing it behind their backs, and that feels like
teamwork. Whether the team likes it or not.

As a sort of peace offering, I've been patient on the Nicholas
Frost front. In part because it's wise to let sleeping immortals
lie, I guess. And in part because I don't feel that same driv-

ing need to approach him just yet. He didn't strike me as the type to respond to prodding. And contrary to popular belief, I do know when to hold back.

For a time anyway.

And tonight I have bigger problems than a surly hermit superwitch.

I glance at the clock. It's six on the dot, but Skip isn't here yet. I convinced him we should just walk up to Nora's, but he insists on picking me up. So we can "enjoy the walk together" when any cursory examination of our history should indicate how unlikely that is. I pull a face, then a few more in the safety of my foyer, because I've got to get all of them out of my system before he gets here.

And I could swear the dragon on my newel post makes them right back.

I have to be pleasant tonight, I remind myself, turning my back on the staircase. While women should never *have* to be pleasant as some kind of currency for male approval, I know that's the only thing that's going to get Skip to slip up. The nicer I am, the more information he'll accidentally give me, because he expects me to be *demanding*. And *shrill*, the all-purpose word to describe a woman's opinions when men don't like them. See also, when women have opinions at all.

It will make it all the sweeter when I defeat him that he gave me ammunition.

I will have to keep reminding myself of that tonight.

I move my pacing to the kitchen, until Georgie comes in and I stop. I don't want to give off the impression of nerves. It's not *nerves* per se. It's the uncomfortable feeling of knowing you're going to have dinner with someone who wants you dead, and while you can handle *them*, it doesn't make the *fact* of a whole murder attempt any easier to swallow.

No one likes a murder attempt.

Georgie smiles at me and puts her hands on my shoulders. No matter how hard I try to act calm and confident, she sees through me. "You're cloaked in every kind of protection we could think of," she says soothingly.

We've been over this. I almost tell her so, but then I realize she's as worried as I am.

"Excellent," I say brightly.

"He won't be able to mark you this time and since we did three thousand layers of protection spells, he won't suspect that *you* know you're a witch. Same with the familiars. The birds will be watching you and he'll think it's just Zander and Ellowyn keeping tabs on you, which is nothing new."

"It'll be fine," I insist. I do not think about the brand Skip put on me. I refuse to, because it makes my stomach feel watery. And because this time I'm going in with my eyes wide open. And my friends have my back.

And, not to brag, but I'm a whole lot more powerful than I was the last time he tried to come for me.

The doorbell gongs. Both Georgie and I go still, staring at each other. I can tell she wants me to back out. I want her to ask me to back out. But I recover my equilibrium. I pull myself together—because this is a battle. I am a Warrior. And warriors of any kind don't *back out*.

"Five minutes late. What a dick," I mutter. Then I shake out my limbs, stretch my head back and forth. Getting ready for the fight.

Because make no mistake here. There will be a fight. Of one sort or another.

"Call for us if you need help," Georgie says. Urgently.

"You know I will," I assure her. Then I march through the house and toss open the front door before I can think better of it. I greet Skip with a huge smile. "Isn't it the perfect night for a walk?"

"I suppose," Skip says, with his own smile, though his is alarming. He offers his arm, but I pretend I don't see it. I head out, walking toward Nora's and letting my arms swing a tad more than they should. Just in case he tries to press the issue.

I concentrate on the lovely evening, not my unfortunate company. It's warmer than it has been, even with the sun setting. It'll be chilly when we walk back, but for now it's a beautiful beginning-of-April evening in St. Cyprian.

Still the greatest place on earth, I think happily. If more magical than I thought it was.

Much like me.

"What have you done to make St. Cyprian better today, Mayor Simon?" I ask, my preferred conversational opener when in the company of local leaders. And also because the silence between us doesn't just make me want to fill it, like I usually do at any business mixer or meeting. It genuinely gives me the creeps.

He puts a hand on my arm and my skin crawls. "We're not in a rush, are we?"

I remember that awful brand he put on me and I want to hit him. But I don't.

"I'm so used to walking *briskly*." I pretend to laugh, then move at a slower pace down the sidewalk. But I let my arms continue to move wildly because it knocks his hand off and discourages any more touching.

I muscle back a shudder. There really needs to be no more touching.

Nora's is doing a brisk business for a Friday night, but Skip has made a reservation and we're led to our seats pretty much immediately. Except the table is in a dark little corner that feels ridiculously isolated. I don't like it at all.

"I'm sorry," I say, grabbing the hostess before she can rush back to her post. "Is there any way we could sit closer to a window?"

"Of course," she replies, then leads us through the tables to one with a view of the street. And everyone else in the restaurant. I hear the whispers and the fake shutter sounds from camera phones, but that's better than being dark-magicked to death in a back corner while they all enjoy a nice soufflé out here.

"I prefer the back," Skip grumbles as I take my seat.

"Oh, but being able to eat and watch the river?" I sigh happily. "What's better than that?"

"I can think of a few things." He sits down grumpily, then flicks open the menu, clearly upset he didn't get his way. And I don't know if that's a sexual innuendo or a confession about his dark-magic predilections, but I don't pursue it.

I need to try to smooth things over. "Have you had the fish fry? Keely sources the catfish—"

"I don't like fish," Skip says. Peevishly. He's looking at me the way he usually does, with petulance and flat-eyed fury. Oddly, that gives me a jolt of courage. Because sure, he tried to kill me and followed that up with a branding, but in all the Skip-and-Emerson skirmishes—the ones I remember and the ones I've only been told about—one thing is always true.

I win.

The waitress comes back to take our order, and I make my requisite small talk, because I can talk to a brick wall if I must. I don't need him to participate. Skip looks more and more irritated the more I chatter on.

I get this sense that it's not just the table. He touched me back there on the walk over, but I'm protected. He must know this is a waste of his time now.

Is that his problem? Does he know I've won—again?

I don't have to feign smiles anymore. I settle in. And I set out to make this the longest night of his miserable life.

After ordering—for the both of us, over his splutters of surprise—I give lecture after lecture on every last locally sourced ingredient this restaurant has ever used. He tries to stop me—oh, he *tries*—but when have I ever been stopped by a blustering male?

I eat toxic masculinity like candy.

I dig into my actual food with almost as much relish, order the chocolate-sampler dessert plate, and linger over every last bite. As I'm lingering, I notice Skip scowl at the entrance. I look behind me, surprised to find not one of my friends ruining this perfect moment for me, but Carol. And a group of people I recognize from various town functions. Gil Redd. Maeve Mather. Happy Ambrose Ford. It hits me as they keep coming. This is the Joywood. All of them.

I know them. They've been sitting on committees with me for years.

My pulse kicks into high gear, but I sit back in my chair like I'm relaxed. Like I might order ten more desserts.

"Did you want to go say hi?" I ask. I wonder how Carol might act in front of her son. Maybe it will give me some clue as to what's going on there if I can watch them with each other.

"Not when she's with all those old fools," Skip mutters irritably, looking over at what's supposed to be the most powerful group of witches alive. And they truly are powerful. I can feel the crackle of it, like static electricity at the nape of my neck. I can see the way they acknowledge—or pointedly don't acknowledge—the people they pass.

There's no question that every single person in this building is fully aware of their importance. Especially them.

"They have a lot of power in this town," I say earnestly

to Skip. *Admiringly.* "So much service to this community. It's really inspiring."

"True power comes from yourself. Not from your connection to others." Skip turns his attention back to me and smiles. "You and I have that belief in common, Em. We're better off going it alone, aren't we?"

I try to keep the easy smile on my face, though my eyebrows want to draw together in a frown. Does he really see me that way? A loner? I'm *constantly* surrounded by my friends. Maybe I tend to take the lead, but I wouldn't have made it this far without their help.

Even before I found out I was a witch.

My friends must know that, even if the likes of Skip do not.

Do they know it? I make a note to incorporate my gratitude into the speech I will inevitably deliver later tonight when we meet up to postmortem this interminable date.

"Skip," I say, with a sad sort of sigh. I'm tempted to reach out and pat his hand like he did to me the last time, but I can't quite bring myself to touch him. "You know I have friends. Do you?"

He makes blustery noises, but I power on.

"You seem so alone," I tell him. "I hope you don't mind me saying this. Friends can be so comforting. And when you find the right ones, really, there's nothing more powerful."

"I have friends, Emerson," Skip snarls at me. "I have *lots* of friends."

In the exact same tone he once told me, in the seventh grade, that he had *seven* girls who liked him, but they all lived across the river in Illinois.

I glance back over at Carol. She's seated now, but closer to Skip's originally requested table. Our gazes meet across the restaurant. She doesn't smile as she nods at me. I beam.

Then she looks at her son and there isn't the faintest shred of devotion there. No helpless love or maternal pride or even affection. I know what parental disapproval looks like.

Skip does too, I think, because he sits up straighter in his chair.

I *almost* feel a pang of sympathy for him. After all, been there, done that. "It's hard when your family doesn't support you the way they should, but the right friends make up—"

"That coven of yours isn't complete." Skip's voice is little more than a nasty hiss. He's leaning toward me, his face mottled red, and I feel the surge of a thick, dark power. I recognize it as his. "And you can't do jack shit without a complete one."

I can tell he didn't mean to say that. Also, it's against witch law to say things like that to the spell dim—I should report him.

But I can't show any triumph. I have to look at him with utter confusion. "My *what* isn't complete?"

"Nothing." His face is even redder. His eyes are way too dark. "Are you done yet?"

"Did you want the last bite?" I ask, and wave my fork in his direction, wafting the scent of really good chocolate over the table between us, like incense.

His jaw works. "No."

"But what did you call my friends? A coven?" I laugh like he told me a joke. "Is that what you call us these days? In high school I'm pretty sure you used other names." I lean in. "I'm afraid to ask what would make our *coven*—" and I say the word like I'm in on the joke, wink wink "—complete?"

"Pitchforks and hangings, Emerson," Skip says pointedly. Some of his usual mean-spirited arrogance is firmly back in place as he stands. "Burnings at the stake. That's what happens to witches."

I wrinkle my nose. "Such male drama, Skip. You're too

funny. I think you know as well as I do that witchcraft is nothing more than a patriarchal construct to undermine female power and punish feminine wisdom."

But in case he doesn't, I hold forth on the topic as we wait for the bill and then I graciously let him pay for my dinner. And I have to bite my tongue to keep from cackling as we walk outside into the dark. This dinner did *not* go the way he wanted.

We head back toward Wilde House, and I get the sensation he's resetting. Determined not to count this dinner as a loss, I guess. I walk faster, chattering nonstop about town things even I don't care about while I'm looking for friendly birds of prey in the shadows—while trying not to look like that's what I'm doing.

I stop at the stone steps up to Wilde House. "Well, Skip, I really had—"

"I'll walk you to your door, Emerson. Don't be silly." He takes my elbow and tugs me up the steps to the porch. It's been dark this whole walk, but this feels darker. Much darker. Less out in the open, maybe, here where the streetlights can't reach. I know I've got an owl and an eagle watching out for me whether I can see them or not, but it doesn't *feel* like it. Can they see me here?

This suddenly seems like a bad idea, even though I've never had a bad feeling on this porch in my life.

There's an odd pain at my elbow, where he's still holding me. Is he breaking through the protections? I'm willing to bet he's trying to. I smile brightly as I carefully pull my elbow out of his grasp.

He doesn't let go easily, but he doesn't hold on forever. He releases his grip at the exact moment a human woman would start to get afraid—and I have no doubt that's deliberate. He wants me afraid.

Skip is one hundred percent that guy.

"That's an interesting necklace," he says. He steps toward me and gets way too close. Crowding into me because he's bigger and he wants me to think about *how much* bigger. Crowding me because he wants me to worry what he might do next.

I scramble backward. I laugh *uncomfortably*. And just barely keep myself from magicking myself safely inside. I'm not proud of that intense biological response, the driving urge for flight, but it is definitely there.

Still, warriors fight. So I don't blast him with my own power. Or succumb to the urge to get the hell away from him by any means necessary.

"It was a gift," I tell him, putting my hand on the door-knob. "Well, this sure was nice. Thanks for dinner. Bye now."

But the door doesn't open. Panic skitters up my spine. "That's...weird," I manage to squeak out. I ring the doorbell, but I can tell it doesn't sound. "These old houses. You never can tell when they'll decide to stick or creak or fall down."

I try the knob again, hoping I look inconvenienced or confused instead of creeped out.

"What about the sixteenth?" Skip asks.

"What about it?" The knob simply won't turn. I turn to look at him and am not entirely surprised to find him smirk-ing. From much too close. He's doing something to my door. But he doesn't think I know he's doing it? Or he's testing me? I don't know, but I don't like it.

"There's a seminar on community building at Wash U." And he sounds friendly now. That hint of a drawl. That good-guy smile. "Would you like to go?"

I stop trying the door. The sixteenth is the full moon.

I am sure he knows that. Is this all some kind of test? Not an attack, but a *test*? I keep my smile in place, but order my-self to stop panicking. Maybe he's keeping me out here, but it's not like he's tried to hurt me. I need to be smarter about this. Less jumpy.

"I love few things more than community building," I chirp at him. "As you know, but—"

The door slams open.

Light spills out from inside and Jacob is there, golden and solid and *him*.

He looks like he might rip Skip limb from limb.

And *really* enjoy it.

"Jacob," I say, not sure if it's more surprise or warning.

Or a little *hallelujah*.

Jacob comes out onto the porch, his gaze never leaving Skip. "The door is sticking again, Em."

He drapes his arm across my shoulders, and for a moment I can only gape up at him. What a stereotypical display of macho bullshit. I wish I wasn't so damn relieved he's here. And I wish the warmth and strength of his heavy arm didn't make everything in me hum so happily.

Just because a woman can save herself doesn't mean she needs to turn her nose up at a man who wants to help her do it.

"And what Emerson is trying to tell you, Skip, is that she's busy." Jacob is growling at Skip in a voice I have never heard him use before. Ever. "The sixteenth and every other day."

Now his arm feels like a patriarchal yoke. My fury is so all-encompassing even *I* can't find the words to counter this territorial display.

Skip seems vaguely amused. "We'll see," he says, with enough menace to make my stomach twist. But he's walking away, the porch suddenly seems well lit and welcoming again, and Jacob is tugging me inside.

And because Skip is leaving me unhurt, I focus all the messy things I've been feeling all night on the biggest load of old-fashioned, misogynistic, unacceptable behavior I've ever witnessed.

The door slams again behind me, violently enough to make me jump. I turn to Jacob, ready to give him a piece of my mind and a lesson on the toxicity of jealous behaviors better suited to baboons. But he charges ahead, fury pumping off of him as if *he* has something to be mad about.

"What was that?" I demand, storming after him.

"That's what I'd like to know, Emerson." His voice is so low and so harsh it sends an odd shudder of foreboding down my spine.

"I was handling him."

He turns to face me, such naked affront on his face that I stop in my tracks. I see Georgie in the living room, but Zander and Ellowyn aren't here yet. I'm not sure if that's good or bad. For them or for me.

"You called out for help," Jacob says between gritted teeth. "Repeatedly."

"I did no such thing."

Except I was feeling a little panicked, so maybe I did and didn't fully realize it. I'm still working on the difference between projecting my every thought and sharing specific ones. I could say that, but I'm too furious that *he's* angry when *I* just suffered through a *date* with Skip Simon. I feel—strongly—that I should be getting nothing but praise.

"You did," Georgie says somewhat apologetically, poking her head around Jacob's intimidating form.

"As you absolutely should have done," Jacob adds, stalking toward the hearth. Then he whirls around—a very un-Jacob-like move. "I'm going to kill him."

Normally I'd think it was one of those silly, men-blowing-off-steam types of comments that's so useless in our post-physical-confrontation-unless-you-want-a-lawsuit age, but the look in his eyes makes me wonder.

He is a witch after all. Maybe witches are less litigious. *Witch justice is old-school*, Georgie told me.

I move to head Jacob off before he can do something irrational, like chase Skip Simon through the streets of town, but he does that hand-flick thing as he mutters a few words and I slide across the floor, out of his way and onto a couch.

Outraged, I hold out my hand and picture a door closing the opening from the living room to the hallway. One doesn't appear, so I offer simple and hasty words: *Block his exit, keep him here.*

Jacob stops abruptly. Clearly he can't get through the magical block I've made.

He looks over his shoulder at me, practically spitting fire. I smirk at him. Probably not my wisest move, but, you know. Check me out. Fighting like a witch.

"Stop it," Georgie scolds both of us. "Childish magic isn't going to solve this."

"No, but murder might," Jacob growls.

"You'd only have to heal him if you hurt him," Georgie says, with a gentleness I don't think Jacob deserves.

"He locked that door. There was no light on that porch. *He was cornering her.*"

"I was handling it," I practically yell.

Jacob glowers. "But you didn't."

That is a terrible read of the situation. I'm offended. I might have let panic get the better of me for a second, but only because I was trying to get something from Skip. If I didn't think I was getting information out of that horrible get-together, I would have totally struck him down like an adlet.

Obviously.

I think better of saying this. "Do you want to know what

I learned having a nice, friendly dinner with Skip tonight?"
I ask instead. "Or will there be more displays of testosterone
poisoning?"

"Sure, every nice, friendly dinner I've ever had has involved me blocking any exit the woman has with my *dark
magic* to do God knows what. So nice. So friendly."

"I was handling it."

"You called for help. Don't be pissed when it doesn't come
exactly the way you want it."

"Jealousy doesn't suit you, Jacob," I shoot back.

He stands so very still. His expression doesn't change.
There isn't even a flicker of emotion in his eyes. "All right."

That's all he says. Two words. Agreement? I think?

Yet I don't feel like I've won.

Because it's followed by complete, utter silence. Jacob's
expression is blank, and when the rest of my friends show
up, he does not sit down.

He stands by the exit.

I feel gross and small and I hate that he can do that when
I know *he* was in the wrong. Not me. I try to focus on why
we're all here. I tell them what Skip mentioned about working together and how I think it means we need a full coven.
How I think it means we *need* Rebekah and Nicholas Frost
on our side before the full moon.

But even as I work through all my points, my eyes keep
drifting to Jacob. And my mind keeps working through that
whole…explosion.

He was wrong. He *was* acting jealous, even if he's not
jealous of Skip, because who could be jealous of Skip? The
bottom line is: he doesn't trust me.

Even if I *did* call out.

"Em?"

Everyone is staring at me.

I've trailed off in the middle of a sentence. I cannot believe I am letting something so *frivolous* rattle me. We'll have a conversation soon enough, and I'll explain to him how wrong he is and everything will go back to the way it was.

Easy. Happy. With only the occasional, fluttery, *what-the-hell-am-I-doing* feeling.

"Let's call it for tonight," I say, because I want to get back to easy and happy, stat. "We'll start early tomorrow. We need to figure out a way to reach Rebekah."

Ellowyn and Zander stand.

Zander gives Jacob a nod toward the door. "You want that beer?"

I have no idea why Zander thinks it's beer time. Of course he's wrong—but I'm shocked when Jacob moves toward my cousin.

"No, he does not," I snap.

In retrospect, maybe a little dictatorially.

Jacob stops. He turns. And he speaks very, very carefully. "You don't speak for me, Emerson."

He says it with absolutely no inflection.

I have never felt smaller or uglier. I want to scream. Or maybe go to my room and cry, but I'm an adult.

I swallow, even though it's hard. And I hate that all of our friends are watching this, looking as frozen as I feel. "We need to have a conversation. Privately."

There is a very tense, *very* awkward silence.

I realize that I have no idea what's going to happen. That I can't control it.

Or him.

Then Jacob takes two steps over to me, takes my hand— not exactly gently—and we're flying.

23

WE LAND OUTSIDE HIS HOUSE. IN THE VAST rolling yard. I cannot *believe* he'd be so high-handed, so utterly controlling, as to just *yank* me here. "What the hell was that?" I demand.

"Trust me, you're going to want to do this here," he says, and at least he isn't speaking in that horrible emotionless voice. He's angry again, and that suits me fine because I am *twice* as angry.

"Why is that? Home turf? Can't handle an argument where I—"

"Because I am furious." He cuts me off with a blaze of temper. Controlled temper, but still. "I have never in my life wanted to kill someone, but I would have ended Skip Simon tonight. That is not who I am. That has never been who I am, but you *called out*, because he had you trapped. You were *scared*." The way he says that makes something crack in me. "And if that's not enough, you're *mad* that I interfered. Like

I'm not allowed to have an emotion about that. You think it's *jealousy*? Over that weasel?"

I'm a little taken aback. He was angry about me seeing Nicholas Frost without telling anyone back in the beginning, but that was different. He was worried. Afraid *for* me.

This isn't fear. Jacob is mad. At *me*.

If I think about that too much—and how I can't remember him ever being anything but eventually supportive, if grim—it makes me feel hollow.

Which is good and fine, because I am mad at *him*. "I cannot believe the childish behavior I'm witnessing. You can't possibly think that just because we've slept together—"

"Don't finish that sentence," he grits out. "We'll both regret it."

I hate that he's right.

Then he laughs, but it's that bitter kind that makes my stomach tie in knots. He begins to pace, and even though I'm right, even though I should be mad at him and he should apologize, I feel...sorry. Nothing but sorry. Like everything has veered off course and I don't know how or why and I *hate* this—

But I am *not* going to apologize.

"Push it all down," he mutters. "Pretend it doesn't hurt. Pretend, pretend, pretend." These are all words he aims more at himself, but then he turns that brilliant green gaze on me. "You're damn lucky I'm a Healer and so fucking good at it."

"I don't know what that means." I know when I say that out loud that I should. There's that weight he carries, that I self-centeredly thought was about me and not remembering our past—but it's not. It's about him. His role. Not what he is. Who he is.

A Healer.

"What conversation do you want to have?" he asks me,

and he's pulled that bright, simmering fury back. I wouldn't say he's hidden it, but he's—

Well. It's what he said. He's pushed it down.

There's a moment where I think I shouldn't answer his question. I should take this opportunity to learn more about that whole Healer thing. And what it really means. But that would be ignoring the fact his behavior tonight is inexcusable.

I don't ask myself why I'm so angry. I know. He doesn't trust me, and he can call it whatever he wants. It's a problem.

I'm used to people not trusting me. Everyone who believed I was powerless, for example, when I told them I wasn't. My parents. The Joywood.

But I concentrate on *Jacob* not trusting me, which feels worse. Partly because I can't remember the other betrayals. Partly because I have been intimate with this man. If that's not a sacred trust, then what is?

"You can't burst into a situation like that and think you can answer for me," I tell him.

"Fine. I won't. Is that all? Feel free to go."

He wheels around and starts toward his house. Like that is in fact *it*. "Where are you going?"

"Away from you, Emerson. I don't particularly feel like being in your company. We'll talk again when I've got a better handle on it."

"Handle on what?"

"You don't want me to say what I have to say."

"Of course I do. I always want you to say whatever you want to say, because *I* actually trust *you*, Jacob, and—"

He turns. He skewers me with one glance.

"I love you," he says, almost flatly. But a sliver of *pain* threads through his words and spears through me. "I have always loved you."

It legitimately feels like the ground has been yanked out from under me. And maybe I should have known, or seen this coming. Maybe I did, but I thought I had time. I thought we could dance around this particular truth for a while. Until after we save St. Cyprian. And convince the Joywood we shouldn't be mind wiped. Maybe figure out how to defeat Skip and his weird dark magic thing. I want to learn how to be the best witch. I want to get ready for whatever comes, including this.

I don't know how much time passes. But I don't say anything. My heart roars around in my chest. I'm not *ready*.

"Told you," he says. Quietly. It's devastating. He turns again. Like the weight of the world is on his shoulders while he walks *away*.

Cassie nudges me in his direction when I didn't even realize she was here. I look at the dog, and she gives me a little growl. *Don't be a dumbass.*

"I am a bit tired of having a rude familiar."

Too bad.

I'm not sure what to think about that, but I can't handle this. We can't leave things like this. We might be a mess, I might not have the slightest idea how to handle feelings or intimacy or *sacred trusts* or *this*, but we have to have moved beyond *walking away from each other*. At least I have.

Jacob goes inside and he moves to close the door behind him, shutting me out, but I block it with magic. He only shrugs. He doesn't fight me. He doesn't acknowledge me at all. He keeps going, like he'll just keep walking until I stop.

Like hell I'll stop.

I charge after him. Up the steps, across the porch, and into his kitchen.

"Jacob…" But I don't know how to fix this. I have no elegant words. No clear checklist of how to handle this. I don't even have the truth, because I'm too scared to look directly at it. I dance around it instead. "I care about you."

He turns back to me, but I am under no illusions that fixed anything. "Emerson, I've heard you give a lot of speeches. To hundreds of people. To people with power and influence. Why did you sound so much more sure then? Passionate. Certain. Like you'd fight the very gates of hell to make everything you love about St. Cyprian a reality. I've never heard you be timid about anything except *Jacob, I care about you*."

I don't particularly like hearing my words in his mouth, particularly the tepid way he says them that matches my tone perfectly.

"I…" I realize in this moment, in a hundred ways, what it is. What it's always been that's kept me at arm's length from Jacob. Even the past few days, having sex. Being together. That was surface stuff. We were attracted. We acted on it. Two healthy, consenting adults.

But I have kept a distance. Facts, not feelings, I used to tell myself. Now I'd convinced myself it was because of my plans. I'd convinced myself I was still dealing with the idea of fate or conduits or soul mates, even while enjoying the easier, more exciting parts of getting close to this man. I thought we could be partners.

On the surface. Where he acted the way I wanted, gave me a few orgasms—okay, a lot more than a few—and never pushed.

And that's something. Maybe even a good thing—I can't judge. But it's not *this*. And at the end of the day, *love*—the kind Jacob is talking about—is the one thing that terrifies me. And always has. It's not only about control, though I can maybe admit some of it is that, yes, I like to be in control. It's about what love does to people. Grandma claimed to love my grandfather, but I don't remember it. And if anything Carol said is true, Grandma gave up things for him. Maybe *she* could have beat the flood if she'd dedicated less time to what women of her generation were expected to do for their men.

Just like Mom always did. Dad ruled the house. They called it love, but he called the shots, and I *hated* it.

Then there's what I remember of Zander and Ellowyn in high school. I always thought it was a bit melodramatic due to teenage hormones, but they did love each other. And practically destroyed themselves in the process.

Plus what Ellowyn told me about *her* parents, who'd ended in cheating and curses and a price their daughter still pays.

Why would I want any of that?

I stare back at Jacob and I don't want to tell him any of those things. It makes me seem weak. Worse, it makes me *feel* weak.

But he loves me. Clearly, he doesn't know what love does to people. He needs to know, I think. To understand what he's saying is all wrong, so we can move back from this edge and stay where it's easy. "All those speeches were about getting what I want. Getting power, not giving it up."

"I don't want any of your power."

"Isn't that what loving someone is? For a woman anyway. You may say you don't want it. Everyone claims they want equality, don't they, but men see equality as a loss. And women do the emotional labor no matter how equal everyone's supposed to be. It's what *happens*."

Something in him softens, like he feels sorry for me, when clearly he's the one in the dark. But he crosses to me in his unlit kitchen. And he touches me for the first time in this whole argument.

His palm cups my cheek. "Not if you do it right."

Something flutters, deep inside me, and it's fear. I know it's fear and I should fight it back. But… "How do…how do you know how to do it right?"

"Because people do," he says. "Your uncle Zack and aunt Zelda? I know they bicker, but they enjoy it. He'd sacrifice everything to make her better. And she'd sacrifice everything to take that pain away from *him*. My parents might not be the most demonstrative people, but they are a team. They've always been a team. My grandparents and great-grandparents too. You, of all people, must know that love is what *you* make of it, like everything else. We get to decide."

That is not the perception of love I have, but there's something about how that's the perception of love *he* has, that has some of that bone-deep fear easing from where it's wrapped too tight around my lungs.

"I don't need…reciprocation." His hand is still warm against my cheek. "That isn't what this is. It's not why I'm angry. You've got entire parts of your life you don't remember. You're only just figuring out all this witch stuff. We have dark magic and floods and who knows what else." This is perilously close to what I was thinking, and it dislodges another great swathe of that fear. "I'd wait a million years on you, Em. But I need you to stop believing that by standing up for you I'm somehow *taking* your power. I will never do anything but celebrate you. I never have. And I can't stand you being afraid of what I *might* feel."

"I'm not… That isn't…" But I'm at a loss for words.

"Em. When you accuse me of things that aren't true, I'm going to get pissed. And when I get pissed, I need to be able to lay out the truth."

I want to say that I can handle the truth, thank you, it's *love* I'm having trouble with, but I still can't seem to speak.

"And maybe I'm not handling that you're not ready for

that truth as well as I could. But I'm not going to stand by and be the biddable puppy when *anyone* traps you in a dark corner and you call out for help. I refuse to be polite in that situation. *You asked for help.* Help doesn't make you less, Emerson. In fact, it'd probably make you more."

I'm having trouble breathing.

I think about what Skip said. About how we're the same, because we're so alone. I knew he wasn't right in the moment. I have friends. I rely on them. I do not consider myself *alone*.

You act like it, though, comes Cassie's voice. And I have to accept that.

Because I don't always ask them for help. And I could have handled tonight better if I'd understood what he was feeling—something he kept from me because he didn't think I could handle it. He was right. Especially when I know I would have done the same thing if the positions were reversed. Maybe that's what scares me.

And I certainly could have handled it better. Like if I'd tried having a conversation instead of throwing out accusations.

I sigh. Heavily.

Jacob fits his free hand to my other cheek, cupping my face. His expression is mostly stoic, but this close, with his hands on my face, I think I see every emotion in his eyes. Frustration, exhaustion, sadness.

Hope.

It's that one that really hurts. Because I don't know how to lay it all out for him like he's done for me. I don't have the vocabulary.

Coward.

I frown and look down. Cassie is there again. Sitting just a few feet away from where Jacob and I stand, her brown eyes not soft and sweet, but challenging.

"Why is my familiar so mean to me?"

Jacob looks over at Cassie. "Familiars don't have to be nice. They're...familiar."

I huff out a breath. "It seems unnecessary."

He smiles a little, but it's sad.

"Jacob."

"Let's just—"

I know he wants to send me away. To shore up his reserves. To harden up that softened heart I've stomped all over. I can feel that waving off him, when I try. When I let myself.

I can't let him send me away. I can't... I can't accept being afraid of the truth. That isn't me. It shouldn't be me.

This man isn't about power, and I know it. He's a protector. A Healer. And he has always, always been there for me.

I'm a fighter. A Warrior.

That means I fight because it's the right thing to do, even if what I have to fight is me.

Maybe especially then.

I reach up and put my hands over his. "I do love you."

My skin gets prickly. All over—head to toe—I don't know exactly what that is. Physical response. Witchy stuff.

He's studying me, probably worried I'm just being nice. But surely he knows me better than that. "I wouldn't lie to spare your feelings."

"I know." His thumbs brush across my cheekbones. "No matter who or what you are, what power you can wield, whether you fail or succeed, what you remember or don't, I will be by your side. I haven't always done loving you right, but I have always been right here, and I will always be right here. No matter what."

All of that is big. Humbling. "I probably don't deserve that."

He shrugs. "Maybe not."

That is not the romantic declaration all those other words are. I can admit, I might have it coming. "Ouch."

He smiles. "But it's true all the same."

Which is very Jacob and very right.

Then he gets serious. Downright grave. "I don't know how much of love is a choice, but you do have one. It doesn't have to be me."

"But of course it's you," I return. Surprised he could even question that. If I'm going to love someone, it's damn well going to be the *right* person.

It's always been you.

It's always been him.

Everything I remember is him. And every memory I know is locked away from me is him. It's been him forever.

And it's funny how accepting that, here and now, feels almost easy. Like the hard part was getting here.

Now there's just Jacob.

I move to my toes to press my mouth to his. His arms wrap around me, but before I can really sink into the kiss, the pain starts. Just like the first time he kissed me. That splitting pain that knocks me out at the knees. I'm lucky I have Jacob holding me up.

"I'm okay," I manage to grit out, because I know he can't come in and heal me or I'll lose whatever this is, whatever's behind the pain. And I don't want him to use his powers to push this back, because he might push too hard.

There's some kind of terrible ripping inside of me, and I have to squeeze my eyes shut and clench my jaw to survive it. But I'm holding on to Jacob, and he's holding on to me.

And I know I'll make it.

"Emerson."

"You have to let me." I keep chanting that, holding on to him. And he holds me upright, when even in the back of my mind I know it's actually painful for him to not try to heal me. Like a physical thing he has to stop himself from doing. Against the grain of everything he stands for.

I feel like I'm going to explode. Into painful, jagged pieces. The pain is excruciating, and I think maybe I might actually pass out.

"Okay," I gasp out. "Just a little. Don't...don't push too hard. Please don't—"

Immediately the pain eases. It doesn't disappear, but I feel like I can breathe again.

And when everything fighting inside me explodes, it doesn't tear me apart. It hurts, and my nails dig into Jacob's strong arms hard enough to draw faint specks of blood, but I'm still here. Still right here.

Still in his arms.

"Emerson." Jacob's voice sounds far away, but I nod as his hands move over me, like he's checking for broken limbs. In the human way, not the witch Healer way.

"I'm going to scan you."

I nod as he grips my hand, but I already know what he's going to find.

I can feel it. The last tendrils of Carol's spell, the obliviscor, are gone. Completely.

I remember everything. No more gaps. No more wondering what else is there.

A laugh bubbles up and out, even though I feel a little deaf and blind. Slowly, everything comes back. I'm exhausted, and achy, but...

I can remember *everything.*

I manage to open my eyes.

Jacob squints, like he's looking into something bright. "Tamp it down, Em. That's too much energy."

I can't speak just yet, but I can make the words go to him

anyway, can't I? I realize that's why Cassie called me a coward. *Tamp what down?*

He taps my temple. "Relax. Breathe. Pull that energy back."

I do what he says, because it feels natural. Breathe. Relax. That hot source of power deep inside feels like it's scalding my entire body. Pull the energy back, Jacob says, but I don't have any energy *left*, at least in my body. I think about that center instead. It should be more like a container. All that power pouring out only when I let it. And slowly, as I concentrate on that, it begins to pull back into its little container.

One I built for control. Not a cage anyone could put me in. I understand in a flash that's why it works.

I let out a breath of relief. I feel spent and used up. I can't stand—Jacob is still supporting me—and my knees feel entirely useless. But I can look at him and remember everything. Whispering about covens. Dancing around each other when we looked a little too long in the other's direction. I remember.

I remember.

Emotion sweeps through me. Because I remember the night Carol wiped me, and how pleased she'd looked while she did it. I can see Jacob trying to jump in front of me. He would have taken that hit. He wanted to. No wonder he blamed himself when he wasn't able to do it.

It's who he was. Who he *is*.

Maybe he's not the one who doesn't trust me. Maybe I don't know how to trust him. Maybe I forgot how.

But I remember now.

"Emerson, I don't feel...any of Carol's magic in you," Jacob says, somewhere between wonder and alarm.

I manage a few croaky words. "I remember. All of it."

All of it.

Rebekah begging me to run away with her. Me refusing because I knew better than the Joywood.

I was so sure I knew better. I wanted her to fight. I couldn't understand running. I still don't understand it for *me*, but I have some empathy for why Rebekah felt she had to.

The memories cascade over me, making my mind whirl until I feel dizzy on top of everything else.

A nap sounds good, but... "Is this the conduit thing?" I ask him. "Is witchdom really so archaic that a kiss breaks powerful spells?"

If fairy tales are real, I'm going to be pissed.

He laughs, but then he presses a kiss to my temple. "Not just a kiss. Love, Em."

I'm not certain I know how I feel about that. But it makes sense. Not his love for me. Not even mine for him. Our love. Together.

"Love is a powerful magic," he says. "Is that archaic? Or is it a fundamental truth of life?"

"Mmm," is all I can manage to say. My limbs are jelly and now my lips won't work. I could totally argue with him, about something, probably.

I have critiques and lectures at the ready.

But he scoops me up, holds me close, and I forget them all. "You need to get to bed."

"I remember everything. *Everything.* And there's so much to do..."

I never finish that sentence. I drift off into a dreamless, restful sleep instead.

And wake up as *me*.

24

ME. FINALLY.

I'm in Jacob's bed, feeling well rested if a little…fuzzy. I'm also alone. Again. This time, there's no note. Only the indentation on the pillow to even signify he slept next to me.

I sit up and frown a little. Outside the window, the sunrise is a riot of pinks and oranges. The water in the river ripples, mirroring those colors. For a moment, I sit in Jacob's bed and watch the path of the river, its ebb and flow, as it meets with two others. The Mississippi. The Missouri. The Illinois.

I look at the confluence, that dark, rippling, sparkling mass of power. And as I look at it, I realize there's something… off about it. Isn't this what Jacob has been saying? There's an imbalance there. Not anything visible or concrete, just a feeling. A very strong feeling.

Looking at it gives me goose bumps.

I have to believe that once we do the flood ritual, we'll fix the imbalance. Maybe it's all connected. Skip using dark magic. The ritual meant to beat back the dark. The very

definition of what a Confluence Warrior is, what I am…
Maybe Skip is what caused all this. And if we stop the flood
and beat back the dark, maybe we beat back Skip too.

Skip.

I look down at my hands. All those things I thought were
accidental, all the times I somehow embarrassed him without
meaning to… I now wonder if was some latent power inside
me all the while. Making him trip. Humiliating him, time
and again. Because those were definitely things I *wanted* to
do, even when I didn't know I had the power to just wave
my fingers and do it.

Is that why he hates me? Because even when I didn't *know*
I had power, I could use it against him?

I laugh, because I hope so. I really, really hope so.

I'm disappointed when I come downstairs to find the
kitchen empty—both of prepared food and Jacob—but I
hum to myself as I start to poke around, looking for coffee.
And possibly pancakes. I'm about to give up and make a cup
appear when I hear the front door creak open.

"Finally," I call out, happily walking out to greet him.

"Sorry, I meant to be in bed when you woke up today."
Jacob looks at me. I'm wearing his shirt, with the design for
St. Cyprian's Christmas Around the World 2019 on the front,
from a drawer in his bedroom with a full selection of festival
T-shirts. He's been secretly sentimental this whole time and
I'm wearing the evidence. He only raises an eyebrow. "Nice."

"Thank you." I smooth out the hem happily. "Farm emergency?"

I assume there must be such things. Possibly cow related.
There always seem to be cows everywhere, and farmers always mutter about them as if they're recalcitrant toddlers
forever getting into scrapes.

He clears his throat uncomfortably, and when I look more

closely I see he has that gray pallor. He must have been out healing someone. Like a doctor, I think. He probably gets calls and has to go.

"I was at your aunt and uncle's house," he says. Carefully. With enough heaviness that my heart trips over itself, but before I can ask, he hurries on. "Your aunt is doing okay. She was in a lot of pain this morning. I did what I could."

I move over to him and take his hand. "You're worn out. Sit down."

I push him into the big armchair by the fire. It's a little chilly this morning, so I flick my fingers and a fire appears. I take a moment—just a brief moment—to admire my work.

Then I look at him. "You need some of that tea you and Ellowyn are always pushing on people. Is there some in the kitchen?" I move that way, but he simply reaches out and takes my hand.

He says nothing. Does nothing. Just holds my hand.

I don't know why a lump forms in my throat, but I…want to take this away from him. The weight. The tiredness. That clear, gray feeling he has that he's failed.

I slide into his lap and lean my head against his shoulder. I can feel the emotional toll this morning took on him. It waves off him. I realize how often he must block that, so no one can see. Because that's who he is. But he can't this morning. He's too spent.

I think about *my* magic, and what I can do. I think about words my grandmother used to say to me when I was worked up about something—because I remember everything now. What she tried to teach me, what Jacob tried to teach me when I thought I might be a Healer. I remember everything.

I touch my hand to his forehead, whisper my grandmother's words like a balm, and while I don't fix his tiredness, I *can* feel him relax a little into the chair.

He lifts my hand and kisses my palm. "Always knew there was some Healer in there." He sighs. "Do you remember what I said about Healers? About why I never pressed this in high school?"

"Well, Jacob, I remember *everything* now, so yes." I think back to that conversation. *Healers should be with Healers*, he said. Often. I lift my head off his shoulder to glare at him. "If you're breaking up with me because of that *now*, you're in for a fight."

He laughs. Tiredly. "No. We're taught that no one can understand. The lines we have to draw, the energy we have to expend elsewhere. It's physical and it's emotional and it means we're not always available for the people we love. It's a bedrock Healer belief that we need to stick to our own. No one understands it and we don't expect them to, but I think you might." And he might be tired, but I can see the shine in his green gaze. "In your own way, you're always trying to heal St. Cyprian. And you take on responsibilities that feel like yours even though they aren't."

I open my mouth to say something but he puts a finger over my lips. "Settle, Confluence Warrior. I like it. I love you."

We sit there for a while, as his energy and power strengthens again. I wait until I think he's almost fully there, with the gray faded completely. Then I slide off his lap. "Let's eat some breakfast."

"It'll have to be quick." But he lets me pull him up and drag him into the kitchen. "I'm behind on chores."

"Can't you wave your magic wand, Jacob? You're supposed to be a witch," I tease him.

"Some things are better done with my own two hands," he says, with a grin that makes me think about how good he is with those hands of his.

I decide that breakfast isn't one of those things that needs hands. I murmur a simple cooking spell and make our breakfast for us with magic. Pancakes. My specialty.

I can tell he doesn't want to go into specifics about my aunt, so I decide to discuss town things. Chatter on while he refuels. He seems to enjoy it and who am I to not indulge him.

"I was thinking," Jacob says after I've exhausted just about every bookstore topic I can think of. "Tonight, let's all meet at the cemetery instead of Wilde House. You had your closest dream connection to Rebekah there. Why not harness the power of your grandmother to do it again?"

I can't decide what surprises me more. That he's making suggestions normally *I* would make, or the possibility... "I can do that?"

"Your grandmother's spirit would have to be willing and Ellowyn will have to guide you, but it's worth a shot."

That sounds like a yes to me. "And Nicholas Frost?"

Jacob's expression hardens. "What would some immortal asshole want to help us for?"

I am unimpressed with this male resistance to the only immortal we know. Even now that I remember my magical education—so what? Just because immortality only comes at a price, that doesn't mean the price is *treason*.

"He's the last piece. Georgie said so, and I think she's right. And clearly my grandmother was okay with him if she linked her charm to his book."

Jacob doesn't look convinced, but he also doesn't argue. I glance at my watch, replete with pancakes, maple syrup, and my delicious view of Jacob, *the man I love*. "I need to get going. I have a call with a local author this morning."

I look down at the T-shirt I'm wearing. I think about the clothes I've got back at Wilde House and call the right outfit to me. Just like that, I'm dressed for the day. I'll fix my hair at home, because I like my brush. I handle the breakfast mess left behind, magicking things back to where they belong. Dishes in the sink. Leftover food in the fridge. Partly because I like to think that I have good manners.

Partly because I'm a witch and it's fun.

Jacob sits back and watches me, his mouth curved. He's amused by my enthusiasm, I know, but the warmth in his eyes is deeper than simple amusement. Because he's in love with me. Always has been. And he believes that love can be what we make it.

I couldn't agree more, now that he's laid it out for me. I suppose even self-made success stories like me need a nudge in the right direction sometimes.

And it occurs to me that Jacob is what makes this whole love thing easy. I can't imagine wanting to choose this—the fear, the worry, the lack of control, and of course the mind-blowing sex—with anyone else.

"I love you," I say, because it all overwhelms me and fills me up until it seems impossible *not* to say.

His smile widens into one of those rare, beautiful, full-fledged ones, and my heart flutters with all that love and a healthy dose of *Holy shit* still mixed in. But I'm not going to let my fears control me anymore.

"I love you too." He stands to drop a kiss to my mouth. "I'll see you tonight."

"You're on food duty tonight," I remind him, then disappear before he has a chance to argue.

I'm grinning when I land in my room at Wilde House. Giddy, maybe. I pack my bag with my own hands for better pen and sticker selection, humming a happy tune. Then I head down to the kitchen for one more mug of coffee.

When I walk into the kitchen, Ellowyn and Georgie are at the table. With doughnuts.

I grab one. Despite the very large breakfast I had with

Jacob and the fact I might be full until tomorrow, I always have room for doughnuts. A woman must have priorities.

"Did you spend the night?" I ask Ellowyn cheerfully as I head to the coffeepot.

"You mean after you and Jacob disappeared in fury? Yeah, I stayed the night. We waited and waited for you to come back." Ellowyn studies me. "You're humming, so I assume you kissed and made up."

I sip my coffee and consider my words. I hold the mug before me like a chalice. "I am in love with Jacob."

My voice rings out grandly.

Neither of my friends really reacts.

"Yes, Em, we know," Ellowyn says with an eye roll. "Tell us something we *haven't* known since the fourth grade."

I might have minded that more if it wasn't true. And I know it's true because I remember. I take great delight in smiling at them. "Okay. How about... I got *all* my memories back."

Now they jump to their feet. There might even be screaming. Georgie wants to know how. Ellowyn decides to test my memory by belting out questions—mostly about the ways I accidentally, or not so accidentally, ran afoul of Skip over the years.

"Fish sticks?" she demands. "How was that anything but a curse?"

I focus on telling them what happened. They each grip a hand while I explain. "Apparently, love is very strong magic," I conclude, a bit loftily.

Georgie sighs dreamily. Ellowyn scowls and drops my hand.

"Fish sticks," she mutters. And when she says it like that, it really does sound like a curse.

"My motives were pure," I tell her. And when I don't turn into a fish stick, despite her baleful glare, I get back to business. "Tonight, we're meeting at the cemetery. Jacob has a theory that we can reach Rebekah easier that way."

"I was going to suggest something similar," Georgie says, excitedly. "I found an old spell in Frost's book. It's about summoning. Ellowyn and I went over it a bit last night."

"I love that we're on the same page," I say. Because it proves that we have major coven potential, doesn't it? I kind of want to rant about it, but I'm foiled by my duties. "I have to get to the store. I'm on the verge of almost late."

"Do you have your crystals?" Georgie asks, as she does every morning these days.

I pat my pocket. "I even know what they're for now."

"She's going to be insufferable if we win," Ellowyn says to Georgie. "Successful and in love? *Insufferable*."

I grin at Ellowyn. "You've been calling me insufferable since the day you learned what the word means. And yet, behold, you suffer along anyway. You'll be fine."

I carry the glow of happiness—memories and love and *me*—through the entire day. Later I meet Georgie and Ellowyn at Wilde House and we fly to Jacob's together. He isn't there, but there's a dinner spread on the table. Probably from his mother, as I can't see Jacob whipping up a couple of trays of lasagna, plus two green salads and a trough of garlic bread. Zander arrives and I tell everyone to eat while I go stand on the front porch and wait for Jacob.

I pace the length of his porch and wonder if this is a glimpse into my future. Waiting for Jacob to appear from some healing call. Isn't this the thing non-Healers aren't supposed to understand? That the people we love aren't just ours.

But I know, deep down, that I wouldn't love him this much—I couldn't—if he was only his. Because I'm the same. We love helping, and that means we always will.

Jacob appears in the yard then. He walks toward me, big

and beautiful and his green eyes so hot. And I don't care
who else's he is.

As long as he's mine.

"Sorry," he says when he draws near. "Broken leg out of
town."

I reach up and touch his windblown hair. "Don't apologize. You don't have to apologize for being you. Ever."

He smiles down at me. Then he runs a hand over my hair.
"You're all right, Em."

Love is powerful magic.

Love is how I know—*I know*—the ritual is going to work.

After dinner we head down to the cemetery with the necessary supplies and our familiars going on ahead. We set up
at my grandmother's grave. I can't say I feel her here, even as
I touch her fox. But I can't really imagine my grandmother
letting her spirit rest either.

Zander, Jacob, and Georgie create the circle. Our familiars fan out to make their own outer one. In the center I sit
with Ellowyn and one lone white candle.

I have the words Georgie gave me, and Ellowyn and I
whisper them together, over and over, as we watch the flame
of the candle dance in the wind.

There's a flash of light that forces me to close my eyes, but
I don't let go of Ellowyn's hands. I wonder if I would have
had that inner muscle memory to hold on to in this moment
if I didn't remember how important keeping the circle is.

When I open my eyes, I look over to the source of this
new, bigger light. Rebekah is standing outside the witch circle, but within the familiar circle.

Rebekah. Plain as day. Right in front of me. She's dressed
in black. Thick boots. A silver nose ring winking in the
light. When the image of her solidifies into corporeal form,
she glares at me.

It's all so *her* I could cry.

"Haven't I told you to stop this?" She crosses her arms and scowls at me. It's just like high school.

"Rebekah, you need to come home. I know it's risky—"

"I am never setting foot in St. Cyprian ever again." She holds my gaze. Hard. "Ever."

"It's important."

She smiles faintly. "It always is. When it's you."

If it really was high school I might yell. Tonight I explain. "You don't understand. St. Cyprian is in danger. There's dark magic and a flood and… We need you. We need you to help fight it back."

I look at Ellowyn. Her eyes are opaque and I'm not sure she'll hear me if I speak out loud. She's the one holding Rebekah here. *Can I drop your hands?*

Five minutes, she replies.

I stand and face Rebekah. I don't leave the circle, but I'm face-to-face with my sister. My sister, who I haven't seen outside of dreams and visions in ten years. And it's a good thing that I know why she left. It is. But doesn't she want to come home?

I want to tell her all the things that have happened since she left. I want to tell her everything about Jacob. I want to curl up on our favorite window seat in Wilde House the way we used to, our legs tangled together, until we end up laughing so hard our chests and jaws ache.

But there's no time for all the things I want to tell her. I focus on the most important.

"We have to stop this flood," I say. "We have to save the town."

Rebekah lifts a shoulder, and though we don't look anything like identical, that gesture is all Wilde. All us. "I'd prefer to watch it all burn, but drowning works too."

She's maddening. Always. "You were there. With Grandma. She said it was our turn."

Rebekah's eyes cloud with emotion, but her voice is flat when she speaks. "She said it was *your* turn. St. Cyprian is yours, Em. I want no part of it."

"Please." I take a step forward but remember myself. I can't cross the line. It'll hurt Ellowyn and maybe Rebekah too.

Her eyes flash. "I made myself a promise the night I left. After what they did? Never again." There is a wealth of pain in those words. A pain I want to heal. But I can't until she comes *home*.

I reach for her, but she's not really there. I have a sense of her arm, but that's all. "I have power, which means you probably do too. I remember everything. I broke Carol's mind wipe. You have to come home and help us. It's your destiny and you know it."

Her mouth twists. Her eyes are too bright.

"If there's a destiny around, I think we both know it's yours. I'm an exile, Em. St. Cyprian spit me out and I don't hate myself enough to go back for more."

"Rebekah—"

Her dark eyes glitter. "It's your town. You fix it."

The projection of her disappears with a violent clap of thunder. I feel a bloom of agony against my heart as I fall back down, hard, to sit across from Ellowyn again.

My sister won't help us.

I am devastated.

Hollow.

And I don't have the slightest idea what to do now.

25

I MEET GEORGIE AT WILDE HOUSE A FEW DAYS later. I tell myself I no longer feel hollow, that I'm committed to our hastily tossed together plan B in the wake of my sister's refusal to help, but I suspect that might just be Jacob's excellent coffee talking. I have a third cup of less stellar coffee in my kitchen as we go over our game plan for today's mission: get the elusive Nicholas Frost on board.

Without Rebekah's help—but I need to stop thinking about her. I need to let her go. Everyone agrees.

"Do you know more about this guy?" I ask. "His actual history instead of all the legends?"

"I did some more research last night, but so much of it is hearsay." Georgie piles her red hair on her head. Absently. "Contradictions wrapped in mysteries and that kind of thing. The only verifiable fact is that he is, indeed, immortal—though no one knows how or why he got that way. He was also involved in teaching on a higher level at some point, a world-renowned Praeceptor. He helped found St. Cyprian after Salem. And he was an advisor to the Joywood, years ago."

None of this really gives me any great insight into how to get through to our immortal friend, especially when he's not shy about throwing his power around so easily. But if I let uphill battles stop me, I wouldn't be the youngest chamber of commerce president in St. Cyprian history, would I? And magical immortality can't disguise the fact that Nicholas Frost is, beneath it all, just a man.

And I have spent my entire life in training for the handling of difficult men.

Like every other woman alive.

Georgie and I decide to walk to Frost House. If anyone stops us, we'll say that I'm on another mission to *do something* about that hideous eyesore of a house. Who would question it? I've been on the same mission for years.

As we walk up Main, we chat about normal things. The store, the museum. I talk a bit about my plans for this year's May Day.

Otherwise known as Beltane to witchkind. For the first time in ten years, I'll be able to celebrate one of *our* rituals. Not just with magic and my memories intact, but as a Confluence Warrior.

As someone who successfully stopped a world-altering flood. Convinced the Joywood they were wrong about said flood, and my mind wipe. And maybe even put together a coven that could replace the overbearing Joywood in the next election, no big deal.

I believe in the power of positive thinking, so why not believe all this will happen exactly the way I want? Georgie and I begin up the stairs built into the bluff. Arm in arm. The house stands at the top. And this time I know what's under the glamour. A glorious old Victorian on the bluff, looking out over the confluence.

My confluence. Because it's in me. It's part of me. I wish my sister felt the same.

But I also know that it would have been easier for Nicholas Frost to set up shop somewhere else, the way Rebekah has. Anywhere else.

Something clicks. "He lives here for a reason."

Georgie makes that Historian noise of thoughtful assent. "For some, their power is stronger closer to the confluence."

"Then the confluence matters to him." And I think St. Cyprian must too. Whether he likes it or not. Why else build a monument where everyone can see it—and then camp out here for generations?

I feel a surge of power inside me. Because if I know what he cares about, that's an in. And as a saleswoman of some renown, I—

"Emerson. Georgie."

That oily voice skitters over my skin.

Georgie's hold on me tightens as I turn, my fake smile in place as we look at Skip down below us at the bottom of the stairs. He's standing on his silly little hover board he likes to zoom around on and draw attention to himself. Helmetless, of course. "Morning, Skip," I make myself say, with as much fake cheer as I can muster. "How are you?"

"What are you two up to?" he asks in return, like we're pals.

Like we habitually chitchat about our plans with the guy who went out of his way to intimidate me on my own front porch, to name only the most recent transgression.

Creep.

But I only smile wider. Next to me, Georgie manages to *look* flakier. It's not a glamour. It's something in the way she holds her mouth, I think—and now I can remember the hours and hours we spent howling with laughter in front of mirrors, practicing ways to hide in plain sight. Because when everyone has magic, disguises that aren't spell dependent are smart.

I focus on Skip and his little motorized mode of transportation he's so proud of.

"Just wanted to have another look at this pile of sadness that's a blight on our charming little town," I say. Merrily. Because cheerfulness is its own reward, and also an excellent mask. "Something has to be done about it, especially since we're about to get into the busy season."

He gets off the hover board and jogs up a few steps. "I told you I'd take care of it."

"Have you gotten to it yet?" I return. I force my smile to brighten, so the question doesn't seem *quite* so antagonistic.

His expression flickers, like he can't quite decide which one to land on. He takes another step up, toward us, but hisses out a breath and falls back. Then he does it again.

"Are you okay?" I force myself to ask, the way a human would. Probably.

"I'm getting a call," Skip blusters, and fishes out his phone. Which isn't ringing. He wheels around and shows us his back, and I *might* have taken that at face value once—because Skip has always been off and weird and unknowable—but I know better now.

Something is preventing him from climbing any higher up the stairs. I study the step that pushed him back, but I can't see anything. I look at Georgie. She looks as puzzled as I feel.

"We'll see you around, Skip," I call. I turn Georgie back toward the house with our linked arms. And I'm sure I hear Skip trying to say something to us as we hurry up to the top of the stairs, but it's lost in the morning breeze.

"That was weird," Georgie mutters. "I'd think Frost had some kind of protection around the house, but we got through without feeling anything."

"Maybe it's a protection against weaselly idiots who barter their souls for black magic."

"I'm not sure an immortal would judge bartering a soul all that harshly," Georgie replies as we make it to the top of the bluff and face the house at last.

I can feel her nerves, and I'll admit to having a few of my own, but nerves are nothing but signs of impending greatness. I know we're doing the right thing.

We whisper the words to lower the glamour together. Like before, it takes a few tries.

"He definitely has strong magic," Georgie says, almost under her breath. "Which is fair enough. It would be embarrassing to live forever and have weak magic, wouldn't it?"

"I wouldn't know," I say. Maybe a little smugly, because I'm feeling like myself again, clearly. "And neither would you."

We wait there for a moment or two, but he doesn't appear on the porch like he did the last time I was here. So I march forward and use the grinning-dragon door knocker to bang against the door. Forcefully.

I do it again.

And again.

"Emerson, clearly he doesn't want—"

But the door opens with a loud flourish, and then he's there. Somehow his cloak is swirling about him like there's a windstorm, but he's standing inside. Just as I remember him. Ancient eyes and distressingly attractive and that sense that he's a yawning abyss of power too great to handle. I tell myself that's his mask, but I'm not sure I'm convinced.

"I'm not interested in Girl Scout cookies, little witches," he drawls.

I roll my eyes. "Are you going to let us in? Or glower there in your fake windstorm?"

"Oh, it's you," he says. I am under no illusions he didn't know who it was. "Do you really want to bother me again? Not much for taking a hint, are you?"

"Not when I don't want to take the hint."

He makes a noise. Not approval exactly. But not negative either. Exactly. He waves us inside. Georgie's eyes are practically anime-sized at this point, and her grip on me tightens to the verge of pain. We follow him down his gleaming hallway, lit to the ceiling with candles. Everything about the house is opulent, old, rich. There are paintings on the walls I know I've seen in books. There is a certain hush, as if the house itself is too stately to allow the sound of a footstep.

He leads us into a giant room that looks like it belongs in a castle. I glance around, not entirely for show, for a throne. He points to an antique couch, and before I know it, Georgie and I are sitting on it.

Clearly, his doing. A little flex of his magical muscles. Men do love to trot out their guns.

Then Nicholas Frost stands before us, looking every inch the forbidding, deathless witch, around as long as anyone can remember. "Let me guess. You found the flood ritual."

He doesn't actually *say* "ho-hum" like a cartoon villain, but…

"Yes. Isn't that why you gave me the book? We've been preparing as best we can, but it requires a full coven to pull off properly."

"And…what?" He looks the closest to amused as I've seen him yet. "You think I'll join your sad little tea party?"

"I happen to throw an excellent tea party," I return, with a smile. "Ask anyone."

He makes that same sound. Not approval. But like I'm making steps in the right direction.

"By my count, if I deigned to join your little teenage drama society, you'd still be short one."

"Technically, yes."

"You won't succeed without a full coven."

"How do you know?"

He shrugs eloquently. Elegantly. "Many have tried. Many have failed."

I'm not many. I'm me. And I like my odds. "Did any of them have what I have?"

He makes an insouciant gesture that has me grinding my teeth. "Perhaps. Perhaps not."

"If we need a full coven, why not join ours?" Georgie asks.

Nicholas Frost raises an eyebrow at her, but she doesn't back down, much to my pride and pleasure. She holds his gaze with that placid, dreamy expression on her face.

"Half of your coven considers me the boogeyman."

"So, show them you aren't," Georgie urges him.

His old eyes gleam. "Perhaps I am, little Historian."

She pales. I try to match his nonchalance, but I can't. Because I care too much. Far too deeply to pretend this isn't *everything*. "Fight for St. Cyprian, Frost. Fight for witchkind. Fight for *something*, for God's sake. It's a worthy fight."

I think I have him, until I say *worthy*. His expression shutters. It's all sculpted blankness. Not even a glimmer of mild curiosity.

"What an intriguing offer," he says, with a lash in his cultured voice. "And I wish you luck. But if we're meant to drown in a few days' time, drown we will. The rivers always win, in the end."

His words make me shiver. *The rivers always win.*

"Not that it matters to you," Georgie says, more sharply than I would have expected. "Because you'll survive either way."

Nicholas Frost shrugs again, and any progress is locked up tight behind that cold facade again. "That is what immortal means. Last I checked."

I stand. "Maybe you think we can't do it without you, or a full coven, but I know what we're capable of. If you don't want to be part of that, it's your loss."

His cruel mouth curves into something cold. "I never lose."

And then, in a dizzying rush, Georgie and I are once again standing on his porch. The glamour of an old, dilapidated house is back, the wind from the river seems colder, and I can hear what sounds like raven laughter from somewhere above us, but hey, at least we're both in one piece.

"Asshole," Georgie mutters.

But he's an asshole we need. I sigh. Zero for two. But that's not a strikeout.

"Emerson, you're thinking out loud in baseball metaphors. That's not good."

"No, it's not," I agree. I frown at the sun in the sky, higher than it should be. Then I look at my watch. "How were we in there for an hour? I need to get to the store in five minutes. I'll have to fly."

"I'll come with you," she says brightly. Too brightly.

"I'm fine, Georgie. Pissed, but fine. Really."

She leans into me. "Don't take it personally. We knew Frost would be a long shot."

I suppose we did, and it's not that I take his refusal personally. He's not Rebekah. It's just that we need to win. We have to win. "We'll figure something out."

Georgie smiles. "Come find me for lunch. I'll be at the museum, researching my face off."

Then she flies off. I step off the porch and take a deep breath. It's nice up here. Quiet. And you can see all of St. Cyprian and the rivers below, spread out like a painting of pretty much everything I love.

I glance back at the house. Whatever Nicholas Frost says, he cares. I know he has to care. He wouldn't be *here* if he didn't.

He's waiting for something, a voice in me asserts with absolute authority. I know it's true.

If only I knew what.

I make a note to add *figure out what immortal witch might wait for across untold centuries* to the appropriate planners and action item list. And I won't lie, being able to magically update everything makes the household AIs everyone has these days seem like a Walkman from the 1980s.

Then I focus on the bookstore. I prepare to fly there, and even get air bound—

But I'm slapped out of the air by something heavy and dark.

What the actual fuck.

I land on the ground—out at the very edge of the bluff—with a bone-rattling thud and a jolting roll.

And then, in front of me, Skip appears.

Clearly over pretending to be human.

His eyes are as red as an adlet's. He looks like one of them. A demon. A monster.

Carefully, I get to my feet. He knocked me out of the sky. *Slapped* me out of the sky. My stomach tilts and lurches. I go cold.

He knows what—no, *who*—I am.

Worse, he knows that I remember.

His mouth twists into a hideous sneer as he stalks toward me. There isn't just anger flaming in his tiny, black eyes, there's hatred. Fury. *"Witch,"* he seethes.

I look around as best I can out of the corner of my eyes. The town is hidden below the bluff. There's no one up here now, early morning on a workday. It's just Skip. And me. No one will see.

At least there's that.

"You already know I'm a witch," I throw back at him "A Warrior at that. And you, Skip Simon, are nothing."

I focus on that heat, on that energy. On the belief that I am so much stronger than this sad excuse for a man. I send out a blast of power that stops him in his tracks.

But it doesn't knock him down.

He stretches a hand toward the ground. "Everyone always thought you were the biggest threat. Emerson this. Emerson that." Something black and oily and *wrong* floats up from the grass, into his fingers. *Dark magic.* "But they didn't know what I could do. You'll know, and then so will they."

"Bartering your blood for dark magic doesn't make you strong, Skip," I scoff at him. Openly. And I'll admit it feels good not to pretend. To be who I really am. "If anything, it makes you weak."

His laughter is a new kind of nightmare, red-eyed and slimy.

"We'll see." He sends a blast of that inky black in his fingers toward me. I hold up my hands to block it, and the black hisses as it meets my magic. My power.

Good power. Honest power.

I was never trained as a Warrior. Even now that I remember the magical training I did have, I don't have the spells or the muscle memory to fall back on. I only have instinct. I only have what's inside me.

But that's enough. I'm sure of it.

I concentrate on the power within me. And send my own blast blaring toward Skip, the way I did to those adlets. I think, *Stop.*

Because I don't wish for Skip to die. He should have to pay for what he's done. He should be judged by his peers.

He tumbles backward, but immediately floats back to his feet. The skies darken around us and thunder rumbles in the distance. I can see he's made a wall—some kind of barrier around us. Does he think I'll try to retreat?

He doesn't know me very well.

Still, it makes me realize I shouldn't be doing this alone. I get the feeling I could, and without too much trouble, but no one will see it that way. No one will champion me going it alone, and really, how many times do I need to learn that lesson?

So I call out to my friends.

Deliberately and loudly.

"My friends are coming," I tell Skip. "Too bad you don't have any. I'm pretty sure I told you back in elementary school that you should probably do a little work on you. Guess it's too late now."

"You want your friends to die?" He laughs again in that nasty way. "I can arrange it. But they'll have to get through my barrier first."

I smile at him. "Then I'll wait until they do to bother fighting back. I want an audience when I take you down."

With a quick move, I send a bolt of power straight for him. It hits him dead center. He launches in the air, flips, and lands on the ground with a thud.

And I might be a grown-ass woman. And a Warrior. But I can't deny that it's satisfying. Hugely fucking satisfying.

It's possible I've wanted to punch Skip in his smug face since he lied about Jesse James in Miss Timpkin's class.

Wishes really do come true.

Yet when he gets to his feet again, he's smiling. It's creepy and gross, and that's without the blood that trickles from his mouth. I don't get the sense I put it there. This has to do with the black magic he's bartered for.

I try to send out another bolt, but he blocks it with one of his own. Then reaches below again. The dark tendrils of black magic spiral up from the earth below me and encircle my ankles. I hack at them with the power I have, but it splits my focus and Skip hits me with a shock of magic that has me falling back and smacking my head.

Hard.

The world grays for a moment and my stomach heaves, but I'll be damned if Skip Simon beats me.

I will be *damned*.

An eagle lets out an angry screech above us and Skip's attention is distracted enough for me to raise myself up to my feet. I float. And I might be a little unsteady when I touch the ground, but I'm upright.

Skip points toward the sky, and before I can get my own shot off, inky black shoots toward the bird hurtling toward him, coiling around it. The eagle tries to fight it off, but it begins to plummet to the river below the bluff with a pained screech.

I feel the power of anger pulse within me. I twine it in my light. "You'll pay for that."

Zander. Take care of your eagle first.

I don't know if my message gets through the barrier. I can only hope that Zander's connection with his eagle means he'll know and help.

That word resonates inside me. *Help*.

Help doesn't make you less, Emerson, Jacob told me. *In fact, it'd probably make you more.*

I can take Skip. I *know* I can, but he's blocking my friends out for a reason. Blocking everyone out. Which means, before I kick his creepy ass, I want to knock down that barrier.

I dodge some of his blasts, block more, all the while revving up my own. I pretend to telegraph my intent, focus on him and point my fingers his way before the power blasts out. I give him the time he needs to dodge the blow.

Just like I want him to.

His smug laughter is exactly what I want.

He flies up and the bolt misses him completely. He laughs again—while my shot sails past him, piercing the barrier he has around us.

Immediately, Zander rushes in through the tear. There's murder in his eyes. Before I can say anything to him, I hear what sounds like fabric ripping—only ten times louder. As I watch, that sword of light from the adlet attack slowly penetrates the barrier, carving its way in until there's a person-sized hole.

My heart immediately feels lighter.

Help is more. Not less.

Ellowyn and Georgie push through, followed by Jacob, sword of light still in his hand. I smile at them.

Like this is another pizza party.

They fan out and take battle stances, like we've done this before. Like fighting evil is our job.

Skip smiles in his same old obnoxious way, but his red eyes begin to dart around. "If you losers want to fight, let's do this."

"Are you in high school?" Zander snaps.

Skip gives him the finger. No magic, just his finger, which is a choice. Then he holds up a clenched fist. He lets his fingers open. A black crystal of some kind lies there in his palm, pulsing in a way that makes me feel sick.

I raise my hands—

But Ellowyn's owl appears from nowhere, swooping down to snatch the crystal, talons extended.

Skip screams in fury, reaching out, black shooting out of his hands. But Ellowyn and Zander send light to meet between them, and form a shield around the owl.

"I'll fight all of you," Skip bellows, but there's more tantrum than magic in his voice. The red in his eyes is fading. "North! You want to fight me. I know you do."

"No," I say. In a voice that carries. A voice that scrapes the sky. As if in response, the bluff thunders, the ground shaking beneath us. "It's my fight."

I hold my hand out to Jacob. My Jacob. "This one is *my* fight," I say, meeting his green gaze. But he doesn't look like he agrees.

"Come on, North. Man to man. You and me. I'll even spare your life. I won't spare hers, so you might as well step in and try to stop it," Skip taunts, louder with every word.

This is his mistake. Jacob's eyes narrow. *He wants me to fight him a little too much. Why?*

I don't know, but let's not give him what he wants.

Jacob nods once, decisively. He tosses me the sword and I catch it easily, like I've been plucking swords of light from midair my whole life.

I don't hesitate. I run at Skip.

Around me, I hear my friends chanting. Creating a circle. The owl flies above and the eagle returns, free of the dark magic that had enveloped it before. Murphy and Cassie shouldn't make the river crossing, but I can *feel* them from the farm—pushing their magic and power at us, to help. To make us stronger.

Skip bellows. He creates his own sword, black and oily. Dark and wrong. It's just me and him now. The Skip-and-Emerson show once again. For the last time, if I have anything to say about it.

And I think I do. Because whatever new horror he wanted to manifest with that crystal, he can't.

I lunge. And it's like a dance I somehow know already. Like every witch who came before lives inside of me, preparing me for this moment. Like Sarah Wilde herself is whispering in my ear. *I chose not to fight but you can.* Block, duck, lunge.

Our swords clash with thunderous roars, but I hear my friends' spell anyway. Inside me and around me. Everywhere.

Protection. Support. Love.

Help.

Skip's sword nicks my shoulder, but I don't feel it. I stumble back a little when it catches my cheek, but he's so proud of himself for making me bleed that he leaves his side open. I swing my sword and it finds him.

With a nauseating *squelch*.

Skip screams. I pull back and swing once more, plunging all the sword's light deep into him. And the sound he makes then…

It's inhuman.

He stumbles back, but he doesn't disappear into black ash like the adlets did. He simply begins to…melt. Like wax. Slow and grotesque.

Jacob hauls me back, away from Skip even as I watch his human form slowly decay into something else. I can feel Jacob healing my cuts, his power shooting into me, lighting me up, but I can't stop watching Skip.

Because he's turning into something.

Something small and wet with matted fur.

A…weasel.

It's like the entire universe holds its breath.

"I always said he was a dickweasel," Ellowyn breathes.

Even the red eyes are fading. He's nothing but a little… rodent. Surrounded by black goop.

I want to laugh but I don't. I don't know what the appropriate response is. To *weasels*.

He begins to scurry, but Georgie whispers something, and a cage appears around it. *Him*. So he looks like a harmless pet, except maybe for the way he squeals. Murderously.

"Who turned Skip into a weasel?" I demand, looking around. But everyone's shaking their heads. "*Someone* had to turn him into a weasel, right?"

We all squint at the Skipweasel in his cage. He hisses at us, which is less scary than he might think.

"That's not what it looks like when someone casts a transformation spell," Jacob says, his eyes gleaming. "You'd know that if you'd ever actually succeeded in casting one."

I can't help grinning at him. I remember that almost-kiss by the pond now, in all its glory. Just like I remember the spell for turning boys into toads. "I bet I'd be okay at it now. Want to find out?"

"Guys," Zander says impatiently. "More important. What the hell do we do now?"

I wish I knew.

But then everything disappears in a flash. Cage, Skipweasel, even the black ooze left behind. I panic at first, but then Jacob takes my arm and points to the top of Frost House.

Nicholas Frost stands on the widow's walk. His cloak whips in the wind while his huge raven perches on his shoulder. The raven lets out a long cry.

Inside.

The command is in my head. As I look around, I realize

it's in everyone's head. We exchange glances, but what else is there to do?

We close ranks, carefully coming together to move as a group. And then we go inside Nicholas's mansion—the glamour long gone.

He's standing in his grand library like he's waiting to hold court. No cloak this time. He's dressed like a normal man, jeans and a shirt, but nothing hides the power of the immortal before us.

Georgie is staring at the books on the walls with wide eyes, but the rest of us are focused on the table at the center of the room. There sits the cage with the weasel within. The little creature has given up its screeching and lies there, curled up like any wild animal that has tired itself out.

I meet Frost's wintry gaze, my pulse a small riot. But I know something about him now. He's not ambivalent. Maybe he doesn't want to leap into participating, but he isn't *uninterested*.

I'll get him yet. "Did we stop the flood by defeating Skip's dark magic?"

He says nothing, but waves his arm. The walls around us disappear for a moment and the confluence is visible. It's like looking through space and time at once, or maybe the whole universe. Into the heart of the power.

That's what these rivers are. That's why we hide them.

Yet threaded in all that golden light of true, good power, is a thick ribbon of black. It slowly gets bigger and thicker. With every second. With every breath.

I look at Jacob, needing to see my horror reflected in his expression. But there's only a grimness to the set of his mouth.

Then it hits me. Jacob sees this all the time. As a Healer, it isn't just witchkind that needs his special brand of powers.

It's the earth, the air, our rivers. He can see the imbalance, the dark magic threaded through. He can *see* it.

And everyone else can deny it, pretend it doesn't exist, because it's easier than facing the problem. And how do you fight willful ignorance?

I know something with a striking clarity I didn't fully have before.

If we don't win, evil will.

Not just Skip-level weaselly evil. But a bigger, badder, scarier evil. Without a face. Without a name.

Whatever is doing this.

Whoever wants this blackness, this dark magic gone wild.

And I know something else. If this darkness wins, that will be it.

The end.

26

"IN THE END, YOU DEFEATED NOTHING BUT Skip," Frost tells us when the walls return. He looks at the weasel, and I swear there's the tiniest hint of sympathy there. "Who was nothing much to begin with."

"Has he...always been a weasel?" Georgie asks, finally tearing her gaze away from the massive library.

"No. And yes." Nicholas lifts a shoulder. "There are things I can't tell you. There are things I won't. But I will give you a warning, so you know what you're up against. The dark magic that made him will have many chances to win. You will only have one chance. One loss, and it's all over. For all of you."

But he only looks at me when he says it, and I have to fight off the cold chill that moves through me so I don't shudder. Visibly.

"You have to help us," I insist. I don't understand how he could think otherwise.

"You don't learn, do you?" he returns, his voice a danger-ous purr. "You are not in charge of me, little witch."

"I am a Confluence Warrior."

There's a moment—just one moment—when I think that might mean something to him. He doesn't move. Doesn't react, but there's a flash of something.

I want to believe it's hope.

"Confluence Warrior, powerful Healer, misguided Guard-ian, cursed half witch Summoner, fantastical Historian. It doesn't matter to me who or what you are. I am Nicholas Frost."

The arrogance is *astounding*. So much so I struggle to come up with words to defend myself and my friends that aren't just an outraged squeak.

"Last time I checked, immortal didn't mean better than anyone, just older." Ellowyn smirks at him. "Nicholas Frost is no better than us. Hear that? It's called a truth test. Throw my curse around all you like, but it's handy when taking ass-holes down a peg."

I want to give Ellowyn the *biggest* high five, but I can *see* the sparks of Nicholas's temper, and we need him. Some-times leadership requires more tact that showing an arrogant man his place.

However satisfying.

"I'll keep the weasel here until such a time you have to face the consequences of your actions. A favor, we'll call it." He's talking only to me. I'm almost positive.

I know I really don't want to owe this witch any favors, but I don't have a choice. That doesn't mean I have to stop there. "The real favor would be joining us for the flood ritual."

Nicholas smiles, and for a moment I think he's actually going to agree.

And then I land with a thud in the living room of Wilde

House. I look around in a panic, but then all my friends appear around me.

We have been dismissed. Against our will. Against *my* will.

I scowl. "I really, *really* don't like him." But he stepped in, didn't he? Can we trust that it was benevolent? In his fashion?

There's no good answer to that question, and now there's very little to do except get on with our lives. I'm late to open the store, so likely Ellowyn is too. Zander might make his shift at the ferry, but it'll be close.

"I know he has more answers," Georgie says, frustration laced through her soft tone as she and Jacob walk with me down Main toward the bookstore, because we all need a moment. "Or, at the very least, his library has more answers. There has to be something we're missing, and I think it's in those books."

I make myself smile. "We'll find it. Whatever it is." We have to, don't we?

She smiles back, but I'm not sure either of us fully believes it. She veers off toward Wilde House, while Jacob walks me into Confluence Books. He's quiet, but it's not that seething silence I've enjoyed before. This is more pensive.

As I'm feeling the same, I don't really know what to say. Except one thing. "Thank you for letting me handle that."

"I wish I could say it was easy." He drops a kiss to my mouth. "Good thing you're a hell of a Warrior, Emerson Wilde."

"Thanks for patching me up too."

"Anytime."

I study his face. I know it so well. "Something's bothering you."

Jacob doesn't deny it. He scrapes a hand over his beard. "I don't know. I feel the same as Georgie, like I'm missing something. Right under my nose. I didn't feel that until Skip's stunt back there."

I rethink my decision to keep that whole *this-is-the-end* thing to myself. If we're all feeling this, maybe we need to talk about it. Isn't that the lesson? Help is more. *Us*, not individuals. I open my mouth to suggest we all gather for a working lunch—

But the front door opens with a discordant jangle and Maeve Mather blusters in. "Emerson Wilde! You are opening up an *hour* late."

"I know, Maeve." And I love a schedule, but it dawns on me that Maeve's obsession with mine, when she's not exactly a big customer, is…not normal.

"I was so worried!"

Neither is the dramatic concern when I know she's no fan. I manage a bright smile. "How kind of you to care."

"Care?" she sputters. "Well, of course! I hope you have a good reason for scaring years off my life."

I feel like I should. Like I should spin a story and charm her right back out of my store, the way I would on any other day. But I'm tired and not in the mood.

"I don't have a good excuse at all." I pat Jacob's chest and lean forward in a conspiratorial manner. "I was *very* distracted this morning."

Maeve makes a distressed sound, and Jacob closes his eyes. I'm not sure if it's embarrassment on his part or possibly thinking I shouldn't have intimated such things to Maeve. Who may be a member of the scary Joywood, but is also a busybody of the first degree.

"The store is open now," I say sweetly. "What can I interest you in today? Some self-help books?"

"The gardening section upstairs just got some new stock,

didn't it, Emerson?" Jacob interrupts. His tone is much, *much* nicer than mine.

And he's in the right of it. To cut me off. To try to get Maeve to leave.

"I can't imagine you have anything *I'd* be interested in," Maeve says with a sniff, then turns with a flounce and walks outside.

Jacob raises an eyebrow at me. "You might want to take a day off if you're going to talk to all your customers like that."

"I can't stand Maeve. I don't care if she's a Summoner."

"No one can stand Maeve. But you're amped. Frustrated." He drags his fingertips down my temple. "And you have a headache. Taking it out on people you don't like isn't going to solve the problem, especially when they basically live in Carol's pocket. Close your eyes for a moment."

"You don't need to heal me, Jacob. It's nothing but little hurts."

"Then it'll be quick and easy to heal them up. Close your eyes, Emerson."

I'd argue. Normally I would. Some of Ellowyn's tea or even five minutes of sitting with Georgie's crystals would likely clear it all up. But Jacob's fingers are on my temples and my eyes drift shut.

He whispers his Healer words, goes in there and soothes the hurts. Each and every one. And yes, it's a lot more pleasant to have Jacob's fingers work their magic than to drink a mug of *tea* that tastes like moss with an attitude problem.

"There now, all better." He kisses my forehead.

It's all very sweet, but I find what I most want right now is to be alone in my store with my ancestors' spirits around me.

And I don't have to verbalize it for Jacob to understand.

"Wilde House for lunch?" he asks.

I nod. I tell him to get everyone there, then I give him another kiss and send him on his way.

I tidy the store. I let the normality of it settle me. I let the history of the stones I walk over seep into me. *Confluence Warrior.* That is what I am. I defeated dark magic today, and even if Skip was only the weaselly tip of the iceberg, it was a step in the right direction.

I help two young mothers carting unruly toddlers around find some books that interest their horde of children. I no longer have to ask myself *Witch or not a witch?* because I remember everything, and I can tell. These women are not witches. Just human women who want books and maybe five minutes of quiet.

Handling them like there's no flood coming and no magic laws I might already have broken, like there's a normal world out there somewhere, soothes me all the more, and I think maybe I'm finally back to feeling like myself when Carol walks in. I can see Maeve across the street outside, watching. Not like she's spying. More like she sent Carol here and is waiting to see what happens.

Meaning Jacob was right to warn me.

Still, I find myself hating both of them, hot and bright, like it's new. From Carol's mind wipe that defied all of witch-kind's protocols back when I was eighteen and foolish. To Maeve always meddling with my grandmother's store. And, now that I have all the missing context, is no doubt the source of Carol's *disappointment* commentary.

Women should lift up other women, but these two have spent years trying to tear the Wilde women down.

Carol smiles at me, and I make my lips curve, but I know there's no warmth behind it.

I beat her son, didn't I? Why can't I beat her too? And why wait for the full moon if she's here right now? She didn't wait for the right moment to wipe my mind. She just did it. I stand a little straighter.

It isn't time yet, sweet pea. Not yet. It's my grandmother's voice. There in my head. She's never spoken like this to me before. Not so directly. It's not supposed to be possible. I stand very still, desperate to keep her talking. *Hide what you are. Bide your time.*

Because it's not clear whether Carol knows I broke through her mind-wipe spell. Maybe she's come to see for herself. Grandma is telling me—very distinctly—not to let her see how I've changed.

I almost panic, but then I think...I just need to be the old me. The me from a few weeks ago, really. And I know what it feels like to be mind wiped from both sides now. Half in and half out. I know what she's looking for, and with my own magic I can make it seem like my mind is fogged over by her old spell. I wrap a good rendition of that blockade around me, just in case she's inclined to take a peek.

Then again, maybe she's here about Skip.

My mind spins around and around, worrying through various strategies, and I almost feel like there's oily residue on my skin.

I can't hide the fact Skip has disappeared. And it's probably best not to pretend I haven't seen him. Best to be as honest as I can be and stay as close to the truth as I can from a sup-posedly human perspective—without inviting some of that harsh Joywood justice.

All of this whirls through me in the space of a smile.

"It's weird that you came in today, actually," I say.

Her hair seems to frizz extra at that, like a dog's hackles rising. "Oh?"

"I need to tell you something. Something very upsetting."

Her eyebrows lift. Her gaze is sharp.

I blow out a breath, and I'm not faking the leftover shiver of reaction. "Your son attacked me, Carol. In broad daylight."

She blinks. Once. "Excuse me?"

"He, well, I really don't want to relive the specifics, but it was bad," I say. I wrap my arms around my middle. "I defended myself as best I could. But..." What would I have done back when I didn't know magic existed? When my mind would have convinced me there was nothing supernatural going on? "It was... It was clearly... I'm going to have to file a police report."

"A police report," Carol echoes.

"I'm sorry," I whisper. "I wish I could make a different choice out of respect to you, but it isn't safe. For any woman in St. Cyprian. You warned me about him yourself, but I never thought he'd get *physical*." I shake myself off, briskly, and something in me aches. Because I know that if this had happened a few weeks ago and I survived it, Jacob would have healed me in the same way, I wouldn't understand what had happened, and I would feel...like this. Determined to rise above what happened to me, yet battling back tears. And the shakes. "I have no choice, Carol. I hope you understand."

She narrows her eyes and I get the sense she's trying to read me. The human way. Then she reaches out and takes hold of my hand. "I am so sorry, Emerson," she whispers.

And I want to believe her, but I can feel what she's doing. Magically. She's scanning me, like Jacob does. Not with the same Healer's finesse, but it's the same idea.

She pulls her hand back, still frowning. She's still suspicious, which doesn't surprise me.

But she isn't ready to accuse me. That does surprise me.

"Emerson, of course I understand. What woman wouldn't?" Carol furrows her brow, sorrowfully. "I'm horrified that my own son could behave like this."

She reaches out and touches me again, putting her hand on my shoulder the way she did in the cemetery. I feel her magic pour into me. And more, this time I know what she's doing. She's weaving a spell.

"You don't need to call the police," she tells me, her voice melodic. Hypnotic. A beautiful, inevitable song that swells inside me. "It would cause unnecessary complications. Let me handle it."

My mouth opens of its own accord. "I'll just let you handle it, Carol."

"I'm his mother after all. Who could handle him better?"

"You know him best," I agree at once.

Inside, it's like I'm wrapped up tight, in a ball, covering myself while her spell moves through me. It's a lyrical, glimmering attack, encouraging me to do as she wishes. And to feel easy about it while I do.

But at heart it's no different from what Skip did.

He wanted to hurt me. She's simply controlling me.

And this time I can't fight. I have to let her do as she likes. I have to smile as a new memory blooms in my mind, of Skip being a little bit testy. A little bit contentious in a chance meeting on the street. Maybe I refused him a second date?

Because of course it's my fault.

If I fight, I'll give myself away. I'll give everything away. It's a lie-back-and-think-of-Salem kind of a thing and there's nothing to do but endure it. Curl myself up tight and wait her out.

I hide the real me deep, safe behind my little blockade, and surrender the rest.

"You'll let it go, won't you, Emerson?" Carol asks in that soft, singsong way. "Like you always have."

Deep inside, I remember. Odd little conversations with Carol over the years. When Skip lit my semiformal dress on fire. When Skip turned my junior-year exam paper into a pit of snakes. When Skip did any number of psychotic things over the years.

Almost, I think now, like they were tests to see what I'd do with the power no one believed I had.

And Carol would roll up each time in the aftermath. *Boys will be boys*, she would say. *Don't you think, Emerson? Boys have these strange urges. Boys can't help themselves.*

Drip feeding my opinions on this literal dickweasel so I laughed him off and considered him nothing more than a punchline. A joke. Annoying but never *dangerous*.

Maybe the only thing that changed here is that Skip branched out on his own and started using black magic. The kind Mommy can't clean up.

But outwardly, I'm nodding along with her. "Of course," I murmur. "Boys will be boys. Especially grown ones."

"Have a good day now, Emerson," Carol says.

I feel that like a bookend. The finish line of her spell.

"You too, Carol," I say brightly. "Thanks for stopping by. I so appreciate your support. I'm excited about tourist season this year. We're really going to put St. Cyprian on the map."

"I can't wait," she says warmly, and for a moment she looks like the benevolent, faintly frazzled, yet always formidable grande dame of St. Cyprian's founding families that I've always thought she was.

And by *always*, I mean while scrubbed of my magic. By her.

I remember that too. I feel it. And there's a kind of grief in me that swells up then, because that Carol isn't real. She was never real. It's not like I confused her for a mother figure, but I had a certain affection for the woman. She represented the best of St. Cyprian to me. I thought we shared the love of this town, at the very least.

I don't wait for Carol to do something else. I bustle back behind the counter and start tidying the area around the computer and register. I do a great rendition of my former self, who would have been—who *was*—totally unaware of it every time Carol "encouraged" me.

And it's only after she leaves, with an airy wave, that I let myself go still again.

Outside, I see her and Maeve put their heads together. I see the looks they shoot back toward the store window. They walk together down the street, out of sight, and only then do I let myself mourn the ten-year-long life of mind-wiped Emerson Wilde.

I've been so caught up in the awesomeness of magic, and falling in love, and Skip and battles and the rest, that I haven't let myself do this.

I do it now.

I hold her close. I let her grieve.

Then I let her go.

And I let myself laugh.

Because boys might be boys in Carol's world. But are weasels...weasels?

It turns out that new me—magical Confluence Warrior me who remembers everything and knows how to bide her time—can't wait to find out.

27

THERE ARE NO NEW ANSWERS THAT DAY. OR THE next. Only questions.

And that's a theme that continues as days pass. Too quickly, marching us toward the full moon. A severe dearth of answers everywhere we look.

I never reach Rebekah again, though I try—with our friends and on my own. She has us fully blocked. Even in dreams. Which, of course, means she has her own power, and should want to come home and wield it, but I digress.

My sister never did take kindly to being told what to do.

Frost too remains aloof. Unwilling to allow any communication. I feel like I could force both their hands if I had more time. To learn, to harness my power, and to wield it effectively. To push in ways I was never taught because I allegedly didn't have *that* kind of power.

Or any power.

But I don't have time. We've run out. The flood is coming.

It becomes clear that something is in the air. A tension even humans feel, and it's everywhere.

Carol reports Skip's disappearance to the human police, but there's a strange lack of urgency about it. In witch circles, it's suggested that Skip ran afoul of magical law—possibly by misbehaving with yours truly. And Carol is seen as a better leader for having treated her own son as she would have treated anyone. *No wonder she can't bring herself to discuss it,* people tell Georgie and Ellowyn and even Zander. *Imagine how painful it must be.*

It's a blessing that no one talks about it to me. Just the strange disappearance of the mayor, sometimes, when people remember to remark on it at all. I assume that's Carol's spellwork in action. But then, day in and day out, I find that playing the role of mind-wiped Emerson makes me almost too aware of the costumes everyone else is wearing.

I'm pretty sure all the residents of this river town sense something big is coming.

My friends and I pore over the ritual. I practice my fighting skills. Jacob and Zander are distracted by Aunt Zelda's worsening health, and Uncle Zack stops allowing visitors. Ellowyn continues to look pale and drawn but when I ask her about it in the tea shop, alone, she says she doesn't know what's wrong.

Since she can't lie, I have to believe her.

I feel Georgie and I are the only ones operating at one hundred percent, and though I try very hard not to let myself worry…I can't seem to do anything else.

I make charts. I make graphs. I write reports. I give PowerPoint presentations. I make lists upon lists.

But the moon grows rounder every night, and we're still only five.

Can five beat back the dark?

Well, I tell myself, again and again like a prayer—we will.

Because we must.

We have no other alternative.

The night before the ritual, we gather at Jacob's to do a practice run. Because we have to be careful, to keep our magic close, protected, hidden. Even while we're holding back the fury of three mighty, magical rivers. Even though, together, the five of us are already more powerful than maybe we should be. We still don't know what it will mean if our magic attracts attention.

We just know it won't be good.

We also don't know who controls the dark magic swallowing the confluence. It could come from anyone. Or no one we've ever met. It could be Frost himself, as Zander belligerently suggested the other day. We suspect everyone and no one.

The only people it can't be is us. This I hold in my heart, like a talisman.

Georgie sets up the circle tonight. Crystals twinkle in the moonlight. Ellowyn organizes a tray of candles, Jacob cleanses the whole area of any potential creeping magic, and Zander instructs the familiars.

I watch the proceedings. I'm not used to standing still instead of acting, but something holds me back. Apart. Not my lack of magical memories this time. If anything, it's the weight of having them back.

Never happy, are you?

I look down at Cassie. Now that I fully remember her, us, I don't think she's mean the way amnesiac Emerson did. I understand instead that, when I'm at my worst, Cassie will remind me to stop. To regroup. In that sarcastic way of hers.

I am decidedly thrilled, I respond in turn, though it isn't true.

I know I'm strong. I killed those adlets without any magical memories. I defeated Skip easily enough, and maybe he was weak—a *weasel*, for God's sake—but he was still bolstered with all that dark magic. I know I'm strong, and powerful. That we all are.

Especially together.

But I also know we've never faced anything like this. And I believed I was special once before, then spent the next decade not even knowing who I really was.

Jacob comes to stand next to me and slips his arm around my shoulders. "Ready?"

I nod. Because I don't know what I might say if I speak.

We won't do the actual spell. The words are too powerful, too sacred. Tonight is about more mapping out how it will all go. We'll hold space for the words in our heads, but we won't risk saying them. Not until it's time.

We all take our places. A pentagon more than a circle this time. Me at the top point, looking out over the river, Jacob and Zander on one side, facing Ellowyn and Georgie, over the array of candles.

Georgie has researched this ritual backward and forward and inside out. "We'll each hold our crystals in our palms," she tells us, demonstrating with an innocuous pebble. "We'll wear whatever charms we see fit. We'll wait for the familiars to create their outer protection circle, and then Emerson will start." She nods at me. "She'll light the white candle, then we'll follow suit around the circle. When all our candles are lit, Emerson will start the chant. We'll add our voices in the same order."

"We're missing something," Ellowyn says darkly.

"What could we be missing?" I counter. "We've prepared and practiced and prepared all over again. We've done all that we could."

I'm not sure I believe it, but I will by tomorrow night.

"Ellowyn's right," Zander says, surprising everyone.

Maybe especially Ellowyn. "I haven't been able to put my finger on what's missing. But I feel it too. Something is missing from the ritual itself."

Georgie seems to take a long time to look at me. A foreboding shiver zips up my spine.

"There's no sacrifice." Her voice is grave. "Every major ritual I've ever done or read about requires some kind of sacrifice."

"Maybe there's no sacrifice needed," I suggest. "We're fighting the dark here. Maybe fighting for the light is enough."

"Sacrifice is always needed," Ellowyn replies, looking pale again. "For balance. It's a basic tenet to everything magical."

It's what we've always been taught. Magic seeks balance, and if it's not offered—magic will find its own. Everything has a cost. What we take, we must give. Like the seasons. Like the moon. Everything returns in its time, in its way. Earth. Air. Fire. Water. But it doesn't sit right tonight. Because what could we sacrifice that could possibly balance out the coming flood?

Maybe no one has an answer because there are no good ones.

It weighs on me, and I can see it weighs on all of us. As we discuss the finer points of the ritual. As we run through it, once and then again. Even as we begin to go our separate ways later.

"Staying here again tonight?" Georgie asks with a smile after Zander and Ellowyn leave, Octavius rubbing his face against her legs.

"Yes." I know she thinks it's Jacob, and it is. But it's not only Jacob. I feel closer to my grandmother here, and through her, closer to Rebekah. The voices of St. Cyprian don't reach me quite so loudly here. I sleep better. "You don't feel alone in that creaky old house, do you?"

"I've never felt alone there. I feel protected. There's a

dragon in the banister." She leans in and gives me a hug, the cat purring between us. "I'll see you in the morning."

Maybe our hug lasts a little longer than usual.

When she and Octavius leave, it's just Jacob and me, standing in the light of the almost-full moon. Cassie and Murphy have made themselves scarce, their work with the ritual practice done. Now it's their time, to recharge or find trouble… whatever it is that familiars do on their own that we lowly witches will never fully know or understand.

It amazes me anew how many worlds exist within the worlds we think we know.

Jacob runs a hand over my hair. I let my hands trail up his hard chest. But neither of us says anything as he leads me inside.

In fact, we don't talk much at all. We get into bed. We turn to each other, urgent and intense. And then we fall into sleep, tangled all around each other. As if it was any other day and we were ordinary people.

But the dream that grips me is not ordinary, no matter how familiar it seems.

There is a storm whipping around me. I hover above the confluence, looking at all that dark and churning water. All three rivers are angry. That thread of black is thicker and stronger than it was when Frost showed it to us before.

I used to have this dream all the time. And I realize that the nonmagic memories I had still included this. Even Carol's spell couldn't strip this dream from my memories. I've done this hovering a million times. I've looked at the rivers, at St. Cyprian, at this pretty little part of the world that means everything to me, over and over.

Tonight I lower myself down, closer and closer to the very center of the confluence. I keep going until my feet touch the cold water, and for a moment I hold myself there. Suspended while the might of three rivers races over my toes. For a moment.

Then I let go—

And I'm sucked in.

I go down, deeper and deeper. And for the first time I can remember ever having this dream, there are words.

Voices.

Whispers.

What will you sacrifice?

What will you give?

Haven't you known all along what you must do?

Warriors do not live in glory, Emerson. They die for it.

I sit bolt upright in bed, breathing heavily, the clawing sensation of drowning still clinging to me. Even as I recognize that I'm in Jacob's bed, beside him. That it's morning, dawn beginning to stretch and yawn its way across the sky outside.

The day of the ritual. The day of the flood. The day of the show, one way or another. It all comes down to today.

There's something swimming on the edge of my consciousness that I can't quite reach. An answer, if I could only get there—

Jacob puts his hand on my back. I must have woken him up and I feel bad about that. But some of the tension loosens at his touch. I can breathe easier. He's helping me relax. Helping me, the way he always has.

"Bad dream?"

I nod, then smile. "You're here. You're never here when I wake up."

His hand is hot and the heat moves through me, chasing away the tendrils of that dream. The water's dark, cold grasp. The insidious whispers. "No healing calls today and it's still early enough to get my chores in before breakfast. We'll count it as a good omen."

I think about my dream. Usually I float down to the water, then shoot back up. Usually it's about flying, not drowning. This time, for the first time, I did not rise from the confluence. I sank deeper.

Jacob kisses me. I wind myself around him because he's strong, safe and good, and best of all, *mine*.

And we'll need all the good omens we can get.

28

IT MIGHT BE THE END OF THE WORLD, BUT I still have a job to do. And maybe I'm a little jumpy, but I refuse to let that keep me from being the best bookseller in Missouri. Character shines in times of peril after all. Still, before I open the store, I stop at Holly Bishop's bakery and coffee shop. The vast quantities I already downed today aren't doing the trick.

I need sugar and fat *and* caffeine. I order the sweetest, thickest coffee drink on the menu and then wait for the barista to put it together, and possibly alert emergency services while she's at it. But as I wait, Carol walks in.

Like she's stalking me, I think balefully.

All my nerves, all my fears, all the whispers of *sacrifice* seem to surround me. But she merely smiles kindly, as she always has.

As she always does, even when she's casting spells and exerting her control.

"Good morning, Emerson." She casts an eye over me. "You're looking a bit worse for wear today."

That's a bit rich coming from someone who could use a glamour, yet *chooses* the hair of a labradoodle.

I pout a little, calling on everything I have to put up a good front. "Am I?"

Carol puts in an order for two coffees. I look out the window to see who she's buying for, and am not at all surprised to see Maeve Mather standing on the red bricks, practically vibrating as she looks down at her phone.

Texting, obviously. Who would take her call?

Carol follows my gaze. Then treats me to what I assume is her version of a maternal smile. "Maeve tells me you and Jacob North have started seeing each other. I imagine there was…some overlap."

She says that last part a little louder than the rest, and out of the corner of my eye I see a table of locals nod sagely. It takes me a long—dangerous—moment to remember the story she planted in my head. And spread around town. Skip may have *"gotten handsy,"* as I was told the police chief said, but I'd had something to do with it. My feminine wiles, apparently, since women have been held responsible for the reprehensible sins of men since the primordial ooze.

I turn my gaze back to Carol and I trot out the guileless smile of spell dim Emerson, who believed everyone on these old bricks was her friend. Or wanted to be. Not for the first time, I think of what a harsh term *spell dim* is and how Carol and her coven use it like a weapon—but this isn't the time to fight *that* battle. If I'm lucky, that time will come later.

I focus on now. And *this* battle. "Jacob and I are a bit overdue, don't you think?"

"What I think is that you, of all people, could do better than a town-hating hermit," Carol returns. "Couldn't you?"

I open my mouth to defend Jacob, automatically and robustly, but there's something about the way she looks at me that makes me realize that's what she's looking for. She's prodding, and she wants to get me worked up.

Because if I'm busy defending Jacob, I can't defend myself, and she can poke around inside me again.

She'll have to work a lot harder today. "You know, maybe you're right," I say with a shrug. I lean forward conspiratorially, but make sure to pitch my voice loud enough for the table of sage nodders to hear too. "But he's excellent in bed."

Carol rears back in surprise and perhaps a little bit of pearl-clutching horror.

I bite back a laugh and merely gaze at her. Like we're two girlfriends chattering about boys, tee-hee.

"How nice for you," she says, clearing her throat. "Will you be at Wilde House tonight?" Her voice is casual. "There's an emergency meeting of the town council at six to address the mayoral vacuum of power. There's a slightly *treasonous* idea being bandied about that we should simply merge with the county."

And I can feel the layers of her spellwork, winding around me, encouraging me to nod along as if the *"mayoral vacuum"* isn't the disappearance of her *son*. As if it's a fuzzy, bureaucratic notion that requires some dry meetings in overheated boardrooms, that's all.

Witches think she's a hero for dealing with her son in accordance with magical law, no matter how painful. Humans, I understand now, have already forgotten she ever had a son.

She's that good.

"It might be necessary to loop you in at some point," she's saying. "I know we all depend on your practical turn of phrase and keen insight, Emerson. It's always such a breath of fresh air. You would never be such a traitor to your town, would you?"

Treason. Traitor. She's not outright accusing me, is she? It's careful. Words planted. Spells cast.

"I'll be home," I return, cheerfully. I take the to-go cup the barista offers. "You know how I feel about properly functioning local governments, Carol. They are nothing short of the true, beating heart of our nation, and ambitious women are an asset to such a nation."

I probably shouldn't talk about beating hearts when my own is making a ruckus. I have to hope she'll mistake it for my usual zealousness about local politics instead of an invitation to mind wipe me again, here and now.

And anyway, we won't be at Wilde House when the Joywood come looking tonight. We'll be at the cemetery. No doubt she'll track us down easily enough, but hopefully we can get the ritual accomplished before the ruling coven descends upon us.

"I'll prepare a few flowcharts," I say sweetly. "And between you and me, Carol, I might just take this opportunity to announce my own mayoral run. What do you think? Could there be a better-qualified candidate?"

And if there was time, I most certainly would have launched into a pocket lecture on how well-qualified women must be to lose to cravenly underqualified men, but I refrain. Only because I'm not really running for mayor.

Her pleasant mask slips, just for a second. "It's a small town. Ambitious women need to be careful they're not lured to a power they can't contain, don't you think?" But the edge in her eyes doesn't make it to her voice, and I can't fully read her. Maybe the anger isn't what I think it is.

For all I know she misses her weasel son and wishes she

didn't spell me so deeply—as far as she knows—so I could probably be more mindful of her feelings.

Maybe I should even ask for her help.

She's the most powerful witch in the world. She's almost certainly worked her magic in me because she thought it was the right thing to do. If she was evil, how could St. Cyprian be a safe haven?

"Take care, Emerson." And *that* sounds like it's a warning. Before I can say anything in return, she's turned and left the coffee shop. I watch as she crosses the street to where Maeve is waiting. They both look back over at me, laughing, and even across the distance I can feel that neither one of them is a safe space.

They wouldn't help me. They wouldn't believe the darkness, the coming flood, is real. Haven't they been arguing with Jacob for years? Telling him that nothing was wrong? That he was imbalanced, not the world? They would think something about *me* is wrong. They probably already do.

And I can't pretend to understand all the weighty magical concerns that members of the world's most powerful coven must have. But I know a thing or two about women. And I know that Maeve and Carol never liked my grandmother. They weren't too hot on my mother either, and they *really* didn't care for Rebekah and me.

We were embarrassments to our family name, something that was clear since elementary school—but neither one of us had the grace to *act* as ashamed as we should have. We were a little too bright, a little too bold. We were too loud. We had opinions we didn't bother to hide. We thought too highly of ourselves, never sufficiently cowed by the fact we couldn't find our magic the way the other kids did.

And it pains me to say this, but there are some women who find younger women threatening. Who try to stamp out a girl's brightness instead of nurturing it. Women who tut and sniff about *rules* and *behavior* because they see something shiny and want to dim it.

I understand them. And more, I know with absolute certainty that if we were all human, they'd hate us just the same.

Because whatever else Carol Simon and Maeve Mather might be, they're small.

Tiny.

I am not.

So no, the Joywood aren't going to help.

It's up to me and my friends to save St. Cyprian.

I'm just a little worried that in order to do that, I'm going to have to sacrifice *everything*.

I walk outside once Carol and Maeve move on. I head down pretty, historic Main Street toward Confluence Books. I look around the town as I walk. *My* town. The birds are singing. There's green everywhere. Crocuses and daffodils. Spring is here and life is beautiful, and St. Cyprian is what it's always been and always will be.

Mine.

Just like that song I've been singing to myself forever. The words Grandma gave me. They were so powerful they existed even underneath Carol's mind wipe.

And I'm not small. I'm big enough to know that when it comes down to it, I'll do what needs doing.

I always do.

I put in a full day's work, thoughts of sacrifice keeping me from feeling fully tethered to the store or myself. Worry and stress tangle deep in my gut, and I know I have to figure out a way to smooth that out—or hide it—before I head over to the cemetery for the real ritual.

If my friends know what kind of sacrifice is in the offing tonight, they'll try to stop me. I can't let that happen.

I close up the store after tactfully hurrying out the last customers for the day. I decide to take the ferry rather than magic myself over to the cemetery. I walk on and wave at my uncle.

He looks tired, but he smiles when I duck my head in the pilot booth. "How's it going, Em?"

"Good. Headed over to Jacob's. How's Aunt Zelda?"

He looks at me for a moment, and there's such a cloud of pain in his eyes. But he smiles. "Not bad," he lies. "Not bad at all."

"Good news," I say, forcing myself to smile. "I'm going to stand out and watch the sun set, but you let me know when it's a good time to visit."

"I will," he says, and I know it's another lie. He doesn't know I remember everything, doesn't think I can understand her mystery illness in my supposed spell-dim mind. And for now, I have to go on letting him believe that, no matter how much it makes me ache.

I walk to the side of the boat and look out at the confluence. I can't see that thread of black.

I frown out over the water. The Rivers family are Guardians. They guard the confluence, the three rivers, the power inherent there. I think about Aunt Zelda, her mysterious sickness. The fact my grandmother died so young—because one hundred and thirty really is young for a witch. It seems too many witches are dying before their time these days. Like my great-great-great-grandfather, who walked into the river. Does it all connect? To that swathe of malignant darkness in the confluence? Jacob can't cure my aunt, not the way things are now, but what if stopping the rising flood can?

Skip *used* dark magic, but he wasn't dark magic himself. Or he wasn't strong enough to wield it against my power or our combined power. Maybe he didn't know how to use it—maybe the dark magic even used him.

So many theories. So few answers. Just darkness and rising water and a flood we all know is coming.

Sacrifice yourself, Emerson.

I don't know if it's the voice from my dream or a voice in the here and now. It's not a voice I recognize. It sounds more like a mixture of voices I know, but none I can pick out for sure. I breathe in. I reach for the center of my power and let it ground me.

I will do what needs doing.

We land, I look back and give my uncle a wave as I exit, and then begin the walk to the cemetery. The last time I walked up this way, I walked to two separate awakenings in one long day. First, my near death. My rebirth. Because without that adlet attack, I don't find my power. I don't go on this journey. I don't find *me* again.

Does that mean I owe Skip a debt of gratitude?

I shake my head as I walk. "No, I don't think so."

That same day, I came back up this path in the evening. Buzzing with the newfound knowledge of who I was and what I could do. The power I'd had in me all along. The witch I was, free at last.

But I was still only half myself, without my memories.

Now I walk through the gates as me. For the first time, all me. I go straight for Grandma's grave. I put my hand on the stone fox and ask for my grandmother's guidance. Her protection.

As for the sacrifice, I'll leave it to the moment.

How very unlike me. Or maybe it's all me, at last.

I feel a presence and look back. Jacob stands back from the grave, Murphy and Cassie at his side. He's giving me my moment. He's good at that sort of thing.

Let's be real. He's good at all the things.

I smile and wave him over. He slides his arm around me and greets me with a quick, hot kiss. Georgie appears next, laden with tote bags and books. Octavius perched perilously on her shoulder. Jacob moves to help her as the cat jumps off. Ellowyn appears next to me, Zander just a bit too close behind her—while their birds circle at a distance from each other up above. Ellowyn moves to help Georgie too, and Zander stays behind with me.

I wish I had time to fix that rift, but I suppose it's a problem for another day. Assuming there is one. I turn to face my cousin. He quickly averts his eyes from Ellowyn's back to me, and smiles.

I'm not sure how I failed to realize how fake that smile is. How much he's always hiding in it. The pendant he gave me warms a little against my skin. I'm not sure if it's telling me something, or it knows its owner. But it's served its purpose for me.

I pull the necklace up and over my head. This morning I moved my grandmother's bluebell charm to a smaller chain I found at Jacob's. Now it makes sense why I felt that need. "You should have this for tonight."

He looks torn, but he bends his head so I can slip it over his head. "You're leading this thing."

"I am, but it's a combined effort, and you are our Guardian. A Rivers. You should wear your family's charm."

"You're family," he says, and takes my hand.

I hold his tight. "We're all family."

Then we walk to join the others to set up for our ritual.

This time we make a circle using the points of our various ancestors to lend us strength. I stand facing my grandmother's grave, and beyond her, the confluence. The moon is rising, and with it, so are the three rivers. Starting in the confluence, then moving out. Slowly. Like a dark, solid, rising wave.

When it crashes, it will destroy everything.

We didn't come here to end the world, but to save it.

Jacob takes his place in front of a great-great-grandfather's grave. Zander stands a few feet away from him with a three-times-great uncle. Georgie positions herself across from him, between two Pendells. She reaches out for Ellowyn, who's standing in front of her great-grandmother. On the witch side.

Jacob and Georgie are on either side of me, and they each reach out for me. We all clasp hands. "Before we start, there are things I want you all to know," I begin.

"No speeches," Ellowyn says. "God."

"You know she practiced it, though," Georgie argues.

She's overruled.

"No goodbyes, Emerson," Jacob cuts them off, a hard warning tone to his voice. "No one sacrifices themselves. That's not balance."

I've let you be the sacrificial lamb before. I can't do it again. I can't, Em.

That last part is just for me. I wouldn't have understood it if I didn't remember everything, but I do. He tried to stop Carol's mind wipe, and I wouldn't let him. With what little power I had then, I stopped him.

Maybe the power wasn't so little. Maybe the power was never so little.

And maybe there's a way to avoid a sacrifice this time around. I certainly don't *want* to die. But I will do what I have to do.

I always do what I have to do.

"This isn't a goodbye," I say, carefully choosing my words. "It's a thank-you. For ten years, I didn't know who I was. I can't imagine what you all went through, pretending to be something you weren't, just for me. You hurt for me—I know that. But you were still my best friends. You still showed up. You never so much as hinted that I was anything less than fully me."

"You were you," Zander says gruffly.

"As much you as possible," Jacob agrees.

"Relentlessly," Ellowyn says dryly.

"We love you," Georgie says, looking a little teary.

"That's the point," I say, though I feel weepy myself. "Love got us this far. Love can do anything. It can beat back the dark." I meet Jacob's gaze. Everything I am was always inside of me, but he had a part in unlocking it. "It has. It *will*."

If I have to sacrifice myself, I'll do it for love. Not fear. Never fear.

"How touching," an unfamiliar voice says sardonically.

We all turn, dropping our linked hands to see Nicholas Frost.

He's appeared behind me, cloak in the wind and disdain etched across his aristocratic face, but he's *here*.

Hope blooms inside of me. He came. He's here. I *really* wish he'd come for the practice run, but maybe he's done this a million times before. And his presence brings us to six. That has to tip the odds in our favor. "Did you *finally* decide to help save St. Cyprian?"

"I'm complicated," he says mildly. "But let's make it a full house, shall we?"

He snaps his fingers and a light shines, too bright to look at directly. We all flinch and shield our eyes.

But when I can drop my arm, and look at the light without my eyes watering, there's a woman there.

"Rebekah." Not an image. Not a vision or a dream. Her real body. *Here*.

She's dressed for warmer weather in a ripped T-shirt that shows hints of more piercings. And she scowls at Frost. "What the fuck?"

He only stares back at her, a faint curve to his arrogant mouth and a gleam in his ancient gaze.

I rush forward, unable to stop myself. I grab her and she's *real*. My sister is *here*.

God, I can't let myself cry but it takes almost everything I have to keep the tears at bay.

"I knew you'd come," I whisper.

But Rebekah is staring daggers at Frost. "I didn't ask to be brought here. I didn't *agree*."

"Who told you that your agreement was necessary?" Frost asks lazily, but with a deep power beneath. "It's time to grow up, witchling."

He inclines his head toward me.

Rebekah looks at me, and her stubborn mouth, a lot like mine, trembles slightly. Then she shifts her gaze beyond me. To the rivers, churning black and oily. The waters, rising in ever bigger waves as a cold wind picks up.

"Oh," she says, eyes widening. "It's even worse than my dreams."

"Help us, Rebekah," I say. Maybe I'm pleading. I'm not afraid to beg—not tonight. "If you leave again afterward, I'll understand. But please stay and help."

I want to tell her what Jacob told me, that help makes us *more*. But I can already see the scornful face she'll make if I present her with what she calls my *slogans*.

"I don't want to help St. Cyprian," she says quietly, and for a moment I think all is lost.

Rebekah looks at the rivers. Then she turns to look at Ellowyn.

Then she looks at me, too many emotions in her dark eyes that are just like mine. "But I'll help *you*."

"We had best get started, then," Frost drawls. "'A rising tide waits for no tender reunion.' I'm sure that's the quote."

Georgie frowns at him. "It is not."

We go back to our places, adding two more people and completing our circle at last. A full coven. I want to *laugh*. Because despite everything, here we are. We are going to stop this dark flood that threatens everything.

One way or another. I know it.

I can feel our power, like the scent of a new season laced through the breeze.

All together now, we follow the words of the ritual. This time, we say the words.

"*We call on the wisdom of history, all souls who came before,*" Georgie says solemnly.

"*We call on the earth, all she is, all she gives.*" Jacob's hand is hot in mine.

"*We call on the rivers, protectors of who we are.*" Zander sends a sideways look at Ellowyn.

She resolutely keeps her gaze on me. "*We call on the spirits, the truth of them and us and everything in between.*"

And with each step around the circle, the candles blaze to life, one by one. And with each new candle, the flames lift higher, twining into a column of light.

Good, solid magic.

Full-coven magic.

"*We call on the future, on all that can be,*" Rebekah whispers, almost as if the words surprise her.

"*We call on time. On power. On all that we are and have been.*" Frost, if anything, looks *bored*, but his words practically boom inside our circle.

And then it's my turn. *"We call on the strength within, ours and our ancestors'. Ours and all witchkind's."*

Together, we say the rest. Together, with all that we've called upon, we start the ritual that will stop this flood.

Because it has to.

"With the moon made full, we seven are the light. With the merging rivers, we seven are ready to rise. We will beat back the dark. We will stop the water's mark."

We are already more powerful than we've ever been before. I can feel it welling up in us like a song.

We lift our faces to the rising full moon, still not high in the sky. Somewhere, the Joywood are making their own plans, but I can't think about that yet. First we have to save our beloved town from an impending doom no one else seems to recognize.

The column of light climbs. Then it thickens. We repeat our chant. Three times. Five times. Seven times. A full coven, weaving our magic into this night.

And then we send all our light straight into the heart of that oily blackness.

Light crashes into dark with loud, thundering booms that shake the ground under our feet. It's a terrible dance, and we have to push our power behind the light as the dark tries to split it, twine around it, and choke it out.

And us with it.

But we dance. We fight.

And get nowhere.

Our power against the dark, strike after strike, is nothing but a shattering stalemate.

All the while, the rivers rise.

You know what you have to do. It's Frost's icy voice inside my head.

I flick a glance at him. Unlike all the other people in the

circle, who have their eyes on the great circle of the moon, he's looking right at me, eyes blazing.

But I find myself nodding. Because I do know. "I have to go into the confluence myself."

"Like hell you do," Jacob growls from beside me.

I don't look directly at him. I know he'll see right through me. I look around the circle, never holding anyone's gaze for too long. It's not that I'm afraid. It's that I don't want them to be.

"I've always had this dream," I say. "I go into the confluence, over and over. Haven't I, Rebekah?"

My sister is alight with a power she shouldn't have any more than I should have mine. "Since we were kids."

"I go into the confluence. It's meant. It's right."

"It's not in the ritual," Georgie counters.

"The ritual doesn't seem to be working," I point out gently. "We need more. This has been in my dreams my whole life. It's *meant*." Maybe it's the prophecy but I don't say that out loud. "I have to go."

"Then let the town drown," Jacob says viciously. "Because you're not doing it tonight."

Zander and Ellowyn murmur their agreement. Sides are drawn.

"You're not going in there," Jacob says, and I know I have to look at him. I don't need his permission, but I need us to be on the same page. It's the only way I have any chance of survival.

If survival is an option.

"I have to do it, Jacob," I say quietly.

The wind is whipping at us. There's a screaming in the distance, and I know it's the rivers themselves. We don't have time to argue. I don't have time to convince everyone.

But I need them to trust me. I need *him* to trust me before all is lost.

"We'll fight the dark some other day," Jacob is saying. "You're not sacrificing yourself. It's not happening. If we have to hold you down ourselves—and Em. Hear me. I will."

"I know you will," I reply. "I know you would."

I know his love is like the earth, solid and welcoming. But this is a different fate.

"She always comes out," Rebekah offers. "Right, Em? In your dreams, you always come out. Wildes always rise."

I didn't rise last night, but I smile anyway. "Always," I say. I turn my gaze back to Jacob.

I know you're scared for me, but trust me. You promised to trust me.

I'm asking too much of him. I know that. But this isn't about him. Or me.

St. Cyprian is mine and I am St. Cyprian's.

I've always known it would come to this, haven't I? Even when I wasn't the least bit magical. I always knew that if this place asked, I would give.

I will.

"I trust you," he grits out.

Because he really does. He trusts me.

And because he loves me. If I don't come back, he'll know that this is the fate I accepted long ago, before I knew words like *soul mates* and *conduits*. This is the love I never feared.

These people who adore me, my marvelous family both born and made—plus immortal Nicholas Frost—will learn how to laugh when they tell this story. And if I know anything about myself, I'll figure out how to haunt them all so I can correct them in the telling of it.

I want to give a thousand speeches, but I settle for a smile.

I pull Rebekah's hand to Jacob's on my other side, to keep the circle intact.

I'm Emerson Wilde, last in a line of powerful witches, and I can accomplish *anything*.

Nothing ever ends. The circle turns, again and again. Seasons change, moons rise.

St. Cyprian is mine. I am St. Cyprian's.

We are what matters. These people. This magic we make. This bright, beautiful love we share.

Fate is a choice and this is mine.

And so I fly out to meet it at last.

29

I FLY ABOVE THE CONFLUENCE. EXCEPT IT'S not exactly the confluence now. Not any longer. There's a thick black column rising from it. That same thick, oily, sickening blackness I've seen way too much of lately.

This is the wave that wants to take out St. Cyprian. And possibly most of the Midwest along with it. Possibly all of witchkind.

I'll have to dive through all that darkness to get to the place I've always dreamed about. The center of everything. Three rivers meeting in power.

It's what I have to do, and if the immortal *also* knows I have to do it, I'd say I'm on the right track.

Fate, something in me says. *Destiny.*

And maybe I'll survive. After all, like Rebekah said, in all the dreams from my childhood about these rivers, I came out every time. Maybe last night I didn't, and maybe that means something. But going in, I'll plan to live.

I plan to live *fantastically*, in fact. Starting here, flying high above everything and everyone I love.

I fit my hand around my grandmother's charm. I ask her and all my ancestors for strength.

Not to survive. But to fight off this darkness that doesn't belong here.

Once that's done, I'll worry about me.

I dive.

The black is a shock of cold, so cold it hurts. I try to let my power warm me, but it's a battle. It's a fight to get through the wave, the flood rising high, the screaming waters all around me. Every inch I manage to accomplish is agony.

But I keep going. Because the pain is worth it.

The black seems to suck me in, like my dream, but it's worse. There are teeth to it. Fangs. And scraping, screaming agony.

When I finally get into the actual confluence, that very place where three magnificent rivers meet and mingle, it's another shock of hideous cold—but only on one side of me. On the other is the sweet heat of *right*. It helps me refocus. Reset.

Breathe.

I open my eyes in the water of the confluence. It's murky and black, but deep, deep down, blinking down lower still, is an ominous red.

I've seen that red before. My body reacts, breaking out in goose bumps, and I feel my power flare. This only confirms what I know instinctually.

I must destroy it.

I try to send out a blast of power, but it doesn't work in the dark, cold water. I try again, calling on all that power, but it doesn't meet me where I am. It can't get through the weight of the pitiless water.

I have to get there myself. I have to touch it.

I start to kick, to try to swim. To launch myself with the power inside of me, but it's weakening. I'm losing against the current. Against the black.

The cold presses into me, crowding me.

I understand then that I am truly alone. The cold whispers that truth to me, and the truth winds its way in deep until it feels like my bones. *Alone.*

And suddenly it's as if I'm being ripped apart, wrenched wide open so I can finally face the truth.

I see a vision of myself as a little girl, sitting alone out behind the house where the wild grasses lead down to the river. Except it doesn't feel like a memory. It feels like I'm there. I look around, sure my parents, my grandmother, Rebekah must be near, but I see no one. I feel the sun on my neck and a chill breeze on my face. I'm no more than four. Maybe five. And I start to walk toward the river, then break out into a full run, even as the part of me that's here, deep beneath the water, screams for that little girl to stop. To turn back around. To *stop—*

This isn't how the story goes, I try to say to the cold, to that implacable truth making my bones feel like lead and regret.

This is the story, it whispers back. *It's always been the story, hasn't it?*

On and on I run, until the river is right there in front of me, beckoning me like my ancestors before me—

But suddenly I'm not a little girl anymore. I'm a teenager, barely fourteen on a cold January day. I'm standing in an empty staircase in school, staring out the narrow windows at the river in the distance. I can hear the voices of my friends, my sister, rising up from the landing we liked to claim in between classes and at lunch, away from all the judgy little witches who smirked at the Wilde girls and their supposed lack of magic. I can smell the cleaning agents on the shiny floors. When I reach out my hand, I can feel the brick beside the window and then the cold glass beneath my palm.

All I have to do is walk down the stairs. My people are *right there.*

But I don't.

Because you're not like them, the cold tells me. *You are always apart.*

I feel it in me, the little whispers of *what-ifs* that the real me knows will lead to me taking on Carol—or trying. And beneath all that, the curling, inky certainty that in the end, it will be up to me. Only me.

That dream, rising in the confluence, has always been about me alone.

And I know something, deep in my heart. Heavier than the lead in my bones.

I will have to do it myself. *I have to do everything myself.*

Emerson Wilde is solitary, always. A powerful woman has to be. To survive. To endure. To succeed.

But I wanted more...

I'm sinking. Farther and farther I go. Down into the deep I am made of lead and solitude, as I have always been—

The images inside my head begin to cascade, except none of them feel like images. I'm there inside them. A little bit older, whispering treacherous things into Jacob's ear, but still understanding that it was up to me alone. That he didn't *fully* understand. That I was apart, always.

That thought doesn't sit right. Something churns deep within me and there's a whisper of something far off, but I can't make it out.

Focus, Emerson. It's that voice from the ferry. Familiar and yet unidentifiable. *Sacrifice yourself. It's the only way.*

That little kernel of certainty glows inside me. It makes

me understand that what I tell myself is noble is really this—that I have only me.

I'm with my sister on the night she ran away, pleading with her—arguing with her—but that hunching certainty within me knows better. She will run. I will stay. There is no coin and we are two sides of nothing. If she doesn't listen to me, if she doesn't fight with me, who will?

Then I'm in Wilde House, but not the version I live in now. I see my parents, packing up to leave. And I know, even in my spell-dim state, that it's wrong. It doesn't make sense that two people so dedicated to our family's history in this town would abandon it. It doesn't make any *sense*—

But it does make sense, the cold tells me.

And a new certainty slams into me like a blow, knocking the air from my body. Making me gasp and kick.

But all the writhing in the world can't save me from the truth barreling at me like a train.

Even your grandmother, comes that same, insidious voice. *She died so young. She could have saved herself, but she didn't. Why do you think that is?*

And I can't avoid it any longer. The train flattens me. The real truth shimmers.

Finally, *finally*, I understand that no one, no one ever has or ever could love me. Rebekah refused to stay and fight. My parents cared only about how little power I showed, never me. Even Jacob just *let me* be mind wiped.

The cold and dark around me embraces me. I let myself sink, because I can't fight the truth. I am alone.

Great Hecate, the self-pity, comes Cassie's voice in my head.

My heart shatters around me. All my dreams, my plans, in shards as I face the bitter reality...

I'm alone, I shout at her, through that link we share.

How I wish that were true, Cassie replies, warm and spiky, as always. The warmth seems to bite at me. Through the cold, through the crushing realizations. *But here we are. And maybe, Emerson, you could stop letting the darkness win.*

It's the truth—

It's not. Her voice in my head brooks no argument. *Even if every single thing you just thought was true, and it's not, you're forgetting that I was always there. Against my will.*

Something in me shifts. The leaden weight in my bones seem to twist, and suddenly I see more. Cassie, waiting for me at the water's edge when I was little. Cassie, just outside the school window that January day, rolling around in the snow. I go back through all the images in my head and there she is, every time.

Think, my familiar urges me, and this time there's no trace of her trademark sarcasm. *Who does it benefit if you think you're a lonely martyr, destined to stay alone forever?*

I remember my fight with Skip on the bluff outside Frost's house. How he blocked out my friends to concentrate on me alone. Separating me from the greatest source of my power. For a reason.

There's a difference between a leader and a lonely fool, I think then.

Because they all came. They always came. Even now, Rebekah might not want to be here, she might not care about St. Cyprian, but she said she'll fight for me. Not the town.

Me.

Fight the outside voices, Cassie urges me. *The darkness doesn't know you. It only knows what you fear. You are a Confluence Warrior. Fight.*

So I do. With the most powerful force of all. I listen to my heart. Still beating, warm and hot.

This iced-over darkness can't claim me. Can't mess with

me so that I fail before I start. I will fight it. I will fight *everything*.

Because I'm the Confluence Warrior. Because my friends are waiting. They need me—and I need them. It doesn't end here.

I make myself rally, kicking out at the blackness. I reach out with all of my strength.

And I remind myself that I have never been alone.

I'm not alone now.

That's the entire point of a coven, my familiar tells me dryly. *Dumbass*.

I need your help, I call out then, sending Cassie my gratitude.

And my coven answers me.

I can feel the circle pour its power into me, strength and light, helping me swim lower. I can feel their chanting in my blood, fueling me.

More, just a little more.

I swim until my muscles feel torn, then I keep going until they're numb. I kick. I pull. Until my whole body is screaming.

Every force of light they've conjured is in me now, and I'm so close.

But not close enough.

I reach out, my energy fading. I can barely keep my eyes open. I feel used up, and my body is slowly stiffening in the cold grip of the water. It's in my bones. It's in my throat.

It's everywhere.

Maybe I can't reach it. Maybe this is the sacrifice. If I let the dark take me, if I bargain with the dark, maybe they'll be safe.

Sacrifice yourself, Emerson, comes that voice from last night's dream. A voice that is many voices. *St. Cyprian will be saved. Your friends will be saved.*

I need a promise.

Only a Wilde sacrifice will stop it all.

If I let go, if I give up…

I want to.

St. Cyprian is mine and I am St. Cyprian's. The words echo inside of me, over and over again, in my own voice this time. From child to adult. Always those same words.

Time is mine until time takes me home. Rebekah's voice. Now. Then. Always by my side even when she was far away. Two sides of a coin.

And then my grandmother whispering into my ear: *Wildes don't sacrifice themselves to lose.*

We rise, I say. I shout. I *know*.

I reach out, blind but sure, and my fingers brush something cold. So cold it burns like fire and I want to snatch back my hand.

But I don't. I've found the heart of the dark in the confluence.

It shouldn't be here. It doesn't belong here.

I curl my hand around it, use all that is inside me to crush it in my hand, pouring all my power into its destruction. It screams. It fights.

It pours into me, that frigid fire.

It consumes me. It conquers me.

But I only crush it harder. It can take all of me, but I don't let go. Because my coven, our familiars, all those ancestors who came together to make *me* are with me. Giving me the last bit of strength to destroy this blight.

I keep my gaze—what there is of it—on the thing in my hand. In my peripheral vision I see monsters and nightmares. They come at me, claws and teeth.

They rend my flesh. They wail in my ears. The pain is indescribable, but there is warmth in fighting it. Jacob's warmth, healing me with all he is. There is protection in the water, in the confluence, Zander guarding me with all the power of the ancient Rivers family. Ellowyn's and Rebekah's past and future are a thread of pure light, keeping me tethered, while Georgie whispers all our histories, a reminder of what we can do when our cause is noble.

When love is at its heart.

I don't look at the monsters. I don't think about the pain. One by one, my circle's magic flows through me and takes them down.

I crush and crush, with the strength in all of us.

All seven become one.

And we are amazing.

Gold infuses the vile red. And suddenly, with a groan like a living thing, it cracks. The sound echoes like madness.

Then it bursts apart, like glitter. And as the glitter spreads out around me in the water, the thick ribbons of black begin to shrink, fade, disappear.

We did it.

And I have nothing left in me.

I've given all I have to give.

I sink.

30

I SINK DOWN, AND MAYBE I WON'T RISE. I'M too tired and spent to even be worried about that. Maybe the rising was metaphorical all along. It doesn't matter.

Because we stopped the dark. In the end, that's all that matters.

There's a part of me that accepts this. The surface is too far away and I have nothing in me. No spell, no stamina, but I did what I was made to do. The dark didn't win—thanks to Cassie, thanks to my coven, thanks to *me*. And there's a joy in that, even now.

I let go.

I give myself to the water. The confluence. These three rivers that made me who I am.

And I hardly notice when I'm not sinking any longer.

I'm pulled up. Painfully, slowly, but with such resolute power.

I'm dragged out of the water. There's the kiss of sky, then I feel land beneath me. There's a commotion, hands and magic all over me, but there's a fog holding me down.

Or maybe I am the fog.

Am I breathing? I think I'm dying.

I'm okay with that. I made my peace with it.

I hear Jacob's voice. His hand is on my heart. He's trying to heal me, but he's already used so much power to help me, he doesn't have the strength.

I try to tell him it's okay. In his mind. Out loud.

Let me go, I tell him. I tell all of them.

But instead of a soft slip into whatever's beyond the fog, I get a hard punch in the arm.

"Emerson, we already made our sacrifices," Rebekah says fiercely in my ear. "Ten years we sacrificed for this place. This isn't your sacrifice to make. *Fight,* damn it."

I cough and water leaks out of my mouth. I feel Jacob's healing might, finding a way.

My head is elevated and cradled in Georgie's lap. Rebekah is holding my left hand, her free hand in a fist. Ellowyn has my right. Zander and Frost are chanting, words I dimly recognize. About rivers and dreams, rising and sorrow. Prayers for life that begin in grief. Songs of lamentation that ease into light.

And Jacob pours his healing power into me, a bright beam, like salve and benediction on fire.

I suck in a deep, rattling breath and manage to open my eyes. The full moon shines high above me. Into me. Into all of us. Without the full moon and all its quicksilver magic, we'd be dead. Lost beneath the river of dark.

I close my eyes again. Breathe it in. Let it sink into me. When I open my eyes again, I see only Jacob. His hands are still on my chest.

He's as empty as I've ever seen him. Pale as the moon. But

his eyes are open and on me. I reach out, but I don't quite have the strength to touch his face like I want to.

"We did it," I whisper.

"You did it, Confluence Warrior."

I shake my head a little. I can't move to look at all my friends in turn, but my eyes track around the circle they've created to protect me. Our familiars in another circle, double protection. "It was all of us. I couldn't reach without you. I'd still be down there without you. The power of seven."

Everyone looks spent. Frail and tired. Even our immortal.

But we won, and even in our exhaustion, there is the *joy* of that deep inside, shining through on all our faces. Our familiars make it sound more like a party, sending up a chorus of screeches, hoots, barks and meows to celebrate.

Because we won. I'm still lying on the ground, but I laugh. "We stopped a world-ending flood." And even though I had all the faith in the world we would succeed—with or without my eventual survival—it is sheer *awe* moving through me. "We *saved the world*, guys."

We really are all that. But then, I've always thought so.

Eventually, I feel strong enough to be helped to my feet. Rebekah and Georgie weave their arms around my waist. Zander and Frost help Jacob get up. No one uses magic.

Maybe we just want to revel in our physical bodies for a moment, having saved…everything.

Maybe we're all a little burned-out around the edges.

"We still have to face the Joywood," Jacob points out. My voice of truth, even now. Always willing to point out the flaws in a plan—but I'm glad that these days, I know that only makes me stronger. Makes *us* stronger. "There's no way a single witch in witchkind didn't feel what happened here."

"Going to stick around for that one, Frost?" Zander asks, but with notably less sharpness than before.

"I am eternal," he replies. Sedately. "I always stick around, river child. By definition."

Beside me, I feel my sister stiffen. "I can't stay, Em," she says, her voice rough. "I'm not supposed to be here. I'm not sure the Joywood will listen if I try to tell them I didn't come back by choice."

I manage to turn my head in time to see the way Rebekah and Ellowyn look at each other, years of their friendship unspoken between them. Ellowyn leans in and bumps her shoulder to Rebekah's, an easy jostle I've seen a thousand times before.

But not in a long, long while.

Neither of them speaks out loud, but Frost does. "Easy come, easy go," he murmurs, though I'm sure I see something like disappointment in his gaze. "I am sure the world waits with bated breath for the return of a powerless witchling. How proud you must be."

"Many a man considers himself a god even without immortality," Ellowyn comments. "Not all of them take it as far as you have. What's that about?"

Frost only smiles. And keeps his gaze on Rebekah. "When you're ready to slink off to your life of mortal glory, do sing out. I live to serve."

Everyone else moves away then, giving Rebekah and me some space to talk. Rebekah keeps her arm around me, and I remember this. Just the two of us against the world—the world that insisted we were less than what we knew, deep down, we were meant to be. I look down at Grandma's grave. This is better. Just the three of us, and I know who we are now.

Who we've always been.

"Are you really okay?" Rebekah asks.

I nod, holding on to her. In another place and time—last

week even—I might have demanded she stay, demanded she let me fix things for her. But in this misty moment while I'm still recovering, I understand what she needs is more important than what I think she needs.

"I hope you'll come home soon. By your own choice."

Her expression is pained, but in the language that is just ours, she promises she will. Then she turns toward Frost, looming beneath the cemetery gates, his flowing cloak intact, his raven on his shoulder. He sighs, then snaps his fingers, and Rebekah disappears.

With the words *Wildes rise* echoing between us.

Georgie comes back to help me stand on my unsteady feet. Jacob leans on Zander. Much like that morning I fought off Skip's adlets. And won. Our familiars are nearby, perhaps recovering themselves.

Wildes rise.

I grin at Cassie. *Damn right we do.* But I owe her more than that. *Cassie, I can never repay—*

Familiars shun such cloying human behavior. Honestly.

I want to cry, but I hold back the tears. Because we won, and now is the time for joy. We earned it. *Thank you all the same.*

She inclines her head, regally. Her eyes are warm, and if I'm not attributing *human* behaviors to familiars, a little misty too. But she lopes off to find some of her own rest before I can point that out.

"Let's go back to Jacob's," Georgie is saying. "Everyone will need to rest up if the Joywood come after us tonight."

"I'll make sure there's no trace of us," Frost says, drifting closer. And it's clear, he isn't overly concerned about the Joywood. Or maybe he can snap his fingers and escape them. I make a note to learn *that* spell.

What matters is that he showed up. He brought Rebekah.

He completed the coven. I turn to look at him. A solitary figure standing in the ruins of the ritual.

"Nicholas," I say.

He takes his time looking toward me, as if affronted by my use of his name.

"Thank you," I say, sagging against Georgie. "Not just for us, but for all of St. Cyprian."

"Your gratitude is my only true reward," he replies.

Mockingly, of course.

But I smile. "You don't know it yet, but you're screwed. You're in the coven. You're ours now. Solitary playtime in your haunted house is over. Mark my words."

The immortal witch only rolls his eyes, but I take that as an acknowledgment. As a victory.

It's only one step, but it's an important one. Another victory tonight.

"Come on, Em," Georgie urges me.

But Frost is looking at me—at us—in a manner I can only call ominous.

"The battle is won," he murmurs. "But the war is another matter."

I frown at him. "That felt like a war already."

But he waves an arm, and a wall appears. A fortress in midair, hiding the remains of the ritual.

And himself.

"Do immortals have to be so opaque?" I mutter.

"I'm pretty sure it's required," Georgie says sagely.

We both smile. But inside, I can feel something in me shaking itself off. Maybe the war Frost means is with the Joywood and the reckoning I know will be coming about the power they claimed I didn't have. Probably tonight. Maybe it's more than that.

Whatever it is, I'll meet it head-on. They can't take us out now. We saved St. Cyprian. Maybe all of witchkind. Jacob said it himself—everyone will have felt what we did.

And Rebekah and I at the center of it.

Maybe a punishment is coming, but they can hardly mind wipe us all after we saved the town. I'll make certain Carol knows it.

Perhaps with a PowerPoint. Or two.

We walk back to the house, soaking in the moonlight. The familiars scatter—they have their own mysterious familiar ways of recuperating.

I feel stronger with every step, but hardly strong. Even when we reach the house, Jacob and I still need help on the stairs, like we've aged a million years tonight.

But I'm starting to find it almost funny.

"We're hobbling around like we're Frost's age," I say, laughing as I make it inside. Barely.

"Hilarious," Jacob says, but his gaze on me is warm.

Deliciously warm.

Ellowyn charges into the kitchen and is back with a tray of mugs before we've even sat down. She hands one to each of us, even Zander. Then she collapses into Jacob's big armchair.

Everyone's sitting. Everyone's got a mug. We're spent. We're exhausted.

But we all look as elated as we do tired, because we did it. We stopped the flood. And maybe there's more to fight, but not right now. Not this minute.

And if that doesn't call for a speech, what does?

I try to stand, but Jacob holds me firm on his lap. "Speech if you must, but do it sitting."

I'm not sure how long I could have stood anyway at this point, though I would never admit that. "When I was down there—"

Ellowyn holds up a hand. "Do we really have to rehash

right now? I remember well enough." She shudders. "I thought we'd lost you. No need to relive."

I survey my friends' faces. Zander stares at his mug, Georgie swallows with tears in her eyes, but when I turn my head to meet Jacob's gaze, it's as steady as ever.

"We did lose you, for a moment or two," he says quietly. "But I knew you'd fight your way back."

My throat closes up, but I force a breath through that. Trust. Love. These are the things that saved the day. Not a sacrifice. Not even a well-executed plan.

"Cassie helped." I realize she was the only one who could in that moment because the rest of them were busy, you know, holding back a whole world-ending flood.

"It's what familiars are meant to do," Zander says. "It's who they are."

The same way we're witches. It's *who* we are, not what we are. I feel that deeply tonight. I pull in another deep breath. Then I raise my mug. "A toast."

"I hope it's to us," Ellowyn says dryly.

"Oh, it's to us. And our kick-ass coven. And saving the town. And the world. It's to us, and—"

Jacob's hand tightens on my arm. *Leave it at that, Em. Whatever comes next will come soon enough.*

He's right, sadly. As much as the Warrior in me is already focusing in on the next step, the next fight, there is something to be said for savoring a hard-won victory.

Besides, the Joywood will make their displeasure known soon enough.

"Here's to us," I say instead of the next rallying battle cry. "And love and trust, and most of all, light winning over dark. We'll make sure it always does."

"Damn right we will," Zander says, shocking everyone

by clinking his mug with Ellowyn's without any snarky comments or pained expressions.

Maybe there's hope after all.

Maybe there's always hope.

We settle into silence, enjoying the simple comfort of each other's company and Ellowyn's restorative tea.

"They'll probably wait until midnight, don't you think?" Ellowyn asks sometime later. "For prime-time mind wiping?"

"Probably," Georgie agrees with remarkably equanimity, sipping her tea. "Which gives us an hour or so to rest."

"The familiars will warn us when they're coming," Jacob says, but his gaze is on me. "Emerson, you should go upstairs and get some sleep."

"Finish that tea first," Ellowyn insists.

And, since I can't even stand on my own two feet without help, I down the rest. I'm ready for a little of my strength back. Jacob does the same. I don't think he likes leaning on Zander any more than I like seeing him so spent because of me.

"Both of you," Georgie insists, patting Jacob's back like he's her cat. "You two used the most energy. Rest, and we'll get you when it's time."

Then we land in Jacob's room with a thump, and somehow don't collapse to the floor. The tea must be working.

"Georgie just sent us to our room," I say, laughing again. Maybe I'm slightly hysterical. Then I think, *our room.*

Jacob's mouth is curled up on one side, and I know he heard that. Absorbed it for what it is. Somehow this has become *ours*, even though it's his.

"Look," he says, and points to the window. He stands behind me and I lean into him as his arms come around me and we hold each other up. This is my favorite place to be. The two of us together, looking out at St. Cyprian. The confluence three healthy rivers now, as it should be. Because we beat back the dark.

We did it.

Jacob does whatever it is he does, so that I can see deep into that pulsing center. That meeting place where I accepted my death. Embraced it. Then lived.

I can see the very fabric of it now. No longer laced with dark, but instead shot through with light. Glittering, beautiful light, powering the town, and the world, and us.

He rests his mouth against my head. "Come on. Rest. We'll need you on your A game when Carol comes to mete out justice."

I don't want to stop staring at the confluence, at this glorious thing we did. I feel like I'm getting power just from that. Just from him.

Just from this. Us.

But with that power comes a clarity. I didn't die.

And now I know exactly how I want to live.

"Do Healers get married in a traditional fashion?" I ask. "Your kind are so secretive, I don't really know."

He makes a choking sound.

I look up over at my shoulder at him, and I can't hold back my grin. I do love catching him off guard.

But he doesn't stay that way for long.

"There are any number of ceremonies we can do. Healer to Warrior. North to Wilde. Once I *ask*," he says pointedly.

I wave a hand. "Don't be so patriarchal."

"Fine. We can ask each other, but I get to go first."

I turn in his arms. "Not if—"

"Emerson." And my name in his mouth stops me. Soothes me. Saves me all over again. "I love you. I've always loved you. I never needed fate to tell me that. It's like breathing. Everything you are is everything I want." He's said the words

before, but they're powerful every time. Beautiful. *Ours.*
"Will you marry me?"

"That isn't *fair.* You can't jump the gun. I have spreadsheets, Jacob. Pie charts. *Stickers.*"

He shrugs. "Too bad."

I scowl at him, but he twines a lock of my hair around
one of his fingers. "You know, there's a story my mother
told me the other day."

"You inviting me to a Healer family dinner is on at least
three of my lists, Jacob. Maybe five."

He grins. "It's a North family story that my grandfather
hates, so it never got passed down to my generation out of
respect for him. But my father told my mother, who told it
to me when she gave me this."

A ring appears in his free hand. It's stunning. It's historical
and charming, bold and magical. A center diamond gleams
like hope, surrounded by clusters of sapphires and more di-
amonds, all of it looking regal and very nearly floral. *Mine.*
I know it's mine. The organized woman in me, who has
already researched everything and anything pertaining to
weddings on the off chance I'd have one someday, knows
the ring is in the Georgian style. The witch in me feels the
power vibrating off of it.

"Way back when, one of my ancestors was the strongest
Healer known the world over. He prided himself on his independence, on dedicating his life to the healing arts and
nothing more. Then one day, he found a Warrior, hurt in
the forest. She was powerful, known across the land for protecting her village and all that chose to seek refuge there in
her light magic. She too had vowed never to marry, never to
split her focus from her people. But she needed his help, because though she'd fought the dark and won, she was dying."

I know it's not our story, but it feels like us. And that

ring seems to pulse in his hand like it's casting its own spell around us.

And this spell I can't surrender to fast enough.

"Though they had made vows of solitude, they couldn't deny that the magic they made together was a grand power in and of itself. They could do tremendous good with it, and more, they were happy together, Healer and Warrior. They married. And he gave her this ring that he made and charmed himself. And together, they lit up the old country with light and love."

It's a story of fate. A much better fate than the one I expected to meet tonight. We were meant for each other. Made for each other all along.

And it doesn't bother me for even a second. Fate did an excellent job. I couldn't have done a better one myself, and I don't say that lightly.

"Your mother is a sage and all-knowing woman," I say, smiling at him.

His grin widens. "She also told me it was nice to see me not being a grumpy bastard all the time, and I'd better lock this down before you get wise. Not *all* fate and love."

But perfect. Somehow, exactly right. I rest my palms on his chest. "If I've always loved you, that's fate. But right now, I'm choosing to love you, because we make each other better, stronger. Because being loved by you is everything."

"Is that a yes?"

"No, it's a counteroffer."

He sighs. "Of course it is. Beat dark magic. Almost die. Counter a marriage proposal. All in an evening's work."

"You were the one who co-opted my proposal after almost dying to save me."

His hand cups my cheek, pain etching across his face. "I would have."

A lump forms in my throat, but I swallow it down. "I know."

His other hand comes up to my other cheek. "And I know you were prepared to die in there. For us."

I'm not sure how comfortable I am with him *knowing* that, but it means more than I can say that he did know. Because he could have pulled me out. They all could have stopped me. Maybe not forever, but six against one in that moment could have pulled me back.

But they didn't. They sent their power to help me do what I needed to do. They trusted me that much.

I keep thinking I know what love is.

Then love raises the stakes.

"Say yes, Em," Jacob says softly. "That's all you have to do."

And he's right, as he is too often. The simplest answer will do. "Yes."

His mouth covers mine, and I am really, really, *really* glad I didn't die.

I pull away a little. "Hey, what about that ring?"

He shifts his gaze down, and I look at my hand. The ring is already there on my finger. Right where it belongs. I sigh happily.

I haven't forgotten the night isn't over. There's still a deep weariness inside of me, but it's going away. Replaced by a new energy, telling me I'm ready to fight the Joywood. And anything else that stands in our way. Whether it's a stubborn immortal, my recalcitrant little sister, or assorted other evils—including the ever-present town bureaucracy.

And maybe I don't want to *rest* all that much with the man I've loved my whole life who just became my fiancé, but there's no time for that either.

I'd love to take a moment to drink this all in, but I'm nothing if not a *doer*. "Jacob, you know I'm not going to wait around for the Joywood to come to us. We needed a few minutes to rest, to regroup, but we have to go to them. If we show them what we did, they can't mind wipe us. We have to be proactive."

He smiles. "I know. But let's take a moment."

"We'll take a few," I agree, staying right where I am, where I belong, with Jacob's arms around me. Together we watch the confluence twist and turn, tangle and dance, golden lights shimmering deep inside for those who know where to look.

Like peace. Like joy.

Like love.

The only things that can ever beat back the dark.

Aside from us.

And as we stand there, watching the ribbons of gleaming water, there's a sudden blast of light. It's blinding and electric, making everything inside me seize up.

I want to fight, but for a breath, then two, I'm frozen. Jacob is like a statue beside me. I hear Cassie barking wildly somewhere outside.

And then, when the light releases its hold, I see them. They're arrayed in a circle out there behind the house. Between us and the rivers. Between us and the town.

Seven figures. Seven faces I've known all my life, in one way or another. Seven people I would have told you I knew inside and out, but never quite like this.

The Joywood have come to play.

But unlike my beloved Sarah Wilde, may she rest in power, I intend to win.

★ ★ ★ ★ ★